JAMES STREET

A NOVEL

SARAH VAIL

ARCHWAY
PUBLISHING

Archway Publishing books may be ordered through booksellers or by contacting:

Archway Publishing
1663 Liberty Drive
Bloomington, IN 47403
www.archwaypublishing.com
1 (888) 242-5904

Because of the dynamic nature of the Internet, any web addresses or links contained in this book may have changed since publication and may no longer be valid. The views expressed in this work are solely those of the author and do not necessarily reflect the views of the publisher, and the publisher hereby disclaims any responsibility for them.

Any people depicted in stock imagery provided by Thinkstock are models, and such images are being used for illustrative purposes only.
Certain stock imagery © Thinkstock.

ISBN: 978-1-4808-4470-4 (sc)
ISBN: 978-1-4808-4468-1 (hc)
ISBN: 978-1-4808-4469-8 (e)

Library of Congress Control Number: 2017905867

Print information available on the last page.

Archway Publishing rev. date: 08/11/2017

ACKNOWLEDGEMENTS

I would like to express my heartfelt gratitude to Sarah Guthu and Elizabeth Lyons for their extraordinary editorial help and valuable suggestions. Particular thanks to Detective Bob Holland, EPD, retired, for his insights into police work. I'd like to also voice my appreciation to my co-workers for their patience and support. Again, thank you all for helping me make this novel a reality.

ONE

The first time he killed was an accident. Now it was such a rush he couldn't stop. He had entertained the thought of killing before. He and Lily Johansson had been married only a couple of months when a tiny thought niggled at the edge of his consciousness. The idea grew and exploded until thoughts of killing her consumed his every waking moment. He even dreamed about killing her at night while he slept.

Lily was all sweetness and light until they were married. Then she turned into a shrew that would put Shakespeare's Katharine to shame. Demanding, angry, abusing him continuously with her vile criticism. No matter what he did, it was always wrong. He hated her. Then, that night four years ago, as he watched her studying the evening newspaper, he wondered how a woman as beautiful as she could be so ugly inside.

He had just settled into his comfortable chair and started to relax from a grueling day at work. She demanded that he get her a glass of wine. He didn't dare complain. He didn't want to start anything with her.

Begrudgingly, but silent, he went to get it for her. He reached into the cupboard for a glass, and he knocked over a small prescription bottle. After pouring her glass of wine, he started to set the bottle upright. Lily had been too lazy to tighten the top, and when the bottle slipped through his fingers, the lid came off. He'd been horrified. Lily would go ballistic and shred him to pieces with her vicious great-white-shark mouth.

He remembered the hot little pop in his brain and the blinding fury that rushed over him, turbulent and boiling, then sudden quiet calm an instant later as he watched the shower of tiny white pills bouncing, clicking, and clattering against the Formica countertop and the floor. One minute he was mercilessly oppressed. The next he saw his freedom.

He should've dumped the glass of chardonnay when three pills from the prescription bottle splashed into the pale-yellow liquid. He didn't. Besides, Lily would've ripped him a new one for wasting good wine. By the time he'd finished collecting the little white tablets from the kitchen floor, the ones that had plopped into the glass had dissolved. *Colorless. Odorless. Tasteless.* Toxic as hell.

Within hours, Lily Johansson had died of ventricular fibrillation. He would've been happy just to be free of her, but the woman had left him a million-dollar insurance policy as a bonus.

Tonight, he sat in the restaurant booth upholstered in plush cranberry velvet at the Skyline Grille. Watching the entry and waiting like a lion in the tall brown grass of the Serengeti. Out of the corner of his eye, he could see the evening lights of Seattle flicker and dance on the undulating waters of Puget Sound. He toyed with the cap from the amber bottle of Lily Johansson's magic pills. When he was sure no one in the restaurant was looking, he took out four tablets. The Skyline Grille was Amber Brown's favorite night spot. Intimate, elegant. High atop the Edison Bank Tower, above the noise and confusion of the city. The crisp, white linen tablecloth reflected the pinkish glow from incandescent electric candles. Outside the window, towering skyscrapers glittered in the moonlight. Against a background of sorrowful strains of violin, gentle piano notes tinkled a melody. The Skyline Grille was indeed a place for lovers.

He glanced down at the face of the gold-and-stainless Tag Heuer he'd bought four years ago, with his insurance windfall. Amber was, predictably, ten minutes late. He poured the expensive pinot gris into her wineglass. With a brush of his thumb against his palm, he deposited four tablets into the wine and watched the tiny pills melt into the alcohol.

Within minutes he saw Amber weaving her way toward the booth where he sat. What a fabulous woman she was! In her sleek gray pin-striped business suit, she looked younger than her thirty years. Her magnificent, shapely legs were smooth and tan beneath expensive silky hosiery.

Other men in the restaurant stopped mid-sentence and gaped, wide-eyed, at her as she bustled past their tables. Amber was gloriously sexy.

"Am I late? I'm sorry, darling." Her throaty voice settled on his ears like a dove. She slid into the booth next to him, leaned forward, and pecked his cheek. All his senses suddenly came alive as he breathed in the luscious scent of her perfume.

He wanted to kiss her, but his rage bubbled up; he caged it behind a teeth-gritted smile. She didn't notice. They never did. Before he handed her the potion, he swirled the liquid around in the wineglass, stirring the toxic mix.

"It's no problem, darling. I'd wait forever. I ordered wine for us; a nice pinot gris, your favorite. Is that okay?"

"You are the sweetest man on earth." She kissed his cheek again and took hold of his arm, squeezing it against her. He closed his eyes and felt his hands involuntarily clench into fists. Violent lust. Violent anger. Both barely contained. When he opened his eyes again, he was amazed how much her profile reminded him of Lily and...

Lily and her glorious money. Soon, he would have control, and the bank account would be full again. Amber lifted the wineglass to her lips and sipped.

TWO

Deputy District Attorney Tim McAndrews pulled the collar of his overcoat up around his neck as added protection against the pouring rain. He snapped open his umbrella and stared at the multistory parking garage from under the shelter of the green-striped awning overhanging Jake's Deli. By now, the girl who had fascinated him for the last seven months would be parked and starting her brisk walk through the garage, down the stairs, and to the traffic light here at James Street, where he waited. Until now they had only shared a few glances, a few smiles, but this morning he vowed to himself that he would speak to her.

Tim had tried many times to screw up his courage and say "Hello." But each time his eyes met hers, and he opened his mouth to speak, the words vanished into thin air, and opportunity disappeared with them. Each time a brief smile would cross her lovely lips, and she would hurry on her way and vanish into the city.

There were lots of cute girls in the city, and there were pretty girls in his office, but she was different. Something about her made him linger here to watch her spring lightly down the stairs, like a dancer from an old 1930s musical. She was like the memory of the movies he'd watched with his mom when he was six or seven, on rainy days, when outside play was impossible.

Unlike this cold and dreary morning, the first time he saw her sunshine had filled the sky and blossoms fragrant and pink burst forth from the trees along the streets of Seattle, contrasting with the hard edges of brick, concrete, and steel. He'd just finished a tough game of racquetball with Bradley Hollingsrow, a prominent defense attorney whom the governor was considering for the bench. Very few of the young assistant district attorneys had this chance. But Tim had worked hard to earn the reputation of a tough, shrewd prosecutor, and many of the older lawyers and judges whose careers were made respected him. Maybe he reminded them of their younger days. Hell, he was smart. Top of his class in law school. He had a great conviction record after only four years at the D.A.'s office and he'd worked hard to get it. He'd earned their respect. That day, the two men had just taken seats under the green-striped awning outside, ready to enjoy a good cup of coffee. Maybe it was the soft clicking of her high heels against the slab stairs--he didn't remember exactly why he'd looked up just at the moment she descended the last few steps from the parking garage--but he had. She wore a summer dress that drifted and swirled around her like a silk scarf in a breeze. Every fluid step announced romance and passion. He'd been completely overwhelmed. So much so that Hollingsrow had craned his neck to see what had captured his attention. When he turned back, a big grin swept across Hollingsrow's face.

"Beautiful, isn't she? Want to meet her?" he'd asked.

"Do you know her?"

"Sure. I handled her divorce about three—maybe four years ago."

"Yes. I want to meet her." Tim had been surprised to find she was single and remembered hoping for a formal introduction. Coming from Hollingsrow it would be like a recommendation. But Judge Mattison had unexpectedly joined their table and the lovely girl crossed the street and slipped away. After that, Tim was handed a big child abuse case, and Hollingsrow was appointed to the Superior Court. Life happened, and they never met. Today, he would make sure they did.

Was it love at first sight? Tim had never really believed in it until that day. Feeling a momentary twinge of insecurity, he checked his image in the storefront window and scrubbed his hand over his short blond hair.

He glanced at his watch. 7:55 A.M. Where was she? She was late.

THREE

Daniela St. Clair pulled her car into the entry of the downtown parking garage and slipped the magnetic card into the scanner that opened the entrance gate. Like magic, the gate slowly lifted. She drove through and found her favorite parking spot. The spaces in the garage weren't assigned, but since she beat the crowd, she grabbed a prime one. Though she could take any parking spot she wanted underneath her building, she followed her father's lead and chose to leave the available parking for her employees and clients.

Finding a good parking spot could be the highpoint of my day! Family and friends said she needed more than work in her life, but she found a measure of security in routine. Joy springs from the heart, no matter life's circumstances.

Unbuckling her seatbelt, she gathered her umbrella and briefcase and left the car. Outside the parking structure, rain poured like water through a sieve. She could hear the runoff from the roof racing through the drainpipes and slapping against the pavement below. Spring rains were the best. The temperature was warmer, and the rain left a fresh scent throughout the city. Even with an umbrella, though, by the time she reached the office she'd be drenched. The thought almost discouraged her, so she willfully cast out the negativity.

She pressed the button on her remote and listened for the click of the auto lock. The shiny gray Lexus reflected the dim orange sodium lights from the ceiling of the garage. This year had been a bonus year, and she'd decided to buy a new car. She considered it a reward for all her hard work. Besides, the onboard GPS and turn-by-turn directions completely intrigued her. What a time saver technology was! Since her father's death after a long battle with cancer, she had managed the family's businesses, money, and properties. She needed every advantage she could get, she thought and laughed to herself. So far, she had been able to provide an excellent living for herself and her two older sisters.

As she walked the length of the parking garage, she made a mental list of all the things she needed to accomplish today. Then she remembered next week was her birthday. In two years, she'd be thirty. *Uggh!* Her sisters were planning a party. It was supposed to be a surprise, but they were terrible at keeping secrets. She dreaded it. Her family was too concerned about her single status. They would be grilling her over her non-existent love life.

Aunt Jane would remind her over and over about the black-as-midnight sta-tistics of her chances of ever getting married again. Not that she cared. Since her divorce four years ago, she hadn't been much for dating. Every time she tried, she'd been so disgusted by the end of the date, she'd stopped allowing herself even to think about love. Carl, her ex-husband, had cheated on her since high school and used her family for the money and position it gave him. Not only was he running around with other women, but he was also caught stealing money from the wineries, putting everyone in the family in jeopardy of financial ruin. She blamed herself for not seeing it. When her fa-ther found out, he brought all Carl's transgressions to light and forced her to acknowledge her marriage was a disaster. She initiated divorce proceedings, and in return Carl had seen to it she was crushed and publicly humiliated in the tabloid press. A writer from the *National Globe,* one Alice Carroll, had taken charge and made her out to be a frigid, cold-hearted villain when it was Carl that never loved her and cheated. She dreaded the ugly feelings that returned in a rush: loneliness, bitterness, jealousy. All a waste of time and energy. Marriage. What a train wreck hers had been! It wasn't true for everyone; she had friends who were deliriously happy. But each time she thought of including a man in her life again, she was filled with trepidation. Besides, with all she had to do, there was no room for anyone else.

At the elevator, a crowd of workers formed and milled about, silently waiting for the car. She thought of saying good morning, throwing out some wisecrack about the wicked weather, but at the last second, she changed her mind. The elevator wasn't for her. Instead, she opted to make quick work of the three flights of stairs to the street. After all, it was much-needed exercise: that stubborn five pounds remained glued to her hips and thighs from last year's holiday cookies and candy.

As she emerged from under the cover of the overhang at the bottom of the stairs, she snapped open her umbrella. The steady beat of giant raindrops against the waterproof fabric filled her ears.

Singin' in the Rain. The musical's words came tinkling into her mind as she danced a side step around a puddle at the bottom of the stairs. For a brief flash, she was tempted to kick and stamp in the water like the movie but decided that would be entirely too playful. All the city-folk around her would believe she'd gone crazy.

She dashed toward the street crossing, but as luck would have it, the light at James Street turned red. The brisk pace she initiated with her blast down the stairway came to a complete halt. Suddenly, she was cold and huddled under her umbrella. The crowd she'd left behind at the elevator caught up to her. She tried to avoid staring at the other people who parked in the garage and walked across James Street with her each morning. They didn't look at her, either. That was city life.

With moments to kill, she turned slightly to check the time and temperature display that flashed intermittent information from the Edison Bank sign. And she caught a glimpse of him. The handsome young man she and her secretary had jokingly named *Apollo*. His dark blond hair was cropped short; his strong jaw was clean shaven, and he was nicely dressed in a suit and tie under a rather expensive looking overcoat. But it was his sapphire blue eyes that captivated her and seemed to draw her in. Fit and tall, he was what she considered pure male perfection. A big, bold smile sped across his face when he noticed she was looking. Quickly, she turned away. She'd seen him here at the light or Jake's almost every morning during the business week. Occasionally, she'd seen him enjoying coffee with her trusted attorney, Brad Hollingsrow, and a fellow member of the board for Seattle's Children's Hospital, Judge Vernon Mattison. Once she'd almost asked Brad about him since he'd often smiled at her in an intriguing way, but an emergency had cropped up, and her question was lost. Obviously, he was a professional-most likely a lawyer, stock broker, or banker-innocently crossing the street and walking in the same direction as she. She shrugged her shoulders and chuckled to herself.

Before the light changed, she peeked at him again and gasped: he was still smiling at her. She must've smiled back because he was moving through the crowd toward her. Surely, she hadn't encouraged him. She felt insecurity rise in her throat. If he spoke to her, whatever would a mere mortal say to a god? Besides, she'd made up a story about him in her mind and would be terribly disappointed if he was just another egocentric bore like her ex-husband had been. She'd done everything in her power to avoid contact with men since Carl had betrayed her.

Looking around nervously for an escape, she bumped into the woman beside her.

"I'm sorry, so sorry," she said, glancing back to see if he was still coming toward her. He was. Just in time, the light changed to green, and she bolted across the street, no longer daring to look back to see if he was there. For some reason, he made her feel disarmed and vulnerable. She hurried along the rain-soaked sidewalk.

Worried that he might follow, she didn't stop at Coffee Corner for her usual extra-tall double mocha. Without looking, she imagined him close behind her. If she weren't wearing high heels, she would've run. It was completely irrational and unreasonable. She would have to have a strong self-talk--once she was safe in her office.

She bolted up the five steps to her office door two at a time, and once inside, leaned against the door to close it. He hadn't followed. She imagined a baseball umpire making the call as she crossed home plate: *Safe!* She was amazed at how rattled she'd allowed herself to become.

Surely, he hadn't wanted to talk to her. She'd let her runaway imagination take her in a completely errant direction. Probably, he only wanted to offer her a sunny smile on a rather dreary day. He meant her no harm. It was just that her experience with men was so dismal. Since her divorce, the only men she'd met were more interested in her money than they were in her.

"Daniela, you look pale. Are you all right?" Karen Muldoon, her red-haired secretary, stood from behind her desk.

"Fine, fine." Daniela gasped for breath. Waving Karen away from her, she went into her office and plopped down behind the desk. Karen, of course, would follow. When Daniela looked up, she could see the worry in her eyes.

"What on earth happened?"

"Nothing, it's nothing. I have a conference call with William Arnot and didn't want to be late. Would you mind going and getting coffee this morning? I forgot to stop. You fly, I'll buy?" Daniela offered her the bribe.

"Of course; I'm dying for another cup."

Daniela fumbled with her purse and pulled out a twenty and handed it to her secretary. Karen was more than just an assistant; she was a friend. "Thank you."

"But first you have to tell me why you're so upset. What just happened?"

"It's nothing. Just raining so hard I had to hurry. Nothing at all," she lied.

Karen stared at her with green cat eyes. Her flaming red curls tumbled down around her shoulders. "Raining that hard and you're sending me out into it? Not buying it. When I get back, I want the truth." She turned and slipped into her overcoat.

Grateful to be alone, Daniela surveyed her office from her wingback chair. Her life was exactly the way she wanted it. She ran her fingers over the smooth oak finish of her desk. Leaning deep into the buttery-soft leather of her chair, she stared at the painting of horses and hounds at the hunt placed squarely in the center of the cream-colored wall across from her and let her mind drift into the rhythm of a canter. The cool green plaid of her sofa and the brass planters of vibrant maidenhair fern soothed her frazzled nerves.

Like her father, she'd taken the simple ground floor offices in their building for practical reasons. Most execs would have preferred the big corner office on the twenty-fourth floor, but she found it was easier to escape to the airport from here. From Boeing Field, she could fly to check on the wineries and cattle ranch. William Arnot had always run the wineries day-to-day and Mark Settle the ranch. She trusted them completely, and that freed her to work on the parts of the business she liked best.

Composed, she sat forward, turned on her computer, and began work on her latest project. She was redesigning the wine tasting room in their Napa Valley location and wanted to add food services since her label had recently become so popular with the public. It was up to her to keep her family in the lifestyle to which they had become accustomed. She'd been incredibly lucky, turning her parent's nest egg into a more-than-comfortable living for them all. When it came to making money, she always seemed to be at the right place at the right time. When it came to men, the opposite was true. She briefly wondered why she was thinking of men and love. *Apollo's smile!* She laughed.

It had been a good fifteen minutes since she sent Karen for coffee. *What's keeping her?* Her mouth watered at the thought of her favorite morning pick-me-up. She wished she'd asked Karen to get one of those delicious scones, too. When she heard the outer office door swish open and click shut, she could almost taste the smooth mocha. She continued to concentrate on the numbers on her screen.

"Hello." The male voice startled her. She looked up and stared into the beaming face of *Apollo.* There he was before her in all his sunny glory, holding a lovely bouquet of dark red roses and baby's breath, the stems wrapped in white tissue and tied with a scarlet bow. A splendid smile, a promise like a rainbow, spread across his handsome face.

Speechless and insecure, she felt her face flush hot with embarrassment and surprise.

"I hope you don't mind," he continued forward into the room, his voice ringing with confidence. "These are for you." He offered the gift.

Flustered by his presence, Daniela stood, accidently brushing a stack of papers from the file in front of her. The bulk of them spilled to the floor. Helpless, she watched the last few pages drift lazily down around his polished cordovan leather shoes.

"Oh, no! Oh dear!" she laughed nervously. So this did happen in real life. She'd never expected to be living a romance novel cliché.

She quickly surveyed the mess and bent to pick up the papers. Like a true gentleman, he responded: he set the bouquet on the edge of her desk, rounded the corner, and stooped down and agilely gathered her papers from the floor. Daniela snatched them from his hand and tried to grab up the rest before he could help her. Those pages contained all sorts of financial information no stranger should see.

"I didn't mean to startle you," he said, easily reaching for a sheet at the same time as she. His cool fingers grazed the back of her hand. He was too close. The fragrance of the roses mixed with his aftershave was heady. She caught herself searching his face. It had been years since she'd been this close to a man who intrigued her. His eyes sparkled, and he glanced from hers down to her lips and back again. She was no child, no innocent; she knew exactly what that meant. Disarmed, she stood too quickly. He was there, supporting her with a strong arm.

"Are you all right, Miss St. Clair?" he whispered, so close to her she could feel the warmth and smell the sweet mint of his breath

There was nothing to be done. The situation was too unbelievable, too clumsy, and too comical. Daniela started laughing--and in so doing she infected him with laughter as well. Slowly, she gathered her composure and brushed the wrinkles from her straight skirt. "I'm fine, fine." She knew she was blushing. "Thank you." She moved to the safety behind her desk. "From where do I know you?" They'd never met, so how did he know her name? Then she remembered the nameplate prominently displayed on her desk

"You don't know me. I'm Tim McAndrews." He reached forward and shook her hand. "We have mutual friends. Brad Hollingsrow?"

Of course, he was here to use mutual friends to sell her something. That was disappointing. He was so gorgeous; she'd almost let her imagination carry her away.

He continued. "I'm striking out, aren't I? First, I frighten you at the light; then I drop by to make it up to you and wreak havoc." He recovered the bouquet from the edge of her desk with one courtly swoop and checked the flowers for damage. Then a playful turn to his lips pleaded for forgiveness, and he gently asked, "Is there any way I can salvage this?" With care, he set the roses on the end of her desk.

"Oh, you didn't frighten me on the street." Geez, he'd noticed her flight. She'd hoped he hadn't. So much for discretion. Embarrassment flooded into her cheeks anew until they were flaming hot.

"I'm glad. I sure didn't mean to. I wanted to say hello. I've meant to for days. I know it isn't proper, but I didn't know what else to do. I couldn't think of another way to meet you. That's why I dropped by."

She had to admire his boldness. "So, how can I help you, Mr. McAndrews?" Since he'd mentioned Brad, she would give him a few minutes to pitch her on whatever he was selling.

"Have dinner with me. I've wanted to ask you to dinner for weeks."

"Me? For weeks? You don't have to take me to dinner. If Brad suggested you see me—then--" She gestured for him to sit down in the chair in front of her desk.

He looked at her as if perplexed. "You must let me make it up to you. I insist. At least lunch?" Now, he was the one coloring with a blush. He didn't sit. Daniela was amazed.

"I'm sorry, I don't have very much free time. Just tell me what you're selling, and we can go from there." She smiled.

"Selling?"

She recognized she'd thrown him off his game. "Securities, an investment account, annuities?" She shrugged her shoulders, coaching him.

He briefly laughed. "Me. I guess I'm selling--me. I'm asking you for a date." His eyes seemed to effervesce with a delightful mixture of sincerity and play.

Surprise was an understatement for what she felt. She studied him for a moment and watched some of that stunning confidence erode. He was even more handsome with a hint of vulnerability in his eyes.

"Thank you, lunch would be..." before she could finish the words of her refusal, his face broke wide open like sunshine after a rainstorm. She lost her words.

"Tomorrow, then. Lunch. I'll come by for you," he beamed. He took one of her business cards from her desk. With a gallant stride, he crossed to the door. "Tomorrow," he called back to her.

"Lunch would be out of the question..." Daniela whispered at the closed door. Astonished, she sank in her chair, realizing she'd just accepted a date with Apollo.

Karen bustled into the room. She set Daniela's coffee on her desk.

"You'll never guess who I just saw on the street-Apollo!" she chuckled. "Wow! He is one hunk of gorgeous man."

"Yes, he certainly is." Daniela still tried to process what had just happened. "Do you know anything about him?"

"I think he's an attorney. I think I heard that. Hey, where did you get the roses? Shall I put them in water for you?"

"An attorney, umm. Would you get Brad Hollingsrow on the phone for me?"

"Sure," Karen said.

FOUR

"You're late for your meeting!" Myra's stern air scolded him. She could put the most obnoxious defense attorneys in their place with one of her wilting stares. Tim snatched the pink message paper from his secretary's hand. He'd learned early on that staying on her good side was easily accomplished with a big smile.

"My meeting?" He didn't remember any meeting. He'd taken advantage of his clear calendar this morning to deliver roses to Daniela St. Clair. He had planned to slip into the office late and unnoticed. But the best-laid plans...

"Well, Dr. Kathy Hope is waiting for you in your office."

"Kathy Hope. That's not a meeting." Tim grinned, turned, and walked briskly down the gray corridor to his ninth-floor office.

He wondered what she was up to; he hadn't seen her for a couple of weeks. Kathy Hope was one of his closest friends, but she was weird. Though he loved her dearly, Tim had always thought so. What did he expect? She was a doctor raised by a pair of biology professors. Weird was probably genetic. When they were kids, she'd spent hours in her father's basement laboratory studying everything that he and his best friend, Scott Renton, found outdoors and brought to her. Bugs. Water from the pond in the park. Leaves from every shrub and tree in their middle-class neighborhood. He'd never admitted it to her or Scott, but he'd enjoyed looking through her father's microscope and learning about the unseen world.

Peculiar and bookish though she might've been, Kathy was the one who taught him what little he knew about biology and physiology. He remembered her patiently helping Renton and him through boring homework when all they wanted to do was play football. If it weren't for Kathy's tutoring, he wasn't sure either one of them would've made it to college.

It seemed they had always been friends--McAndrews, Renton, and Hope. He thought of the treehouse in the backyard his dad had built for them. They'd spent most days after school and summers meeting there, making up mysteries, and superhero games in grade school. And later meeting there to discuss their trials and tribulations with the opposite sex during high school.

They had gone separate ways in college. He and Scott Renton pursued degrees in law, while Kathy got hers in medicine. And now, after several years, they were back together socially and professionally. It amazed him that three scruffy kids could turn out to be such regular, upstanding citizens.

"Kath, how are you?" Tim asked as he entered his office. He peeled off his overcoat, hung it on the rack by the door, and leaned his umbrella against the wall.

Kathy's smile collapsed into a frown. Her posture hinted at the serious business she'd come to discuss.

"I take it this isn't a social visit?" he asked, seeing the expression on her face. She'd only been with the medical examiner's office a little over a year, and she'd developed a reputation. Young and woman and smart weren't adding up to the popularity it should. He moved behind his desk and sat.

Tim was a little ashamed that he and Scott didn't do a better job of standing up for her. They knew how bright she was. She'd clued them into a homicide by cyanide poisoning her first week with the M.E. If she hadn't, the case would have been dismissed, and a greedy, evil woman would still be out on the loose. Kathy claimed she could smell the almond scent lingering on the dead body. She insisted the emergency room doctor had missed it. She had nagged Tim so relentlessly he'd authorized the police lab to run the expensive toxicology test for the poison just to get rid of her.

Bingo! Death by cyanide. A loving wife had murdered the man on Kathy's autopsy table. Tim and Scott received kudos from the D.A. Kathy got nothing but lip.

Down at the station some of the cops still joked behind her back that they could hire and train her as a drug-sniffing dog. It was cruel. Tall, lanky, and lean, she reminded him of a female scarecrow. Her too-thin legs were finished with feet so large they looked out of place. But she *was* strange. What kind of woman wanted to be a medical examiner? Sometimes Tim found his stomach wrenching when he had to look at photographs for court, let alone the real thing.

"So, what's this all about, Kathy? Another cyanide?" She had the guts and brains to muscle her way through medical school, so he guessed she had the guts and brains to muscle her way through police officers, too. She ran her free hand through her short shock of straw-blonde hair.

Sometimes Tim wondered if the guys at the cop shop would be unkind if she were a beauty like Daniela St Clair. He nearly drifted into fantasy but forced himself to pay attention to Kathy. Today, she sat in front of him now feminine and frail in a lacy pink dress, looking like a little girl.

"I want to wait for Scott. Tell you both at the same time."

"Okay." No surprise. He suspected that Kathy was still in love with their longtime best friend. She'd had a hefty crush all through high school.

Kathy and every other woman on the planet. Scott Renton was tall, dark, and good-looking. When he was promoted to police detective, he became a chick magnet as if it were part of the job description.

"Have you had coffee this morning? I'm dying for a cup."

"Sure, I'll have one," Kathy answered.

Tim buzzed Myra on the intercom and asked her to bring two cups.

"You're sure you want to wait for Scott?"

"Are you too busy? Is that what you're getting at, McAndrews?"

"Never for you." He was too busy after goofing around all morning delivering flowers like the pathetic love-starved puppy he was. He wouldn't brush Kathy off. She wouldn't be here, fidgeting in the chair across the desk from him unless she needed him. She couldn't help it if she liked to cut up dead bodies. Tim tried to keep himself from shuddering.

Once, while working on a particularly gruesome homicide, he'd asked her over drinks how she could stand her job. She had blinked at him with those pale blue eyes as if she couldn't believe he didn't understand. "To me, it's science. The life, the spirit has gone, and it's not a person anymore," she'd answered.

Myra brought coffee in ceramic mugs and handed one to each of them.

Tim grinned his thanks. With the subtlety of a Mac truck, Myra winked back at him as if she believed Kathy was his girlfriend. Tim shook his head and sighed. Maybe he should just let her think it. She was always prodding him, trying to fix him up, and reminding him that married men live longer. Myra lumbered out of his office as Detective Renton finally breezed in.

"Sorry, I'm late. Did you start without me?"

"No. We waited." Tim noticed how Kathy changed with Scott's appearance. Her pale cheeks suddenly flushed with color and she was...pretty. If he were a betting man, he'd put money on Kathy being madly in love with the six-foot-two detective since her tenth birthday. Scott had given her a microscope. Scott's parents bought the gift without his input. But Kathy was sure he'd selected it and understood her. Scott Renton always had the luck that way. He could make the shyest of the ladies feel completely at home and comfortable. A knack that, judging by this morning's fiasco, Tim sorely lacked.

"So, Kath, what have you got that's so urgent we had to meet this morning?" Scott took off his brown tweed overcoat and tossed it across the remaining empty chair in the corner of Tim's cramped office. He leaned his backside against the edge of Tim's cluttered desk and expectantly waited as Kathy fumbled through her files, handing each of them a neatly typed page. To counter all the garbage she took from everyone, she always came prepared for battle. Kathy was a fast learner, and she knew she'd have to defend her position.

"I've got two bodies, guys."

Scott turned to face Tim; his left eyebrow arched with intrigue. "Do tell, Kath. Fill us in," Scott encouraged.

"The second one came through yesterday morning. I thought I was losing my mind. Or dreaming. I lifted the sheet and freaked because I just did an autopsy on this woman. Then I realized it wasn't the same woman but another who looked just like her or-at least, so close they could've been sisters. They were beauties. Great physical shape. Young, too; I'd say the early thirties. They had the hearts of eighteen-year-olds."

Tim looked at Scott and shrugged his shoulders. Scott rolled his eyes and studied his watch. Tim recognized the message; he didn't have time to wait through one of her stories. "Come on, Kath, get to the point."

"Hear her out, Scott." Tim always gleaned great information from her tales. Later, he could use the physiology of the death that she would describe in the courtroom to significant effect. Was she presenting evidence for serial murder? His heartbeat quickened. A high-profile case would be challenging. Lately, he'd been stuck training new law school recruits on DUII detail. He remembered how he'd felt when he'd won the Senchal abuse case last spring. Putting that sadistic pedophile away had been sweet!

"I began to wonder why women in great shape like this would be dying of sudden heart attacks; when there was no evidence of heart disease. I had the lab do toxicology on the latest victim, Amber Brown. I had them look for everything, *including* the kitchen sink. We found traces of desipramine. That's no big deal. A lot of women take antidepressant drugs, especially ladies approaching mid-life. Depressed about getting older, you know. It was the look-alike thing that kept needling me. I pulled the chart of the other woman and had toxicology run the same screens."

"You're telling us some depressed chick ended up on your table. Was it suicide?" Scott asked, playing with a pen, clicking the ballpoint in and out, in and out.

"Two. Two depressed chicks, Scott. Two depressed chicks who look alike. That's a strange coincidence. But that's where you come in," Tim asserted himself.

Nervous, her narrow hands trembling, Kathy took a swallow of her coffee. If there were a perp poisoning women out there, they had to get him off the street and fast. "I'm listening, even if Sherlock Holmes here isn't." Tim pushed his weight back into his swivel chair and twisted it from side to side.

Kathy sighed and picked a piece of lint off the pink dress. "I want Scott to talk to Amber Brown's sister, look through her stuff to see what he can find. Right off the bat, the doc in the emergency room thought it was an overdose. He had the sister go to her house and tell him all the prescription meds she found. It makes treatment easier; sometimes there's an antidote. All she had were some stale dated antibiotics. There was no suicide note."

"How did Ms. Brown get to the emergency room?" Tim reached across the clutter for his mug of coffee.

"She collapsed at The Backstreet Boutique. A salesgirl called 9-1-1. The paramedics brought her to the hospital. Apparently, she had a seizure, fell into a coma. She went into v-fib at the emergency room, and they couldn't save her. Emergency doc was baffled. As far as the family knew, Amber was successful and happy. They pressed for an autopsy." Kathy peeked at Scott through the veil of her blonde lashes.

"You're sure it's this drug, not some scary new virus?" Tim asked. He took a yellow legal pad from his right-hand drawer and began to write down notes.

"I'm sure, Tim. I think we have a poisoner on the prowl."

"It's a defective batch of medication. Or she could've bought it on the street. Designer drug for the designer woman." Scott countered with an argument that sounded like Goddard. He mimicked the gruff D.A. down to his voice and hand gestures.

"I thought of that. But desipramine is not a street drug. I already checked around with other doctors to see if they'd had any similar cases, heard about a recall in progress, anything like that. I even called the pharmaceutical company and asked if there were reports on record of any problems like we were seeing. I asked if their plants had been broken into recently, or if supplies were stolen. Nada! I'm telling you boys; we have a killer. Believe it or not; that's up to you. But it's my job to report it to you."

"You think a drug company is going to tell you they have bad stuff?" Scott stood, reached for his overcoat, and settled back down against the edge of the desk as if he was planning to leave.

"Not necessarily. That's why I told them I was calling the FDA and the CDC just in case they decided to lie to me."

Scott opened his mouth to speak, but Kathy interrupted him. "It could be product tampering, but both women used the same drug. It takes a prescription; neither of them had one, no histories of depression or substance abuse. Other than alcohol, a lethal dose of desipramine's all we found drifting around in the victims' blood." She sat tall in her chair, daring another contradiction.

Tim was impressed by her thoroughness.

Scott's mouth spread wide with an approving grin. He took a long, pondering pause before saying, "I don't have time for a wild goose chase, so I hope you're right."

"If you don't take this case, I'm going over your heads. I thought you'd want to be heroes again. I thought you'd want to head up this investigation." Kathy started to pack her briefcase.

"Whoa! Kathy! Don't be so hasty! I believe you," Tim defended himself. "How about you, Scott? Are you going to look into this? I think Kathy has enough for you to do some snooping. She's almost done all of your job for you. Do you want me to run it by Goddard?" With the district attorney's blessing, and if this panned out, Tim might get the chance to try another capital murder case in court. He was ready for the work and challenge. He flicked the intercom button on his phone.

"Myra, do me a favor and see if Goddard is in. Call me right back."

"I'm in. I'll investigate." Scott's blue eyes sparkled. "If this turns out to be one of your B.S. missions like when we were kids, I'll have your head, Kath. You know I love ya, but I swear, I'll have your head." Scott couldn't hide the fact he was teasing her; his smile broke out like too much popcorn under the lid of a skillet.

"If this turns out to be B.S. you won't have to have my head, Goddard will do it for you. But, I feel it in my bones. I'm going to have another body in the morgue before the month is out. We have got to get on this. I think we have a stone killer on our hands."

"Before the end of the month? Are you sure? Maybe I better investigate *you*."

"Any time, Scott. Investigate away," Kathy sang out. Was she flirting? Tim had never seen Kathy flirt. But she was, after all, a woman.

"Your place or mine?" Scott handed it back at her, stood, and pecked Kathy with a quick kiss on the cheek. "I've gotta go. Hand me one of those reports so I can sell the captain." He grabbed a folder from her hand and his coat. He breezed out the doorway.

"You believe me, don't you, Tim?" Kathy's cheeks were bright red from Scott's kiss, and she fumbled with the papers on her lap as if she'd lost some of her conviction.

"Kath, if you say you have something—I think you have something. Scott will see what he can find. That's his job." Tim stood and navigated through the small space to the doorway. Kathy rose from her chair.

"Do you think Scott thinks I'm an idiot?" Her thin lips twitched with dejection.

"Naw. We've know you too long to think that. He's just busy." Tim put an arm around her bony shoulders and gave her a reassuring hug. Obviously, what Scott thought of her was paramount to Kathy. With all the ladies chasing the detective around the planet, he hoped his friend wasn't in for heartbreak.

FIVE

He discovered her. First as an image, a fleeting glimpse beside him at the traffic light. Now, he watched as long, shapely legs and dainty feet in red high heels emerged from her pristine, candy-apple red Mercedes 450 SL. He felt heat race through his body. She wore a red miniskirt and matching jacket. She turned. As she did her glorious mane of honey-brown hair flowed all around her shoulders and down her back. She combed her scarlet-tipped fingers through the silk, raking it back and away from her face. She was heart-stoppingly beautiful. His pulse was pounding in his ears. He'd been hunting for two weeks. Unable to resist, he turned right into the parking lot when the light flashed green.

Keeping her in sight, he pulled into a parking space three cars away from her, then became a shadow. She must never know he was following her, watching her. She bustled into The Backstreet Boutique. She was on a mission. Shopping was an obsession for some of these women. They chased after agelessness as if they could find Persephone's beauty cream in the mall. As he passed her car, he memorized the license number. She was one of them: rich, sassy, gorgeous. Having it all, knowing it all. He could tell by her confident gait.

Quickly, he got out of his car and closed the space between them across the rain-misted parking lot. He wasn't afraid she'd notice him. They never saw him before he wanted them to. He followed a safe distance behind, the fragrance of her designer perfume lingering where she'd passed. He entered the store, carefully studied the patrons, and finally allowed himself the pleasure of looking at her. She was more exciting than he had realized at first. Standing at the circular dress rack, she scraped metal against metal as she drew dress after dress, hanger after hanger into view. Obviously, she was bored with shopping, dismissing each item quickly, as if she were on a mission to satisfy an insatiable greed. Wealthy and beautiful and bored; a completely useless human being.

After a few minutes, she finally found something she liked and lifted the crimson frock out and away from the others. She moved over to the full-length mirror and held it against her body, twisting from side to side as if contemplating whether the dress was stylish enough to buy.

"I'll try this one," she said to the salesgirl who followed her like a puppy. The tinkle of her laughter alighted on his ears, and he savored the sound.

He almost let her see him. But instead, he waited, prolonging his anticipation of the moment of contact. Stalking his prey had become as delicious and addictive as killing them.

Nearby, still tracking her, he sampled men's cologne as she entered the dressing room. He wished he could see her. Would she be wearing a scarlet lace bra that cradled and lifted her exquisite breasts and the thong panties he imagined in his fantasy?

She emerged and bought the little red dress; he had been right about her. He moved back to the display of men's sweaters on her exit path from the store. His senses revved into high gear. Sight. Smell. Taste. Sound. As sharp as a diamond cutter's tool. *See me. See me.* He repeated the magic chant in his mind. Briefly, he glanced her way, catching the flicker of a smile that passed across her full, come-kiss-me red lips. She was looking him up and down. He lifted a navy-blue sweater and inspected it more carefully. She tossed her saucy little head, and it sent ripples through her glossy hair. Thirty seconds. He made a bet with himself. Thirty seconds and she'd approach him. Putting on his most perplexed frown, he became the irresistible frustrated-by-shopping male.

"Oh, no. That's the wrong color for you," she flirted.

"Do you like this one?" He'd been wrong--sooner. She was hungry. He was hungrier.

"This one would be much better."

"Do you think so?" He sidestepped to where she stood. He studied the garment, holding the pale-yellow sweater up against his chest.

"Yes. Yes, that's the one. It suits you." She was radiant.

"Thank you. You've been so much help." He looked deep into her pretty face, focusing his attention on her lips as if he were kissing her. "This may sound presumptuous of me--and forgive me if it is, but can I buy you a glass of wine?"

"Why, I would be delighted," she said.

SIX

Daniela had been so distracted this morning with her Napa remodel she'd forgotten she'd been railroaded into lunch with Mr. McAndrews until she overheard his clear, cheerful voice ask Karen if he could see her. She glanced at the clock on her wall and saw that it was almost noon.

Oh, no. She grabbed her purse and fumbled through it for a mirror. *My God!* Horrified at her washed-out appearance, she applied some lipstick in hopes it would brighten her pallor. If she'd remembered, she would've worn another outfit. Something far less drab and dowdy. The soft electric ring of her telephone intercom insisted that she hurry.

"Yes?" she choked on the word, mashing the top of her lipstick in its cover. This man made her come apart at the seams!

"There is a Mr. Tim McAndrews here to see you." Karen Muldoon was entirely too enthusiastic. When Daniela returned from this disastrous lunch, Karen would be waiting for a full report. She would have nothing to report, other than the fact that the Marsala restaurant had great food. That info Karen already knew.

Reluctantly, she stood from behind her desk. She squared her stance, hoping to bolster her courage. She tugged at the bottom of the cream-colored linen vest, straightening it over the waistband of her chocolate-and-cream-checked skirt. No matter how long she waited, courage didn't come to join her. She swallowed the lump of pure anxiety lodged in her throat and slid her arms through the sleeves of her wool blazer. *Might as well get this over with.*

Tim looked up just as Daniela emerged from the door to her office. All morning he'd been thinking about her. Entertaining fantasies about touching the lustrous skin of her cheek, brushing his fingers through her long, golden-brown hair. Today she wore it pulled back and tied with a brown silk scarf. He wanted to untie that bow and watch her hair fall long and soft about her shoulders.

"Good morning," he said.

"Is it still morning?" The nervous smile that quivered on her lips delighted him. She was so feminine and her blue eyes were captivating.

"For five more minutes. Am I too early?"

"No, not at all." He watched a pink flush race into her cheeks. Maybe she was as excited about this date as he was—or else dreading it. He guessed he'd find out soon enough.

"I'm looking forward to lunch; I seldom have time for Marsala's. I love the calamari. The way they prepare it is amazing: sauté it right there at your table. Great stuff." He opened the door for her. As she walked through, he looked down at her. She was the perfect height, perfect weight; she was the perfect woman. He imagined her in his bed, resting in the crook of his arm. He hadn't felt this way about any woman ever before. Wonderful. Exactly as he'd dreamed. He decided. Hell, he decided last spring when he first saw her at the James Street stoplight. He was going to marry Daniela St. Clair.

Intimate dining at its finest, Daniela thought as she stared at the reserved table. It was very private, with a spectacular view of the islands in the Sound. Mr. McAndrews had thought of everything. A lovely red rose, still sparkling with droplets of water, had been carefully arranged on the starched white tablecloth between her fork, knife, and spoon. Her place setting-*Oh, my!*-was just a little too close to his. She tugged at the collar of her white cotton blouse. Suddenly, the neck felt entirely too tight. She shot the maitre'd an agonized glance. He wouldn't help her; his huge, tell-tale grin confirmed that he was McAndrews' co-conspirator.

She really shouldn't be complaining. McAndrews was wonderful to look at, and his cheerful, confident manner was so refreshing. He was tall--over six feet, and his broad shoulders and slim hips looked great in the navy pinstripe. Underneath, she expected he'd be as buff and beautiful as a Michelangelo. But all the effort he put forth was intimidating, and it only fueled her cynicism. Too good to be true always was just that. Brad Hollingsrow had said he was a brilliant prosecutor, but to Daniela, that only meant big ego and that kind of ego could quickly translate into cad and cheater.

Slowly, she slid into the booth, making her way to the too-close-for-comfort place setting. She stopped short and moved the silverware and napkin to her preferred distance. This problem with men was hers and hers alone. Any of her lady friends would have been delighted to share a meal with Mr. Sunshine. It was a hangover from her miserable marriage and even more miserable divorce. And it was fear, fear that this good-looking man could inspire her to fall in love again. By the look radiating from his eyes, she understood that love was what he had in mind. But deep down she feared it was money he was after. Did her father know that the blessing he'd left her was a curse?

The waiter handed her a menu. She lifted it in front of her face, hiding while she screwed up her courage. The air was full of the smell of roasted garlic, vegetables, and meat. Her stomach reminded her that she was truly hungry. *This is a one-time thing. One lunch, and it's over. Life can go back to normal.*

"Okay." She lowered the menu and beamed at Tim with everything she could give. "Let's have some of that fantastic calamari."

As it turned out, Tim was a great guy--and funny. Lunch hadn't been nearly as awkward as Daniela expected. They talked much longer than they should have. He told her about his job as deputy district attorney, and as they walked back to her office, he pointed out his window on the ninth floor of the city tower. The mirrored surface reflected the sun and sky, and she wasn't sure which one he meant, but she'd listened.

Through lunch, he'd made her laugh. He was not at all the scary monster she'd pretended he was going to be. He was fun. Once, a long time ago, she'd thought she might be fun. But that part of herself she'd put away and allowed to become cluttered with cobwebs and dust. Suddenly, he made her wonder if she could resurrect it, or if the playfulness she remembered was buried too deep to bother.

Unexpectedly, he turned around and walked backward up the five steps to her office, as if he liked looking at her. He reached out his hand. This wasn't real! She felt as though she had been transported to another time when men could think of women as ladies. In the confusion, she almost let him take her hand. Thinking better of it, she withdrew, balling her fingers into a fist. He bit the bottom lip of his smile as if he understood her hesitation. Did he understand her? His eyes said so.

When they reached the top step, he opened the door for her. It was as if her reserve inspired him to try that much harder. All this effort touched and awakened emotion. He was going to make her think of love in spite of herself.

Karen wasn't at her desk. She was both sorry and grateful and was confused by her feelings.

"Dani? May I call you that?" Tim asked, searching her eyes for a yes. She nodded.

"Dani. I enjoyed this. Can I see you again? I want to see you again." The door closed behind him, and she was suddenly aware she was without the protection of the meandering city crowd. Karen wasn't here to run blockade for her, either. She backed two steps away from him.

"Yes." She hadn't thought she would want to see him again, so it shocked her as the word tumbled out.

"Tonight? Dinner? A movie?"

"No, not tonight." She could feel anxiety racing through her. She wasn't ready for another date. She needed to think. What had she done?

"Tomorrow, then?"

She shook her head quickly. She had to fix this somehow.

"Are you blowing me off? You don't want to see me again, do you?" His grin told her he knew perfectly well that she did want to see him again. "You need to give me a chance, Dani. I'm not that bad a guy."

"I know." She stopped herself from fidgeting with her fingernails.

"See me again." The pause was horrible, an eternity. But she needed time to sort through her feelings and her fears.

"Okay." Her voice trembled. Dating was stupid! She should've never let this get this far.

He took a bold step forward and turned her chin with a flick of his fingers so she would look up into his face. He started to say something but didn't. His eyes were full of passion. She felt as though she'd lost all sensation in her body. Was he going to kiss her? She found she wanted him to. The heat of a full-blown blush raced all the way from her toes. Confusion was in charge. He smiled at her and backed up a half step, as if forcing control over a longing he didn't want to restrain.

"Tomorrow night?" he asked again.

"Tomorrow night," she answered. His smile was infectious. She resisted, but to her dismay, she found one toying at the corners of her mouth.

SEVEN

Tim sat at his desk. The cases stacked messily on the right corner needed his attention, but he couldn't open a single file. Why hadn't he followed through and kissed her? Dani needed kissing--and for a brief moment, and in spite of her formal behavior and her resistance, he knew she wanted to be kissed. He closed his eyes and imagined what it was going to be like when finally they did.

A quiet knock on his door snapped him quickly out of his daydream. He had to get back to work.

"Come in."

Paul Goddard filled the doorway. The district attorney was a big man, almost as broad as he was tall. His dust-brown suit nearly matched the color of his thinning hair and full mustache. A young woman followed him. "Good afternoon, Tim. This is Jenny Mattison. Jenny, my best up-and-coming prosecutor, Tim McAndrews."

Goddard's compliment both surprised and flattered Tim. "Hi, Jenny." He stood, reaching out his hand to shake hers. She was tall, with brown hair that curled just under her chin and big brown puppy eyes. Her navy-blue suit hung on her thin frame, so unlike Dani's delicious curves. Mattison? He wondered for a second if she were Judge Mattison's daughter, following in the family tradition.

"Jenny thinks she wants to be a prosecutor," Goddard chuckled. "She's joining us."

"Good for you, Jenny," Tim said. "Welcome."

Jenny was staring at him, her lips parted as if she wanted to say something, but instead was embarrassingly tongue-tied. He remembered his first day, how intimidated and lost he'd felt, and sympathized immediately.

"You'll do fine. It's scary at first, but we'll all help you through," Tim offered.

"Mr. McAndrews, is it? I've met so many people today, I'm sorry."

"Tim," he answered.

"Tim," she repeated, almost as a whisper, an awkward blush rising into her cheeks.

He smiled at her and nodded. But she stared too long. He had seen that kind of a look before. It quickly reminded him of his college days: the girls newly on their own and hunting for husbands. This girl was going to be trouble. He looked over at Goddard for rescue. But Goddard lifted a skeptical eyebrow instead, letting him know he was on his own.

"Wait for me, I'll be right back," Goddard said. Glancing back as he left Tim's office with Jenny. Goddard shook his head and silently mouthed, "'No." Confused, Tim followed them to the doorway. He watched as Goddard passed Jenny off to a couple of the secretaries, spun on his heel, and headed back.

He closed the door after he'd passed through. "Hands off, McAndrews. She's Judge Mattison's daughter. He's a big donor to my campaign, and we're not going to have any scandals."

Surprised, Tim tried to think how he'd given the wrong impression. Was there anything about Jenny that appealed in the slightest? She was cute, but not like Dani, a beauty, a dream, everything he'd ever wanted a woman to be.

"Did I do something wrong?"

"No, but I wanted us to be perfectly straight. You're single; she's single. Jenny is out of bounds, Am I clear?"

"Yes. Of course." Tim could swear Goddard's eyes said otherwise. The message was confusing.

"You've always behaved appropriately, but I hear the talk." Goddard was stern.

"Talk? About me?" Tim was shocked and knew his faced showed it. Unlike other ADAs he hadn't dated anyone from the office. He'd even avoided working lunches and after-hours get-togethers.

Goddard chuckled, "Yes, talk about you. Nothing like a good-looking man to get the women all cackling like old hens. Just remember: Jenny is off-limits."

"I've got it, sir." He shrugged it off. Besides, at this point, he couldn't think of any woman other than Daniela St. Clair.

"Now, do you have anything new to report on this serial killer case?"

"Nothing new from the police. No suspects. Not even sure it's real," Tim said, rubbing his hand through his short, blond hair.

"Keep on top of this, keep me informed. Do whatever you have to do—day or night—am I clear? But get control of this. If it is real, we've got to put a stop to it immediately."

"Yes, sir," Tim answered.

EIGHT

The jangle slowly brought Tim out of a most satisfying dream. At first, he thought the sound was the alarm on the nightstand, and he pressed the OFF button five times before his mind registered the noise as the telephone. It was 2:30 in the morning

He lifted the receiver and spoke into the earpiece. "Hello?"

"Tim?" The voice was a million miles away. He turned the handset around.

"This is Tim. Who's this?"

"It's Scott."

"Scott, what's up?"

"Kathy Hope called. There's another body at the morgue. She thinks it's connected to our killer."

Tim felt his stomach flop over. Ever since the medical examiner brought her suspicions to their attention, he had hoped she was wrong. Though he wanted the recognition a high-profile case would bring, he didn't want anyone to die. When Goddard had told him to get on top of it, he'd called Kathy and Scott and told them he wanted to know if anything came up, no matter the time of day or night. Kathy had given instructions to the emergency room to wake her if any suspicious cases showed up.

"I'll be right there." He was wide awake now. He hung up the phone and scrambled from the blankets and sheets. He grabbed the navy-blue sweats he'd worn last night before stripping for bed. He glanced in the mirror on his dresser and scrubbed his knuckles through his hair, trying to straighten the jumble. One side had been mashed in sleep and stood on end. All he needed was some wild color, and he'd look like one of the punk-ass kids he prosecuted in court. He opted for a Seahawks baseball cap.

Like every other hospital morgue he'd ever had the misfortune to visit, this one was in the basement. It had something to do with environmental issues, but the only one Tim could think of was making sure the environment was plenty creepy. The cinderblock walls were painted gray-green, windowless, and unadorned. The mottled gray vinyl floor added to the impersonal chill that hovered in the hallway like a Halloween mist. Tim wondered if the spirits of the newly departed were suspended in the air above him. He looked up at the ceiling and adjusted the baseball cap on his head. He didn't much believe in ghosts, but he wanted to be respectful just in case.

Long before he saw Kathy and Scott, he heard the eerie echo of their footfalls in the empty corridor. He expectantly turned as they rounded the corner. Kathy was dressed in green surgical scrubs; Scott had also apparently rushed here from a sound sleep: he wore blue jeans, a rumpled T-shirt under a leather jacket, and slip-on boat shoes. He'd failed to bother matching his socks, and wore argyle on the left and solid blue on the right. It was three in the morning; who cared?

Both Kathy and Scott carried paper cups with steam rising off the surface. Tim's sleepy mind longed for the taste of coffee on his tongue. He could sure use a jolt of caffeine.

"Did you bring me one?" he asked, staring hungrily at Kathy's cup.

Kathy looked at him and gave him a guilty grimace. "Umm. You can have a sip of mine. Or you can run up to the cafeteria and get your own."

"Yours." Tim took the paper cup she offered and gulped the weak-brewed lukewarm coffee. "God! That's worse than the crap at the cop shop."

"I forgot, Mr. GQ needs espresso," Kathy teased and received a chuckle of agreement from Scott.

"So, what have we got?" Tim said, searching the hallway for a drinking fountain to rinse away the lingering bitter taste.

"Another woman. I'm sure she's compliments of our guy."

Tim watched Kathy turn the key in the autopsy room door. She knew what she was doing, but still he hoped she was wrong.

"You're sure it's the same guy?" Scott shared Tim's fears. Maybe they thought if they asked the same question repeatedly the answer would be different, like spinning the numbers on a roulette wheel.

"I'm sure. I didn't call you bums until everything was back except the DNA." Kathy was grim. They all stared at each other for a moment, voicing their mutual anxiety in their silence. Scott had just started to piece together the bare shreds of evidence. They didn't have a suspect. There would be more bodies.

Kathy wrested open the heavy metal door. "Here's what we know about him. I matched the semen I found to the samples from all the other bodies. He's a Type-A secretor. He's a white male; pubic hair samples confirm that. Now all I need is the DNA, and we have him linked to all the victims."

"Then he assaults them?" Scott asked.

"No. There is no evidence of a struggle, no ligature marks. I think they are willing participants. Then, he poisons them."

"Oh, lovely," Tim said sarcastically.

Before entering the room, Kathy flipped the switch by the door, and they waited as the fluorescent lights blinked and crackled, slowly illuminating the room in a greenish glow. There were three work areas in the center of the room, side by side. Each included a large stainless steel table. They reminded Tim of the sacrificial stone altars of the ancient Mayans. Trays of gleaming sterile instruments were ready at each station. A trace of antiseptic cleaners lingered in the air. Huge clusters of surgical lights hung from the ceiling, giving the room an otherworldly appearance. A body draped in a green sheet lay on the third table, waiting for Kathy to practice her gruesome art. Tim imagined her wielding her polished knives under the dark cover of a new moon. He swallowed the lump in his throat. He could never be a doctor. Thank God he'd studied the law.

"I thought you warned the emergency room to be on the lookout for this kind of a thing," Scott complained.

"I did. This one was just a tiny bit different from the others, and I guess that threw the staff off the scent. The woman came in with an irregular heartbeat. She was carefully monitored. She seemed to recover, and they released her. I'm as frustrated as you. But the emergency room staff didn't drop the ball. I remembered something about desipramine: It's an insidious little drug in overdose."

"Insidious how?" Tim needed to know.

"I'm getting there. This woman came to the emergency room with heart palpitations and then recovered. I didn't immediately recall this effect of the drug. But I had one of those vague feelings that I was missing something, so I looked it up. There can be a rebound--a delayed effect. Everything apparently normalizes, then bam! A few hours later, the patient dies of a massive heart attack. That explains why we only found minute traces of the drug--the body had metabolized most of it."

"The guy's a doctor. A nurse. A pharmacist. He knows this stuff." The sudden illumination frightened Tim. Even medical professionals could be evil.

"Maybe. I thought about that angle. I wondered if it was a mercy killing, you know like she had terminal cancer or something." Scott said.

Tim and Scott's eyes locked in a breathless stare. From the formless void, in the dim, misty mirror, the killer would slowly take shape. They had a new lead, one that left Tim swallowing back bile. A person with a medical background might also be clued in to police procedure.

"Did she? I mean--have terminal cancer?" Tim followed Kathy to the table. She lifted the sheet covering the body. Tim felt as if a vise-clamp tightened around his stomach. *It's just science. They aren't people anymore.* He tried to make his mind feel the essence of Kathy's words, but he couldn't seem to go there. He hadn't been able to detach himself from his revulsion.

"No. No cancer. So, who's he having mercy on? Not these beautiful, healthy, women. Why would they need mercy?" Kathy mused.

"Another thing: none of these gals were married. All single. None had a boyfriend that the families were aware of," Scott added.

Kathy finished folding back the sheet that covered the dead woman. Tim screwed up enough fortitude to look. The shock sent adrenaline rebounding and reverberating through his system. On the table before him lay a gorgeous woman. Her eyes were closed as if she were sleeping peacefully. Her pale cheeks were smooth and unblemished. Long brown hair spread out straight and shiny against the steel table. Her body was slender, shapely, and youthful.

"Damned shame. Nothing but a damned shame," Scott repeated over and over, shaking his head in dismay.

Damned shame?! Tim backed away, bumping, and knocking a tray full of instruments crashing to the floor.

"Damn, Tim! Be careful," Kathy scolded him.

"Sorry," he offered. But this woman looked strangely familiar. *Jesus!* This woman could have been Daniela St. Clair's sister!

NINE

Daniela's membership in the Sevens Athletic Club began as an investment in a building: a friend suggested she put some money into the project. She read the prospectus and decided it was a great idea to cash into fitness. After all, people wanted to live forever. Four years ago, just after her divorce, she dug into her piggy bank and was glad she did. Her meager investment had turned out beautifully. The group purchased a grand old building from a failed savings and loan. They refurbished the structure inside and out, managing to retain much of the bank's luxurious interiors. Sweating and burning calories between the elegant walls, with their polished hardwood wainscoting and crown moldings, somehow made workouts easier. The investment had a twofold benefit: the club lined her pockets with silver, and the workouts redefined her body.

Daniela felt sweat form into beads and trickle down the center of her back. She pressed the soft cotton of her tank top against her skin, allowing it to absorb the moisture and adjusted the waistband of her loose-fitting shorts. The invigorating workout melted away the tension in her body like ice cubes on hot pavement. She wiped her forehead and draped the white towel around her shoulders. Was it lunch the other day with Tim McAndrews that had made her so edgy? After only a few minutes at their cozy table, they had talked easily as if they'd known each other for years. He certainly wasn't the ogre she'd tried to make him out to be. In fact, all his gentlemanly attention might be making her lose sight of reality; she'd agreed to meet him for dinner later tonight.

"Let's go to the weight room." Her friend and workout partner Katrina Collins tightened the tawny ribbon holding her yellow curls up and away from her pretty face. She stretched from side to side in her animal-print leotard. Katrina was as agile as a cheetah.

Daniela and Katrina's parents had been best friends. Robert Collins had saved her father's life in the battle for Khe Sanh in the Vietnam War. When Robert "Bert" Collins developed lung cancer years ago, he'd approached Daniela's father for help. The medical bills were staggering, and Bert worried he would leave his family destitute. And there was no way on earth Simon St. Clair would let the Collins family suffer. Dani's father would've given his friend whatever he needed. But Collins was a proud man and wouldn't allow him to take on his medical expenses. Instead, he sold Simon his 200 acres adjoining Delight Valley Wineries. When Collins died, there was a falling-out between the families that Daniela's father had never explained. Nevertheless, Simon kept his promise. He set up a trust for his friend's family. The Collins family would live, rent-free, on the land; Delight Valley would buy their grapes and maintain their property as if nothing had happened. When Daniela's dad died, she became the trustee of the trust and carried out her duties without question as she was charged to do. Dani had even financed Katrina's Back Street Boutique here in the Seattle when she'd brought the proposal to her. Fashion and Katrina were a great mix. Katrina had developed a reputation and helped many professional women dress for success.

"I'm dying to see if Gary Warden is there," Katrina giggled. She always had one guy or another in her sights. Katrina wanted more than anything to be married, and she picked her prospects, researched them, and made her moves as if it were her life's goal.

"I need to cool down. Can we walk on the track for a few minutes?"

Katrina managed to stay amazingly unruffled by the vigorous exercise. Compared to Daniela's damp, overheated mess, she looked as though she'd just arrived for her workout, not just finished one.

"Okay." Though she consented, Daniela could tell by the hesitant toss of her saucy curls that Katrina wanted to make straight for the weights and her romantic rendezvous. Time was wasting, after all. Dani always thought Katrina's aggressiveness kept her single. She could be too forward and downright scary. But after her marriage failed, what advice could Daniela offer anyone else?

"Don't let me hold you up. I can catch up with you in a second."

"Oh, it's no big deal. I'll wait and walk with you. It's just that Gary brought a friend. I think you'll like this guy."

"I don't need to meet a friend of Gary's, Katrina. Thank you for being concerned about my lack of a love life, but I'm fine. Really." Daniela laughed as she shoved a wet strand of hair back into her long braid.

Katrina narrowed her eyes at her, almost as if masking anger. "I just want you to meet him, not marry him. You have no sense of adventure!"

"I have too much sense, period!" Daniela answered, but under her mirth her words were lies. If she had so much sense, why had she agreed to meet Tim again? Though she wasn't going to admit it, she had enjoyed being with him. Every cell in her body resonated like the tines of a tuning fork at the memory of her arm in his. Earlier as she'd walked past the downtown department store windows on her way to the club, she almost stopped in to buy flowery canisters for her kitchen. Tim was inspiring all her feminine urges. Wasn't it just like a man to make a woman feel like a woman!

But just as she'd stepped to the shop's door, reality had showed up and rained on her parade. She'd glanced down the street and, walking arm-in-arm up the sidewalk, was Carl, her cheater ex-husband, and his latest babe. Probably out spending the money she'd been obligated to pay him up until last month. She seethed. That was the real reason for the agitated workout. *That's how relationships turn out! In the rubbish bin!*

Daniela and Katrina walked around the specially designed indoor jogging track. The floor was covered with a blue rubberized mixture that cushioned each step. Katrina was talking to her, but Daniela found it hard to focus.

"I think he's going to ask me out," Katrina said, flexing her arms in bicep curls.

"Who? I'm sorry, I wasn't listening."

"What's with you today? You are so—lost."

Daniela laughed, "I guess I am lost. Oh! Yes. You were talking about Gary. Go on." She wanted Katrina to keep talking. Then she could continue agonizing over Tim McAndrews and the way he looked at her. When he left her at the doorstep to her office after lunch, he'd almost kissed her. He wanted to; she was sure of it. If he had, what would she have done? Let him? Left town for a while? And she'd agreed to have dinner with him tonight. They were going to make contact after they had both worked out. What if he kissed her tonight? God, she was so mixed up.

Suddenly, Tim appeared at the entrance to the indoor jogging track. Of course he'd be a member. He was the young professional type they'd marketed memberships to. It was like her thoughts evoked him in the flesh. In his workout shorts, he was every bit the Greek god she'd imagined, all his muscles tight and trim as if he'd been chiseled from marble. His lapis eyes sparkled with surprise.

"Dani, hi! I didn't know you belonged here. I haven't seen you here before." He was radiant.

"Hi." Daniela was suddenly aware she was a total disaster. She raked her fingers through the damp strings of hair that had worked their way loose from her braid. She'd been trying to cool down and seeing him sent a wave through her body, rocketing her temperature right back up.

Katrina stopped, her mouth gaping mid-sentence.

"Have you decided where you'd like to have dinner?" He stretched his arms over his head, preparing for his run.

"The food's great upstairs. We could meet there after we work out," Daniela answered.

"Sounds good. Oh, hey, before you sneak off I have tickets to the symphony Saturday night. It's a charity affair and formal. I know it's short notice, but would you join me?"

"Sure, okay," she said, blushing and anxious. After all, Katrina was standing there.

"Dinner upstairs, say seven o'clock?"

"All right. It's a date." Daniela looked at her speechless girlfriend. Tim hadn't even noticed Katrina. This was treatment she was not likely to take lightly. Katrina was used to being the center of male attention.

"My name is Katrina." She shoved her right hand forward.

"I'm sorry Katrina, this is my friend, Tim McAndrews." Daniela quickly tried to make up for the social breach.

"Hi, Katrina." Tim shook her outstretched hand and briefly smiled, but focused immediately on Daniela. "I better get after this run, or I'll be late for dinner." He hesitated before jogging off as if he might kiss her. Daniela almost panicked at the thought of being kissed right here, in public, by him. She wanted him to, she didn't; which? Tim seemed to read the discomfort in her eyes. He didn't kiss her.

"See you at seven."

Daniela nodded as he ran off ahead of them and was surprised by the reaction she had to Tim.

"I'll see you at seven? I'll see you at seven? Why didn't you tell me you knew Tim McAndrews! I've been dying to meet him for months; every other single girl at this club and me. You know him and didn't tell me!" Katrina complained.

"I just met him." Daniela made her way to the weight room, leaving the tidbit of information hanging in the air like the blue haze of smoke. Katrina wouldn't be able to stand it.

"Wait a minute. Hold on a second." Katrina caught up to her. "You have a date-date with the notorious Mr. McAndrews, and you didn't tell me?"

"Notorious?"

"You don't remember? It was all over the TV news and in the papers. He tried and won the Senchal abuse case last year. Everyone says he's up-and-coming in the prosecuting attorney's office."

"That's not notorious, Katrina. Notable. Notorious is bad."

"Oh, whatever. I can't believe you have a date with him. You're sure not his type. You're kidding me. It's just business, right?"

"What business would I have with the prosecuting attorney's office?"

Daniela laughed. She wanted to be but wasn't insulted by Katrina's put-down. She was right, after all. She wasn't any man's type. "You think he's too good for me, is that what you're saying? Real friend you are, Katrina!"

"Oh, I didn't mean that. It sounded like that, didn't it? I just can't—"

"Can't imagine him with me, or can't stand that you didn't get to meet him first?"

Katrina said nothing but returned a pout.

"It's nothing. Don't worry. You still have a chance. We're just friends." Daniela picked up two ten-pound weights from the rack in front of the mirror. Katrina was distracted, and her mouth turned down in a forlorn frown. She didn't notice as her dreamboat, Gary Warden, approached from the other side of the weight room. Gary was every bit as handsome and fit as Tim McAndrews. Well, not quite, but he was still very good-looking. He had brown hair, blue eyes and a great, winning smile.

"Hello, babe," he said, bending forward to peck her cheek.

Katrina managed a grin. Daniela knew she'd be unhappy for hours. She would get over it by morning. It was Katrina's competitive nature that was so perplexing; why couldn't she be happy with what she had, rather than wanting something else?

In the corner of her eye, Daniela caught sight of the tall, dark-haired man who made his way toward the group. He was pleasant-looking, fit and trim. She turned to face him. This must be Gary's friend; the one Katrina had been in such a hurry to introduce to her. He smiled, and his even, white teeth showed between nicely shaped lips.

"Katrina, Daniela, this is my friend and co-worker, Bill Fraser. Bill, these are the ladies I was telling you about." Gary slid his arm around Katrina's shoulders and squeezed her against his side.

Daniela found herself transfixed by Bill Fraser's eyes. They weren't green. Nor were they brown but gold. Gold like cat's-eye marbles.

TEN

Like cards shuffled by an expert blackjack dealer, the rush-hour traffic merged onto the busy freeway. Tim pressed the accelerator of his silver Mercedes and kept even with the brisk pace. Sunset painted the undersides of the rain clouds with brilliant color. The same reds and oranges shimmered off the windows of the glass and steel towers of Seattle and rippled over the surface of the smooth waters of the Lake Union. He glanced at the digital clock on the dashboard. He was right on time; dinner reservations were set, the symphony tickets were in his tuxedo pocket, and Daniela would be waiting for him at her downtown office. He caught his off-key voice singing along with the lyrics playing on the radio. It had been some time since he'd noticed a sunset, and even longer since he found himself singing. He marveled at life: for months everything had ticked along in the same boring routine. And one day, you see a beautiful woman dancing down the stairs at the James Street parking garage, and life takes off in an entirely new direction. Dani had changed his life and the way he felt about everything. He couldn't wait to share it all with her. And in a few minutes, he would start. He'd whisk her away for the evening. He had big plans.

The other night as they dined, he noticed the simple toss of her head when she laughed, and how moonlight glinting through the restaurant window played on her silky brown hair. He recalled his fascination with a single tiny freckle that rested just atop the curve of her lip. He dreamed of kissing that freckle. The thought sent long, slow pulses of excitement through his body. He shifted in his seat. After dinner tonight, he wasn't going to chicken out. He vowed to himself he would kiss her.

The sudden shock of his cell phone vibrating in his jacket pocket and the Bluetooth screen ringing in his car was like cold water poured on his fantasy. He'd forgotten to turn the damn thing off. The screen announced: KATHY HOPE 206 998 7567. He trusted she hadn't found another body.

He pressed the ANSWER button on his steering column. "Kathy? This is Tim," he said hesitantly, hoping it was just an invitation to meet her and Scott at McTavish's.

"Better get over here. I've got another victim," Kathy panted excitedly into the phone.

"I've got a date."

"And your point is? You're the one that said update you day or night, remember?" Kathy was stoic. She didn't ever have dates, of this Tim was certain. So, she'd have no sympathy for him if he had to break his.

"I don't want to break it."

"Bring her."

"Bring her? That would be impressive: 'Hey babe. Want to go to the morgue before dinner?' Geez! Kathy!"

"Do what you have to do, McAndrews. We have another murder."

"Did you call Scott?"

"Before you, sugar. See you in a few minutes—ah--with your date." Kathy chuckled into the phone.

"Yeah, great. Thanks." Tim stared at the CALL ENDED message on his screen. So much for the long, lingering kisses he'd planned. Daniela was only two short blocks from here. Since he had to cancel the date or postpone it, he figured he should do so in person. Asking a woman to dress in formal attire wasn't a small thing. He sure didn't want her to think he was making excuses. Who knows? Maybe she wouldn't be put off by the idea of going to the morgue before dinner. *Right.* All he could do was find out.

ELEVEN

He slid up the stairs to the third floor of the refurbished old building over Jake's Deli and across James Street from the offices of his newest prey. Since he'd first seen her, he thought of little else. He had to have her. So he'd rented a small one-bedroom apartment here.

The dim light from the amber wall sconces barely chased away the shadows in the hallway. He looked both ways before he carefully unlocked the glass door to the ancient emergency box. He reached up, felt behind the folded fire hose for the plastic bag he'd stashed there earlier. Inside the bag were protective booties and a green cotton surgical gown he'd stolen from the hospital. He knew all about forensic fiber evidence, and he wouldn't be caught so easily. In California, he'd learned how meticulous the police could be. He'd found out just in time that they had discovered Nomex fibers on two of his victims. Nomex would lead them to the fire department and straight to him. Some stupid flunky at the police department leaked information to the press, and the news of the break in the case had flashed all over the newspapers and airwaves. Lily's money had made it easy to move on.

This time, the police would find only generic cotton, the hardest fiber to trace. In addition to the pleasure of ridding the world of selfish, money-hungry bitches, killing stopped the endless, aching, emptiness he couldn't explain. He loved the chase. In California, he'd competed with the homicide detective assigned to the cases, sometimes leaving distracting clues for him. When the detective got close, he vanished. He wondered whether he would have a worthy adversary this time.

He'd been scouring the newspapers for information, but they hadn't even linked the chain of murders together yet. That was the beauty of poison: his victims died of seemingly natural causes. It would take a while to uncover-if anyone uncovered it at all.

He unlocked the door to his apartment and opened it just enough to snake through, closing it quickly but silently behind him. No need for nosey neighbors to note his comings and goings. Instead of switching on the light, he let his eyes adjust to the semidarkness. He could make out the shape of his camera on the tripod like some strange skeletal creature silhouetted against the pale city lights that reflected through the window. The curtains billowed; the fresh breeze filled them like spinnakers. Tonight, the wind off the Sound carried the scent of iodine and salt, and he briefly wondered why he'd never been sailing, why he'd never done the normal things that were billed on television commercials as providing happiness. He smiled to himself. He doubted his favorite sport would ever be used to sell aftershave and beer.

Below, on the street, he could hear voices. The night people were beginning to emerge as sunset faded to darkness. A memory tried to surface, dark and brooding, and he shook it off.

He slipped the booties over his shoes and the surgical gown over his clothes. From the pocket of the gown, he extracted cotton gloves and covered his hands. With a clean white handkerchief, he wiped the door handle, whisking away traces of oil his fingers had left behind. He savored all the minute details that kept him away from the camera, away from seeing into her office. It was like a tease, exhilarating. The tension built pleasure like a crescendo. He imagined watching her die. This time, he would be there to savor her slow death.

At last, with all the cleaning and fussing complete, he pulled the apartment's one furnishing, a straight wooden chair, into position and sat down. To his surprise, the office across from and below him was empty. He'd watched her leave her car at the parking garage and followed her until she'd crossed James Street and unlocked the door to her office. Many times in the last week, he'd watched her through the camera as she worked at her computer long after the business day ended. Why wasn't she there?

Angry, he slumped back into his chair. Then he noticed the light in the outer office snap on. He pressed his eye to the viewfinder of the camera. *Ah, there she is.* He snapped picture after picture as she moved through the doorway to her office, peeling away a black coat. She sat at her desk and changed out of the flat shoes she'd worn from the parking garage. He licked his lips as she slipped small stockinged feet into black high heels. He let his gaze travel up the slender ankle to the calf of her lovely legs. The long, wispy skirt kept him from seeing any further. Tonight, she wore an evening gown. *Going somewhere special, my darling?* He would follow her. He was hungry to know all about her. She stood, and he caught the sparkle of her beaded top and the shine of her honey-brown hair, braided into a neat chignon. She hurried to the outer door.

A man! My beauty, you have another man in your life! The tall blond dressed in a tuxedo followed her back into her office as she collected her coat and purse. He leaned against the stiff wood spindles in the back of the chair. Excitement thrilled though his body. *So. There will be more competition. No matter, my darling; I will win. I always win.*

TWELVE

Tim opened the car door for Daniela. He took hold of her hand, helping her across the rain-filled gutter to the sidewalk. He was glad they'd decided to drop her car before the miserable side trip to the morgue. It gave him this chance to drive her home. The morgue! Geez. He almost couldn't believe he'd asked her to accompany him. She'd taken it in stride, giving his career the importance it deserved. In that regard, too, she was different from other ladies he'd dated. She'd read magazines in the hospital lobby while he'd taken care of his grim business with Scott and Kathy. At least Dani hadn't let it color the rest of their date.

He pressed the LOCK button on his keys and kept her hand in his. As they meandered up the long walkway to her front door, he had an impulse to twirl her as if they were dancers. So, he did. The recent shower had left a shiny film on the pavement, and it reflected the street light and their silhouettes back up to his eyes. Daniela was taken by surprise but laughed with him as her silk skirt swirled up and then settled around her legs. He did it again, this time making sure she ended her spin in his arms.

He held her firmly against him, looking down into her upturned face. He couldn't remember being with a woman that made him feel so wonderful, so much in love.

"I had a great time tonight. How about dinner tomorrow?"

"Mr. McAndrews, you're spending too many evenings with me. Don't you want a break?" she teased, pulling away from him and wistfully twisting from side to side, making the silk skirts float and drift with her movement.

"I don't want a break. I want more." He grabbed her hand and pulled her back to him.

"You're going to give me a big fat ego. I'll be impossible to be around if you keep treating me like I'm a princess."

"You *are* a princess."

She tried to pull away again, but he wouldn't let her. He could see a hint of anxiety in her eyes as if she knew he was going to kiss her. Maybe she didn't want him to? Briefly, as he stared down at her, he worried that it might be too early in their relationship. But he did. He let his lips barely touch hers, and he lingered there, lost in the misty world of awakening desire. The pleasure was exquisite, and his body responded hungrily. He wanted more.

Daniela moved away. Her reaction was what he expected. *Too soon.* Her cheeks flushed with color, and she seemed flustered as if conflicted. Maybe she didn't like him? Could he change that?

"Come back here," he whispered, gently tugging her to bring her lips back to his.

"I better go in now, Tim. You'll have me all bewildered if you kiss me again."

"That's what I want: you, unable to resist me." He kissed her again, losing himself in the delicious cravings. She let him. She tasted like honey, and a subtle trace of her perfume teased the air, stirring desire even more.

"I *am* unable to resist you," she laughed and leaned back against his arms. "That's why I'm going into my house right now." She danced away from him. The playful tease made him follow her up the wide porch steps. She fumbled in her beaded handbag for her keys at the elegantly carved door.

"Do I get to come in?" He braced himself against the door jam, wanting more kisses, grinning down at her. His imagination ran hot hands over the curves of her body.

"No. Like I said, I'm unable to resist you. I'm going in, and you're going home, like a good boy."

He wasn't going to get what he wanted tonight. She was worth waiting for. "Thanks for putting up with the morgue. I didn't plan that as part of our date, but…"

"It's okay. We all must do our jobs. I'm just glad it's your job, not mine." She finished unlatching the door and opened it. She stepped up onto the threshold, turning back as she did.

He was going to marry her; that was all there was to it.

"Good night, Tim." She gave him a wistful smile that glinted from her eyes like moonlight on a high mountain lake. Did she want him? He could only hope.

"One more kiss: A good-night kiss." He stepped onto the threshold and took her around the waist. He kissed her tenderly and lingered at her full lips as long as she would allow. He felt the heat begin, and he pressed her against the entryway wall. His kissed her ardently now, letting the excitement build. She was responding, her long, red-tipped fingers tracing up his arms. She pressed her palms flat against his chest.

"Good night, Tim. You have to go."

He studied her. He wanted her so badly, but, knew that to rush her would be wrong. *I can wait. I really can wait … Can't I?*

"Okay. I'll go," he laughed and stepped back from her onto the porch.

"You never answered me about dinner tomorrow night. I'll take you anywhere you want to go."

"Dinner will be lovely. We'll talk in the morning. Good-night, Tim." Her smile was dreamy and hinted that she like kissing him. But her words were firm.

He didn't want to say it, didn't want the evening to end, but he finally conceded: "Good-night."

She closed the door. The latch clicked quietly into the recess, and he heard her fasten the deadbolt. For a long time, he stood staring at the door, imagining what it would be like to help her out of her clothes. He untied his black bow tie and let the ends hang loose about his neck. He unbuttoned the top button of his white tuxedo shirt as he turned and strolled to his car. He remembered how she felt, her scent, and was tempted to go back, to beg her to let him in. He leaned against the inside of the open car door. Waiting would require a healthy dose of restraint.

So this is what Dad meant when he said, "You'll know when the right one comes along." The others he'd dated before never made him feel like this. His dad often told the story of seeing Mom for the first time. He'd told Tim and his two older brothers that at that moment he knew he would marry her. He'd never wanted anyone else. Dad shared that kind of story while the boys, Tim and his two older brothers, had helped in his woodworking shop in the back of their property. And that's how Tim had felt when he first saw Dani. He didn't want anyone else. *No doubt; Dani is the right woman.*

He started to get into the car when he noticed the man in the gray hooded sweatshirt, jogging from the shadow of the street trees, padding almost silently up the sidewalk. He could see the puffs of his breath condensing in the crisp night air. Tim hadn't noticed him earlier. *Must have been too busy.* He chuckled as he remembered Dani's kisses.

"Good evening," he called out as the man passed by, straining to get a look at the face obscured by the shadow of the hood.

"Good evening to you, too," the jogger replied. Tim suddenly had the impression he'd seen the man before. He couldn't place him. *Somewhere— somewhere else. Tonight.* Tim turned and watched as he disappeared around the corner in the distance. He climbed into the front seat of his car, but he didn't start the engine. For some reason, he felt uneasy. He stared into his rearview mirror, but the jogger never returned to the sidewalk.

THIRTEEN

He watched the silver Mercedes until it finally drove away. From the cover of the leafy hedge, he emerged and crept back to the edge of her property. His rival had made progress courting Miss St. Clair this evening. But that wouldn't last long; when he finally made his move, he would enjoy sweeping the young man from the field. He always won the ladies with little effort. The competition with the blond only added spice to the game.

Tonight, he'd shadowed them, haunting the lobby at the hospital, the archway at the symphony, blending into the crowd, stalking them from a distance. He watched them kiss and watched Daniela dismiss his rival from her doorstep. He chuckled aloud. Miss St Clair was the type that would insist on a commitment, and he doubted that handsome young man would be ready to give her one.

Agile as a cat, he sprung to the top of the concrete wall along her property line. He perched on the top ledge, hidden in the overhanging branches of the dogwoods. The window coverings of her house were drawn shut, and he couldn't see in. Not even a silhouette. He'd hoped for more. Wanting the thrill of watching her undress for bed, something to fuel the need and the rage, he watched the closed windows. Like a junkie, emotions were an addiction.

From under his sweatshirt, he plucked binoculars and checked each window at the back of the house. He could see only the warm glow of light from inside at the very edges of the blinds. He heard a click-snap and jerked right, adjusting the lens as he turned. Two dogs appeared through a pet door into a fenced run. They barked furiously at him. He froze. Would she investigate? He dropped low on the wall and waited until the persistent animals stopped their fray.

Ears peeled for sound, he strained to hear the dogs retreat into the house. Satisfied, he once again topped the brick-capped ledge and squatted, muscles taut, weight balanced like a tightrope walker. He stared through the binoculars and took mental measurements of the doggy-door that fed into the run. It was about a foot wide and two-and-a-half tall. He twisted his body, working out how he could wriggle through. The six-foot chainlink fence around the edge of the run would be a breeze to climb over.

Monday morning, while she worked, he would scramble over the fence and get in. By the time they had their first date, he would know more about her than she knew about herself.

FOURTEEN

Morning came glorious and pink, and Daniela woke early, smiling from the inside out. She felt beautiful. She touched her fingers lightly across her lips, remembering Tim's silken kisses. He was the most romantic man she'd ever met. She snuggled back into her pillows, pulling the thick goose down comforter up and under her chin.

If he'd persisted in kissing her any longer last night, he would most likely be waking with her now. *Wouldn't he be surprised to know I'm thinking that!*

She stretched her arms overhead and stirred the gray striped kitty curled at her feet. As if on cue, the dogs roused awake, cheerful and exuberant at the thought of breakfast. She threw back the covers and breezed to the kitchen, twirling in her white cotton nightgown as if Tim were still dancing with her.

"Tim McAndrews is fantastic. Did I tell you that, kids?" she asked as she opened dog and cat food tins. The two dogs listened with ears pricked forward while the cat purred and wound himself back and forth against her legs. She knew they cared, her darling pets, but did they understand what she was saying? It didn't keep her from talking to them.

"You should've seen what he did! After the symphony was over and we were waiting at the light to cross to the parking garage, the street was soaked, and there was a huge puddle spread almost three-quarters of the way across." She spooned food into their dishes. Now she had their full attention but certainly not for the story she told them. "He scooped me up into his arms and carried me over!" She spun in place, the spoon held high, remembering the surprise and delight of being lifted and carried in his arms. "It was—wonderful! I heard another woman complain to her husband about not doing the same." She placed the feeding dishes at strategic distances so there would be no battles. The animals dug in as if they were starved. "Oh, pooh on you; you bums don't care. You only want breakfast," she laughed.

Daniela decided to treat herself to a bubble bath. *The luxury of a lazy Sunday morning.* She would relax and savor the beauty of her life. No doubt about it, she was standing on the precipice, primed and ready to fall in love. No, it couldn't be, not her. With Tim? *He's only a nice fantasy for a Sunday morning.* She stripped and slipped into the steamy, fragrant water.

After whiling away a good half hour in the bath, she dried, briefly fussed with her hair, and dressed in casual, comfortable jeans and T-shirt. Now for a great big cup of coffee and food. As she turned to the kitchen, the dogs barked an alarm at the front door. Who would come calling this early on a Sunday morning? She dashed to the door and peeked through the visor.

Daniela opened the door and stood barefoot on the hardwood floors of her entryway, completely surprised. "Tim?"

"Hi." He handed her the Sunday newspaper he'd gathered from her front step. "May I come in?" He wore charcoal gray sweats that smelled fresh as he passed by as if he'd just pulled them from a warm dryer. His eyes and the set of his strong jaw was tense. She felt worry cloak her shoulders like a thick winter coat.

"Is something wrong? Are you okay?" She readily admitted to herself that no matter why he was here, she liked that he was. She took the paper from him, hugging it to her chest.

He pushed the door closed quietly behind him and gulped a swallow of air. Whatever he'd come to say was serious, indeed.

"What? What's wrong? Tim?"

"Dani." He raked his hand through his short blond hair. "I couldn't sleep—I couldn't sleep at all—for thinking of you. I needed to see you." He attempted a smile, but it collapsed quickly into a disquiet as if he was afraid he'd overstepped the boundaries she'd set last night. Had he? She was all tingly inside. She absently set the newspaper on the mahogany entry table.

"Oh? Oh! You're teasing me. Is that all? By the look on your face, I thought the world was ending or something," she laughed. He grinned, running his hand over his lips and she felt the muscles in her body tighten as his gaze fixed on her eyes and drifted hungrily down her face to her mouth. At once, she understood what he'd come for; she was just unsure what she was going to do about it. He was in turmoil, lust barely reined in, like one of her racehorses pawing and foaming at the bit at a starting gate. *This is not good.* It had been such a long time since a man wanted her, she was confused. *I can't do this.*

"When I went to hang my tuxedo this morning, your scent—your perfume, was all over... all over my clothes." He closed his eyes briefly and took a breath through his parted lips as if every sense trembled on the brink of spilling over.

Seeing him in this state made her light-headed. Pangs of desire squeezed at her. It had been so long since a man had stared at her with such passion. Words stuck in her throat and finally materialized only as a sigh: "Oh, my." *I should send him away. Right now!*

"Don't be mad. Okay?' He stood tenuously before her as if barefoot on broken glass. His beautiful blue eyes radiated a compelling vulnerability. In spite of not wanting to encourage him, Daniela felt her face soften into a smile. She caught herself and frowned; she needed to change the direction this freight train was heading in a hurry!

"Would you like some coffee? An omelet?" she offered, breaking the awful silence, unable to think of what else to do. Her body was quivering inside like a butterfly. Tim was excited; his eyes burning, intense, electric blue, consuming her, making promises her body clearly understood. The wonder and agony he inspired overwhelmed her. Pulses of white-hot longing rocketed through her. *I should stop this. I should tell him to go.*

"I could fix breakfast," she fumbled. None of the *I-should* thoughts formed into words and she found herself wondering why.

"Uhh, no—I—I shouldn't have come here. I'm losing it—this is crazy. You don't want this. I'm sorry. I just—I'll call you later." He scrambled for the words. Self-conscious, Tim started to leave. Dani knew if he did, he would be so embarrassed she might never see him again. She closed her eyes, not sure what she wanted to do.

"Stay. Please stay," she whispered and gasped at the realization. She couldn't take her words back. Did she want to? For an endless moment, anxiety ran rampant. Through her confusion, she understood precisely what she had invited him to do. He turned back, and a sigh escaped from her lips. Time slowed. She was in the clouds, surrounded by the mist of her yearning. He reached for her shoulders and gently pulled her to him until they stood inches apart. Fingers of heat from his body touched her skin like the warmth of springtime sunshine. She could still send him away, couldn't she?

"Dani, I want—I—I have to—your scent—your scent was all over my clothes."

She reached out and brushed his lips with the tip of her index finger. He didn't need to say anything more. She ached for his touch, couldn't speak. Transfixed, she nodded. *Yes.*

His lips found hers. And they were kissing as if they hadn't stopped last night. Spinning and drunk with the taste of his mouth, her body aching for him, she yielded to his embrace. As he swept her up into his arms once again, she was amazed at how fabulous and reckless it felt to give in to him. He carried her down the hall, stopping only to lose himself in kisses, fueling the passion that already burned like wildfire.

As if by some earthy instinct, he easily found her room. With one hand, he tore back the white quilt and covers from her bed and tenderly set her back on the crisp cotton sheet. He brushed all the decorative white ruffles-and-lace pillows aside. He kicked off his shoes and peeled away his sweatshirt. Daniela watched him, knowing she should stop this. Right now. If ever she was going to. But he slid next to her and enfolded her to his body. The flesh over the muscles in his arms and chest was tight and hard from weight-lifting. He was kissing her throat, pulling the cotton tee free from where she'd tucked it into her jeans. His masculine hands caressed her bare stomach with a touch as light as silk. He pulled her to a sitting position. Within moments he lifted her t-shirt off and unclasped her white lace bra, sliding the straps down her arms and over her hands. He stared and said nothing, studying her face, her eyes, and letting his gaze course over her curves. She was hot with embarrassment and grabbed at the sheet to cover herself. With a firm grip on her wrists, he stopped her and shook his head no.

"You are so beautiful. I need to look at you," he whispered. With the back of his fingers, he traced down her cheek and throat, over the soft rise of her full breast. His touch was exquisite, and her body strained to feel the lightness of it as if a sun-drenched breeze were caressing her. He unfastened her jeans and slowly slid the zipper open. Daniela marveled at how easily he undressed her. His were the hands and this the touch of an experienced lover. A very experienced lover.

She shut her eyes, squeezing them tight against the panic that tried to take over. At the edge of her mind reason sought to intrude. *Stop now. Stop now.* But then she felt the tender, wet, warmth of his mouth as he licked and nibbled at her breast. Each tender bite sent torrents of pleasure through her. It had been too long, too many lonely nights. As frightened and hesitant as she was, he was confident. He knew exactly how and where and when to touch her. Common sense got lost somewhere; finally and completely, she gave in to him.

He encouraged her back against the pillows. Standing beside the bed, he peeled away his sweats. She tried not to look at him, but he was every bit as she'd imagined, and she couldn't stop staring, memorizing every angle of his firm body. It was as if he were fashioned from molten gold, from her wildest, most sensuous dreams. Slowly, he pressed open her legs and climbed onto the bed, kneeling between her thighs. Daniela marveled at how incredibly sexy her lover was and reached for him. He groaned as his splendid erection throbbed up against his firm belly. She begged him with her gentle touch. Quickly, he was over her, his eyes glistening and dark, like sequins in the moonlight. She arched up to meet him. He pressed inside her, and she felt her body tighten around him. He shoved into her, hard and driven, passion exploding with desperate need.

"Dani." He whispered her name, and she surrendered herself to the delirium of pure pleasure.

FIFTEEN

Tim stirred awake and quietly, carefully, untangled his body from Dani's. Wanting to absorb every part of her and carve the memory deep into his brain, he studied her. Her skin was like porcelain, creamy and flawless, except for one freckle. God, he loved that freckle. The lashes that framed her eyes were dark against her pink cheeks. Her hair was like billions of long threads of shimmery light brown silk mixed with strands of pure gold. Lips so full and lush he wanted to linger in kisses forever. He lifted the corner of the sheet and memorized the feminine symmetry of her body. He had hoped for this, longed for it, but it was hard to believe that he was here: in her bed, in her arms.

Unfortunately, he reminded himself, he had to go into the office this afternoon. He could dash in and write a memo, then spend the rest of the day with her. Already it was afternoon! The morning was long gone. He chuckled to himself. *What a morning!*

Still sleeping, Dani repositioned herself, tugging the big quilt up around her shoulders. He'd better get going. That memo to Goddard wasn't going to write itself.

"Did I wake you?" he asked, as Dani curled up sleepy-eyed against his side.

"No, not really. What time is it?" She stretched and yawned like a contented cat. She was sweeter in real life than she'd ever been in his most treasured fantasy. He was so in love.

"Two." He combed his fingers through her shiny hair, pushing it away from her face. He kissed her lips and remained close. "I've got to go in and write a memo to my boss. Want to come?"

"No. I have so much work to do," she sighed. "No town for me. It's Sunday, and I've got to get ready for Monday."

"I know, but I've got to ask for an FBI profiler for a case I'm working on, and I don't want to leave you."

"An FBI profiler? Don't profilers figure out the personalities of serial killers?" She pulled the covers closer around her body.

Tim felt his stomach flop over. *Damn it!* They had agreed; no leaks to anyone until they were sure what they had. "Yes—serial killers, rapists, molesters. Scum."

"Is that why we went to the morgue last night? Is there a serial killer?" Dani sat up. "Here in Seattle?"

"I won't let anything happen to you. I'll watch out for you. You don't have to worry." The covers fell away. Her body was exquisite, and he wanted her again. But, he could read fear flash in her eyes.

"There is a serial killer?" She swallowed hard. "Were you going to tell me? Why isn't there anything in the papers, on the news?"

"We're not sure, but it's time to find out, and if there is one, I'll protect you. I promise." The image of the girl on Kathy's autopsy table surfaced in his mind, transposed over Dani's pretty face. He shook it off. He wrapped his arms around her. Right now, wasn't the time to tell her the victims were beautiful business women with long, golden-brown hair just like hers.

"You'll be my guardian? I feel safer already." She cuddled closer to him, settling her head against his chest as if listening to his heartbeat.

"That's me. Your special guardian. The champion of truth and justice. Defender of the American way," he laughed, curling his free arm, making the muscle bulge.

"Okay, Mr. Hero. Go write your memo and get that profiler." She kissed the edge of his chin, and he moaned as desire swept through him. He dropped his chin, so her next kiss met his lips.

"Darling, Dani, I'll never get to the office if you kiss me again."

"You are too sexy, Mr. McAndrews."

"You make me hot," he said. She moved back from his embrace and rested her head on her hand. The turn of her lips told him she was skeptical. He'd prove to her he meant every word. "I could pick up Chinese and bring it over for dinner on my way back from town. Do you like Chinese food?" Not waiting for her answer, he untangled himself from the bed covers and pulled on his sweatpants.

"I like Chinese." The hesitancy in her voice wasn't the tone he wanted. Was she going to tell him not to come tonight? For a moment, he waited, expecting her refusal. He sat back down on the edge of the bed and stroked her hair. He thought about telling her he loved her. He decided to wait. If he overwhelmed her, he might scare her away, and he had to pull this part of his life together. He wanted Dani in it.

"Then I'll be back with dinner," he said. She nodded yes.

SIXTEEN

Daniela watched Tim leave. She was overwhelmed; he was too perfect to be real. Entirely too ardent. She tried to find a flaw as if it would protect her. *Well, there is one, even if I can't see it now. It will surface.*

She dressed in her T-shirt and blue jeans. She tore the sheets from the bed. As she carried them to the washing machine, she breathed in the mix of Tim's aftershave and sex. *Mmmm.* She was set adrift in a sea of delicious memories. Was she in love? Maybe--in lust. Either way, it was wonderful after her miserable marriage and four long years alone. *Four years? Had it been that long?* Tim opened the bitter truth of her life like a skilled surgeon, and she could see how lonely and solitary she'd become. The gauntlet had been thrown down before her: all she had to do to heal her heart was be a complete fool for a gorgeous man who would never stay with her. It hurt just to think about it. So she wouldn't.

There was work to do. She couldn't worry anymore about Tim. She needed to toss herself into something else. Something to keep her mind off what she'd done and where it would or wouldn't lead.

She rummaged through her briefcase and placed her purchase bid for the new vineyard on the oak table in her kitchen nook. Resolved to work on the contract, she sat down in one of the oak chairs. She read the words, but they didn't stick in her brain, and she gazed through the window. Outside in her rose garden, a butterfly fluttered from pink-tipped petals to red. New plants sprouted everywhere, opening flowers to the kiss of sunshine. The rained-washed sky was as bright and sparkling as blue topaz. And Tim's eyes. *So much for not thinking about him!*

The doorbell rang, and the dogs went crazy. Tim couldn't be back already. He'd promised he'd bring dinner around five; it was only three.

"Oh, for crying out loud! Who is it this time?" She complained to the dogs. Not that she minded what had happened between Tim and herself. Warmed by the memory, she scooted the chair back from the table and once again found herself looking through the peephole.

"Katrina?" She opened the door. To her amazement, her girlfriend stood on her porch step with Gary Warden and Katrina's I'm-going-to-fix-you-up-friend, the golden-eyed Bill Fraser. *What? Why?* How was she going to get rid of them before five and Tim's return? Katrina barged past her. Gary followed with grocery bags, and Bill lifted wine, a bottle in each hand.

"Won't you come in?" Daniela called to Katrina's back as the uninvited guests paraded through her hallway to the kitchen.

"I knew you'd be working on work, so I brought dinner. Gary's going to barbecue some steaks, where's your grill?" Katrina fingered the contract on the nook table. Daniela quickly swept the papers together and shoved them into their manila folder. Katrina scowled at her. Dani could tell she wanted to see. *Better to keep financial information private, even with friends.*

"In the garage; I hadn't thought of dragging it out yet. It's still rainy," she said, stuffing the contract into her briefcase.

"Have you looked outside? Not today--it's fabulous!" Gary chimed in. Daniela felt a blush flash over her cheeks as if they might have the power to know how she'd spent the last few hours. She combed her fingers through her hair, wondering how red-faced she was: strawberry or vine-ripened tomato.

"Are you kidding? When Daniela gets involved in work, she doesn't know if it's day or night," Katrina laughed.

"So, where is this grill of yours? We'll get it out and set it up for you," Bill said as he slid one of the wine bottles on its side and into the empty middle shelf of her refrigerator. "We should open this one." He held the other out to her, his face creased with a trace of a smile that let her know he felt a little bit ashamed for barging in on her like this. But with Katrina as their leader, he had no choice but to acquiesce; Daniela knew that as fact.

"Katrina, I have plans."

"Oh, stop it, Daniela. You were just going to work. The grill's this way." Katrina led Gary and Bill through the laundry room to her garage.

Daniela resigned herself to her dinner party. Tim would understand. At least, she hoped he would.

"While the boys are doing that, help me with the salad, okay?" Katrina tossed her blonde curls, and they bounced around her lovely cheeks and chin. Daniela knew what Katrina-the-matchmaker was up to and prepared herself. Katrina couldn't last even five seconds without a man on her arm and assumed no other woman could either. If her latest and greatest love turned out not to be interested enough she'd accuse him of being gay and barge on to the next one. Remarkably, there was always one waiting in line. Katrina's men seemed to be interchangeable. The current one, while in favor, was granted the title of the love of her life for as long as she put up with him. Katrina then began to find horrible flaws that she would've noticed early on if she'd taken more time. But Dani had no business judging her-not today, not after what she'd just done.

Dani stepped back into the kitchen and pulled a large stainless steel bowl

from the cupboard. "This is a surprise. What if I wasn't home? Or busy?"
With Tim McAndrews? she added silently. Thank goodness she'd been able
to straighten things before Katrina took over the afternoon. But then she
remembered when Tim stripped her for bed he'd tossed her jeans and tee
on the floor. She wondered if she was rumpled and quickly checked herself
over. Too bad! If she was a mess, there was nothing she could do about
it now.

"I knew you were home. You're always home. What do you think of
Bill? Isn't he handsome? Gary likes him. Pour me a glass of wine, will you?"
Katrina grabbed a knife and sliced tomatoes on a cutting board.

Daniela reached for glasses and set five on the counter. "He seems very
nice." Bill was good- looking and fit. But she was stuck in some crazy other
dimension—a lost world where it would be okay for her to love Tim. While
she was in this state, no one else on the planet stood a remote chance of
getting a second of her attention.

"Five? Can't you count? There are only four of us," Katrina teased.

"I'm expecting someone. I had other plans when you steamrolled in.
So we'll all have dinner together," Daniela laughed.

"Other plans? Who were you expecting?" Katrina waited with her
mouth hanging open.

"Is it so hard for you to believe that anyone would be interested in me?
Geez, Katrina, am I that horrible?"

"I didn't say that. Bill's interested. You know, you are gorgeous, it's just
that you are so—well—so introverted."

"Tim McAndrews," Daniela blurted out, staring at her hands, twisting
the emerald-and-gold ring on her finger, knowing Katrina was going to go
off like dynamite under a blasting cap.

"TIM MCANDREWS? Are you kidding?" Katrina stood squarely
in front of her; tomato drenched hands firmly on her hips, seeds and juice
dripping down the leg of her tight blue jeans. Instantly, Dani read jealousy
in her eyes. "You aren't kidding," she confirmed. She grabbed a towel from
the counter and cleaned up.

"No, I'm not kidding," Daniela said, watching her friend press her lips
together in a thin line. Katrina's blue eyes flashed like firecrackers.

"You're seeing him? I knew it! Daniela, he's …"

"He's only coming for dinner," she lied.

"Daniela, he's a cad. You can't go out with him; he's awful. His reputation is—terrible. You've got to be careful! Besides, I don't think we have
enough steak. I didn't plan for him."

Katrina's accusation unsettled her. She had none of her resilience. Men weren't interchangeable to her. She wanted only one. One love. And she was already worried making love to Tim had been a mistake.

"He was invited; you and your friends were—a surprise." Daniela poured them each a glass of wine, knowing that with all the food Katrina had brought and Tim's Chinese there would be more than enough for them all–and twenty more.

"I see. We should leave." Katrina loaded the seeded French baguette back into a brown paper bag, a full-blown pout forming on her abundant lips.

"Stop it! We can all eat together, can't we?" She took Katrina's hand and pressed the wineglass into it. It was seconds before Katrina's fingers curled around the stem and Daniela could let go. Katrina could be such a brat.

"Bill will feel out of place. If you'd told me, you were involved with Tim ..." Katrina needled her, prying for more information than Daniela was willing to give, her brown eyes searching Dani's as if trying to read the thoughts behind them.

"Give me a break. I don't know what I'm doing with Tim. He's coming to dinner. That's all I know." Daniela broke the tension with a healthy laugh.

"God! Daniela! I can't believe you're such a jerk. He's got a bad reputation as a skirt chaser. I've heard about him from lots of women at the club."

"Katrina, stop it. I'm a member, too." *Not to mention an owner*, Daniela thought. But that information Katrina didn't know. "And I haven't heard a bad word. Not one. Except you, just now. And just the other day you said you'd wanted to meet him for months. Isn't that what you said? Is he a chaser? Is he?" She felt angst tighten her stomach. All she needed was to get involved with another hound dog. Once was more than enough. She remembered Tim's experienced hands on her body and dread started to trickle in like a slow leak.

"You're defending that scoundrel! Do you remember Ellen Mason from the club? Talk to her before you get involved. What are you doing?" Katrina's chastising grimace curled the corners of her red lips. Suddenly, again, Dani had the distinct impression that Katrina was jealous. That would be just like her: she expected every man to fall only for her. Because they usually did. Katrina was beautiful.

"I don't know. Let's drop it, okay? Whatever is going to happen, is going to happen." She wasn't going to share what had already happened.

"I was hoping you and Bill would hit it off. He and Gary are so close. And we, well, we *used* to be best friends." Now Katrina was threatening to withdraw her friendship! Sometimes Daniela could just smack her. She gave her a hug, instead. All the while, her thoughts rolled over in her mind until she felt nauseated.

"We still are friends, aren't we? Or are we only friends if I date Mr. Fraser?" Katrina was probably right. Tim would surely break her heart. The question now was only when and whether she could stand it. She sighed.

"At least give Bill a chance; he thinks you are so pretty," Katrina said.

"Isn't this crazy? I've been single for four years, now all of a sudden--"

"Tim McAndrews is after you; I knew it!"

"I don't know what he's after. Right now, we're friends," Daniela lied. No use arguing with Katrina. When she made her mind up, it was her way or no way at all. And she was backing Bill Fraser.

SEVENTEEN

"Hey, Tim. Over here." Scott slid out of the booth and stood from behind the maple wood table in the dark corner of McTavish's. Mic's was a favorite of the cops and was convenient, occupying space in the lobby floor of a building close to the county courthouse and Tim's offices. Mic's was an artfully decorated dive, a dark hole-in-the-wall kind of place with big screen TVs here and there tuned to the sport of the season. Though the building was less than a year old, Mic's already smelled of spilled beer.

Tim slid into the booth across from his friend.

"You asked Goddard for the profiler?"

"Memo's in the middle of his desk, waiting for him as we speak. He'll have it first thing."

"Thought you should know: newspaper boys caught wind of the killings, don't ask me how. They were snooping through police reports this morning, asking all kinds of questions. It'll hit the press soon. When it does, we'll have a heck of a time." Scott motioned the bartender to bring over another bottle of Full Sail Amber.

"You worried about being famous?" Tim chuckled.

"I'm worried about being wrong. Besides a cop's fame is always short lived. What about you? Plans for political office?"

"Oh fuck no. Wouldn't mind more money, though."

"We solve this one, and you'll get a raise. Have you thought about what happens to us if Kathy's wrong?" Scott took a long pull on his bottle of beer.

"She's not wrong." Tim ran a hand over his chin. At least, he hoped she wasn't wrong.

"If she is, it wouldn't be the first time Captain Stick-up-the-Butt called me a screw-off." Scott sighed, smoothing a finger over his dark mustache.

"It's not too late for me to go get that memo. I thought we were all in agreement."

"Three bodies—all alike. We're in agreement. Sometimes I worry, though. Kathy can be so ..."

"So bullishly self-assured?" Tim supplied the end to his sentence and Scott laughed.

"She's brilliant. I don't want her hurt by a wrong call, you know." Scott toyed with the label on his beer, pulling it free from the glass.

"I don't either. My rear is on the line too, so if we go down, we all go

together." Tim leaned back into his side of the booth as the bartender set
a cold, frosty bottle in front of him. "Ah, hell; better safe than sorry. How
would we feel if we hesitated and a serial killer got away with murder?"

"That would be unspeakable ... Oh, on my tab," Scott said to the
bartender.

"You're buying?" Tim was delighted; he'd spent all his cash on last
night and had forgotten to go to the bank machine this afternoon to replace it.

"My turn," Scott said, watching the barkeeper lumber back to his
station.

"Tomorrow Goddard is going to want to know what we have and what
we intend to do. Kathy's report is already typed and on his desk. What have
you got?"

"I've interviewed the victims' families to see if the ladies had any
friends in common. None. They didn't see the same doctor or shop at the
same pharmacy. This week, I'm checking to see how many prescriptions
have been filled in this town for Desip-whatcha-ma-call-it. There could be
thousands. I'll interview them all. Lab boys found some fiber on the latest
woman. But said it's generic cotton. I've got to have a suspect before I can
match anything up. There are no fingerprints. Kathy's sent off the semen
for the DNA match. Until everything comes back, we're in the dark. I hope
the profiler can give some insight into what kind of sicko I'm dealing with.
This morning, I wondered, is it a guy? Or a jealous woman, killing after
she catches her man in his—extracurricular activities? There was a case like
that in Oklahoma a few years back, and poison tends to be a woman's M.O."

"Possible; I never thought of that. That's what I like about you, Scott.
You act like a goof-off. Instead, you're right on." Tim lifted his bottle in
toast and drank a bubbly swallow.

"Yeah, well, tell me that again in three months when we're still fum-
bling around." Scott's jaw looked tight.

"Speaking of Kathy." Tim noticed a softening around Scott's eyes. A
warmth turned the corners of his mouth just at the mention of her name, a
reaction Tim hadn't seen before.

"Isn't she something? The way that steel-trap mind of hers works
just amazes me. And have you noticed how gorgeous she's looking lately?
There's a sparkle—a glow to her." Scott paused to drink his beer as if pondering Kathy's merits. Geez! Kathy wasn't exactly what Tim would call
"gorgeous," but she had inner beauty.

"Only when she's around you. Look, that's what I wanted to talk to
you about; you and Kathy."

"I know what you're thinking. I don't have the best reputation in the world. And when we were in school—well—we were pretty out-of-control."

"Pretty out-of-control? We were mutts," Tim laughed.

"I'm not like that anymore."

"We've both grown up since then. I just thought I'd let you know Kathy's got it pretty bad when it comes to you. Always has--I don't want anyone to get hurt." Tim felt a frown fold the flesh between his eyebrows and hoped he wasn't too serious.

"You mean you don't want *Kathy* to get hurt," Scott snickered and leaned back into the red leather booth.

"I don't want any of us to get hurt. If our friendship hits the skids, we all get screwed."

Both men took a drink of beer as if on cue. "Don't worry about Kathy. Worry about me. Lately—well—she's been driving me wild." Scott set his forearms on the table, his voice little more than a whisper.

"Kathy can be a little pushy when she gets on a case. Remember the cyanide one? She badgered me relentlessly until I agreed to sign my name to her homicide report."

"I think about her all the time. Can you believe it?"

"I don't think you can let her get to you. It's just her way." Tim shrugged his shoulders.

"No, buddy. What I'm trying to tell you is that I haven't been able to imagine my life without her in it. I think I'm in love with her."

Tim gasped, and the swig of beer in his mouth headed right down his windpipe. He coughed and sputtered it clear. He stared, getting Scott's full attention.

"Are you okay?"

"Fine." Tim's voice was weak, and he cleared his throat. "You and Kathy? You've been dating? Where have I been? I didn't know."

"We haven't exactly been dating. Not formally. 'Let's go for a beer, Kath.' 'How about a movie before we go home?' 'Have you had dinner yet?' All last-minute stuff. But, hell, look how long we've been friends." Scott absently sipped his beer. "I haven't seen anyone else for over a year. And it hit me months ago, that the reason was, I love Kathy. And if I don't make a move, some other guy is going to come along and snap her up. Yesterday afternoon, I bought her this ring." He passed a black velvet box across the table to Tim. "Tell me what you think? Do you think she'll say yes?"

Stunned, Tim stared at Scott, his mouth hanging open. When he realized, he closed it, running his tongue over his teeth. After a few moments, he snapped open the case. Inside was a lovely solitaire. A respectable one-carat diamond set in gold. "I never imagined—you and Kathy. Don't you think you should date first?"

"Kathy? If I don't know her by now, I never will." Scott's statement was true enough; she was the one woman they both could say they understood. Kathy was an easy friend, as comfortable as a broken-in pair of tennis shoes. Of course Kathy would marry Scott; there was no doubt in Tim's mind.

"She'll say yes. Why wouldn't she?" Tim liked the idea of his best friends together. It was sweet.

"She'll probably laugh in my face, you mean. She knows me. She's seen what a jerk I am. She knows about all the other women."

"Kathy will marry you. It's written all over her every time she sees you. I'm surprised with all your training you haven't seen it. If you're ready to settle down and make a commitment, she'll marry you. I couldn't be happier," Tim said.

"Would you be there for me? Tuesday night we're meeting for drinks and dinner. I was planning to ask her then. You could bring Ellen Mason. Kathy likes Ellen, and I could use the moral support."

"I don't see Ellen anymore. She gave me the big steel-toed boot." Tim grimaced. It wasn't that he cared-he didn't. It was just that Kathy did like Ellen. Would she like Dani?

"Now I'm the one in the dark. When did that happen?" Scott stood and gestured with two fingers to the bartender to bring more beer.

"About a year ago. I didn't say anything. She was just another woman throwing me out, on the long list of women who threw me out. I guess I'm used to it. I deserved it." He *had* deserved it. Ellen had been like most of the women in his life: she'd pursued him and initiated all contact. He, Scott, and Kathy had been wandering the waterfront on one of their very few days off. Spontaneously, they decided to take the ferry over to Bainbridge Island. There was a coffee shop on the other side with a great brunch menu. Ellen was on the ferry with several friends. Kathy was the one that brought it to their attention that the girls were checking them out. They'd been out all night for a bachelorette party, still tipsy, and were a little forward. Ellen was sweet. And she took charge. Relaxing into that kind of liaison was easy. It seems he'd always been doing that. He only remembered once, in high school, when he'd made an actual effort and that had been such a spectacular failure, he'd stopped trying until Dani. Letting women choose him was stress-free. But as time went on in the relationship, it never turned out that way. Tim was more devoted to his success, whether it be scoring the highest grades in law school, or making top prosecuting attorney now. And then inevitably the nagging came, the endless demands that he give up the time he spent preparing his court cases for something Ellen wanted to do. She'd wanted him to move in, but he hadn't ever spent the whole night with her. He was always home before midnight, sleeping in his bed, at his loft. Even weekends. Ellen was never invited there. Why she'd put up with him for as long as she had was a mystery. Finally, she accused him of being selfish. He knew it was true but Ellen wasn't enough of a reason to change. She deserved better, someone who loved her. The proverbial handwriting had been on the wall.

Then there was that day. That weird, wonderful day when he saw Dani dancing lightly down the steps at the James Street parking garage. She hit him like a tsunami, and he found himself thinking of her unbidden when he shouldn't. He knew then he had to have her. That's the day he stopped hearing Ellen's complaints. He tuned her out like pressing the MUTE button on the TV remote. Ellen's demands became threats she'd leave him. And he let her.

"Good. I mean, are you all right with it? Oh, heck, I never liked her," Scott chuckled.

Neither did I," Tim laughed. "Buddy, neither did I."

"Remember your Mom's lecture on the night of our first high school prom?"

"Yeah." Tim smiled at the memory.

"Ellen always reminded me of the kind of girl she warned us about. What was it she said? 'Easy sex from a forward woman. Trouble always follows.'" Scott laughed. "Ellen was too possessive. Almost scary. Every time we got together I was afraid you'd tell me Ellen was pregnant. I was sure she was going to trap you, one way or another."

"My fault, really. She wanted more than I was ready for or willing to give. We never were on the same page." Tim cringed, remembering.

Scott seemed to understand. "So, we're on for Tuesday? You've got to be there. Kath would want you there; I know it."

The bartender set two full bottles of beer on the table and whisked away the empties.

"So much for our grade-school we're-never-going-to-get-married pact," Tim grinned. "I never believed that, even then."

"Me either." Scott held out his hand for a high five from Tim. They erupted with laughter.

Tim was going to enjoy seeing Kathy's face after Scott proposed. She was going to be the happiest girl on the planet, though she might not appreciate Tim being there for the proposal.

"Don't you think you should ask Kathy in private? You know, something romantic?"

"Kathy? Heck if I did something romantic she'd think I was sick and send me to emergency. She'd want you there; I'm sure of it."

"You think so?" Tim hesitated. When he proposed it would be private and somewhere romantic. But, Kathy—what would she want? Maybe she'd want him there.

For a few minutes, they drank from the amber bottles without speaking. Tim listened but didn't hear the sports commentator on the TV in the background. He thought about Dani and loving her. He thought about having a life with her like his best friends were about to find. He glanced at his watch.

"Oh, hey, I've got to run. I have dinner plans," he said.

"Aha! No wonder you aren't that upset about Ellen; there's someone new?" Scott raised an eyebrow.

"Yes. And this lady is the one." Tim rose from his chair.

"Do we get to meet her?"

"Tuesday night," Tim answered.

EIGHTEEN

Tim stood at Dani's door, arms loaded with bags of Chinese food. The smell of deep fry and hot vegetables reminded him he was hungry. His stomach rumbled in anticipation. He pressed the doorbell with his elbow. *A quick dinner and then back to bed.* He savored the thought of touching her again and felt heat rising through out his body.

"Hi, baby," he grinned, stepping up the one riser into the house as Dani opened the door. He leaned forward to kiss her and lost all interest in wasting time on dinner.

"Goodness! You brought enough food!" She stepped back from him, bit her bottom lip, her eyes sparkling as if wondering how they would ever eat it all.

"You know Chinese; always too much. But I figure we'll be hungry again in an hour." He handed one bag to her and then reached for her free hand, pulling her back to him for a kiss. "I missed you." He'd always thought when it finally happened to him, that he'd be frightened by feeling completely in love. But with Dani, he was home. Color raced up her neck and into her cheeks. She looked away from him as if she weren't sure how to react to his advances. He knew he should back off the gas pedal just a little, give her some time, but he didn't want to.

"Uh, hump!"

Tim turned, and Dani's friend from the club stood at the end of the hallway, hands balled into fists and planted solidly on her hips.

"You have other guests, Daniela," Katrina Collins said in a tone so gruff it startled him. Now he understood Dani's reluctance to kiss him: she had company.

"Hi. It's Katrina, isn't it?" Tim settled the bag of food on his hip and approached her with an outstretched hand. Katrina shot him an icy glare. He tried to thaw her with a big grin, but she only responded to his greeting by dropping a limp hand in his and withdrawing it immediately as if she might catch something fatal by touching him. She spun on her heel and walked ahead of them. Tim wondered what he'd done to piss her off. Live?

"Am I interrupting something?" he whispered to Dani as she caught up with him.

"No. Katrina popped by unannounced. They are interrupting *us*," she said so low only he could hear, pushing her lips into a seductive pout. "I didn't have the heart to send them away. It's okay, isn't it?"

"They as in, more than just Katrina?"

"Yes."

"Then I hope *they* don't stay long," Tim said, watching her mouth turn up at corners. She agreed with him. Just a little smile and he felt his desire surge. He'd be polite, but he couldn't wait to be alone with her again.

"Come on; I'll introduce you."

Katrina had crossed the room and stood beside the sofa, her hand resting on the shoulder of her beau. Tim remembered him from The Sevens Club. Gary something; he couldn't remember. The other uninvited guest in the party sat in a wingback chair across the room, leaning forward, captivating both of Dani's dogs with generous attention. Instantly uncomfortable, Tim wondered if he was the outsider at this soiree. For Dani's sake, he'd make the best of it. Dani took hold of his free hand, giving him a shot of confidence.

As the memory of their lovemaking raced into his brain, he warmed and glanced at her. Their stare locked for a moment too long, like he'd seen other lovers do. Her lips parted, as if she were remembering, like he was, the heat of their kisses. Her baggy blue T-shirt and jeans didn't fully disguise the feminine curves he knew were underneath. They had company; he needed to control himself.

For a distraction, he looked around the room. So, this was the rest of Dani's house. The afternoon sunshine filtered through the windows and drenched walls so pale pink as to be almost opalescent with warmth and light. The gleaming hardwood floors from the entry hall gave way to a cream-colored carpet. The high ceilings and baseboards were finished with elegantly carved wooden moldings, painted an impeccable white. Dark cherry and mahogany furniture contrasted with the light walls. The chairs and sofa matched each other in rich cranberry, navy, and forest-green prints. White bookshelves full of leather-bound editions reached from floor to ceiling, bordering a fireplace framed by a magnificently carved antique cherry mantle. Past the shelves, a dark cherry cabinet on hand-hewn claw feet stood full of trophies, ribbons, and pictures of Dani with horses. One picture stood out from all the rest: Dani wore a wispy blue dress, bareback astride a magnificent gray horse, like a fantasy from a movie or a dream. He looked at it and briefly wondered if he'd ever seen a woman more beautiful in all his life.

"Tim, this is Gary Warden and Bill Fraser. This is Tim McAndrews," Dani sparkled. Tim quickly imagined her at his house, at his table, helping him entertain—which of course would help his career.

"Hello, Tim. I think we've seen each other around--at the Sevens Club," Gary said, rising from the sofa to shake Tim's hand. Katrina stood beside Gary, linking her arm through his, still firing frigid sparks from her brown eyes. She was a dangerous woman. Pretty, but in a fake, Hollywood sort of way. Her blonde hair was from a bottle and her snug, low-cut tank top advertised Wonderbra cleavage and availability. Any man foolish enough to get involved with her would pay a hefty price. All for Katrina and nothing for him, except maybe grief!

"Yes, at the club," Tim said, finding himself unsettled not only by Katrina's chill but by the stare he received from Bill Fraser, as he turned to greet him. "And where do I know you from, Bill? You look so familiar." He tried to shake off the impression he was being sized up, evaluated as if by a leopard from the shadows.

"The club, too," Bill answered easily. But he narrowed his weird, amber eyes. *Was Dani dating Fraser, too?*

"Sure, sure. That must be it," Tim said, staring back, not giving an inch. Tim turned to read Dani's face as a twinge of jealousy shot through his system. She was innocent. Oblivious to her sensuality and unaware of the stir of masculine competition circling the air above her like a vulture. Even Gary Warden was affected, though Katrina clung to his side. By the end of the evening, Tim had to see to it that everyone understood Dani was his.

"At least we all have that in common. The club and healthy living!" Katrina said.

"Well, excuse me. I need to put our healthy dinner together," Dani grinned at Tim and let him know she expected him to engage in conversation with the men. She took the bag of food from his arm.

"I'll help you!" Katrina followed Dani to the kitchen, intentionally ignoring Tim's smile as she passed and succeeded in making him feel as unwelcome as possible. He smoothed a hand through his blond hair.

"So, I understand from Katrina you work for the district attorney's office. That must be fascinating." Gary made conversation, shoving his hands in his pockets and rattling the keys inside. Tension soaked the air like the humidity before a thunderstorm. *Am I misreading Dani? Could she be dating Fraser?* The question kept spinning through his mind. Fraser was certainly good-looking, apparently established--maybe even wealthy. Tim noticed the designer logo on his red polo shirt, the expensive gold watch and chains sparkling at his wrist and throat.

"Yes, work's great. Very interesting," Tim said, shaken by the unspoken threat boiling in Bill Fraser's glare. *Did I take Dani away from Fraser?* Tim's attempts at conversation were as awkward as a high-school kid meeting his date's father for the first time.

Dani eased some of the tension when she brought him a glass of wine.

"Thank you." Tim tried to find the secret to Fraser's hostility in her eyes, but instead, they mirrored back the wonder of blossoming love. Love for him.

"You're welcome! I'm off to help Katrina." Tim watched Dani return to the kitchen.

"We work for the city. Bill and I are firefighters and paramedics," Gary said. They had to get the career comparison out of the way. "So, you working on anything big? Any big, bad murder cases?"

Momentarily taken aback by the question, Tim replied, "Just a lot of DUIIs I'm afraid. I'm sure your job is far more interesting than mine." He studied the two men and shook off suspicion. "Maybe that's why I thought I'd met you elsewhere, Bill. Have you testified in court for me before?" Tim returned his attention to the conversation.

"Nope, not yet. But I'm sure I'll get the opportunity: someone will drink and drive, I'll rescue them, and you'll prosecute them. We'll be seeing each other," Fraser laughed. "Now that you're here we should slap those steaks on the grill; I'm starved." Bill stood from the jewel-toned wingback chair, grabbing up his glass of white wine. Dani's dogs followed him.

"You coming?" Gary offered the invitation.

"Sure. I think I'll get a refill first." Tim didn't join the men outdoors. Instead, he wandered into the kitchen.

"May I bother you for another glass of wine?" Tim asked, careful not to earn one of Katrina's wintry looks.

"Certainly." Dani wiped her hands on a clean white dish towel.

"Wow! Quite the feast you girls are putting together," he said, grabbing a juicy tomato off the top of Katrina's salad and popping it into his mouth.

"Stop it! Not until dinner!" Katrina swatted at his hand as if he were a pesky fly.

Dani poured wine from the bottle into his glass. They stood only inches apart. He stared down at her, wanting to feel the softness of her lips against his. He almost kissed her, almost forgot Katrina was in the kitchen with them. "I missed you," he said just above a whisper.

"Me, too," she answered. Dani was That Girl, the magic one on the gray horse, a dream he had to have since the first day he saw her.

"Shoo! Out! Go help the boys!" Katrina snapped. Under ordinary circumstances, Tim would've believed she was teasing him. But not tonight. He took his glass of wine and strolled to the patio door.

"I know when I'm not wanted," he laughed playfully.

"Apparently not soon enough." Katrina shot him another hostile glance.

"Did I do something to upset you?" Tim asked. A flush of color raced into Katrina's cheeks. Maybe no one had ever confronted her about her rudeness before. Maybe she didn't understand how she was coming off.

"Of course not. Katrina's only teasing. I bet those steaks are ready," Dani intervened, handing Tim an empty platter and squeezing his hand to bolster him.

"I'll go get them, then." No matter what Katrina wanted, Dani had made it clear she wanted *him*. He had no choice but to be gracious and slowly stepped out onto the patio.

"Katrina, what's the matter with you? You're being mean!" he heard Dani say.

"He almost kissed you, Daniela! He almost freaking kissed you!"

Tim quickly closed the door behind him.

NINETEEN

Tim frowned across the dinner table at the enemy. Throughout his life, he'd always been able to fit into any crowd. So, tonight was a solid slap in the face. Dani's friends were not going to accept him. All he could do was endure. Oh, he'd survived miserable dinner parties before in his life. Awards banquets with overcooked roast beef and back-slapping speeches. Uncomfortable cocktail parties with political wannabes pontificating their party's mundane talking points as if they were an original thought. But this--tonight topped them all. He'd had enough of Bill Fraser's hostile stares. Katrina Collins' thinly veiled insults had him hanging on the edge. If he hadn't overheard Dani politely challenge Katrina's behavior, he would have left long ago. But that's what Katrina wanted him to do. And he wasn't about to give her the satisfaction.

"Can I help clear the table?" Tim stood and gathered the dishes in front of him, hoping to bring this miserable party to its end. As he did, both Bill Fraser and Gary Warden rose from their chairs to pitch in. Katrina glowered at him; his intentions weren't lost on her. She clambered from her chair and stormed to the kitchen without a word.

Tim brought the dishes into the kitchen, setting them carefully on the granite countertop beside the sink. Katrina met his gaze with hard, unyielding eyes. He countered with the biggest, toothiest grin he could muster. *This was war.*

He returned to the dining room. Warden and Fraser had retired to the family room and flipped the TV to the basketball game. Tim was reluctant to join them.

"I don't think your friends approve of me," he whispered to Dani as he collected another stack of soiled dishes from the dinner table.

"That's Katrina's doing, nothing you have to worry about. She's trying to save me—fix me up with Bill Fraser." Dani set a plate on top of the ones he already held.

"Aha! Now I get it; I wondered what she was up to. Why does she hate me so much?"

"I doubt she hates you. How could anyone hate you?"

Tim set the plates back on the table and wrapped his arms around Dani's waist. As he pulled her body against his, he could feel his arousal and nibbled at the back of her neck.

"I take it Katrina doesn't know I'm crazy about you. I'm just curious: what do you think of Bill Fraser?" Jealousy licked the edges of his mind like fire on tinder. He wanted reassurance from Dani that he was her only one.

"He's handsome, very striking," she said, turning to face him, her eyes full of mischief.

"Really?" Tim dropped his hands to his side. "Am I handsome?"

"You?" she paused making him wait for an answer. "Very. You're not possessive, are you?"

"Very. You're mine. All mine." He touched her hand, but she danced away just out of reach.

"Am I? *All yours*? Umm. We'll see."

Tim felt insecurity crumbling his confidence, but Dani's eyes hinted at a tease. After a few seconds of silence, she rolled up on her tiptoes and kissed him. The kiss ended as he heard Katrina's footfalls on the hardwood floor, heavy and hurried. He groaned.

"Let her walk in and see me kissing you. She's got to know eventually," he laughed.

"She knows." Dani's mouth turned up at the corners, and she still pulled away. "Dishes, now. Kisses, later." With that promise, he rolled up his sleeves.

"Oh, there you are!" Katrina exclaimed in overloud, fake surprise. "Gary, Bill, and I thought we'd go see a movie. Why don't you come, Daniela?"

"Without me, isn't that what you mean, Katrina?" Tim asked. Katrina met his challenge with a tight-lipped stare so stony it could have stopped the sun mid-heaven. Tim grinned. "You don't like me much, do you, Ms. Freeze?"

"I don't like any smart-mouthed, self-absorbed, overconfident, pretty boys like you, Mr. Big-Time D.A."

Dani stepped between them. "That's enough of that! I have work to do, and I won't be able to go to the movies with you." She laughed and then scowled at both Tim and Katrina, her kind eyes coursing first over Katrina's face then Tim's as if searching for the answer to the mutual hostility.

"We're leaving, then. I'll talk to you tomorrow." Katrina addressed Daniela, spun on her heel, and left the room in a huff. The battle lines were drawn: his fight to gain Katrina's approval would be like climbing Everest without a coat in a 200-mile-an-hour blizzard!

Dani sighed, shook her head, and followed. As a gracious hostess, he knew she would need to see her guests to the door. Tim stayed behind, loading his arms with dishes. When he heard the front door close, he was amused by his small victory. He was alone with Dani; Bill Fraser was not. No matter what pressure Katrina had added to the equation.

He finished carting the dishes from the dining room. Dani was silent as if weighed by deep thought. She filled the sink with hot water, the fragrant dish soap bubbling and foaming under the stream.

"You aren't angry with me, are you?" Tim asked, knowing when he finally crumbled under Katrina's hostility, he'd breached common decency. Dani was such a lady; she might fault him for his rudeness. He shouldn't have joined in the mean talk and called Katrina "Ms. Freeze." That comment should have stayed in his unspoken thoughts, where it belonged.

"No, of course not. Whew! You hit it off with her: 'smart-mouthed, self-absorbed, over-confident, pretty boy'?" She laughed, shaking her fingers as if she'd scalded them in hot water, the wet bubbles dripping back into the sink.

"You forgot 'Big-Time D.A.' I wish I knew what I did to piss her off."

"Katrina thrives on control; you weren't in her control. She had a plan for this afternoon, and you ruined it. Not to mention, you didn't fall head over heels in love with her. Most men do."

"No one could fall for an ice queen like that. She's not my type. Besides, I'm—I'm already head over heels—for you." His voice trailed away.

"You say the sweetest things." Dani turned to face him. He took her in his arms and kissed her long and slow until he felt water from her hands dripping on the back of his neck.

"Forget the dishes. I'm taking you to bed," he said.

TWENTY

Angry and agitated, he aimlessly walked Third Street, turning right, and heading down James. The city was completely different under night skies, as if an altered species, a subset of human, prowled the streets, insatiable and wild. The hole-in-the-wall clubs, closed during daylight, brimmed with night people, giddy with alcoholic cheer. Their laughter spilled out to his ears through closed doors and windows, punctuated by the muffled backbeat of drums from live bands. Lingering in the shadows, detached as if outside of life, he watched the night people like a movie flickering by. The scent of fresh garlic and olive oil wafted across the street from Geppetto's Italian Restaurant. Though tempting, he wasn't hungry for food.

Restless, he moved on. Deeper into the city. Deeper into the darkness of the seedier side. The older brick-and-stone buildings in this part of town were stained black from the mold that grew unchecked through the cold, wet winters. Even now, as a balmy spring breeze whispered up from the Sound and through the streets and alleyways, he could smell the musty damp. There were fewer people in this part of the city. Instead of the laughing crowds, a rummy drunk in crumpled, filthy clothing huddled in the doorway of a closed antique shop, singing slurred words to himself. Up ahead at the mouth of an alley, a lithe silhouette melted into the darkness. He could see only the orange glow at the tip of her cigarette when she took a drag. But he knew her; deep down inside, he knew and despised her.

"Hey, handsome. Do you want a date?" she asked as he passed by. He glanced to his side. She stood there, leaning against the cold stone, a sloppy pout on her painted full lips, slender thighs showing under the too-short miniskirt, long brown hair spilling over a bare right shoulder, where her partially unbuttoned blouse fell away. Her intent was to be sexy, enticing. She was anything but. He couldn't resist.

"Are you talking to me, miss?" he replied softly, coaxing her from the gloom of her alley to the sidewalk on the street.

She sidled up to him. "Do you want a date, darlin'?" she drawled, her voice cooing, dove-sweet. She was stoned. Her pupils were pinprick-tight against the faint city lights. Now that she was close, he could see she was no more than eighteen: a girl. A child. But her face was drawn and tired under the heavy makeup and heroin. She smelled of drug sweat and cigarettes, like a memory he hated but couldn't place. She was trash on the street, just like the crumpled candy wrapper that scurried noisily along the gutter in the eddies and whirls caused by the hot wind of a passing car.

"Sure, I want a date." He felt an impulse flare in the dark, an anger that burned at his insides like red–hot molten steel. He would kill her, this rag of a girl. He would kill her, and no one would care or miss her. As he followed her back into the murk of her alley, he slipped his left hand into his pocket feeling for the amber pharmaceutical bottle and the switchblade knife. He clasped the knife, feeling his body relax at the security of having it.

"My place is only a few yards from here, darlin'," she said, linking her arm through his.

"First, let's go for a glass of wine," he offered.

"Well, well, darlin', aren't you the classy one?"

TWENTY-ONE

"Court will reconvene at one-thirty." With the resounding rap of the gavel, Judge Simmerhorn declared a noon recess. Tim glanced at the round clock on the walnut paneling behind the judge's bench. An hour-and-a-half to see Dani. Quickly, he packed his briefcase and brushed his hand across the prosecutor's table, wiping away the sprinkling of dust.

"I think we've got this guy. Want to go for a sandwich?" Tall, willowy Jenny Mattison waited for his answer, her big brown eyes full of that know-it-all, fresh-from-law-school confidence he remembered very clearly. She had yet to be knocked down by the reality of losing a case she should've won. That time would come, soon enough.

"We might have this one, this time," he answered, in his most I'm-seasoned voice.

Jenny stood back from him, shoving her horn-rims back in place. She didn't need them, but she told him she thought they made her look more serious. "How stupid would you have to be not to convict this guy? He crashed straight into a cliff less than fifty feet from a stoplight and less than a mile from home. He had a pickup bed full of empty beer cans; he was drunk!"

"His injuries prevented a breathalyzer. Juries can be unpredictable."

"Thanks for the warning, Mr. Experience." She placed her hands on her nonexistent hips, bunching the too-big pinstriped skirt that hung off her thin frame. She hitched at the waistband. Jenny was two pounds heavier than a war refugee, and she ate like a horse.

"You're welcome, Miss Inexperienced," he grinned.

"Sandwich? Or no?"

"No. See you at one-twenty."

"I thought you were supposed to be my mentor."

"I bet you can figure out how to eat lunch on your own," he chuckled at her exaggerated pout.

"We have three more of these today. One-fifteen," she countered.

"Yep, but you won't be hurrying the judge. One-twenty." He grabbed up his case and shoved his way through the swinging gate that divided the court from the benches for observers. Dani's office was three short blocks from here. He had to get there before she left for lunch. He hurried through the slate-gray marble hallway between courtrooms at a pace just short of a jog.

"Where are you headed in such a rush?" Jenny panted, catching up to him as he shouldered through the lobby doors. He snapped open his umbrella against the light rain. Jenny didn't have one, so, he handed it to her.

"Lunch." He took the courthouse steps two at a time, hearing Jenny's high heels clattering on the concrete as she fought to keep up with him.

"And not with me? Why can't I go?"

He didn't answer and stopped at the large white tent at the bottom of the stairs, where a street vendor sold flowers.

"Those," he pointed to a nosegay of pink roses and lavender. He set down his briefcase, retrieved his wallet from inside his suit coat, and paid.

"Wow! Who's the lucky girl?" Jenny tilted into his face, her body bending like a palm tree in a hurricane. He seized his umbrella from her clenched fist. If Myra hadn't been on a mission to see him fixed up and married, he wouldn't have to run this gauntlet with the women from his office so often. He'd been the subject of gossip by his coworkers and knew it; why else would the hens stop their whispering when he walked into the breakroom?

"You don't know her. But you can report to the gals that I'm dating someone. See you at one-twenty."

"You mean I can't go?"

Tim blinked at her in disbelief.

She giggled. "One fifteen," she countered.

"Twenty." Tim bit the bottom lip of his smile. He left Jenny standing at the foot of the courthouse steps. Briefly, he wondered if she'd be overwhelmed by curiosity and follow him. The temptation to be the first in the office with new gossip might be too captivating. But he didn't care what they found out about Dani. He had a mind to parade her through the office some morning to put an end to all the speculation.

Glancing behind him as he climbed the five steps to Dani's suite, he found Jenny wasn't there. He shook out his umbrella before opening the door and once inside, caught Karen packing her lipstick back in her purse.

"Hi, Karen. Dani left for lunch yet?"

"I usually go first. Want me to stay so you can take her out?" Karen set her purse on top of the desk and started to slip from her stylish overcoat.

"No, you go ahead." He slid his umbrella into a big clay pot Dani kept for the purpose by the doorway and wiped his feet on the entry mat, careful not to track dirt on her cream carpet.

"Ooh. She'll like those." Karen raised her eyebrows as if delighted by the bouquet. Tim hoped Dani would feel the same. "Awfully romantic," she said.

"You think so? Good. Now, if your boss thinks so."

"She will. I'll see you later." Karen picked up the phone.

"Wait; don't announce me. I want to surprise her."

"As you wish, Sir. Daniela, I'm off to lunch now! See you in an hour!"

"An hour or so?" Tim suggested after she'd replaced the phone in its cradle.

"Really? An hour or *so?*" Karen gave him a thoughtful look and smiled. "You're naughty, Mr. McAndrews. Naughty, but very romantic."

Tim liked that Karen thought he was romantic. He was! He needed one of Dani's girlfriends on his side since Katrina Collins was as hostile as the Gobi Desert.

Without knocking, he walked through Dani's office door, closing it behind him. He headed straight for the window facing the street and twisted the rod that closed the blinds. Dani looked up from her desk, a curious smile teasing her lips as she watched him shut out the city.

"Hi." He pulled the flowers from behind his back. "Have time for lunch?" He rounded her desk, sitting on the edge so he'd be close to her. She raised an eyebrow; she understood lunch wasn't exactly what he had in mind.

"This is a surprise." She leaned forward, placing her elbows on the desk and her chin in her hands. "The flowers are lovely."

"How about lunch?"

"Karen just left. I shouldn't go until she gets back."

"We could order in."

"It's okay. I don't have time today. Thank you for these." Rolling her chair back from the desk, she stood and accepted the flowers from him. He grabbed her free hand, pressing the fingers to his lips. Like the delicate pink roses in the nosegay, her cheeks flushed with color. Dani seemed to be where he was: lost in the spin of desire. Their eyes locked, and passion arced between them like electricity. Silky and warm, her lips brushed his cheek. The simplest touch from her sent longing racing through him. He drew her into his arms.

"I'm not hungry for lunch; I'm hungry for you," he whispered.

"Aren't you in court today?" Dani asked, pulling back, trying to change the subject, resisting the irresistible. He couldn't let her and followed her as she found a vase from a small antique cabinet in the corner of her office. Tim peeled away his suit coat and tossed it across the back of one of her office chairs.

"Yes, I'm in court today."

"Umm." She started to arrange the flowers, placing them in the vase one by one. He reached for her, pulling her tight against him.

Dani sighed. He studied her. Though she outwardly opposed it, the symmetry of her face, the deep-water blue of her eyes, the permissive turn to her mouth, made him ache to have her.

"I want you so much," he said. She closed her eyes, her lips parted in invitation. His body pulsed with new urgency. He thought of sweeping the paperwork away from the desk. Instead, he coaxed her back to the desk and sat down in her swivel chair. She stood before him, a branch of pink roses clutched in her hand.

"I need you, Dani." He inched the long blue silk skirt up over her knee, wondering if she'd stop him. She crushed the flowers in her hands, and the scent of roses quavered on the air. Flower petals drifted down around her feet. She didn't pull away. His heartbeat quickened with anticipation.

"Tim, don't. This isn't the place for this. Karen will ..." she pushed the skirt back into place.

He stood and covered her mouth with his, kissing her long and hard until he felt her muscles soften, her body yielding. She needed kissing, lots of kissing. As he slowly sat down in the chair, he pulled her onto his lap.

"We're safe. Karen's at lunch." He toyed with the buttons on her blouse, undoing them one at a time between kisses.

"Tim, no. We shouldn't ..."

"We can lock the door." Need defied reason, and he followed his overwhelming instincts. He had to have her.

A weird vibration at this hip snapped his thoughts back to reality.

"What? What is—my phone? My phone?" The magic of the moment was lost. "I forgot to turn the damn thing off."

Dani laughed at him. "They found you! They knew you were trying to have a quickie!" She stood and fastened the buttons on her blouse. "It's the business day, after all. We'd better tend to business."

Reluctantly, Tim reached behind him and fished the phone from his pocket. Pressing the display button, he checked the number. His gut slammed down to his shoes. Kathy Hope.

"Geez. Myra was supposed to tell everyone I'm in court today."

"Who is it?" Dani sat back against the edge of her desk, her arms folded across her chest. She'd noticed his anxiety.

"The medical examiner." He rubbed his hand down his face and over his chin. "I'd better call her."

Dani moved aside, sliding her telephone close to him. "Is this to do with the serial killer case?" Her brow was creased, and she brushed her long hair back away from her face.

"That or dinner tomorrow night. Maybe a break in the case." *Maybe another body,* he thought but didn't say.

Dani leaned forward and touched his cheek with the back of her fingers in sympathy. Savoring the feelings stirring inside him, he closed his eyes. Loving Dani softened his hard edges. Holding her was so much better than thinking about another victim. Another victim; he shuddered. He grabbed her, making her sit in his lap, hoping the warmth of her body would chase away the sudden chill. He decided to use Dani's desk phone. He could use it hands free and he wanted to use his hands for something else. He dialed Kathy's number.

"I love you, Dani," he said, waiting for Kathy to answer the rings.

Dani nestled back against him, and he buried his face in her fragrant hair.

"Marry me," Tim whispered against her ear. She straightened immediately. And he had to fight to keep her from standing. When he wouldn't release her, Dani settled back against him. He heard the click of the phone as Kathy picked up.

"Kath, it's Tim. What's up?" he pressed the button for the speakerphone and set the handset in its cradle. Brushing her hair aside, he kissed the back of Dani's neck.

"Myra said you were in court today, but Tim, Scott was called out on a homicide this morning. Brutal. Awful. I think our killer's gone violent." Kathy's voice trembled with worry.

Tim sat forward, and Dani rocketed from his lap and wheeled to face him, the blue skirt swishing around her legs. He grabbed the phone, cutting off the speaker function as he wrestled the handset to his ear.

"What? God! Are they bringing the body up right now? All right. I'll get there as soon as I can. This morning's case is ready to go to the jury; I'll have to stay for that. But I'll call someone to cover the others ... I will, as fast as I can." Did Kathy think his being there would hasten the killer's capture? "See you in a few." Tim stared at the handset for a moment before hanging up the phone. "I'm sorry; you shouldn't have heard that, Dani. We don't know anything. We have squat for evidence, no suspects. Until the profiler gets here tomorrow, we don't even know what to tell the press. We have no idea what to warn the public to be on the lookout for."

"It's bad, isn't it?" Dani's stare followed his movements, reading from them what he didn't want her to know. She sat on the edge of her desk.

"I've got to go. I don't want to go." He stood, bent down, and kissed her lips. He lingered there, treasuring the moment. Lately, he'd imagined winning all his cases for her as if protecting her from all that was wrong with the world. "Would it be so bad?" he asked, suddenly, tucking his shirt inside his trousers.

"Would what be so bad?" she cocked her head slightly. Her brown and gold hair settled around her shoulders.'

"To be married to me?"

"Tim, you bring up the craziest things at the most insane time! You need to go!"

"Would it?"

"I don't know—how awful are you?" she chuckled. But underneath the mirth, Tim saw pain in her eyes. He saw it, but he didn't fully understand it. She'd never told him what went wrong with her marriage, and he'd never asked.

"I'm not your ex," he volunteered.

"That's for sure! Not even close. You are a person, good and bad. A person I don't know well enough yet to marry."

"Don't be so practical! Do you love me? Even a little?"

"I think—a lot." Dani was exposing her vulnerability. Her honesty moved him, and once again he engaged her into his arms.

"Marry me." The scent of her hair, the warm perfume radiating from her throat, made him lose all sense of time.

"I like this. Just the way we are. Can't we leave it like this for a while?" She stroked his cheek with the back of her fingers, and he closed his eyes.

"We can. It's just that I want so much."

"Beautiful dreams," she whispered.

"We can have them, Dani. All we have to do is reach out and take them." He wondered how he could convince her, what could heal what had happened before, short of time.

She stared deeply into his eyes as if trying to ascertain if his words were truth or lies. "You need to go make arrangements for your cases this afternoon. We can talk about this later."

"Tonight?"

"Tonight," she answered, and he felt a flush of hungry desire in his veins.

"I can't wait."

"Mmm. Me either."

He kissed her long and slow.

The door to the outer office slammed shut. Karen was obviously letting them know she was back from lunch. Tim glanced at the door.

"At least you know how I feel," Tim said. He glimpsed his watch and groaned.

"You better go, I have work." Dani brushed at the random creases pressed into her blouse by the warmth of his body.

"I'm not sorry about wrinkling your top," he laughed. He loved forging secret, intimate memories to relish and savor. He loved being in love.

"You're not! At least I don't have meetings today. You do, and you're a mess," she teased him.

Tim surveyed the damage. Pants and shirt were a little crumpled and in disarray. Not bad. He shrugged his shoulders. "Nothing I can do about it now. I can't seem to help myself around you. Fun, isn't it?"

"Yes, fun …" her words drifted away.

"What does that mean?" Tim stepped to the mirror on the side wall of her office to straighten his tie. Adoration in her eyes, Dani watched his reflection, triggering a memory: this was the way his mother had looked at his father when he was a child. He was surprised and charmed all at once. The puzzle pieces of his life finally fitted together.

"I feel like a kid. A teenager," she chuckled.

"That's good, isn't it?"

"Yes, good. I was wondering, though: Are you going to leave that big red lipstick kiss on your cheek?" she laughed.

"Should I? What do you think—would it help or hurt my case?"

"Um, might not hurt your case, but your image—ruined!"

"I thought it might help my image!" He slipped into his jacket.

She pulled a tissue from an ornate box, dampened it, and wiped his cheek. "There. Better."

She was falling for him. He could see it in her eyes, her smile. Perfect.

"Gotta maintain that image!" Tim scruffed his hand through his hair. "God, I'm starving. Do I look okay?"

"A little rumpled. You should've had lunch."

"I had better than food. I've got to go; I need to be back in the court-room in five minutes. And I've got to make arrangements to meet with the M.E. I'll pick you up tonight at seven o'clock?"

Dani nodded yes.

"Happy?" He lifted a handful of her long brown hair and pressed the ends against his lips. Even that touch was exciting and sweet.

"Very."

"Marry me." He knew the answer would be left unspoken for now. But an impulsive thought raced lightning-quick through his mind: She would marry him. He didn't know how, he just knew she would.

Tim dashed up the courthouse steps, cell phone to his ear, his briefcase banging against the unopened umbrella with each step like a drum in a marching band.

"Kathy Hope believes this murder is connected. I don't know how. Won't know until I get to the autopsy. Chuck Radoe can try these DUIIs as well as I can, tell him to use my outline. No. Jenny's too nervous; she needs more time. Yes, I'll finish this one. It's about to go to the jury. I think the defense has about five minutes of testimony left. All right. Then I'll be at the morgue. If it's not connected, *I'll* kick her skinny butt; you won't have to." Tim disengaged from Goddard and stuffed his cell phone back into his breast pocket.

The morning's mist yielded to sun breaks and the ornamental cherry trees along the streets had exploded into pink bloom. Tim felt so good he tossed five dollars and change into the shabby hat belonging to a beggar stationed outside the courthouse lobby. Before opening the door to the courtroom, he checked the time. 1:19. He pulled open the door and breezed down the aisle. Jenny paced the edge of the prosecutor's table as if she'd believed he wouldn't show. He shook his head; he was in love, but not irresponsible.

"You're late." She tapped her watch, her brows scrunched together as she scolded him with a frown.

"I'm not." He pointed to the clock behind the judge's bench just as the long hand clicked one more minute away. "One-twenty on the nose."

Hands planted firmly on her hips; she gave him a once-over. "What the hell happened to you, a wrestling match with the waiter?" She straightened his tie as the jury filed in.

"Chuck Radoe is going to finish this afternoon…"

"Radoe! Why? He's a moron," Jenny protested.

"There's a new development in another case I'm working on. Goddard wants me to get down to the morgue."

"Eeww."

"Goddard is very hands-on, Jenny. He oversees the M.E. and the cops. When the time comes, you'll have to go to places you don't want to. Get used to it."

"You can't leave. I can't do this without you."

"Wasn't it just yesterday you were itching to be a lead prosecutor? Here's your big chance to show Goddard what you can do. You can work with Radoe."

Jenny was clearly annoyed. She narrowed her eyes at him.

Grinning at her, making sure he ratcheted her irritation up one more notch, Tim took his place behind the prosecutor's table. The jury was seated.

"Lipstick? Is that *lipstick* on your shirt collar?" Jenny grappled to keep her voice to a whisper.

Tim looked down to see the tiny smear of red on the triangle tip of his white collar. "Oops! See, you *have* to present the rest of today's cases without me. Can't let a jury see lipstick."

"Oh, God! You're awful, McAndrews!" she grimaced.

"I am. And you can tell that to the gals in the break room," he snickered, knowing a bad-boy reputation would soon jet around the ninth floor. Maybe when Myra found out about his lady friend he could at least get her off his back.

Before Jenny could reply the bailiff announced, "All rise." And Judge Simmerhorn took his seat at the bench.

TWENTY-TWO

"Not every homicide in this city is going to be committed by our guy, Kathy!"

Tim heard Scott's voice clear out in the hospital hallway. Kathy didn't reply, at least not at Renton's volume. Sheepishly, Tim rounded the corner to her small hole-in-the-wall office next to the morgue and peeked through the doorway. He didn't want to enter if their argument had reached a full boil. Kathy seethed behind her metal-and-Formica hospital desk. Arms folded tight across her chest. *Uh-oh.*

"Sorry, I'm late. What have you got, Kathy?" Tim slipped into the green room and sat in one of the padded metal-frame chairs across from Kathy's neatly organized desk. A whiff of formaldehyde assaulted his nostrils, and a shudder ran along the top of his shoulders. "It's cold as a refrigerator in here."

Kathy pushed a file toward Tim. "I thought you were going to be here for the autopsy." The thought of autopsy wasn't his favorite, but it would have caught him up on the killer's M.O.

Kathy's pale blues were charged with anger, especially when she looked at Scott. They were engaged in one of their notorious battles, all right.

"Jury took longer than I imagined," Tim sighed, then turned his attention to Scott. "Is it bad?"

Scott's face was stony, giving no clue as to what he might find inside the folder.

Tim opened the file and groaned, setting his elbows on Kathy's desktop and leaning into his hands for support. "Geez. I'm glad I missed the autopsy." Just the glimpse of one of the photographs was graphic enough to gag a maggot; the real thing would've been a gut-twisting catastrophe. Tim felt tiny beads of sweat breaking out on his upper lip and wiped them away quickly with the back of his hand. This was why he worked so hard to put anyone who could do something as depraved as this behind bars.

"It's not our guy. Kathy! This perp stabbed her at least eighteen times. She's a known prostitute. A known heroin addict. It's her pimp--or drug-related." Scott stood from his chair and paced back and forth in front of her desk, raking his hand through his dark hair. "She's not what our guy is after."

"What *is* our guy after?" Kathy countered, with a lift to her left eyebrow and a smile that said she had no confidence in Scott's hypothesis. Tim wondered how long they'd been arguing about it. All afternoon, most likely.

"The others were older, rich, respectable. This poisoner isn't the only weed in the garden, Kathy; there's a whole crop of them," Scott said.

"Okay. That's a good reason to think she's not a victim of our guy. Your turn, Kathy; convince me" Tim leveled his gaze to meet Kathy's. She returned his stare with unblinking certainty.

"This morning I took one look, and I knew. See beyond the gore," she answered, a pretense of calm barely cloaking the fact that she was totally ruffled by Scott's challenge. Good thing Scott was proposing on Tuesday; if he asked her tonight, she might refuse him on principle.

Tim swallowed hard. He steeled himself. Then spread out the photos side by side on her desk. Thank God he hadn't had lunch! He looked.

"See what I mean, Tim."

Tim tried. His brain screamed at him to divert his eyes, but he stared as long as he could. "Ah, God." He stood and paced in a circle behind his chair. Kathy calmly handed him a plastic-lined trash can over the desk. He lifted both hands in front of him, hoping to signal he was all right. "I could never be a doctor," he finally said.

"See," Kathy pointed to one of the photos. "Long brown hair, slender body. I know you can't tell now, but under those gashes was once a pretty face. The bone structure is very symmetrical. She's his type. The other women were older, but still youthful." Kathy replaced her arms across her chest; her mind made up. Case closed. Sitting there in that white coat she looked professional, no longer the little girl who used to share his treehouse after school.

Tim glanced over at Scott, wanting him to rebut Kathy's theory. Scott was silent, his face anxious. Underneath the bullshit, Scott realized Kathy was right. "You think she's right, don't you, Scott? You're giving her crap, but you think she's right."

Scott tightened his mouth, the muscles in his jaw firmly set. He thought it; he just wasn't going to give Kathy the satisfaction of saying so.

"I'll be damned," Tim said, just above a whisper.

"Something happened last night. Something triggered the rage." Kathy's voice was somber, resigned to the horrible reality. "Like I told Scott at the scene: her heart had stopped before he stabbed her, or there would have been blood everywhere. She was poisoned first, dead when he knifed her." Tim's mind raced. He was here; Dani was alone. The thought put him on the edge of panic. He needed to protect her from this monster.

"Can't be our guy," Scott objected, but there was no conviction behind his voice. It was as if he'd whispered a prayer. Tim shared it. "Hopheads are always killing each other," Scott added in a mumble.

"I've fast-tracked the toxicology. It'll be up any minute." Kathy wriggled back into her chair, chin tilted in defiance. Tim understood where Kathy was leading: he'd killed the prostitute with poison first, then mutilated the body. Every day-day in, day out-his office dealt with this, and yet he still wasn't used to it, could never turn off his empathy.

"What makes someone do this?" He shook his head slowly from side to side. "Incredible. Did he have sex with her?" Tim asked.

"No."

"That's different from the others," Scott volunteered.

"Yes. But we all agree he's involved in the medical profession in some way. He's not likely to risk having sex with a prostitute, a heroin addict. She was enough like the others to kill, but not to have sex with," Kathy said.

"He risked HIV by stabbing her if that's where you're headed," Scott said matter-of-factly.

"Just a case of a look-alike girl being in the wrong place at the wrong time," Tim mused.

"What a sick, perverted fuck!" Scott's words smoldered like embers in a hot campfire, ready to explode into full flame with the slightest breeze. Tim had seen this before. Scott would set all his other cases aside.

If there was poison—the antidepressant—then the killer was acting out a rage that left every woman in the city vulnerable. Every brown-and-gold-haired beauty. Dani. Tim groaned at the thought; he couldn't let her out of his sight.

"Dr. Hope?" A young man dressed in a white lab coat brought a file and passed it over the desk to Kathy. "These are the results of your tox screens. Sign here."

Tim watched as Kathy scribbled her name at the bottom of his clipboard.

"Thank you, Carlos." Kathy wiped her hands across her face and down her chin.

"Damn it, Kathy! Open it!" Scott inclined forward, bracing his weight against her desk, leaning into her face. Owl-eyed, she stood in defense.

"That anxious for me to be wrong?" Challenging Scott with a glare, Kathy turned up the manila folder's cover. Tim watched her gaze drop to her desk and course back and forth over the typewritten page, line by line. "Heroin, alcohol." She looked up, her words catching momentarily in her throat, voice dropping an octave. "Desipramine, 500 mm. The lethal dose. Same as the others."

Tim expected her to shoot Scott a victory smile. She did not. She slumped down into her chair, her mouth grim.

TWENTY-THREE

Daniela watched the white cotton sheet rise and fall with the rhythm of Tim's breathing. Tangled in her linens, Tim slept. Daniela couldn't. Instead, she sat beside him, looking down at his peaceful face. She almost reached out and touched his cheek. Almost. But she drew her hand back. Everything would be fine if he'd just come to her as her lover if he didn't ask for anything more. But he already had. It was that time in life; of course he'd want to be settled. She understood. At his age, with a solid career in place, he would make a good husband and father.

What could he possibly see in her? Already tiny crow's feet were there at the edges of her eyes. She saw them, no matter how many pounds of lotion or beauty creams she applied. He needed to find a younger woman to love and have a family with. But--if he left her now--she moaned.

Too late; she'd sipped love's wine and was intoxicated. Whether or not she wanted to, she was on the roller coaster, going for a ride. Four long years. Four lonely years she'd kept these feelings at bay. She was afraid, and tired of being afraid. In the morning, she'd have to tell him she wasn't a candidate for mother. She'd buried the memories so deep; she'd almost forgotten. Almost. Her unhappy marriage had produced a child in its fourth year. At his birth, the stillborn baby had taken all her other chances with him. She would have no children of her own. As perfect as he seemed, not even Tim McAndrews would be able to stand that!

"Whatcha doing?" Tim stirred and reached for her.

"Thinking." Swallowing back the memory and the pain, she burrowed down into the sheets. She couldn't tell him, not now, in the dark. She wanted this night; then she'd let go. The tears were there filling her eyes. She didn't want to let go.

"Don't do that. Come here, sleep. Let me hold you."

She slipped into his arms. His warm skin against her and his masculine scent filled her with comfort and security. Still, underneath, she knew her heart wasn't safe.

"What's wrong?" Tim pulled away as if he could read her thoughts by looking into her face.

Daniela tried so hard to mask her fears and yet each time he saw through them. He was sensitive to her, drew her out, loved her.

"Nothing," she lied. In the morning, she would tell him there would never be children. Wide awake now, he rested on the pillow. She hadn't intended this.

"Something's wrong. Tell me so we can solve it." He moved so that his lips touched hers and they connected in a tender kiss. She felt tingling warmth all through her. Was he for real? Daniela retreated and adjusted her head on her pillow.

"You're worried about something." He traced a finger over her brow, smoothing away her frown. "Talk to me."

"I can't have children," Daniela blurted out. Expecting rejection, she rolled onto her back, away from him.

Scooting next to her, he propped himself on an elbow and gazed down into her face. "Oh. Is that all?" He pulled the sheet away from her body and pressed his palm flat against her tummy. "I wondered about this." He walked his fingers along the faint incision scar at her bikini line.

"You're not disappointed?"

"No. I'm kind of—well—selfish. I haven't ever really thought about kids. Don't get me wrong, I would do it; I'm sure I would enjoy kids—I just—I'm selfish. And my brothers have plenty to carry on the family name." He grimaced as if waiting for her to scold him. He'd been chastised for these feelings before.

Daniela felt herself squinting at him in disbelief. Was he going to dispute all her objections with these perfect answers? And with such openness? Tim knew who he was and accepted it. Not like her, tossed by a wild sea of guilt and insecurity.

"You don't believe me," he chuckled. "You'll see, very selfish. Now, let's get some sleep. Work tomorrow." He slid an arm under her neck and pulled her close to him. Daniela felt herself wanting to slip into the comfort of mutual love. Closing her eyes, she curled up against his skin, kissing his throat.

"I love you, Dani," he whispered and drifted back to sleep as she watched. She couldn't sleep.

TWENTY-FOUR

Daniela set the freshly brewed cup of coffee in front of Tim on the breakfast nook table. He glanced up at her and smiled his thanks. He was so "classic attorney" in his gray slacks and crisp white long-sleeved shirt, his only rebellion the rich color in his grey-and-jewel-toned tie. He had court today. Daniela was schlepping, still in her thick terry-cloth robe, trying to decide if she'd go into the city today or not. She was on cloud nine; maybe they were going to get to have a real grown-up life together.

"Happy?" Tim asked, a dreamy look in his sapphire eyes.

"Yes. Are you?"

"Deliriously," he answered. "You make it all worth living. Meet me for lunch?"

"Um. Okay."

"I'll only have an hour and Jenny-ugh, Jenny will be pestering me to tag along. But by lunch, I'm going to need to look at you." He laughed. "Wish Radoe had the Jenny-duty rather than me."

"Is she that bad?"

"No. Not really. She's going to be a good lawyer. Just sometimes, the way she looks at me is unsettling, predatory. Got any good friends we could fix her up with?" he snickered.

"Bill Fraser?" Dani offered.

"Perfect. Especially if it keeps him away from you. I think I need to parade you around the office, let all the gossip girls know I'm spoken for. I'm yours, aren't I?"

"Completely mine. I know I'm yours."

He closed his eyes and sighed. "Dani. I'll never make it to work. I love this."

"Better get going, or you'll be late. You look so handsome; no wonder Jenny stares at you," she teased.

"I'll meet you at the Coffee Corner. Judge Perry always recesses for lunch at 12:30 sharp." He grabbed his briefcase and took hold of her hand so she'd walk him to the door. He opened it and stepped out. "This is real *Leave it to Beaver,* isn't it? You and me, and a life." She nodded, and he kissed her cheek. She waited in the doorway, flushed, and feeling all dreamy until he drove away.

Leave it to Beaver? Anything but! She knew it was time to let Tim know all about her. When it came to suitors, she'd learned to mete out this part of her life carefully. Hoping to keep herself safe from the smooth operators who would feign love for the money and the lifestyle that went with it. Tim hadn't asked her much about her work, other than if she'd had a good day. He'd probably assumed she was a lower-level manager for S.C. Holdings. That's what her business card said: S.C. Holdings, LLC; Daniela St. Clair, Manager. She knew he'd not realized that the entire twenty-six stories above her offices were the throbbing heart of her business. From there, St. Clair Land and Cattle shipped their beef and the Delight Valley label wines worldwide. When he found out, it would change everything; it always did.

She'd chosen this house, this neighborhood more for location than anything. She considered it her city house, the place she used when she had to conduct business in Seattle. It was more comfortable than a hotel, and the penthouse suite at the top of the twenty-six story building brought back too many bad memories for her. The family had lived in the penthouse during the long hospital stays when Mom and Dad were in their last days. And then there were the rumors that turned out to be fact, that Carl had used the suite to wine and dine his paramours. Now when she went to the penthouse, sadness haunted her. She'd thought about redecorating it to see if that would change things, but it just wasn't a priority.

What Tim didn't know was that when she left this house for the office, a full staff would swoop in to clean and put everything in order, leaving pre-cooked meals she'd only have to microwave if she wanted. The house was in the perfect location between her city offices and the airport. She could easily fly to the ranch and wineries from here. She tightened the terry-cloth robe around her waist and turned indoors. She needed to get dressed and to the office for an hour or so before meeting Tim for lunch.

Out of the corner of her eye, she noticed a hooded jogger padding quietly down the other side of the tree-lined street. Assuming it was one of her neighbors she had yet to meet, she waved. He waved back.

TWENTY-FIVE

Tim was beginning to question his judgment. What was he thinking, planning a quiet lunch with Dani? Jenny had followed, invited herself to join them, and was now yammering at him like they were best friends. He knew he wasn't going to be able to keep Dani a secret forever, didn't want to. He knew that. But Jenny-how did he stop her from talking?

"Do you know how rich she is?" Jenny asked.

Tim looked at her and shook his head. "What are you talking about?"

"Daniela St. Clair. Do you know how rich she is?" Jenny was walking beside him, taking the courthouse steps two at a time. "She funds some of the same charities as Daddy."

"That's nice; means she's generous--not wealthy, Jenny."

"You're so funny," she said, stopping at the top stair. "Oh. My. God. You *don't* know, do you?"

Tim felt uneasy. No. He didn't know about Dani's finances. All he knew was that he loved her and had since the first day he saw her. He shouldered past Jenny, scowling as he overtook her.

"She's the head of St. Clair Land and Cattle. Ring a bell? How about Delight Valley Wineries?"

"*Should* I know? Are they under criminal investigation?" he joked. "Of course I've heard of them. I like a good Delight Valley cab with a steak dinner." He intended to be dismissive. He opened the lobby doors for Jenny. But her talk did slow him down. He and Dani had never talked about money. Her house was elegant, small, but richly appointed. Now that he thought about it, it was in one of the most desirable neighborhoods in the area. He'd been slow to notice. None of these things mattered to him; he wanted the girl and would if she were dirt poor. He opened the doors to the courtroom.

The bailiff approached. "The trial is postponed until tomorrow," he said. "Judge Simmerhorn is ill."

Tim nodded. "Hey, Griff, is he going to be okay?" Simmerhorn was one of Tim's favorite judges. He was smart, no one could pull anything over on him, but he was also fair.

"Not sure. Everything is postponed."

"Thanks," Tim said. "Let's go pack it up, Jenny."

In silence, they took the elevator to the ninth floor. As the doors opened, they stepped through. Jenny headed to her cubicle, Tim to his office. He took the case box and set it inside his office door.

Tim sat at his desk. Was Dani the head of St. Clair and Delight Valley? Did that change things? He was just a middle-class guy from a middle-class family. Sure, his Dad's finish carpentry and cabinet shop had made it so Mom could stay home and raise their kids, but until his older brothers joined the business it had only barely made a living. He booted up his computer, and after staring at the screen for a few minutes, he typed DANIELA ST. CLAIR into Google's search bar and pushed ENTER. The page of results flashed on his screen. He clicked on the Delight Valley Winery web page. There she was, a lovely picture of her face, and the words, "Daniela St. Clair, heiress and manager of--donates the new pediatrics wing to Seattle Children's Hospital." *A whole wing?* Was Jenny right?

Before he had time to consider how he felt Goddard appeared in the doorway.

"Got a minute, Tim?"

"Sure." Tim followed Goddard to his office.

"Close the door."

Tim was worried. Had he done something wrong? When he closed the door, he saw Judge Vernon Mattison, Jenny's father, seated at the small conference table by the window of Goddard's office. It had been weeks since he'd seen the judge. Now that Brad Hollingsrow had been appointed to the bench, he didn't seem to show up for coffee at Jake's as much as he used to. He couldn't remember the last case he'd presented before Mattison.

The judge stood offering his hand. "Hello, Tim. Sorry to bother you in the middle of your day," he said as they shook hands.

"No problem, Your Honor," Tim said, looking from the judge's face to Goddard's and back again. "How can I help you?" He couldn't imagine what he'd done and wondered if Judge Simmerhorn had passed away.

"Goddard assigned Jenny to you for guidance?"

"Yes, sir." Tim felt uneasy. What had Jenny done or said now?

"She's my only child. Spoiled rotten, I'm afraid," the judge began.

Tim wondered what this was about.

"When she's home at dinner I can't keep her from chattering about you. 'Tim did this; Tim did that. Tim said this or that.'" The judge chuckled. "She's very impressed by you." Tim felt himself cringing inside, but let only a small smile tick up. "So, I was wondering how she's doing?"

"Oh. You want a report card, so to speak."

"So to speak, yes."

"She's very smart. She's going to make a good lawyer, sir," Tim answered. Whew. *Is that all!*

"Good, good." There were smiles all around. Judge Mattison beaming with pride, Goddard grinning with satisfaction at his choice of mentor, and Tim felt himself smiling with relief.

"Can you think of any areas where she might need special help?" the judge asked.

"We've only been working DUII. But she's a fast learner. I think she's ready to move up to bigger cases."

"Well, yes. From what I see here ..." Mattison thumbed through some pages from a report on his lap. "You've won them all, so far."

"Yes," Tim nodded. "If they're guilty, we convict them."

Goddard and Mattison looked at each other. *Uh-oh.* He wondered if he'd just sealed his doom.

"Jenny trusts you, Tim." The fact that Mattison was calling him by his first name was unsettling. He and Mattison hardly knew each other. They'd had coffee a couple of times with Brad Hollingsrow, but Mattison seemed to join them spontaneously, and it was never planned. Mattison was now smiling at him like they were friends. That couldn't hurt, could it?

"So, we thought she could assist you on your bigger cases, give her a taste of what the prosecutor's office is all about," Goddard grinned.

Tim nodded. Yep. He'd stepped in it now. *Stuck with Jenny? Lovely. Great. Just what I need. Damn!* "Whatever you think is best," he conceded.

"She asked for you. She likes winning. Your conviction rate is well over 96%, that's better than any of the other prosecutors in this office, better than the national average."

"Sir, Jenny's new. She doesn't understand I only recommend we try the cases we're sure to win--the cases where we have enough evidence to convict. The rest we plea out. That's why my percentages are high. I'm in the reality business. I have to balance the evidence of a crime against the resources provided us by the taxpayers and their need for us to maintain a civil society." Tim answered.

"Ah, well said, McAndrews. How old are you?" The judge asked.

"Twenty-eight, sir."

"Awfully young for such insight. You are a politician, after all."

Tim never thought of himself as a politician, but more as one of the good guys maintaining law and order. He hated political bullshit.

"Don't diminish your accomplishments, Tim," Goddard interjected. "I trust your judgment."

"So, you're the right man to mentor my Jenny," the judge grinned. "Whatever Jenny wants, Jenny gets."

Tim felt his brows pinch together. He studied Goddard's, then Mattison's face. What the hell did that mean?

"Speaking of politics, we think you should be at Goddard's fundraiser this Thursday night," the judge said. "You and Jenny should make an appearance." He set two tickets on the edge of the desk. Tim tried to hold back the shock; it was a thousand-dollars-a-plate dinner! That was way out of his league.

"I've already donated the money," Mattison quickly added.

Tim had made a rule for himself never to date anyone from the office. It could go bad and turn his life into pure hell. Jenny already had a crush, and he had no interest in encouraging it. He was desperate to find a way out. He quickly decided on the truth: "I'm not such a good politician. I think I might be in big trouble with *my girl* if I take Jenny to your party."

"Oh?" The judge looked him up and down. "Oh, yes. Of course, those are for you and your date," he added, but there was a hint of disappointment in his voice. He looked at his watch and stood. "See you Thursday night, young man."

Mattison patted Tim's shoulder as he left the office. Tim stood in front of Goddard's desk.

"That profiler you requested will be here tomorrow morning," Goddard said straightforwardly as if he just hadn't violated his no-fraternization policy and tried to make a date between Tim and Jenny. "I heard your case got postponed; why don't you take the afternoon off?"

"Thank you, sir, but I have plenty to catch up on. Did I misread the judge? Were you expecting me to escort Jenny to the fundraiser?"

Goddard looked up and grinned. "You don't miss much. It wouldn't be the first time a man married to advance his career."

Married!? He felt the shock wave. He hadn't even considered Jenny in that light, ever. "Sir, I--?" Tim found he was slowly shaking his head no.

"Don't worry about it. It was a good test of your integrity; a lesser man would've conceded to the judge's wishes, even if it cost him his girl."

"What about his job? Is *that* on the line?"

"Oh hell no; you're my best prosecutor, for God's sake! Now get out of here and get back to work."

Tim turned and left, but *"whatever Jenny wants, Jenny gets"* kept circling through his thoughts.

TWENTY-SIX

Scott Renton was so nervous he couldn't sit still. He kept standing and watching the door to McTavish's as if they'd never waited for McAndrews before. Kathy stared at him as he sat down once more.

"Who are you looking for? McAndrews is always late," she griped.

"He said he'd meet us here at seven." Scott looked at his watch, popped up once again from his chair, straining to see over the heads of the happy-hour crowd.

"You're so nervous I thought you were looking for your new girlfriend or something," Kathy complained. She felt silly; she shouldn't be here; she wasn't up to meeting Scott's latest lover. Her heart couldn't take it. Scott would never see how much she loved him. If he ever did see it, he would run for the hills, and their friendship would be lost. The dilemma was agony.

Kathy took a gulp of her drink, hoping for tequila's pain-dulling magic. A couple of margaritas and she could face anything. Scott sat down for the umpteenth time. But this time he stared at her with such intensity she felt shivery, even lightheaded. All her life, at least since she could remember having feelings for boys, she'd loved Scott-that was, of course, when she wasn't in love with Tim. They were her boys next door and absolute dreamboats. She was a skinny dork and had never had a chance with either. She was lucky they were friends.

"What?" she asked defensively. Scott just shook his head, as if she should know something she didn't know. Why did he always assume she had ESP?

"There he is!" Scott jumped up and waved an arm in the air. Kathy glanced up and felt relief flood through her. It was Tim whom Scott was waiting for, not some new girl that just-so-happened-to-be-here-by-accident and would-it-be-all-right-if-she-joined-them? Kathy wasn't going to have to endure watching someone new ogle Scott and hang on his every word as if it was an utterance from the gods. Tim approached the table.

"Hi, guys." Tim was grinning ear to ear, his blue eyes sparkling with a happiness Kathy hadn't seen before. "Kathy, Scott, this is my friend, Dani St. Clair. Dani, this is Dr. Kathy Hope and Detective Scott Renton."

Scott had warned Kathy that Tim had a new lady. As she looked up to greet her, Kathy's heart slammed up to her throat. Tim was holding hands with a woman she'd met before: Daniela St. Clair, the heiress of the Simon St. Clair fortune. Ms. St. Clair wasn't wealthy like the tech moguls of Seattle but well-heeled enough to have donated all the money for Seattle Children's new pediatric wing. Tim had been through his share of relationships; Kathy understood she was being introduced to his friend. She even heard herself repeating the standard niceties.

But this woman's familiarity caused her to almost tip over her margarita. Daniela was fashion- model-beautiful. Under her turquoise-blue knit dress, Kathy could see her body trim and sculpted by exercise. Her face was even, her skin clear and smooth, her full lips nicely shaped. Her long golden-brown hair fell straight and shiny across her shoulders and down her back. She was so much like the poison victims. Kathy felt each throb as her heart pulsed blood to her brain.

She gulped and tore her gaze away. She searched for Scott's face and their eyes locked for a second. Was Scott feeling the same wave of nauseating incredulity? Tim scrunched his brow at Kathy as he pulled out the chair for Dani. Kathy understood she was acting goofy, but she couldn't stop. She tried on a smile but found herself gawking again. Tim's friend shifted uncomfortably. Kathy knew she had to say something. If only words would come!

"I'm sorry," Kathy cleared her throat, "I don't mean to stare. It's just that you look familiar. Like someone I recently aut—met," Kathy fumbled.

Scott choked on his drink. He glared at Kathy; then she followed his gaze as he looked Dani over. At least she hadn't said it: *recently autopsied.* Wouldn't that be a great start to an evening?

"We've met," Dani said, smiling softly. "At the hospital fundraiser, about a year ago."

"That must be it." Kathy worried and fussed with the hem of her skirt. Tim sat across from her, chatting happily about the weather and smiling lovingly into Daniela's eyes. For just a fraction of second Kathy's mind flickered through the photographs of the dead women. The concept sped Kathy's heartbeat up. Tim shot Kathy a glare that demanded to know: what's-up-with-you-tonight-anyway? He was clearly annoyed.

"Dani, shall we dance?" Tim asked, taking hold of Daniela's hand. Kathy managed a nod. She understood her awkwardness had driven them away, but she didn't know how to fix it.

"What's the matter with you?" Scott asked, pulling his chair close to hers, taking hold of her hand. "Your face is completely white. Too many margaritas?"

"I've had *one.* Did you look at Tim's new girlfriend?"

"Yes. She's nice, very pretty."

"I thought so. You didn't see her. I mean really *look* at her."

"Kath, what's the matter with you? You're talking nonsense."

"Scott, for crying out loud! She's like the victims, the poison victims!"

Scott sat back in his chair for a moment. Slowly, he turned from Kathy and strained to see through the crowd to the couple on the floor. "Well, I'll be damned! I thought you said that earlier. 'You look like someone I recently autopsied.' You almost said that, didn't you?" he chuckled.

"I almost said it. Tell me something: tell me Tim hasn't turned into a mad killer!"

"Kath, stop it. Snap out of it. Don't be ridiculous! Of course Tim's not a killer. You've known him all your life."

"The girl, though she's the killer's type. Tim's type. He always dates this type of girl."

"Wait. Kathy. Hold on, slow down. Ellen Mason was a chubby blonde."

Kathy sat perfectly still, her mind racing. "Who the hell is Ellen Mason?"

"Tim's last girlfriend, babe. Remember her? You liked her."

"Okay. Yes, I remember."

"You're losing it. You need to get away from this case," Scott scolded.

"Oh God, I know. I know." Kathy sighed and took a big icy swallow of her margarita. The cold headache was instantaneous. She stared out at the dance floor as she rubbed her brow. "Of course Tim isn't the killer. I'm nuts."

"I need to ask you something, something important. So, if you'd stop making Tim the mad poisoner of Seattle for a minute," Scott teased. Talking hold of her left hand, he tenderly stroked her fingers. The gentleness drew her complete focus. She couldn't think about Tim anymore, even if he *were* the mad poisoner of Seattle. Incredulous, she stared into Scott's eyes. His expression was kind, his blue eyes moist with longing. *Longing for me?* He only looked at her and felt that way in her daydreams, fantasies she needed to put behind her.

Scott cleared his throat. He looked down at their hands with a shyness she had never seen in him before.

"*You're* not the mad poisoner, are you?" she laughed. He started to speak but choked on the words. "What?" she insisted.

"Kathy, will you marry me?"

"Wha—what did you say?" she'd heard something, but he couldn't have said what she thought she heard him say, could he?

"Will you marry me?" Was he slipping a ring on her finger? There it was: a huge, sparkling diamond. When she looked at her hand, it dazzled in the light. At least, she thought it was there. She tried to clear her mind, but Scott had dropped to a knee. She was so embarrassed she couldn't say anything. Her mouth hung wide open. Scott stood, put his hand under her chin, and tilted her face up, so she had to look into his eyes.

This wasn't one of his jokes, was it? The ring looked so real. She stood. He was sincere, the muscles of his jaw tight like when he was a little boy and didn't get his way.

"I love you, Kathy. I think I always have … Aren't you going to say anything? I'm proposing to you." How long had she dreamed of this moment? Made it up and rewrote it over and over again. If she didn't say something soon, he'd be mad. She swallowed the lump in her throat. Scott leaned forward and kissed her. The warmth of his lips against hers melted her resistance and disbelief. He'd kissed her before, when they were fourteen and had gone steady for a week. Since then only a quick peck on the cheek, now and then. But this--wow! Kathy couldn't tell if she'd said yes or just thought she had. She was still waiting for her bedside alarm to go off and wake her.

"Kathy, will you?"

"Yes. If this is real, yes. Yes. Yes. Yes." Scott grabbed her up, twirled her around, and hugged her so tight she could hardly breathe.

Tim led Dani back to the table. Scott and Kathy were sitting face to face, knees touching, lost in each other. Tim grinned; Scott had done the deed and Kathy had obviously said yes. At least he'd waited until they were out dancing; when last he'd talked to Scott, Tim had feared his best friend would pop the question in front of them.

"I think we'd better dance again." He turned and pulled Dani out to the floor, spinning her twice as they went. The song changed from a rock hit to a quieter love ballad.

"Is something wrong?" Dani slipped into his arms. She felt so good there.

"Something's *right*: Scott just asked Kathy to marry him."

"Oh!"

Tim slid his hand up Dani's back, bringing her closer to him. "And Scott—Scott is your best friend?" He could feel her velvety lips against his ear. This was right. So right.

"Yep. Known them both since grade school," he answered. Her cheek was against his. Smoothest skin he'd ever felt, deliciously soft. He closed his eyes. Being with Dani was such a pleasure.

"Now I understand," she whispered.

He leaned back away from her, smiling into her big blue eyes. "What do you understand?"

"Your best friends are marrying, and you think you should be doing the same. That's why all the proposals the other day." She laughed, tossing her head back, leaning her weight into his arms. He pressed her close. She might be right about his motive; he found himself considering the possibility. But no--he'd wanted to marry Dani the first day he saw her dancing lightly down the steps at the James Street garage. That was almost a year ago. He spun her around and captured her against his body.

"I'm capable of independent thought. I think it's time I settled down, yes. I want to get married now because I found *you*."

Dani laughed, hugged him, and released him. He was pretty sure he'd said the right thing. Dani stood near him, eyes closed, letting his words wash over her like warm water.

"Come on, let's go buy Scott and Kathy a bottle of champagne," she said, taking hold of his hand.

"Great idea. It's their moment."

Tim let her lead him to the bar. He loved watching the pale lights shimmering on her hair as she moved in front of him.

"Daniela! Daniela! Hi, over here!" A male voice called out from the crowd. Tim stopped and searched faces.

"Hey Tim, isn't it?" Gary Warden stood at the bar, just in front of them, Bill Fraser at his side. The inseparable twosome. Tim squinted against the jealousy he felt inside.

"Hello," Dani greeted them warmly, "How are you?"

Dani hadn't dropped his hand. Tim was reassured and grateful for that. He scanned the surrounding area for his enemy, but Katrina Collins wasn't there. At least he wasn't going to have to battle Ms. Freeze tonight.

"Out slumming tonight?" Dani asked.

"No, we were at a search-and-rescue meeting. Sheriff's Department likes paramedics to volunteer. We decided to come here after for a beer." Bill concentrated on Dani, looking down into her face. Tim felt a twinge rise from the depths like the Loch Ness monster.

"Would you care to join us?' Gary asked. "We have a table over there." He pointed to a large table across the room with a group of firefighters, some of whom Tim knew well, he nodded his hello.

"Thank you, but we're here with friends, celebrating their engagement." Dani squeezed Tim's hand. "Maybe another time."

"Sure. I'll call you if that's all right," Fraser offered, his hungry cat-eyes devouring Dani's lips, coursing over her breasts. Tim barely subdued a sudden urge to punch him. Fraser was pushing his luck. Dani was surprised, but Tim guessed she was too polite to show it.

"Well, we'd better get back to our group. Nice seeing you again." Dani reached out to shake hands. Warden shook her hand, but when Fraser's turn came, he lifted her fingers to his lips. Dani quickly pulled her hand away, cutting his kiss short. Fraser narrowed his eyes at Tim, issuing a challenge. Tim glowered back. But no matter what Fraser did to provoke him, he couldn't respond--at least not with fists. They acknowledged each other as rivals, sizing each other up, like two bull elk in rut.

Dani tugged at Tim's arm. "Shall we order the champagne at the table?" She seemed aware of the tension and adeptly diffused it.

"Sure," Tim answered. He slipped his arm over her shoulder, nudging her body close. Then bent down and kissed her, long and slow. Color raced into Dani's cheeks.

"Oh, my!" A smile tickled across her lush mouth as they turned from Bill and Gary. "You *are* possessive."

"Very. He started it."

"Indeed. And you finished it." She lifted an eyebrow. "He seemed to be spoiling for a fight; who kisses the hand of another guy's lady?"

"I thought he was, too. Are you angry?" Tim asked.

"Not with you." Standing on tiptoe, she teased his lips with hers.

"Dani." He closed his eyes, letting passion sweep over him like bands of summer rain across a grassy meadow.

"Let's order that champagne, pay our social dues quickly, and go home."

Tim had to remind himself to breathe. "My thoughts exactly."

TWENTY-SEVEN

He strolled the long stretch of the waterfront. The closed marketplace was a dark, dirty image of its daytime self. The smell of rotting fish hung in the thickening vapor. As if lamenting its loneliness, a foghorn brayed in the distance. Diffused by mist, the globes of the streetlights cast an eerie, pale reflection that shimmered on the wet streets.

He hunted. Like a tomcat in the back alleyways, he searched for prey. Tonight, he couldn't find her; she wasn't anywhere. Hungry, insatiate, he prowled the streets where the horse-drawn carriages started their daylight tours through the city: no one.

As a damp, salty murk settled like a curtain over the building tops, he wandered back to where he'd found the girl. Two new hookers stood at the mouth of her gloomy alley. He glared at the blondes; they didn't approach him. Tonight, he was invisible. He heard a scuff of leather against the moist pavement and wheeled around on silent feet. Backing into the shelter of a lightless doorway he waited, thigh and calf muscles coiled like cobras, ready to strike.

A beat cop appeared out of the mist, looking for something out of the ordinary. Looking for him. He held his breath. *Invisible.* In his mind, the word formed and disappeared like a wisp of steam.

The police officer passed by. Hesitated. Slowly turned on his heel. Seconds pulsed by like heartbeats. A shudder gripped the policeman's shoulders. Pulling the collar of his blue uniform jacket up around his neck as if against a sudden chill, the policeman reversed direction and continued on his way. When the officer's footfalls no longer echoed against the brick buildings, he emerged from his hiding place. The thrill of adrenaline left his body trembling. He wanted to laugh, laugh out loud.

He crept forward again. Slowly, with each crepe-soled step, he remembered he had watched them kiss. At McTavish's, Tim McAndrews had taken Daniela St. Clair into his arms and kissed her ripe, red mouth. Right in front of him. For a second an image tried to surface in his consciousness. He couldn't let it and shook it off.

The silver Mercedes was parked in her driveway again tonight. The thought sent a bolt of anger flashing through his veins. Brushing gloved fingers across his lips, he let his imagination take him to her home, to the back wall, through the secret doorway, to her bedroom. He wanted her.

He could taste the need like sugar on his tongue. He had to make his move. Now. Before he lost his chance forever.

He zipped his dark leather jacket closed against the fog. He'd never killed a man before. He would do it if he had to.

TWENTY-EIGHT

Elias Cain was a giant of a man. Tim didn't think he'd ever seen a man as tall, except on the basketball court. Cain walked into the conference room with his huge hand wrapped around a venti to-go cup from Starbucks and an ear-to-ear grin peeking from under his handlebar mustache. Elias took his seat at the head of the smooth mahogany-look Formica conference table. Even seated his presence loomed like the Rocky Mountains.

Everyone was here. Kathy sat pensively on the very edge of her chair, her hands stacked one on top of the other in front of her, the new diamond ring sparkling in the light like blue-white snowflakes under a pale winter sun. Tim smiled at her.

Goddard slouched lazily, huge belly straining at the middle button of his suit coat and arms spread back across the top of his chair. Scott, relaxed but attentive, was as neat and pressed as Goddard was sloppy. Captain Martin sat upright, rigid and tight-lipped in full uniform, his eyes following Cain's coffee as if he'd kill for it with the slightest provocation. Tim eased down into his chair.

Goddard sat forward. "Everybody, this is Elias Cain. Cain is a twenty-year veteran of the Behavioral Science Unit of the FBI; he's here to help us find our poisoner."

There was a mumbled greeting.

"I've already emailed him Dr. Hope's autopsy and pathology reports except--yesterday's, and all the evidence we have so far. Which is darn little, I might add." Goddard's glare had a domino effect: His eyes scolded Captain Martin, who then glowered at Scott, who sheepishly eyed first Kathy, then Tim. At this moment, Tim didn't envy his friend; if they didn't get a lead soon unfounded charges of incompetence could soon start flying around like paper airplanes in the hands of ten-year-old boys.

"Elias, do you want to take it from here?" Goddard asked.

Goliath stood. "Yes, I'll take it from here." His bass voice rumbled in his throat. "Well, kids. You've got a real creep in your neighborhood." He ran a fat finger over the mustache, twisting the waxed end a little tighter. "The unknown subject--'unsub'--of our investigation is a white male, late twenties to thirty-five years old. He's in the medical field: doctor, nurse, technician. He knows the effect of desipramine mixed with alcohol. He might enjoy the excitement of a code. He might even be working in the emergency room. That way, he can see to it that his victims never recover."

Kathy, Scott, and Tim had already surmised the medical background. But they hadn't guessed it might be someone right under their noses in the emergency room. Tim scooted forward in his chair, resting his elbows on the table.

"He believes he's above the law, or that he's so great he'll never get caught. And he hates women. Women with a certain look. Christine Murdock, Amber Brown, and Jillian Garner were the type. Beautiful, good jobs, fashionable. He's increasingly enjoying the act of killing. That makes him ever more dangerous. Now, I believe he's good-looking and very sociable, a real charmer. Most of his victims are wealthy, pretty. Our man has enough going for him that he appeals to the classy type. He's after their money," Cain continued. "He wants that rich lifestyle. He blends in with society. If you met him on the street, you'd never know he was a killer. As for motive, it's not reasonable: he believes he deserves their money, that they owe him. He's insane. Cold. Detached. Organized. He's living out some fantasy repeatedly as he kills.

"His killings are not random. He selects the same type of woman. He stalks them, courts them. He may have married one or more of his victims. The drug he uses can be easily be mistaken for suicide. So, we're looking for a guy who might have had one or more wives 'commit suicide.'" Cain emphasized his point by lifting his hands and making air quotes with his fingers. "He may have killed far more women than you know. He's smart, both academically and streetwise. I'll bet he's anxious to know what we know. So, we're also looking for someone who's curious about the case's progress, curious about police procedure. He may even offer to help."

"Could he be a paramedic?" Tim blurted out as the thought struck him. He had always thought of paramedics as heroes. It was hard to entertain another perspective, but the image of Bill Fraser kissing Dani's hand fueled him. *Fraser and his weird eyes. Yeah, he could be a killer.*

"Could be. Firefighters are always popular with the women," Cain answered. "I'm betting on a doctor, though. Paramedics can't write pre-scriptions, and he has to have a way to get access to desipramine. It's not a drug you'd find on a medic unit. We may be able to catch him that way. Scott, you'll need to contact pharmacies in the area."

"I've already started on that," Scott replied.

Tim glanced at Kathy. Her brow furrowed. He imagined her sorting through a list of her colleagues, wondering if any were capable of murder.

"You say it's a man. Could it be a woman? A woman following her lover and killing the competition?" Kathy voiced the same concern Scott had brought to Tim's attention just the other day.

"Yes. That's possible. Women often use poison. It's a more passive form of violence." Elias pondered her input, running a hand over his thick handlebar. "Let me think on that."

"The killer has escalated his violence. The latest victim was poisoned and then stabbed eighteen times. This is the girl you don't have information on yet," Tim offered, wincing at the memory of those horrible photographs.

"She died of the poison first, though. She was dead when the suspect mutilated her," Kathy added.

"Humm. That puts things in a different light. The unsub subdued the victim with the poison cocktail first. Why? Is he weak, small, or just trying to avoid any injury? Living out a fantasy? I'm putting my money on a man. Call it a hunch or whatever you like. He wants compliance, not a fight. The material point is that he is going to slip up, sooner or later. Leave us something more to go on. They always do."

"Scott said there was a similar case in Oklahoma. The woman killed her boyfriend's lovers."

"Yes, the Ratcliff case. But Mary Lou Ratcliff is on death row. Scott checked her status just the other day to make sure she was still there. This is someone new," Captain Martin said, folding his arms back across his chest.

"A copycat?" Kathy asked.

"Maybe. The Ratcliff case was highly publicized."

"Do you think you know who's doing this, Kath?" Tim needed to know.

"No." A frown ticked once across her lower lip. Tim wasn't reassured; it wasn't like Kathy to withhold information. They were all struggling with this.

"When we have a suspect, the woman theory could be raised by the defense. There would be reasonable doubt. We'll need to make sure we have all the evidence possible to convict. Be meticulous, Renton," Goddard warned.

Scott nodded. *Of course, he'd be thorough*, Tim thought. In every case they'd worked together Scott had been a master, never leaving any possibility unexplored. This was going to get nasty. Very nasty.

"That's all I have. Goddard has been gracious enough to give us this conference room as there can be no leaks to the press. Is that understood?" Cain pressed his weight into his hands, leaning onto the table, looking at each of them in turn. Connecting. Ramming home with his glare the importance of secrecy.

"The press has already been going through police reports. Someone is going to connect the dots and come to a conclusion, right or wrong." Tim recollected. Scott had said as much in one of their first meetings.

"Get control of it. When we're ready, we'll drop tidbits to the reporters. We need to make sure we don't give away too much. My feeling is this guy will run if he thinks we're on to him." Cain was adamant.

"That won't be a problem, we don't know anything," Scott grumbled.

"What about the women in this community? If we're silent, they won't be able to defend themselves." Tim worried aloud.

"It's a fine line. If he runs, where ever he lands, the police will have to start over. We have to get him here." Cain answered.

"I want to know why he—or she--went crazy Sunday night." Kathy raked her thin fingers through her hair, and the short stands fell messy and tousled against her forehead.

Elias stared at her, the wheels spinning behind his eyes. "Frustrated. I'll bet he honed in on a target and was thwarted in his attempt to get close to her."

Tim bit his bottom lip. Sunday night. His thoughts raced through memories as if watching a slide show. Sunday night Bill Fraser was unable to get close to Dani because Tim had been there. Suddenly, Tim stood and paced a tight circle behind his chair. His heart was thundering in his ears. He didn't want to think it. Or did he? One thing he knew for sure: until this was over and the killer apprehended, he wasn't going to let Fraser get within a hundred miles of Dani.

"Did you have something to add, Mr. McAndrews?" Tim's actions had obviously surprised Elias and everyone else at the table.

"No. I'm sorry." Tim slid back into his chair. Scott shot Tim a hard stare. His furrowed brow let Tim know that when this meeting was over, he was going to get the third degree. Tim ignored his intensity. Sure, after they were done, he'd talk to Scott about Fraser. Wait, no! He couldn't. He couldn't drag Scott into this. This was serious; he couldn't waste Scott's time if this was only jealousy. But Fraser made his skin crawl.

The meeting broke up. As Cain set up a board with the victims' pictures in the conference room, Scott followed Tim to his office. He closed the door.

"All right. What was all that about in there? What do you know that I should?" For the first time, Scott pulled up a chair from the corner of the room.

"It's nothing. Nothing important enough to waste your time with," Tim explained.

"Tim. When this case hits the fan, we're going to get tips from everyone and their uncle Joe. They know somebody that did it. It's gotta be their most hated brother-in-law. And they know he did it because he looked at them the wrong way on Wednesday. And we'll chase down every one of those leads. So, tell me what you think you know." Scott pushed his weight against the front of Tim's desk.

"We all know that Dani's the killer's type."

"Kathy and I thought it, but I didn't think you were aware. What's your theory?"

"Bill Fraser," Tim said. Scott raised a skeptical eyebrow. "Hear me out: he shows up out of nowhere. He joins the club where she works out. Makes friends with her workout partner. He's a medic. He's good-looking. Sociable. And I'm the jealous fuck that's accusing him because he kissed Dani's hand last night in front of me. "See what I mean?" Tim chuckled, shaking his head at his bad behavior.

"What else? Think back." Scott prompted him. Tim was surprised that Scott didn't balk at his jealousy.

"He was at Dani's Sunday night. He kept trying to flirt with her, but I was there. That's the night the prostitute was murdered. That's what I know." Tim tried to read Scott's expression but he couldn't. Deep in thought, Scott tapped his index finger on Tim's desk.

"He was one of the medics who transported the vics—all of them--to the emergency room when they were complaining of arrhythmia. I interviewed both him and Gary Warden to see if they remembered anything," Scott added. Looking straight into Tim's eyes, he said, "Can't be ruled in. Can't be ruled out. Not yet."

"Then you think?"

Scott threw his hands up. "It's a place to start. What else do we have?"

TWENTY-NINE

Tim detested political fundraisers. But with Dani at his side, he was sure he could endure it. Dani fit into this world of political ambitions and charity fundraising as if it were her second nature. She effused grace and charm, and she knew half the people in the room. They all greeted her as if she had power. And, he guessed, she did. Money was power, wasn't it? He watched her navigate the room, a glass of her own wine in hand, as one politician after another took her aside to ask her for money. When they had first arrived, she had been on his arm, his girl. He'd introduced her to all his friends and acquaintances, and she'd done the same, but now they'd been separated by the crowd and could only catch each other's longing glances across the room.

Suddenly, someone decided to dim the lights, and the room changed: it was warmer, glittery, the lights in the ceiling twinkling like stars. Electric candles flickered to life on the tables. Tim had made chit-chat with all the familiar players: Brad Hollingsrow, Judge Mattison, and Simmerhorn. And had finally found a haven--or so he thought--with colleagues. Tim searched the crowd for Dani. She was still engaged in conversation with a politician looking for St. Clair money for his campaign.

"So, McAndrews, how does it feel to be Mr. Daniela St. Clair?" Jenny asked, her tone sarcastic and bitter. He turned, shook his head in amazement, and softly laughed at her affront.

"Great! Have you ever seen such a stunning woman?" he asked, aware of Jenny's jealousy. He also knew he was meant to be Jenny's date tonight and Jenny wasn't getting what Jenny wanted; she'd had to come here with James Rudolf instead. A great young prosecutor--as ambitious and smart as Tim had been when he'd first started four years ago, Rudolf was Jenny's age and better suited to her. Besides, he was single, unattached, and available.

"Well, if I could afford a Jane Worthen original, I'd look beautiful too," Jenny pouted.

So, that was a Jane Worthen original. Tim searched for Dani so he could look. He hadn't had a clue, nor did he care. All he knew was that Dani looked great, very sexy in her pale pink cocktail dress. The designer frock had a solid lining that hugged Dani's curves, covered by a layer of sheer fabric decorated with intricate beadwork that sparkled in the diffuse light. The neck was high, and the hem dropped just below her knee, but it had been made for her, and it fit perfectly. Unlike Jenny, Dani had delicious curves. Tim felt a smile turn his lips as he contemplated holding her in his arms.

"I think you look beautiful," James interrupted. But Jenny dismissed him as if weren't there, failing even to acknowledge he'd complimented her.

Tim scolded her with a harsh glare. "What the hell, Jenny? Your date just paid you a compliment." He looked past her, keeping an eye on Dani.

"Thank you, James," Jenny said, clearly trying to please Tim. He frowned at her. He wasn't sure what to do about her crush. He decided to ignore it, hoping it would go away. Tim looked around the room and noticed Dani searching for him. He held up his wine glass asking if she'd like another. She nodded. It was their agreed-upon cue that she needed rescue.

"Excuse me. Dani needs another glass of wine."

"That's what she's reduced you to: the top prosecutor in our office is now Daniela St. Clair's go-fer!" Jenny scowled. Her dig meant to offend him. It didn't.

"Willing go-fer," Tim laughed. "I invited her; at least I can see to her comfort."

"Tough work if you can get it. Where can I sign up for the job?" James added. That James found Dani attractive aggravated Jenny even more. She was glaring at him.

"That's not all you see to," she quipped.

Rudolf gasped and stood wide-eyed and stunned that Jenny would suggest such a thing to one of her bosses.

Tim chuckled and shook his head. He wasn't going to acknowledge her meanness. But he was sure she wasn't the only person in the room thinking it. After all, what would Daniela St. Clair be doing with a lowly public servant, if he weren't seeing to her *needs*? There were always going to be speculations, rumors, and gossip that he was after money. Even after he married her, life would be marred by it. No wonder Dani had withdrawn from people. Tim ordered a glass of wine from the bar, paid, and tipped the bartender. He looked for Dani and headed to her.

"Hi," he said handing her the glass. "Doing okay?"

"Yes." She linked her arm through his. "Samuel Fletcher, do you know Tim McAndrews? He's an ADA with Paul Goddard's office." She smiled, but Tim could tell it was strained as she introduced them. Tim shook hands with the man. "Mr. Fletcher was just explaining to me his plans to announce his run for the Senate," she added.

"Congratulations on your decision," Tim said tentatively. He wondered if Dani supported Fletcher's views. Personally, Tim thought Fletcher was an idiot. He was completely anti-law enforcement, seemed to think you could stop crime by being nice. Maybe you could on the planet Fletcher was from, but not here on earth. Tim wondered what he was doing at Goddard's fundraiser. The two men couldn't have more different stances. Then he realized this was another subject he and Dani hadn't yet broached. And that was his fault. He was the one who had carried her off to the bedroom before she was ready. Did he regret it? Not one bit. But did *she*?

"Will you excuse us, Mr. Fletcher? I think they're going to start dinner service now." Tim kept Dani's arm linked through his.

"Oh, thank you, thank, you! I thought I was trapped," Dani whispered, looking up into his eyes. He was overwhelmed by a sudden urge to make love to her. He enjoyed the way she made him feel and gazed down into her face.

"I'm going to kiss you," he said, watching her close her eyes then slowly open them … as she sighed. He did. It was a tender kiss, lingering too long to be appropriate for this venue. He knew it and didn't care. They walked toward their table, exchanging glances.

"Get a room, McAndrews," Jenny snapped as she walked past.

"Sorry," Tim explained to Dani. "She's been sniping at me all evening."

Dani tipped her head to the side. "Why?"

"She's mad at me for something." He pulled out a chair for Dani.

Dani set her wine glass on the table. As she sat, she whispered, "She has a giant crush."

"I don't know what to do about that." He was concerned, but he really didn't know what to do. He sat and turned his chair to face her.

"Is it anything you need to *do* something about?" Dani asked.

"I think Goddard and Judge Mattison expected me to escort Jenny tonight."

"Oh, my."

"All was forgiven when they saw you." He winked at her. "Donations before family," Tim laughed.

"Ah, yes. *They* forgave you; Jenny didn't."

"No. So I suspect she'll keep digging at me all night. Lucky she's not at our table, or it could get ugly."

"We could take her advice."

"Her advice?"

Dani bit her bottom lip, and he could tell she was teasing. "Get a room."

Tim grinned. "Oh! Great idea!"

He turned his chair as the table filled up, and other guests began to introduce themselves. This was as much a networking opportunity for the donors as it was fundraising for the campaign. Tim made nice but kept thinking about getting that room.

Dani knew she'd had too much wine when she found herself staring vacantly at the speaker, unable to concentrate on a word he was saying. Under the table she and Tim held hands. She glanced at her watch. Soon the speeches would be over, and the live band they'd hired would start playing old Neil Diamond tunes for dancing. She braced herself for the tedium. Maybe she could talk Tim into leaving. They could say a nice good evening. She could even say she was headed for the ranch or one of her wineries and had to leave. Earlier, when Tim had explained he had been expected to be Jenny's date, she'd decided to contribute to Goddard's campaign. She didn't want Tim's career beholden to the whims of a judge with a vindictive daughter; she knew Mattison well.

She also remembered the night they'd stayed up talking and Tim had told her about his parents sacrificing, scrimping, and saving to put him through law school. He'd told her how he'd worked extra hours to pay them back so they would have a retirement. He was a hard-working and responsible man. Tim had an inkling what he was up against; she'd seen that in his worried look when he'd explained Jenny's barbs. How could a regular guy stand up to the political machine if it turned against him? She remembered her father's lectures and frustration at the System, with a capital S. Goddard's comment about a man making a place for himself by marrying the daughter of someone politically powerful left her cold. But Goddard would know, because that's what he had done. Rumor had it he'd broken his long-time engagement for State Supreme Court Justice Marvin Logan's daughter. She looked around the room and noticed Maxine wasn't here. Of course, she understood Jenny's attraction; she had her own. And as always, she found herself fascinated by how handsome Tim was and how unaware he was of his effect on the women around him. Even now, several of the ladies at their table were staring wistfully at him.

Dani was no stranger to this game. Even Carl, her philandering ex--who was nowhere near as attractive as Tim--had a bevy of women chasing after him. But Tim was different, so self-assured, making it clear he belonged to Dani and--that she belonged to him.

The boring speech was finally over. Dani excused herself and headed for the powder room. She almost ran into Jenny as she opened the door.

"I'm sorry. How are you, Jenny?" she smiled. Jenny narrowed her eyes.

"You won this one, but don't count on the next round," Jenny scowled.

"Won? What are you talking about, Jenny? Were we competing for something?" Dani smiled, fluffing her long honey curls in the mirror.

"You know we are: Tim." Jenny stood with her hands on her hips.

"Oh, I see. I didn't realize."

"Well, now you know. He's fair game," Jenny announced. A threat formed like a thunderstorm in her eyes.

"Okay, now I know," Dani said, then asked, "does Tim get a choice in this little competition of yours?"

"He's a man, what would he know about anything? My dad will see to it he comes around." Jenny again narrowed her eyes to emphasize her point.

Dani turned to face her. Jenny had always been a spoiled brat. "Would you hurt Tim's career?"

"All's fair in love and war."

"You do want him to love you, don't you? Then you'd better re-think that strategy. If you threaten his job, he might just hate you for it." Dani forced a smile and got a scowl in return. She lifted her hands in surrender. "Go for it, Jenny. Good luck on your competition."

"Bitch. You think I can't win him?"

Dani stared at her. "Of course you can. I'm a free-will kind of girl. I don't want a man who doesn't want me."

"He won't stay with you. Just ask Ellen Mason." Jenny looked like she'd won a small victory.

This was the second person who'd brought up Tim's former affair. Dani felt a twinge of concern. *What had he done to the poor girl?* she wondered.

"Okay, so, what makes you think he'd be any better to you if he was so mean to Ellen Mason?"

"Ellen Mason didn't have my Dad." Jenny glared.

"Touché," Dani laughed. "Like I said, Jenny, I wish you luck."

That was a weird confrontation! she thought as she headed back to her table. She'd never been challenged so openly over a man before. With Carl, it had always been in secret, her playing the fool. She understood Jenny's desire for Tim. He was beautiful, like one of her purebred Arabian stallions. She decided not to think about it anymore. If Tim was going to stay, he would freely stay. And if not, she would let him freely leave.

THIRTY

Dani was so different at the ranch. No sparkling designer gowns, no princess slippers. Just T-shirts, blue jeans, and riding boots. Tim cherished her like this. She belonged here--but did he?

The ranch was beyond anything Tim could imagine. When they rounded the last curve in the driveway, the main house came into view. He had seen pictures on the ranch's website, but even that hadn't prepared him for the rustic log-and-natural-stone mansion sprawling out before him. When they drove up to the covered entryway, he almost expected a valet to park his car and a bellhop to take his luggage. The house was as big as a hotel. Huge natural stone pillars held up giant log beams supporting the peaked roofs of dark green metal. The entry door was magnificent: carved wood with etched glass sidelights. The entry gave way to a large living area with a floor-to-ceiling fireplace made of river rock and surrounded by a carved log mantel. There was an intriguing hint of apples and cinnamon in the air, reminding him of coming home for the holidays and having one of his mom's fresh-baked pies. Beyond the fireplace, two hand-hewn log stairways, one on the left and one on the right, curved to the second story. The fireplace was a pass-through, and on the other side the living area opened to a huge room abutting a wall of windows that formed a big triangle and framed beautiful mountain views to the west. There were three furniture groupings of sofas and chairs, and coffee tables--all color-coordinated and standing on top of expensive hand loomed oriental rugs. French doors opened to covered decks that vaulted out over the pastures and orchards some thirty feet below.

Dani took hold of his hand and led him up the stairway to his right.

"On the right side are the family quarters; to the left, employees," she explained.

"Everyone lives here?"

"Yes. There is always work on a ranch, and we're so far from town, we must house employees and their families. It's part of their compensation package. There are six apartments beyond the horse barn, too, for the other families," she said. The family's quarters were like a separate house inside the whole. There was a large living room, kitchen, dining room, and four spacious bedrooms, each with its own bath. Dani's personal bedroom had the best view of all. Tim stepped out on the wooden deck. The railings were made from the same polished and finished logs as the main house. A thousand feet beyond the newly mown pasture and a small apple orchard, the Cascade mountains began their steep rise from the valley floor. It was as if tree-covered hills around about hugged the ranch. He was overwhelmed and intimidated. Tim had little to offer a woman who had everything. He was out of his depth and knew it. He hadn't expected to feel this way.

She joined him and leaned against the railing next to him. He watched her; her eyes were deep- water blue and her full lips parted in an inviting smile. She was happy and at home here.

"You seem quiet. Is the ranch too much? Not for you?" she asked softly and closed her eyes as if she knew and feared his answer.

"I'm just a little awestruck. I didn't expect all this." He gestured with a sweep of his hand. "I've never seen a place like this, except in magazines." He looked down at the new cowboy boots Dani had encouraged him to buy. Not really his style. But she'd explained they were for safety. He'd understand if he had a thousand-pound horse step on his toes.

"Does it change things?"

"A little." Tim wasn't going to lie. Still, he wasn't sure if it was good or bad. "You're never going to need me, are you?"

"Isn't wanting you better? Besides, there are different kinds of need. But in terms of needing you to support me in the traditional sense: no." She was steeling herself. Tim could see it. He reached for her hand to reassure her. She smiled, but was sad, as if she expected him to leave her. "I thought you knew who I was when you brought me roses. You didn't, did you?"

He shook his head. "No."

"Now I'm the one asking for a chance. Don't throw me away. I'm not that bad a girl," she said, repeating his words back at him. A wan smile turned the corners of her lips.

He remembered and chuckled. He'd asked for a chance when they had first begun. He took her hand and brought her close. "Dani, I love you. I wouldn't care if you were dirt poor," he whispered against her neck between kisses.

"I wouldn't care if you were stinking rich." She kissed his mouth, and he was lost in passion so overpowering he couldn't resist when her body yielded in his arms. She fit perfectly.

The ranch was in what Dani called "full summer mode." The farm crew would spend the days of summer preparing the ranch for winter.

She'd made certain the hay barns and grain silos were full and watertight. Tim trailed her as she took inventory of the shavings barn making certain there would be plenty for bedding. She made sure that the paddocks were covered with a thick layer of bark to keep mud from winter rains at bay. He carefully observed how she pitched in, from helping organize the stacking of the last truckload of hay to cleaning horse stalls. But what he found the most surprising was how the animals responded to her. He stood in a stall doorway and watched. She loved them, and they loved her back. When she left the stall the gray stallion she called Bugsy came with her. No halter, no lead rope. Tim backed out of the way. He'd heard that stallions were unpredictable and could be mean, so he gave distance ... admiring him from afar seemed safer. In the sunlight, the stallion was brilliant white and his coat smooth and shiny like wedding gown satin. But it was his beautiful face that interested Tim. He'd seen horses, but never like this. His face was broad between huge brown eyes and slightly dished, giving him a very intelligent and discerning appearance. His small ears were pricked forward and were fluted and refined as if an artisan had intentionally sculpted them. The horse looked like the ideal; a horse of imagination, not reality. The horse was scrutinizing Tim. His nostrils flared as he breathed in his scent. Tim realized the animal was deciding if he liked him. Dani encouraged Tim to keep up and took hold of his hand. Tim hesitated, but when the gray followed along with them, the stallion stayed at Dani's right side opposite him as if haltered. She led them to a stand of blackberries and when she stopped the horse begged for her gentle touch and for her to pick blackberries for him. At first, Tim was afraid he'd bite his hand off, but Dani showed him how to keep his hand flat and aside from the mashed purple stains all over the leather gloves she'd given him, he enjoyed becoming friends with such a large animal by bribing him with blackberries. After a few minutes, Dani led the stallion to a paddock, where he went to graze. She closed the gate and stood to admire the horse for a minute. That was easy; Tim felt encouraged. Maybe he could be a rancher after all.

It was only when Mark, Dani's foreman, brought out two saddled horses that Tim began to sweat. He was immediately reminded he was completely out of his element.

"This is Corrigan. He's a sweetheart. He will carry you safely anywhere you want to go. I'll be riding his sister, Princess Petrina," Dani said. "Are you game?"

"I'm game, I guess. But I think he'll know I'm scared and will rub me off on the nearest tree," Tim laughed nervously.

"Not these guys. Scared means they will want to take care of you."

They mounted. Tim felt unbalanced and unsure. The big dappled gray seemed to sense it and squared his stance as if helping him, just as Dani said he would. Tim still didn't trust him and reached down and stroked the horse's neck. Corrigan's muscles were firm under his smooth coat. A pleasant scent of leather and citronella radiated from the warmth of the horse's body and Tim forced himself to relax.

"We'll go in the arena for a bit while you get comfortable." She rode beside him. Tim noticed how her blue jeans fit neatly into knee-high black riding boots and how the tails of her long-sleeved checked pink shirt were easily swept away from her body in the breeze, revealing the tight pink t-shirt underneath. Even now she made him think of sex. He let out a breath.

Dani leaned forward in her saddle and opened the gate to the large arena. A thick layer of shredded bark covered the ground. Good. At least if he were bucked off, it wouldn't hurt so bad, he thought.

"Now, there's a tendency to want to curl up. Resist it. Think of pushing your weight down into your heels, like this." Tim looked at her. She was sitting deep in the saddle, straight and tall. He copied her. They walked around for a few minutes. "Don't let your feet slide through the stirrups; that's a good way to get seriously hurt! So just the balls of your feet and heels down."

He nodded.

"Now, want to trot?"

"Sure."

"Okay. Sit deep in the saddle. Remember, weight in your heels and don't brace against the movement; go with it." Once again, she showed him. And when he asked the gelding to trot he was surprised at how easygoing he was. Instead of the jarring he remembered from riding stable rental horses, he quietly rocked side to side. She taught him how to ask Corrigan to turn right, turn left, stop, and back up.

After a while, they were ready to head out on the trail. It was a narrow road, about ten feet wide, mowed on either side. Down the center a small strip of grass eked out a living. The road edged a big hay field, green from an early rain, and wound around a hill on the west side of the property.

"We'll only walk for now. Surprising, isn't it, that only a hundred-and-fifty years ago, this was our transportation? In those days, all men were horsemen." She maneuvered her horse so they rode side by side.

"An art lost on us city boys," Tim chuckled. He was uncomfortable and knew he showed it.

"So, what did you do, growing up?" she asked, patting her horse's neck.

"Baseball, football, dirt bikes. In winter, we would ski."

"That explains your great sense of balance. You'll make a great horseman."

Tim laughed, reaching down, and stroking his horse's neck. He figured if he were nice, he wouldn't get dumped. "So, do you use horses for your cattle roundups?"

"These days, most of the roundups are done with ATVs, not horseback."

"That's good news; that I can do," Tim snickered and shook his head. He wasn't certain horses were going to be his thing.

"Be careful, I might enlist your help when the time comes," she laughed.

They rode side by side for several minutes. Tim relaxed. It was quiet, except for the horses' hooves pounding out a four-beat rhythm on the trail and the whisper of the breeze tickling through the leaves. The wild cottonwood, oak, and sugar maple tree branches arching across the path created a cathedral of greens and golds. Sunlight filtered through, and shadows danced on the ground. The air was fresh with the scent of wild herbs, mint, and the sugar of ripening blackberries. It had been such a long time since he'd been out like this. He was surprised at how much he liked it. He could adjust to this … maybe. There was a soothing peace to the natural world lost in the skyscraper canyons of the busy city streets. He even found his body starting to feel the sway of the horse's movement as they rode along, a tempo like music.

They wound up the side of a hill where, through a break in the trees, he could see the pastures, ranch houses, and outbuildings below. Meticulously kept dark wood fences stood out against the deep green pasture grasses, dividing them into big squares. The ranch and its buildings struck him as practically a private community.

When they reached the top of the hill, Dani stopped and dismounted. Tim followed suit. He lingered behind Dani, trying to help as she moved the horses into a small paddock. She removed their bridles and saddles, hanging them on some racks built especially for that purpose. She let them eat from feeders filled with hay in a shelter constructed for them. Every comfort, animal and human, had been designed into the ranch. He was starting to believe he belonged here, too.

"This was planned?" Tim asked as she closed the gate.

"When you agreed to come to the ranch with me, I had Mark and his boys set it up." She tenderly smiled at him. "I knew you hadn't ridden in a long time, if at all. I wanted to make it easy for you."

"All this effort for me?" He tipped his head slightly, grinning.

"For you and any of our guests," she teased. He knew it was especially for him, but also that she wasn't going to admit it.

She led him to a gazebo that overlooked the pastures and ranch below. When he climbed the two steps to the main floor, he realized it wasn't a gazebo, but a small cottage. The main room had a stone fireplace in the west wall. Two comfortable dark brown leather recliners stood side by side in front of it. Behind, a stainless-steel kitchen was appointed with an oven, stovetop, microwave, and small refrigerator--all the amenities anyone could need. He peeked behind a closed door and found a full bath with a shower. A winding metal staircase to the right of the fireplace led to the loft above, with the bedroom. The north-facing walls were sliding glass doors that opened onto a deck. Tim stepped out onto it.

The view was spectacular: he could see the verdant pastures full of cattle and horses grazing peacefully. The big farmhouse and barns sprawling below looked small, like toys from this height. And it was quiet. There was only the sigh of the breeze through the trees--unlike the city with its constant din of traffic noise and sirens. He didn't miss it.

The sky above was bright blue, marred only by wispy clouds high in the atmosphere. Out on the deck, he found a small table set for two.

"A catered lunch?" he asked, looking at Dani in wonder.

"No. Just bread, cheese, fruit, and wine. Is that okay?" She hoped he was pleased. He could see it in her raised eyebrows, waiting for his response.

"Amazing." Tim worried. He could easily get spoiled by this. Wherever he went on the ranch every need was anticipated and luxuriously met. He felt surreal. He was used to his hungry edge. It drove him to achieve. It motivated him to work hard on his cases and made him feel like a man. *Will I lose all of myself, loving her?*

She stepped up to him and peered deeply into his eyes. His body responded, and he couldn't think of anything else. He closed his eyes as the need for her rose again.

"Am I trying too hard?" she asked, as she set her head on his shoulder. "Am I scaring you away?"

"No. Dani, no; I'm here." He bent forward and kissed her long and slow, letting the ache build and his fears subside.

"It's going to rain tonight," Dani said, looking out over the valley. "See the high cirrus clouds? My dad used to call them mares' tails. When there are mares' tails, it will rain in one to three days, he used to say. I hope so; we need the rain. Are you hungry?"

"Very." He watched her go and wondered how she was going to react to his middle-class family. Their house was nice. His father's woodworking skills had made their home quaint and a work of creativity. His father and brothers had even helped him spiff up his loft with finished wood touches, but it was nothing like the elegance and opulence here.

She went inside and came back with two trays, one with meats and cheeses, and the other with a choice of home-baked bread. There was a bowl of red and gold apples and pears on the table with a bottle of red wine, an opener, and glasses.

"All the food you see is grown here, or from one of our farms."

"You make cheese?"

"Oh, yes. Before my father died, he bought an interest in a large dairy. He wanted the finest of everything served at his wineries. Each winery has a tasting room and restaurant. He hired the best vintners, chefs, and cheese makers, and served grass-fed beef from our ranches, and vegetables and herbs from our gardens and greenhouses. I've tried to keep up his tradition. But many of the local farmers are so much better at growing vegetables and fruit than we are, I buy from them instead."

She handed him a glass of the rich red wine. "If Dad's watching from heaven, I hope he isn't angry," she laughed.

"Dani, your dad couldn't be anything but proud." Tim took a drink from his wine glass. "Wow, that's nice," he exclaimed.

"It's not one of mine; it's a Malbec from Lodi, California. I'm glad you like it. They want us to distribute for them. We agreed to bottle under our label for a portion of the profits."

"You aren't anything like I thought you'd be," Tim admitted. She was an amazing woman, better than he'd ever expected to have. But she scared him. What would it be like to negotiate a business deal with her? She was formidable, he speculated.

"Are you disappointed?" She was concerned. Was she finally starting to love him? He hoped so.

"Not at all. But I wasn't expecting an international business woman." He grinned, but he was apprehensive. "Dani, I'm just a middle-class guy. A government lawyer." Briefly, he wondered if she was comparing him to her ex.

"Are you wondering if that matters to me? Tim, it doesn't. I inherited all you see. I'm not like you; I didn't earn my life. It was given to me. Don't get me wrong--I'm so grateful. But you, you worked for yours. You earned it. Everything you have is all from your effort, your intelligence, and your hard work. The only way I can prove my worth is to make all of this a little bit better than when Dad left it." She took a sip of wine. "I read you were top of your class at Harvard Law."

"I was. But Dani, I had to be. My parents worked and sacrificed to give me the chance to be something. I had to give back. Trust me; they weren't exactly thrilled to hear I'd come home to be a prosecuting attorney in Seattle. They wanted me to be some famous Perry Mason or F. Lee Bailey. But it only took me a few months to figure out Perry Mason wasn't real, and that most perps were pretty much guilty scumbags. We're lucky as hell to live in a society with a constitution that bends over backward to protect individual rights."

Dani cocked her head and leaned in on her elbows.

"Innocent until proven guilty is an amazing concept. America is a place like no other." He picked up a slice of cheese and ate it. "When I bring a case to trial, I'd better have compelling evidence, almost ironclad--or the accused walks. Because of that, the hope is that government can't railroad the truly innocent. I think the intent was to never again have political prisoners. Free thought and free speech are wonderful concepts. But liberty is fragile. Sometimes I wonder if the freedom we have here can endure against the relentless tide of corruption."

"My Dad would've loved you," she said, reaching over, and touching his hand. "He talked about that, too."

"How about you, Dani? Do you love me?" Tim asked boldly, leveling his gaze at her.

She stared back and the moment lasted too long for his comfort.

"I ... I want to love you," she finally said, a pretty smile turning the corners of her mouth. But he saw the barely perceptible hesitation in her eyes. He wanted to kiss her, kiss that tiny freckle at the curve of her lip. He wanted to make her love him.

"So, that spiral staircase, the one next to the fireplace--where does that lead?" he asked, as if he didn't know.

THIRTY-ONE

They made it back to the main barn in the valley just as Mark, Dani's hired man, was letting one of the stallions loose in the outdoor arena. To the west, Tim spotted the dark, brooding rain clouds gathering and slowly advancing east. Dani was right: tonight, it would rain. They dismounted, and Mark's two boys appeared from the barn and took their horses away. Dani grabbed Tim's hand and led him to the arena. She climbed up and sat on the top fence rail. Tim joined her. They watched as the gray stallion played with a giant blue ball. He reared, grabbed it up by the cover that protected it and threw it over his back, spun, and chased it. Mark joined them on the fence, sitting to Tim's left.

"I never knew horses played like that," Tim marveled.

"Yes. They're very playful creatures," Dani explained.

After a few minutes, the stallion walked up to them and turned so Dani could slide onto his back.

"Is he offering you a ride? I thought they didn't like to be ridden." Tim was shocked and looked first at Dani, then at Mark. Mark pretended not to hear but tossed him a dismissive smile when Dani slipped off the fence and onto the stallion's back. The horse seemed to wait patiently while she situated herself. Then she asked him to walk.

Tim was amazed that she not only walked the horse but that she asked him to trot and then to canter.

"No saddle? No bridle?" he asked Mark. The man nodded but stared ahead at Dani. He made no eye contact. Tim wondered what was up with that.

Mark was dressed like a true cowboy: faded but clean blue jeans; dusty, well-worn boots; a long-sleeved checkered shirt with cowboy snaps (not buttons); and a sweat-stained straw cowboy hat.

"Fantastic, isn't it?" Mark asked, more a comment than a question. Their gaze briefly locked. Mark turned away to watch Dani, making it crystal clear he didn't approve of him. Tim shrugged it off.

"Wow." Dani's horsemanship truly impressed Tim. He remembered the picture at her house in the city; blue wispy dress, hair cascading in honey-colored curls around her shoulders, bareback on a dappled gray like a dream. He wondered if this was the same horse.

"She raised him from a foal. They're friends. This is like dancing with a partner; the colt loves her as much as she does him. They have a bond."

"I've never seen anything like it," Tim commented.

"These horses love her. I think they would carry her through fire if she asked them to. She raised each one of them from the day they were born. They belong to her, and she belongs to them, especially the one she's riding," Mark explained. "This was all she did until her father died and left everything for her to manage. Every day she'd work with the stallion. Her ex used to say she loved the horse more than she loved him. He was right. But Carl also didn't know she'd discovered he was cheating on her; I think she found solace with the horse-much more than any man."

Tim looked at Mark. The dig was meant for him. But this was more of Dani's life story that he didn't know. Part of the mix of good and bad, happiness and pain, making her the woman he loved. He liked learning about her.

"You ever been married?" Mark suddenly asked.

"No. I haven't."

Mark stared now, sizing him up. After a few minutes, he'd made his decision. Tim wasn't sure if it was good or bad. "Now, watch this," Mark instructed, nodding toward the arena "Horse and rider as one." The stallion picked up a canter without any apparent prompting from Dani.

"Now he's going to do what we call a half-pass at the canter."

Tim watched as the horse cantered from one corner of the arena across the center to the other on a perfect diagonal as if measuring it with a chalk line. Then he and Dani turned and executed the same maneuver in the other direction.

"Now they'll come up the center doing what we call tempi canter. That's where they change leads every stride; looks like dancing."

Tim nodded dumbly. He didn't know you could do this with horses. He was a city boy, after all. "Until today, my experience with horses … not so great." Tim beamed a big grin, trying to win Mark over.

"If you're around for a while, I'll teach you." Mark smiled, but it was cold, leaving Tim with the impression that he wasn't sold on their relationship. "It appears Daniela likes you. But--and I'm only going to say this once, bud--you screw with Daniela, you break her heart, I'll kick your ass."

"Good to know," he answered. *Precise and to the point,* Tim thought. "You don't like me much, do you?"

Mark stared; he didn't have to answer, the tick to his right eyelid said it all. "Have a good afternoon," Mark said. He climbed down off the fence rail and tipped his cowboy hat as he walked away.

Dani rode over to Tim, jumped off the stallion's back, she was all aglow and hugged the horse. "You are such a good boy!" The horse responded as if her words were pure love washing over him--which, Tim guessed, they were. One of the Mark's sons brought Dani an apple, and she gave it to the horse.

"Ryan, this is my friend, Tim," she introduced them. The boy was a miniature of his stocky father, with his same penetrating eyes. Tim offered him a hand shake. Shyly, Ryan shook his hand and then ran off.

"So, this is ranch life? I could get used to it," Tim said.

"It's a good life, but can be a hard one. Last winter we lost power for four days in a freezing rain storm. Lucky for me I had put in a full back-up generator. Without that, it would've been miserable. A lot of times you are just responding to whatever Mother Nature throws at you. You can never be prepared for everything." She laughed, gazing into his eyes to make sure he understood it was sometimes a hard life. He wasn't sure he understood; they seemed to have everything. Finally, she hooked her arm though his.

They walked to the main house. Dani was looking up into his face as if she were really in love. He knew he was.

THIRTY-TWO

Another Seattle sunset, blood-red light reflecting off the glass-and-steel buildings like hell's fire. Saturday afternoon was fading into black. It was a strange transition, as if the drones who worked during the day traded places with a new shift of disgusting drunks and easy hookers who invaded the streets at night. Even though they washed the dust of a dry summer from the air, the early rains and the cool breeze over the Sound whispered a threat of more and colder weather on the way. He felt it, smelled it on the wind.

All day he had searched for her. His need was building, unrelenting. He went to his apartment and spent several hours looking through his camera without success. Disgusted, he drove to her house, parked, and jogged the tree-lined street over and over. She was not at home. He worked out at the Sevens Club, but she never arrived. He'd even gone to McAndrews' condo. The silver Mercedes wasn't there. He could only conclude they were together. McAndrews had no right. His hands clenched into fists until his knuckles hurt. McAndrews would never have her. *Never.*

Now he walked the streets, hunting. He stepped inside one of the waterfront bars, took a seat, and ordered a glass of wine. When he turned on his stool, he saw lots of pretty women here, but all were safely in the company of men. He quickly downed his glass of wine. Ordered another. This time when he turned, he saw his mark standing alone in the corner of the room. The blond young man lifted his glass in a toast. His stomach churned in disgust. The gay boy was flirting like he would with a woman. Rage boiled up. He smiled back. It had the right effect. The young man crossed the crowded bar and stood next to him.

"Hi. I saw you were alone. I'm new here; would like some company?" the young man asked. He couldn't be more than twenty-one. He was a pretty boy: even feminine features, full lips, deep blue eyes. His body radiated the scent of expensive aftershave and alcohol.

"Absolutely. May I buy you a glass of wine?" he answered. A dark memory tried to edge its way from the depths into his consciousness. He shook it off.

"I'll have what you're having."

"Another merlot," he said to the bartender.

"Do you live around here?"

"I do," he answered, handing over the glass.

"Maybe we could get a bottle and go to your place," the boy suggested.

He tipped his head to the side and lifted an eyebrow, crushing down the fury. "What a lovely idea. Finish your wine."

The blond complied, almost gulping it down in anticipation. He watched him, feeling the anger roiling like a tempest. Rage, barely controlled, twisted his lips into a smile. "Shall we go?"

He stood. He was taller than the young man. Good. He hadn't expected to be. The stranger nodded for him to lead and pulled up his hood. At first, they walked together under the streetlights. A light rain started to fall, and the drops streaked downward, sparkling.

"I know a shortcut. This way," he said. They ducked into a dreary alley lit by a single bare bulb in a cheap reflector hanging from a fire escape. Carefully, he slipped his hands into the leather gloves in his pockets. When they were deep into the alley, he moved behind the young man, placing his arm over his shoulder and holding him still. He pressed his lips up to his ear. The young man sighed as if overpowered by lust. "I'm not one of you," he said, quickly slicing the knife through the flesh from one side of the young man's throat to the other.

In his mind, he transposed McAndrews' face over the boy's. He was surprised at how easy it was, how deep the sharp knife cut. And how quickly death came: as he swiped the knife away, a startling mist of arterial spatter hit his black jacket with the coppery, metallic smell of blood. He let the limp body fall to the ground. Then the rage hit him, he bent over the body and stabbed over and over until he couldn't anymore. He staggered back and stood. Transfixed, he watched as the blood pulsed, pooled, and mixed with water on the sidewalk. The rain picked up. Big drops pelted the rooftops and pounded on the metal trash bins in the alley, ringing in his ears. Still, he watched as the puddles merged and became a red-tinged stream rushing from the sidewalk to the storm sewer. Suddenly, he realized he'd stayed too long. He adjusted his hood and hurried from the alley. When he reached the street, everyone was hustling to get out of the downpour. He made his way to the apartment, slipped up the stairs, found the key, and unlocked the door, closing it behind him. He stood for a moment, reliving and relishing the moment. He waited. In the distance, he heard sirens.

THIRTY-THREE

The patter of rain on the wood deck outside the open sliding glass doors stirred Tim from sleep. He remembered he was at Dani's ranch. A cold breeze made him want the extra blanket folded at the end of the bed. He felt Dani's warm body up against his side. He reached for and pulled the cover up over them. With Dani, he was content. He was home. He relaxed deep into the pillows and put his arms around her, bringing her even closer.

"Are you awake?" she asked.

"Your rainstorm woke me up."

"It woke me, too. Sometimes I can just listen to the rain for hours," she purred.

"It's good thinking music," he laughed, petting her hair.

"Tell me what happened between you and Ellen Mason?" she asked, moving away to consider his face.

"Ellen Mason? I haven't seen or even thought about Ellen for over a year."

"Last night at the fundraiser Jenny mentioned I should ask Ellen what happened between you. And once before, Katrina Collins said the same." She kissed his shoulder.

Tim let out a deep sigh. "I think it's more what I didn't do that they are all upset about."

"What didn't you do that you should've?" She breathed in, almost a gasp.

"I didn't marry her," Tim answered.

"Should you have?" She lifted an eyebrow as if reading his expression.

"No. No way."

"Was there a baby?"

"No, no baby. Her friends were all getting married. She wanted to; I didn't. Dani," he adjusted himself so he could look in her eyes, "I didn't love her. At least, not in the way I want to love when I get married. Like now, with you." He touched her cheek.

"Tell me."

"So, how do you want this, the unvarnished truth or a cleaned-up version?"

'Truth," she said, propping herself in some pillows so she could get the whole story.

He wanted that part of his life left buried, but Dani should know and then they could let it go. "I had just started with the prosecutor's office. They loaded me up with so many cases I didn't have time to even think about girlfriends. They hired me on probation, and I needed to land a full-time position. I wasn't looking for a relationship; I wasn't ready. Ellen and I met on a Sunday morning on the Bainbridge ferry. Scott, Kathy, and I were spending one of our very few days off just knocking around together. Ellen was with friends; they'd been up all night for a bachelorette party. I think they were still drunk. They started flirting, mostly with Scott--he was always the chick magnet. Ellen started talking to me. It was okay. She gave me her number. I didn't call her." Tim stroked Dani's hair. "You're sure you want to hear this?" he asked again.

"Yes."

"A few weeks later we ran into each other one evening at the Sevens Club. I realized I hadn't called her and felt like a real shit. When she asked me out, I accepted, more out of guilt than anything. We went out for dinner, drinks, and dancing with her friends. The whole date I kept wondering how was I going to get out of it. She invited me up to her apartment. I knew it was a bad idea. I wasn't that attracted, but it was easy sex."

Dani inhaled. "Tim!"

"I've done things I'm not proud of. You said you wanted the unvarnished truth; changed your mind?"

"No." She kissed his shoulder. He felt desire racing though him. Dani wasn't Ellen.

"I tried to leave that first night before anything happened. But she said no strings attached. She was lying. I knew it, then. But it had been awhile. You'd have to be male to understand that. I knew there were going to be strings; I just thought I could get out of them."

"How long were you together?"

"That's the problem: I never considered us together. But we saw each other on and off for about a year. She kept saying we were just friends with benefits. Dani, I never stayed the whole night. I never used the toothbrush she bought for me. I was always home by midnight. I made the excuse that I had court in the morning, even when I didn't. I used her; she used me. When she needed a date for something-or-other, she called me. When I needed sex-- Dani, do you really want to hear this?"

"Yes. If people are going to bring up Ellen, I need to know your side of the story." She propped herself up on her elbow stared down at him and then softly kissed his lips. "Keep going."

"When you kiss me, I can't think about Ellen."

"Okay, I'll stop."

"No, kiss me. Let's forget about Ellen, I certainly have."

"Tim, tell me."

He didn't want to think about Ellen. She was a great gal, but not for him. "About six months in she started telling me she loved me. I couldn't tell her that. I didn't feel the same. I started to see less and less of her. She'd call, I'd be too busy."

"Even when you weren't?"

"Yep. Bad, I know. In college Scott and I used to call it slithering. When a girl we'd taken advantage of wanted more, we'd slither away like the snakes we were."

"You were that bad?"

"Dani, you have no idea. We were such hound dogs. In our junior year, Scott and I ended up swearing off women. Girls would just throw themselves at us. They wanted love; we wanted--anyway. I needed to study. I needed to get through with good enough grades to get a scholarship. I couldn't just screw my life away."

"Literally?" she asked, laughing.

He chuckled. "Literally."

"Back to Ellen," she said.

"Slithering was better than listening to her tell me I was selfish. I already knew that; she didn't have to remind me. Besides, it wasn't right. Something was missing. Deep down I knew I could settle, but I couldn't say I loved her. She was a nice girl. She deserved someone who did."

"That's not selfish."

"Isn't it? I kept having sex with her, knowing eventually we'd break up. I wasn't letting her go, letting her find someone who wanted what she wanted. Then one day, I'd ducked into Jake's to grab a cup of coffee with an attorney friend. I looked up. I don't know why. And there was this beautiful woman coming down the stairs at the James Street parking garage. Oh God, Dani, you hit me like a tsunami. I just stood there like a big dope. I had to have you."

Dani gasped.

He knew he had to continue. "From then on, I went to Jake's every morning to get coffee. Just to see you. One morning, just before we broke up, Ellen followed me. She saw you and my reaction to you. She accused me of cheating."

"You cheated on Ellen with me?"

He laughed. "Hell, I didn't even know your name. But I guess I was cheating. She told me she was leaving me and I let her. It took me another seven months to gather up the courage to talk to you. Ellen and I were long over. I kept expecting we'd meet somewhere--you and I--but we never did. I had to do something."

Dani was studying him. "Me?" she asked, incredulous.

"I made a decision. And that's the day I brought you flowers. I wasn't going to meet you any other way. Are you sorry?"

"Me? You wanted me?"

"Desperately."

She kissed him, letting her lips linger at his, barely touching, He could feel every sense waking, every second ticking off, drunk with her and she with him. Tim had never been so in love.

"I'm not a very good guy, Dani. But with you, it's so different. Don't hate me; I was terrible to Ellen. I don't deserve you. But I can't--I won't--give you up. Stay with me anyway."

Dani stared at him. "Okay," she whispered.

THIRTY-FOUR

When Tim opened the door to his office, he was surprised to see Scott and Kathy there. But lately, it had become their meeting place. The police department was too busy, and there was no privacy. And the morgue, the morgue was just plain creepy.

"This is becoming a habit," he laughed, motioning to Kathy to give up his chair behind the desk. He set his briefcase just inside the door. He peeled off his suit coat and hung it on the rack next to Scott's tweed and straightened his tie.

"Where have you been all weekend?" Kathy walked past him, staring hard at his face as if he wasn't allowed to have weekends off. She'd obviously been working and was in clean hospital scrubs.

"Dani's ranch. I even rode a horse. Me, on a horse!"

"Well, yippee-ki-yay!" Kathy teased.

Tim wrinkled his nose at her in a pretend scowl. "Why? What did I miss?"

"Ugly weekend. Along with the usual thefts, rapes, domestic and drug-related violence, a young man got his throat slit in the alley just off Third Avenue," Scott said. "Victim was gay, so Captain Martin believes it was hate crime."

"What do you think?" Tim asked.

"I think all murder is a hate crime, but he could've been killed because he was gay. There are a lot of sickos out there. There were no slurs at the crime scene, none of the usual hate-crime garbage." Scott's brow was pinched with worry.

"Was he robbed?"

"Nope. Wallet was in his pocket, money and credit cards in his wallet. The vic wasn't from around here. San Fran. Took us hours to track down his family," Scott said. He traced a finger over his mustache and adjusted his leather shoulder holster.

"The perp was taller, right-handed. From the wound, I think he grabbed him over the shoulder with his left hand, pinned him, and then slit from left to right." Kathy demonstrated on Scott.

"Oohff." Tim flinched and felt his stomach turn. He wasn't going to want to see the pictures. Thank God he'd been at Dani's ranch; It kept him from having to see the body.

"We've gathered the surveillance videos of the street. But there are no cameras in the alley where the body was found. A building blocks the street camera, and you can't see people coming out. It's almost like the killer knew it and took advantage. And the storm--it was raining so hard everyone on the street was either under an umbrella or in a hoodie. We're interviewing bartenders all along the waterfront to see if they recognize the vic and maybe who he was with," Scott added.

"Did you go to Goddard?"

"Left that for you," Scott answered.

"Okay," Tim nodded. He picked up his phone. "Myra, can you set me up with Goddard this morning? Thanks." He hung up. "Anything new on our poisoner?"

Scott shook his head.

"Well, at least he didn't kill anyone this weekend," Kathy said.

THIRTY-FIVE

Dani entered Paul Goddard's office. He stood from behind his large oak desk. She didn't remember him being such a big man, so stout and rather gruff, at the fundraiser and she felt slightly intimidated. Maybe she shouldn't be trying this?

The county hadn't spared any expense in furnishing his office. It bordered on opulent. Behind his huge desk, matching credenzas lined the back wall and were surely filled with case files. Beautiful red-and-brown hand-loomed oriental rugs covered the hardwood floors. *Taxpayer dollars at work*, she mused. He had an incredible view from his ninth-floor office. The fastidiously groomed city park across the street was in late summer bloom; last night's rain had cleaned the dust away, and everything was bright with color. She studied the pictures of his family prominently positioned on his desk. A pretty wife, a teenage son with Goddard's same brown hair and eyes, and a daughter with his wife's good looks were staged like props in his life. She hadn't seen his family at the fundraiser and briefly wondered if he and his wife were still together.

"Miss St. Clair, to what do I owe this honor?" he asked. She suspected he knew why she'd come.

"I thought perhaps you might need some financial assistance with your campaign." She played coy.

"How thoughtful of you," he grinned, motioning for her to have a seat. "Would you care for coffee?"

"No, thank you," she demurred in a soft voice, trying her best to ratchet up her courage. But Jenny Mattison had left her no choice. She had struck a chord. Dani hated stark-naked injustice and unfair political pressure.

"Do you mind if I have one?"

"Not at all, Paul. May I call you Paul?" She delivered her sweetest smile. "Yes, of course."

She could tell he was charmed. Step one in successful negotiating accomplished.

"I don't want to be crude, but how much were you thinking of giving?" Goddard asked, a sheepish grin on his face.

She took an unsealed envelope out of her purse and slid it across the desk to him.

"May I?" He gestured.

"Of course," she answered. She had given the legal limit for an individual and for each of her corporations, carefully following her accountant's stern warnings.

He looked up at her, beaming. "Miss St. Clair, with this you just put us over our goal."

"Indeed? How lucky," she said, in a tone that let him know she knew exactly how much he'd needed. "Now Paul, I need a favor from you."

Goddard's eyes narrowed. Obviously, he'd expected this! He smiled at her.

"I heard somewhere that it isn't unusual for a young man to marry a politically connected man's daughter to advance his own career." She waited a few seconds to let the impact of her statement to sink in. "I was wondering if my donation is enough to make certain that Mr. McAndrews isn't in any way hurt by the romantic aspirations of a certain judge's daughter?"

"Miss St. Clair, that was a mistake. We had no idea he was involved. We would never have suggested--"

"At your fundraiser, a young lady made me aware of her desires, as well as the power her father would wield on her behalf. You are aware Mr. McAndrews is not from a politically connected family. I want to make certain I--I level the playing field, so to speak. I would hate to think of a hard-working young man and one of your best prosecutors not getting what he deserves."

"Miss St. Clair, what are you suggesting he might deserve?" Goddard sat forward, peeking out from under his bushy eyebrows. "Chief Deputy, perhaps?"

She pressed her lips tightly together and then brushed an errant curl from her cheek. She was shocked, but couldn't show it. Could she have bought Tim a career? She had no intention of doing that. If Tim ever found out, he would hate her for it. "I'm sorry, you misread me. I'm not asking that you give him any particular position. Just that he gets what he truly earns. Nothing more, but certainly nothing less, no matter what kind of pressure comes to bear."

"You have a deal, Miss St. Clair. I will talk to Judge Mattison about Jenny." Goddard sat back deep into his brown leather chair. "I was thinking it's time Jenny was moved so she can learn all about the vice unit."

"Thank you," Dani stood. "Oh, and if you need it, Delight Valley would be happy to host a fundraiser and wine tasting at our Seattle tasting room. Just name the day."

"I'll have my campaign chairman give you a call." Goddard grinned like he couldn't believe his luck. Dani was still skeptical; she hoped she hadn't done more harm than good.

Tim gathered up the folder Scott and Kathy had left him. He hadn't looked inside. Didn't want to see the crime scene or the autopsy photos. He would have to, but he decided to wait if he could.

He pressed his intercom button. "Myra, is Goddard free?"

"I think so, looks like his meeting just broke up."

"Okay, I'm on my way." Tim stood from behind his desk. It had been two years since they'd actually had a verifiable hate crime. He blew out a breath and rubbed a hand over his brow. If this was one, the publicity and pressure would be ugly. The whole prosecutor's office would need to get ready for the unrealistic and unjust accusations of discrimination. Right in the middle of Goddard's campaign--crap! *A hate-crime, a serial murderer, how much worse could it get? Never mind*, he thought. *It could always get worse.*

He opened the door to his office and Dani was there. He was delighted. "Hi, what are you doing here?" She looked fabulous. The pale gray suit she wore was all business, but the knit accentuated her curves perfectly. "Wow. You look gorgeous," he added.

"Thank you." She tipped her head slightly. "I was donating to your boss's campaign. And I thought I'd stop by and see you. Say hi. You'd said you didn't have court today."

"I didn't think you cared much for Goddard's politics."

"I believe in law and order. I just don't like fundraisers, and I'm tired of old Neil Diamond tunes. But more than anything, I was donating to bribe him into being nice to you." She turned and walked with a saucy stride into his workplace.

Tim loved the mischievous tease in her eyes. "Well, good. I need all the help I can get," he played along. But then he wondered: *would she do that?*

"This is it, my grand office." He laughed and leaned against the door, closing it. He set the file down on the desk. He grabbed her hand and spun her into his arms. "Glad you aren't a defense lawyer; I'd be so distracted. You look ... wow!"

"I know you're busy, but I couldn't leave without seeing you."

"The murderers were busy this weekend," he sighed.

"Oh, no." She reached up and touched his cheek with the back of her fingers. Her touch was cool and exciting. He took hold of her hand and kissed her fingertips.

Tim studied her. "Stay with me at my place. I have court tomorrow, and I want to--hell, we should just get a place together. I don't want to spend any nights without you. You really do need to marry me. I'm perfect for you! I can even sort of ride a horse now," he said, with a lighthearted chuckle.

"That's your argument, counsellor?"

"Best I can do."

"Um. Maybe," she answered, her long lashes sweeping up as she looked into his eyes. It was one of those looks that set him spinning.

"Maybe? One step closer to yes. I like that," he said. They kissed, and he felt like one more kiss and he'd take her right here on his desk. He had to put a stop to it; he was being irresponsible. "Dani, no more kisses. I have to go meet with Goddard."

"Okay." She stood on her tiptoes and kissed his cheek. He held her, his eyes closed. "See you tonight," she said.

"McTavish's. At six? I'll have Myra make a reservation."

"Yes."

"Dani?" She turned back, her mouth parted softly. "Goddard--you didn't really ask him to be nice to me, right?"

She didn't answer. She just rolled her eyes and grinned. He was almost reassured. Almost. She reached for his hand. They left the office together, holding hands until they had to part. Tim headed for Goddard's office and she to work. Tim glanced around, and the whole office staff seemed to be looking at him. He was doing what he always thought he should do: parade Dani through so they would stop trying to fix him up with their sisters, nieces, and daughters. He wanted it understood in no uncertain terms: he could fix himself up.

THIRTY-SIX

Dani closed the door to her building and looked over at Karen with desperation. "I think I just screwed up, big time."

"What? What did you do?"

"I just donated to Tim's boss's reelection campaign."

"Okay. How's that a screw-up? You donate to lots of stuff." Karen rounded her desk and followed Dani to her office.

"I attached strings." She peeled away her gray jacket. Karen took it and hung it in the closet.

"What does that mean?"

"I told you that Jenny Mattison had been pretty much throwing herself at Tim? He's been worrying about it."

"Yes."

"Well, she confronted me about Tim at the fundraiser Thursday night, acted like we were in some kind of competition." Dani put both hands over her face and groaned. "Goddard volunteered to move her to a different department when he saw my checks."

"Good. That puts an end to it."

"Tim doesn't know. I hinted that I'd bribed his boss to be nice to him ... he thought I was joking, so I let him think it. But just as I left he asked me if I'd *really* done it. You should've seen the look on his face. If he finds out, he's going to hate me."

"I bet he'll be grateful."

"He's his own man, Karen. I think he'll hate me for trying to influence things. Well, what's done is done. Hope he never finds out. I think--no Karen, I'm sure--I don't want to lose him."

THIRTY-SEVEN

"So, what's so urgent, Tim?" Goddard asked, looking up from his computer screen.

"Detective Renton thinks we may have a hate crime." Tim passed the folder across his boss's desk. He still hadn't looked at the photos and watched carefully as Goddard reacted with disgust.

"This is bad," Goddard said, tapping his meaty fingers against his coffee mug on his desk.

"Scott says the press is on to it--story will break tonight at six. P.D. was able to hold them off until then. Thought you'd want to be ready to make a statement," Tim said.

"Good. Yes. All right. I'll get my speech writer on it right away." Goddard scrutinized him. "You seem to be the cops' go-to guy."

"Detective Renton and I grew up together, went to college together."

Goddard pursed his lips and rubbed his chin. "I've been doing some thinking, McAndrews. With you as lead on the poisoner case and now this, I'm moving you to the major crimes unit. Farland is retiring next year, and we'll be needing someone to fill his spot. You're just the guy for the job," Goddard grinned.

Tim felt weird. He'd spent some time hoping for a break like this, but on the heels of Dani's donation, it left him a little cold. "Thank you, sir. But aren't there more experienced lawyers?"

"McAndrews, you have the best conviction record in the office. You're one of my best prosecutors. Are you saying you don't want the job?"

"Not at all. I'm grateful for the chance."

"The cops trust you; that's a plus." Goddard tapped his fingers on the edge of his desk.

"Did Dani St. Clair ask you for this?" Tim knew it would be better not to ask. But worry had come to haunt him again; was he going to lose all of himself by loving her?

"Hell, no!" Goddard was emphatic but his eyes told a different story. "McAndrews, stop being such an idealist. Such a boy scout. Would it be so bad if she did? You work harder than anyone in the office; you win more often in court. It would only be bad if you hadn't already earned it." Goddard passed the file back across the desk to him. "Take this on for me, okay? I've got the campaign, and I know I can trust you."

Tim nodded his consent. "All right. I'm on it."

"I'll tell Farland. He'll be happy for the help and to know we won't be asking him to stay on when he hits retirement age," Goddard chuckled. "Do you want a new office? Bigger one?"

"I think I'm fine where I am." Tim stared. *How about the moon and stars?* he thought.

"No. You need a bigger office. You know you get a raise with the position, right?"

Moon and stars, coming right up, Tim mused.

"Who do you want to take with you?"

"Myra, of course. Does she get a raise? She could use one: by herself, with three kids at home."

"Yes. Want any of the new ADAs?"

"James Rudolf is really good."

"You've got it. Oh, and I'm assigning Jenny Mattison to vice. She needs the experience there."

"She's not my charge anymore?"

"No. Jenny needs to learn to fly on her own. You think I don't see what's going on in my own department? I might have you check on her from time to time, but I think she was getting entirely too dependent. If you know what I mean."

"Okay." Tim was surprised. Before the fundraiser, Goddard had been all for Tim serving as Jenny's mentor. He lifted an eyebrow.

"All right. Time to get to work."

Goddard was done. Tim picked up the folder and left. He went back to his office and sat down behind his desk. He thought about opening the case file. Didn't. He dialed Scott's cell phone instead.

THIRTY-EIGHT

"So, what's up? You sounded freaked on the phone," Scott asked. He took a bite out of his burger. "God, I love Nina's. These are the best burgers in the world."

Tim scooted down the picnic bench in front of Nina's Food Cart until he sat across from his friend. Nina's stainless-steel exterior reflected a strange image of the ferry maneuvering into the dock below. Scott had removed his suit jacket and carefully set it down the bench from him. He sat across from Tim in shirtsleeves and was garnering stares from passers-by. Tim guessed it was the fully exposed shoulder holster and .45 caliber Smith & Wesson, that caught their eye.

"It's Dani. She donated to Goddard's campaign and suddenly I get promoted to major crimes; offered a bigger, better office; my choice of the new ADAs; a raise." Tim shook his head.

"And your complaint is?" Scott wiped some mayonnaise from his mustache with his fingers. Tim absently handed him a napkin so he wouldn't ruin his new tie.

"My complaint is it feels weird. I should be the one--"

"Look at it this way: Dani has money; she's doing what she can to help you. No different than Kathy, it's just Kathy doesn't have money. She brings us cases instead. The Senchal abuse case last year, the cyanide poisoner eight months ago. She gives us the best stuff, things that make our careers. Why is it okay for Kathy to help, but not Dani? Because Kathy's poor? Do you think if Kathy had money, she wouldn't be 'donating' to get the best for us? That's what friends do." Scott swiped a French fry though a pile of ketchup and ate it.

"You don't feel--emasculated? Shouldn't we be taking care of them?"

"Yes. We should be taking care of them; I've always felt that way. But that's our dads' world, not ours. Hell, I need Kathy--she's smarter than I am. I'm trying to hide that I'm a Neanderthal. Help is help. No one makes it alone," Scott said.

Tim laughed. "Neanderthal? I'm afraid I'll lose myself."

"In a way, isn't that what happens when you--when *we*--fall in love? But it's not losing oneself; it's giving all of yourself, merging together, and getting something far better. Before Kathy, I was a sleazy dog. When I'm with Kathy, I'm an upstanding citizen. I'm a better man. *I* even like me better. I understand it might be scary with Dani--she has what we're all working for, what we think we want. She doesn't seem to need you. But Tim, she does. There's more to life than money. When you're in love you complete each other."

"You've become quite the philosopher," Tim observed. Scott had really grown up since their college days. They'd done a whole lot of pretending and very little thinking when it came to love then. Even now, Tim wasn't sure Scott's advice would help. But, as ever, his constant and unconditional friendship would.

"That's me: Plato. Hey, I went through all this when I first realized I loved Kathy. You should've seen me. I was a train wreck. I had all these beautiful girls calling me, wanting to have sex. They're calling me, and I don't want anything to do with them. I'm in love with Kath. I can't live without her. She knows me. *All* about me," he chuckled. "How do you win the girl that really knows you? The first few months I thought I would go nuts. But then, I just decided; it was Kathy I wanted. You have to decide. Do you want the real, living, breathing Dani or do you want what you made up in your imagination instead? Because the imaginary girl isn't anywhere, you'll never find her."

Tim stared at his friend. "I want Dani."

"Then when she helps you, let her. Pretend you don't know, that's what I'd do. Unless you think you can't live with it. Then you're more fucked up than I knew."

"Big help."

"Tim, how many nights did we drink in our frat room wishing we could meet some rich babe to set us up in life? How many?"

"That was so we didn't have to work so hard. Now, I love it. When I win a case and send some scumbag to jail for the rest of his crappy life, I love the way that feels." Tim grinned at the thought. "I'm one of the good guys, like we dreamed about when we were kids."

"Dani asking you to give that up?"

"No. Not so far."

"Yeah, not so far. And she's not the kind that will. My advice? Throw away the old-fashioned horse hockey and keep the girl."

Tim laughed.

THIRTY-NINE

With two cars between them, he followed her. *Where are you headed?* he wondered. He followed her down past Washington Street. Past Fifteenth, then left on to the I-5 south. He coursed through traffic, passing the same cars she passed, slowing when she slowed, and speeding up when she increased her speed. *Right off the freeway to where?* Where was she going? Ah! King County airport. He continued until she stopped in front of the charter office. She parked, removed a small cordovan leather suitcase from the trunk of her car, and briskly walked to the small aircraft terminal. He followed, staying well behind, meandering slowly, and making sure she didn't see him. She hurriedly walked through the small building and waved to the man at the counter.

"Good afternoon, Miss St. Clair," he heard the man say.

"Hi, Gerald. How are you today?"

"Mitch's out on the tarmac, can I take your bag for you?"

"No, thank you. It's light." She dashed out the glass doors to the waiting airplane.

He followed and watched as she boarded the sleek Cessna 340. He pulled a high-speed digital camera up to his eye and clicked off numerous pictures. He memorized the shape of the aircraft and its call numbers as it taxied to get in line for the runway. He watched the twin-engine roll, gathering speed until its wheels left the ground and she was off. *Where to?* he walked up to the man at the counter. He was exactly what he expected a charter service pilot to look like: dressed in khaki Dockers and a cream-colored T-shirt with MCGOWAN'S CHARTER SERVICE AND AIRCRAFT SALES printed neatly under the pocket. He was clean-shaven, and his haircut was almost military.

"Was that Daniela St. Clair?"

"Yes, it was."

"That must cost a pretty penny. How much to charter that 340?" he asked.

"That's not a charter. We charter here, but we also sell and service most of the private aircraft. I'm a Cessna dealer."

"So, that's Miss St. Clair's private plane?"

"Yes."

"You'd think with all her money she'd have a jet."

"Oh, she does--a Gulfstream, but you can't land a jet at the vineyards or the ranch, so she bought the Cessna. Miss St. Clair is very practical," Gerald said.

"So, where is she off to today? The ranch or the vineyards?" he asked.

"Vineyards; looks like her flight plan is Napa. Can I take a message for her?"

"No, no, Gerald--it is Gerald, isn't it? I'll speak with her later." He reached out to shake Gerald's hand.

"And you are?"

"Michael Sanborn, *Seattle Times*," he lied. "I was trying to catch up with her to get the scoop on her new wine release. Her secretary said I might be able to catch her here. But looks like I missed her instead," he laughed. "I'll have to interview her later. Thanks for your time."

He strolled to his car. He wasn't going to get to connect with Daniela tonight. He contemplated what he should do. He decided to head for the Sevens Club for a workout.

As he returned to the city, he realized that until now, he'd only been inside Daniela's house during daylight hours. The thought of a nighttime visit sent excitement thrilling through him, energizing him. But the one thing he liked best of all was that Daniela left town without Tim McAndrews. Unless he was meeting her later? One way to find out: he'd follow his rival.

FORTY

This was the first evening in two months that Tim had spent alone. Dani was in Napa on business, and with a killer skulking the streets, he couldn't go with her. She hadn't asked. *Why hadn't she asked?* He couldn't linger on those thoughts or his confidence would be ruined.

Spirit sagging, he jogged around the indoor track at the club. Each time he thought of spending the night at his condo, he missed Dani more. He'd gotten used to waking in her queen-sized four-poster, nestled in the deep layer of the down comforter, and feeling the warmth and weight of Dani tangled in his arms. Lately, he'd only been home long enough to grab clean clothes. He wondered if he'd recognize the place.

As he rounded the bend in the track, he saw Katrina Collins at the entryway ahead of him. He felt the muscles in his body tense, his running step hesitate. She was one woman he could do without. Each time she'd called Dani over the last few days, she'd done nothing but harass her, trying to fill her head with lies. She was still in there pitching for Fraser, even though Dani had politely refused to date him.

Katrina stood in the doorway, bending down tightening a shoelace. As always, she made sure her work-out top was so low cut and tight that every man in the club could see the perky curve of her breasts. Wanting to pass her without incident, he sped up. Without Dani to stop him, he might just speak his mind.

"Tim." Katrina stood and reached out as he passed by. "Tim, stop. I need to talk to you." He felt the weight of her hand on his arm. *Damn it!*

He stopped and turned, feeling the muscles in his jaw clench tight and dread oozing out of him like sweat.

"Tim. I'm sorry." She did an aw-shucks shuffle. "I want to apologize for the way I've behaved. Can we have a drink together and talk this out? I *am* Daniela's best friend, after all; we need to get along." She whined, yet her tone was accusing, as if the hard feelings between them were his fault.

"I didn't start this. We don't need to have a drink. You can just accept that Dani and I are together." He narrowed his eyes at her. He didn't like or trust her.

"Oh, come on, Timmy. You can't stay mad at me forever. Just one little drink?" She prowled up to him like a cat in heat, her long red fingertips stroking his arm. He recoiled, moving out of her reach. What a gamester.

He felt sorry for Gary Warden. He imagined she wheedled what she wanted out of him with her sugary talk.

"Not tonight, Katrina. Call Dani and set it up. We can all go for a drink sometime." Hoping that was the end of it, he pivoted to resume his workout.

"Wait, I--"

Closing his eyes in annoyance, he angled to face her.

"Not tonight? Um, I'll call her, then." She bestowed a fake, almost scheming smile on him. The curls tied in her ponytail bounced around her face as if they were made of yellow elastic. "I want us to be friends." She replaced her hand on his arm, drawing the fingertips gently back and forth through the blond hair.

He studied her. Her lips were full and wet, and she blinked up at him, a vain attempt at seduction. He'd been here before. Wondering what Katrina *really* wanted, he managed a closed smile.

"Friends?" She lifted her shoulders. *Right. She's about as shy as a wolverine.*

"Okay. Friends." His offer was skeptical. He spun and jogged briskly away. He made certain to keep up his speed to discourage her from tagging along. His impression remained unchanged: Katrina Collins was a dangerous woman.

After his run, Tim showered and dressed in the navy pin-striped slacks and long-sleeved white shirt he'd worn to court earlier. He didn't bother to put on his tie and carried his suit coat over his arm. Even though he felt refreshed from the workout, he missed Dani, wondered if she missed him. He faced his night alone with an emptiness in the pit of his stomach. He grabbed up his briefcase and workout bag and shouldered through the swinging door to the club's lobby from the men's locker room. It was almost eight o'clock, and he hadn't even thought about dinner. He crossed through the foyer toward the parking garage, trying to decide if he wanted a steak or if he should settle for McDonald's.

"Hi, Timmy."

"Oh no," he groaned, closing his eyes, and grinding his teeth together at the sound of her voice. Slowly, he reversed to face Katrina.

"Friend, will you walk me to my car? I'm scared to go alone." Her wool jacket slipped off her left shoulder and underneath her tight, low-cut blouse failed to cover the black lace that peeked out. Skimming the jacket back away from her like a runway model, showing off the fitted black jeans accentuating the smooth curve of her hips, she slunk up to him. *Rock-star sleazy* automatically registered in Tim's mind. She was up to something, something that wasn't going to serve him well. "I know you're going that way. I'm parked a couple of cars up from you," she added, jingling the gold bangle bracelets on her wrists.

He almost changed direction, almost said he was going to dinner in the restaurant upstairs, but then she might invite herself along. A short walk to the parking garage would be the easier of his two torturous options.

"I'm going that way," he conceded. Katrina tried to thread her arm through his, but he wouldn't let her and guided her with his gym bag, forcing her to walk a few paces ahead.

"Are you working on anything sensational these days—a juicy crime scandal?" Katrina glanced behind her and paused so he would catch up. Tim eyed her. Why would she be asking *that*? Katrina Collins the poisoner? Yeah, he could believe it.

"Nope. DUII detail." He opened the outer door, holding it for her. She passed him, brushing her backside against his thigh. She didn't need to touch him; there was plenty of room. *Friendship? My big toe!* He had to get away from her as soon as possible. At the landing at the top of the stairs, he paused. She spun to face him.

"I'll have to drink and drive, then." She tossed her head back and then leveled a seductive gaze his way.

"Whatever," Tim laughed. *Dumb shit. If she were caught, that would be about a ten-grand tab,* "I'm right over there. I'll see you later."

"Walk me all the way. What if a mugger's on the other side of my car, waiting to grab me?"

"Scream, I'll come running." He couldn't keep the sarcasm from his voice.

"It won't hurt you to walk me." She grasped the end of his briefcase, pulling him along with it. He could imagine the case flying open and his briefs spilling all over the garage floor. He went along until they reached her car.

"Okay. We're here. Goodnight, Katrina."

"Are you afraid of me, Timmy? Her dark lashes fluttered. She was pure poison.

"Listen, Katrina, I haven't been Timmy since I was three. No, I'm not afraid of you. I've just got to go. Turn my briefcase loose, okay?"

"You are! What are you afraid of, Timmy? Afraid I'll--" Katrina moved on him. Before he could react, she was on her tiptoes, kissing him, touching him where she should not. He dropped his briefcase and gym bag and grabbed her wrists, forcing her away. Did she know how close she'd come to getting punched out? He stared down into her upturned face, sucking air through his teeth, checking the impulse. She leaned toward him, offering her lush red mouth, breath heaving the small rounds of her breasts up at him. As a younger man, he might've gone for this. *Easy sex with a forward woman.*

"You're hurting me," she whimpered, straining against his tightening grip, the gold bangle bracelets jingled against his knuckles. He didn't let her free. Didn't want her touching him again.

"You'd do this to Dani? You'd do this to your best friend?" He shoved her back against her car, releasing her hands as he did. "Not with me."

She glowered at him, watching him recover his briefcase and bag, and brush the dirt from his suit coat that had fallen on the oily pavement.

"You'll be sorry," she spit, like a cornered wildcat.

"For not taking you? Not in a million years," he laughed.

"I'll make you sorry."

Anger bubbled to the surface and his jaw tightened against the menace. "Are you threatening me? Don't you dare threaten me." He glared at her, and just as he expected, the gesture alone was enough. Katrina slid along the side of her car, leaving a clean trail in the dust with her butt. She fumbled for the door handle. He watched the comedy as the panicked woman clambered into her car. She ground the car's starter twice before she realized the engine was running, slammed it into gear, and squealed the tires as she tore out of the parking space, almost hitting him as she whipped the car around. Tim jumped to the side, slamming his shin against a bumper.

Suddenly she threw the car in reverse. Tim slipped between two cars for safety. She stopped short when the open passenger side window was even with him, her face twisted in a vicious grin. His thoughts raced: *Did she have a gun?* Heart pounding in his chest, he pulled his briefcase up for cover.

"I'll make you sorry!" she hissed and punched the gas. The tires screamed all the way through the curve ahead, and he could taste the rankness of burnt rubber.

"Cunt!" Tim growled.

FORTY-ONE

Still angry, Tim slid onto a barstool next to Scott. Dark, cave-like McTavish's suited his mood. "Double crown, Mic," he called out to the bartender.

"Hey, bud. How's it going?" Scott sat back and Kathy waved hello from Scott's other side.

"Hi, Kathy. Scott, don't ask." Tim briefly glanced at them and then swigged down his shot of whiskey. The fire in his belly ignited the anger. *Katrina Collins. That bitch.*

When Mic looked his way, Tim tapped the rim of his glass. Mic brought over the bottle.

"You and the lovely lady have a tiff?" Kathy rose from her stool and stood between Scott and Tim, setting a gentle hand on Tim's shoulder.

"No. She's out of town."

"Ah, that's the problem," Scott laughed.

"What are you two lovers doing out? Shouldn't you be home—in bed?" Tim shot back.

"Working late, our favorite. You had dinner?" Kathy mothered and Tim didn't mind. He shook his head. "Bring my cantankerous friend a prime rib, medium rare." She stepped behind him and massaged his shoulders. "Want to tell the doctor all about it?"

"Nope." All the way here to McTavish's he'd stewed over what Katrina had done, why she'd done it, and what she was going to tell Dani. He was baffled: what made a woman behave that way?

"You're in a mood," Kathy rubbed his back.

He twisted in his barstool. "I came here to think and belt back a few in peace. Dani's out of town, that's all."

"I haven't seen you for days. You're lying."

Tim felt his eyes narrow into a glower. She knew him too well.

"Leave him alone, Kathy." Scott pulled her to him. "You need to pay attention to me anyway, doc. My back hurts."

"Okay, okay, you big baby." Tim watched Kathy sink her fingers into Scott's muscles and couldn't help but laugh as Scott wrenched himself away from her grasp.

"Ow! Damn it, woman!"

"There! Finally, Tim's laughing," Kathy giggled in triumph.

"Sadists! Both of you," Scott said, shaking his head from side to side, lifting one shoulder then the other as if to stop the lingering pain.

"So, tell the doctor what's wrong."

Tim sighed. Kathy wasn't going to give up. "Dani has this so-called friend. She came on to me."

"Uh-oh." Scott said, hunching down in his chair. "Not another Missy Warner."

"Far worse than Missy Warner," Tim grinned.

"Missy Warner?" Kathy leaned in tight, grin as big as a full moon on her face.

Tim picked up his shot glass and drained it. In college, while his girl Amy French was home with the flu, he'd joined the guys for a beer. Missy Warner, Amy's best friend, came on to him. She offered and he took, following his hormones right on down the wrong road. He'd really liked Amy French. She dumped him when she found out--and rightly so. He'd been a disloyal, immature jerk.

"Scott?"

"Don't ask me, Kath. I don't know nothing 'bout that." Scott leaned against the back of his stool, barely contained laughter sputtering from his lips.

Kathy gasped. "Tim McAndrews! You didn't!"

"You remember Amy French?"

Kathy nodded yes.

"That's why Amy broke it off with me; I thought you knew. Everyone knew. I sure believed I was something else in college." Tim shook his head, amazed now at the conceit of his youth.

"Tim, since you were in grade school the girls have been chasing you all over the place. Don't you remember?" Kathy teased.

Tim didn't remember it that way. But he'd never really had trouble getting dates; it was getting them to stay that was the problem.

"Everyone did Missy Warner," Scott said, candidly.

"Oh, careful buddy. I think you just stepped in it," Tim laughed.

Kathy pressed her lips into a pout and went back to her bar stool. "Great! My girl is mad at me and yours is going to be!"

Tim stood and wedged himself between his friends, arms over their shoulders. "Glad you two were here. I can always count on you to help me lighten up. Mic, another round for my buds."

"See, Kath? I told you if we were nice to him, he'd buy drinks."

"So, what did you do? How much trouble are you in?" Kathy asked.

"I didn't do anything. I shoved her off. Boy, is she pissed! Said she'd make me sorry."

"She won't do anything. That's all talk," Scott said, leaning back into his stool.

The prime rib dinner Kathy had ordered for Tim arrived and the smell of the perfectly roasted beef should have piqued his hunger. The waitress set it on the bar for him. He sat down, picked up his fork to eat, but found he'd lost his appetite: he was ready for war in the courtroom, but not in his personal life. Katrina Collins wasn't going to ruin this for him, he wouldn't let her. Dani was worth fighting for.

With that decision, hunger returned and Tim ate his dinner.

"That witch will lose a friend if she pushes her luck. Dani's got to know what she's like." Kathy nodded her head once for emphasis.

"And truth and justice always win out in the end," Tim added sarcastically. It should be true. Dani would see that Katrina chased after him and she'd sever their friendship.

"Fifty bucks says the tramp slinks back to her snake pit and never says a word to Dani." Scott eased off his barstool, emptying his pockets of bills for his share of the tab.

"I agree. And if she says something. I'll—I'll," Kathy sputtered, lost her words, and broke down into a spasm of giggles.

"Don't listen to her, she's drunk," Scott said.

"Well, yeah. What do you think she weighs, a hundred pounds? And she's had three shots since I've been here. Mic, a round of cabs, please," Tim laughed. "We're all drunk. We're gonna hate each other in the morning!"

"Not each other; just you. It's all your fault." Kathy pointed a boney finger at Tim's nose. "You and Missy Warner! Boy! I have the goods on you, McAndrews. Can I bribe you? No. Blackball you? No, that's not it."

"Do you mean 'blackmail me'? Have you ever seen this woman this drunk? Are you sure you want to marry her?" Tim helped Scott support Kathy as she clambered from her barstool. Two cabbies waited at the doorway.

"He does. He loves me." She took hold of Scott's chin and squeezed it.

"Whatever you say, doc. Your chariot awaits, madam." Scott chuckled. "And hey, buddy, forget about that sleazy broad."

"Done," Tim said. He knew Katrina was not a friend to Dani like Scott and Kathy were friends to him. The alcohol had taken the edge off, but Katrina's threats were real. He'd have to deal with it, no matter what came. He just knew he couldn't lose Dani. Not now.

FORTY-TWO

The photographs were superb. Beyond his wildest dreams. Clear. Precise. Damning. On his computer screen, he could see that the digital shots of Katrina Collins with her greedy hands all over Tim McAndrews had turned out perfectly. He laughed out loud; somehow, he'd known it would pay to follow McAndrews. The jerk was bound to do something stupid while Daniela was out of town. Katrina Collins, the little slut, had provided the perfect weapon to destroy the blossoming relationship.

Miss St. Clair wasn't likely to tolerate a philandering man--not after the stories he'd heard of what her husband had done to her. And when she dumped Tim, he'd make his move.

He opened the pictures in a sequence. If he reversed the order...he created a spread of the photographs side by side, shifting them with the mouse so that it looked like McAndrews was participating--no, enjoying--Katrina's grope. That was it! When Daniela received these, it would be over. He'd be there to console her. Poor baby; he'd pick up the shattered pieces. To make sure they looked authentic, he added the date and time at the bottom of each picture, mimicking the stamp he imagined the parking garage's camera would display.

He decided to print pictures as well as delivering them on a thumb drive. While waiting for the photos to print, he donned a pair of surgical gloves. He took a clean, lint-free cloth and meticulously wiped the surface of a new manila envelope he'd recovered from the left-hand drawer of his desk.

On his computer, he typed Daniela's name and office address and printed a clean, untouched label on his laser printer. He set the label on his desk and looked at the letters under a magnifying glass. Each letter was dark black, evenly saturated with ink: no repetitive printing flaw was going to lead anyone to his door after he killed her.

Before slipping the photographs into the envelope, he looked at them again, spreading them out on his desktop with gloved fingers. Satisfied, he leaned back into his wingback chair. His choice was critical. He couldn't make any mistakes. Winning Daniela and getting her vast fortune was his priority. For a moment, he fantasized about the lifestyle, the world, the freedom her money would give him.

He dreamed about kissing Daniela in his imagination. This would be a long, slow seduction. She was the big prize. This one had to last awhile; his bank account was running low. He mapped each move out in his mind's eye.

When he emerged from his reverie, he slipped the photographs and the thumb drive into the envelope, sponged the adhesive along the flap with water, and sealed it closed. Carefully, he set the package on the edge of his desk. Usually, he did his work in the apartment on James Street, never from home. But this morning, as the darkness retreated from a rosy sunrise, he hadn't been able to wait. He knew it was dangerous, so he once again wiped the outside of the envelope. He peeled away the surgical gloves and dropped them in the wastebasket.

He stood and slid his arms through the sleeves of his camel-colored microfiber trench coat and smoothed his fingers into the dark-brown leather gloves in the pocket. He lifted the envelope from the corner of his desk, carrying it between his thumb and index finger, holding it out in front of him as if it were too hot to handle.

After she received the package, she'd be easy pickings. He enjoyed that he'd had to work so hard to get her. Maybe he was even a little sorry the game was over. He licked his lips like a tiger salivating at the thought of his prey. Daniela St. Clair and her money were his.

FORTY-THREE

The tan manila envelope almost pulsated with each of Daniela's heartbeats. She stared at it. Trying her best to hold back tears, she opened it again. She knew the more the anger washed over her the tougher she'd become, until she no longer cared. For now, though, the thought that she had allowed herself to trust Tim--to let herself start to fall in love again, only to be betrayed…sheesh! *No one likes being made the fool!* She raked her fingers through her hair.

"Hi, Dani," Karen said, peeking around the corner of her office. "I'm heading out for another cup of coffee, do you want one?"

"Please." Dani heard the distinct quaver in her voice as she spread the photos out side by side on her desk. She realized that Karen heard it, too. She cleared her throat, trying to mask the fact that she'd been crying.

"Wait a minute; what's wrong?" Karen asked, coming back into the room, and plopping down in the chair across the desk from Dani.

"Nothing new. Just me being a complete idiot!" Dani turned the photos so Karen could see.

"That creep!" she gasped.

"There were no commitments. He wasn't obligated to be faithful to me. I just wanted … well, you know … wanted something more. I am so disappointed. So heartbroken … This is why I stopped dating in the first place. Are men just incapable of faithfulness?"

"You deserve something more! That, that … oohh! And to think I used to think he was Apollo! He's just another shit! *You're* not obligated to stick around, either." Karen was angry.

"I'm not going to stick around. Being married to one crappy, cheating man was enough. Why would I take on another? I'm lucky he showed his real self before this went any further." Dani sank deeper into her chair. "Oh, damn it!! What was I thinking?" she exhaled.

"Are you going to be all right?" Karen stood, moved to the side of her desk. "Need a hug?"

"Fine. I'll be fine." She pressed her lips tight together and tried to blink away the tears. "I let myself love him. I wanted the dream. What every girl wants … Karen, just the other day, he was in here begging me to marry him. Just think how I'd feel now, had I said yes! Oh, well. I have work to do. It's almost harvest time, so I'd better get to it." She sniffed back her tears, gathered up the damning photos, stuffed them back into the envelope, and shoved them into her top drawer. "We need never speak of him again. Never. It's over. Done. Finished."

Karen reluctantly left and closed the door to her office.

Only a minute passed before Dani's intercom buzzed. "Yes, Karen?"

"He's here to see you." Her tone was tense, angry.

Dani's first response was to say she wasn't in, making it clear to him she was rejecting his visit.

"Can he hear?"

"No, I've picked up."

"Remind me to give you a raise. Might as well get it over with," Dani said.

The door to her office opened. She was taken aback by Tim's handsomeness: perfectly groomed blond hair; deep, expressive blue eyes; chiseled face; tall; strong; well-muscled, even when covered up in a business suit. That in itself was the ingredient that gave him license to be unfaithful. She ground her teeth together against the pain.

"Mr. McAndrews." She greeted him coldly, in as professional a tone as she could muster.

"Hey, when did you get back?" His eyes, his smile were warm and inviting.

"This morning, early."

"Were you going to let me know you were back, safe?" Suddenly defensive, his brow creased with tension as he picked up on her angry vibe. She wanted him to; she was mad and he might as well know it.

She felt her eyes narrow and her jaw clench, "Yes, eventually."

He cocked his head slightly as if trying to read her. "Eventually? Is something wrong?"

Dani lifted her chin. She reached into the drawer, pulled out the damning photos, and tossed the envelope across the desk to him.

"What's this?" Dani knew her expression was clearly confrontational. She didn't say a word, but could tell he wished he hadn't asked. He opened the package, shuffled through the pictures. "It's not what it seems, Dani. I didn't do anything!" he protested. The shocked look on his face was so genuine, it made her more furious. *And the award for best actor goes to …*

"Mr. McAndrews."

"Hell, Dani--you can't call me Tim?" He rounded the desk and gently pulled her to her feet. She had to look into his face, and all the memories of passion came flooding back. She wanted to wake from this nightmare, and to return to the sweetness she felt before. Her heart was pounding with desire and anger. A strange mix.

"Katrina came on to me. I didn't do anything." He tried to take her in his arms but she refused, shrugged him off, and escaped to the front of her desk.

"Mr. McAndrews, it seems we don't have the same goals. I am flattered that you considered me a notch in your bedpost. It was even fun earning it. But I think I'm going to have to decline any further contact with you." She squared her stance and folded her arms across her chest.

He was angry. Seething. He smiled as if barely keeping emotions in check. He was so practiced. "Wow. That's harsh. Will you at least let me explain?"

"A picture is worth a thousand words, isn't it? I realize we didn't have a commitment. You weren't obligated in any way. So, the problem is mine, not yours." In the past when she caught her creepy ex cheating, taking the blame always seemed to diffuse the situation. She expected it would work this time, too.

"The problem is mine. I love you, Dani; I want to be committed to you."

Now, that was unexpected. Though she wanted to believe him with every fiber of her being, she didn't. If he looked at her again with those I'm-innocent eyes, she could almost be talked into listening. She covered her face with her hands and resisted. "Indeed; you have a strange way of showing it."

"Where did you even get these?" He waved the envelope in the air and a small thumb drive clattered down to the edge of her desk. Tim picked it up, studied it, and pocketed it. *Great,* she thought. *He can just have the damn thing. Hope he enjoys reliving the moment. Maybe he could make a screensaver out of the pictures. That way he could have Katrina all over again!* she thought, fuming. God, she hated being jealous!

"They were on my desk this morning when I arrived. I assume someone from the club staff took pity on me and thought I should know what you're all about. It isn't like I haven't heard the rumors."

"What rumors?" Tim was obviously stunned.

"Mr. McAndrews, really ..." She hated that her voice clearly said he should know.

"What fucking rumors, Dani?"

Dani suddenly realized the only rumors she'd heard of his bad behavior had come from Katrina Collins. That was troubling. But, boy was she right! "I can't. This is why I avoid this dating crap. I don't want my life cluttered with distrust and jealously. I can't do this. It's such a waste of time and energy. Please go, Tim. Leave me alone."

"No. Dani, we need to talk. To work this out. You have to listen to me! I won't give up on us; I can't. Not over that bitch Katrina Collins." His face was contorted with disgust. He tossed the envelope back on her desk. She tried to walk past him to take her seat behind her desk, but he cornered her. "You can't possibly believe I wanted to be with her."

"That's exactly what I believe. And who knows who else."

He sucked in a breath as if she'd slapped him. Tim was clearly shaken, his blue eyes stormy with hurt. She didn't want to hurt him, but he'd hurt her, so she lashed out. He stood before her now, speechless, as if deciding whether to walk away. The longer he stood there looking at her, the closer she came to melting. She couldn't give in. She could distinctly remember how miserable she'd been with her cheating husband--how lonely, angry, bitter, and jealous she'd felt. All emotions she didn't want to feel again. Reaching deep inside, she gathered her resolve. "You want Katrina? Go for it. I won't stop you. I can't do this."

Instead of leaving, he took her in his arms and kissed her, tenderly at first and then with such fervor, her body surrendered. God, she wanted him, even if he was a terrible cad. But it was better to forego pleasure, knowing the pain that would surely follow. When she opened her eyes, he was searching her face for a hint of understanding.

"You need to go. Now," she commanded.

"Promise me, we will work this out?"

She let seconds tick by, saying nothing. "Please go."

"Tonight, after work. Meet me at McTavish's. Five-thirty? We can talk. Dani, I can't lose you. Please Dani, I love you."

She nodded consent, but her eyes were tearing up and she couldn't let him see her cry; anything but that. He stared at her for a moment, as if assessing her truthfulness. They both knew she would never keep that date.

"Dani, please. Don't do this. Hear me out," he said quietly, as if trying to salvage something. He was resigned to her anger. "I love you." It only made her madder. He turned and walked out.

Dani swallowed hard. That handsome face, those pleading eyes; were they to be the last memory she'd have of Tim McAndrews? Oh, uggh! The tears came now, unwanted and unstoppable.

Dani walked behind her desk, sank into the chair. She opened the envelope and spread the pictures out again, side by side, in a row. They were time-stamped, each one a few seconds after the other. She studied them. Tim was lying to her: the evidence was here in full living color. She reversed the order. In this new sequence, it did look like Katrina could've been the aggressor. No way; the garage camera had no reason to lie.

FORTY-FOUR

Tim blew past Myra, not even looking at her. He was furious. Katrina Collins had made good on her promise. He remembered her hissing the words at him as he held his briefcase in front of his chest, fearing she would shoot him. He stormed to his office. He had to fix this! How could Dani believe he'd willingly touch Katrina? He loved Dani so much, he couldn't imagine being with anyone else ever. But there was Jenny coming toward him from the other end of the corridor.

Damn it! Last thing in the world he wanted to deal with right now was Jenny.

"Tim, can you look at this file with me?" she asked, smiling nervously in a way he read as flirtation. *If one more woman flirts with me!* He wasn't sure what he'd do.

"Not now, Jenny."

She followed him anyway. "You're in a mood," she observed. As if he didn't know.

"You have no idea," he grumbled.

"Can I help?"

"No." He stared hard at her, hoping his expression was angry enough to warn her off.

"Okay, grumpy. I have to be in court in two hours, and I just wanted to make sure everything is in order," she said, effectively countering his anger with common sense and work.

He motioned for her to come into his office and sit down in front of his desk. He set his briefcase down and booted up his computer while she waited.

"Let me see it." She passed the file across his desk. He had taught her to use his outline, so if she had followed his instructions, this should be easy. He read the criminal charges and quickly matched her evidence with the collaborating witnesses. Jenny had a solid case. He looked up at her. "Good job, Jenny. I think you're getting the hang of this."

"Do you think I'll win?"

"You never know with a jury, but this is a substantial argument." He nodded his approval and Jenny beamed. "Run with it," he added, hoping she would leave, but she didn't.

"Then you'll come by court and help me?" She grinned again and toyed with a pen on his desk. Her body language was clearly sexual. It was wasted on him. He was not amused.

"No. I have my own case going for jury selection this afternoon. Goddard told you he wants you on your own, you know that."

She leaned across his desk, a know-it-all-grin turning up the corners of her mouth. "So, tell me why you're so grumpy."

He narrowed his eyes at her. "Leave it, Jenny."

"None of my business?"

"Yep."

"Geez, I guess I'll need to go to Goddard and tell him you won't help me with my case because you had a fight with Ms. Daniela St. Clair."

He fought the impulse to stand. Instead he studied her, running his tongue over his teeth. "You following me?" he accused her.

"No. Not exactly. But I did you see you go into her office as I was walking to work."

Dani's office wasn't exactly on the path to work. You had to intentionally walk a block west. Jenny *was* following him. His mind raced in crazy directions. There was something terribly entitled to her demeanor, as if being Judge Mattison's daughter gave her privileges ordinary humans didn't get. Was she the culprit behind the pictures? He could easily imagine her being that mean.

"Go on, go try your case. I have work to do," he said. He tried a smile, but suspicion of everyone and everything colored his world.

Jenny stood, but her wistful gaze lingered too long. Her crush was obvious and he had no idea what to do about it. "I told you she'd never stay with you."

He glared at her. She lifted an eyebrow and backed out of his office.

When she closed the door, he called Scott and invited him to lunch. He needed to find out who had sent Dani the pictures and the drive. Who was trying to ruin his relationship and for what purpose? Bill Fraser came immediately to mind.

Nina's Burgers had every kind of hamburger known to man, and if she didn't have it on the menu, she'd still make any combination you could imagine. Tim waited at the picnic table under the awning Nina had set up to shelter her customers from the sun--and rain, now that he thought about it. He glanced at his watch. The judge had cut their usual hour-long lunch short, so he hoped Scott wouldn't be late. He had to be back in court. It wasn't too long before the unmarked white Crown Victoria pulled up to the curb. Scott jumped out of the open passenger-side door.

"About an hour--unless you want a big, greasy burger instead of a salad," he laughed to his partner. Anna Marringe was a tiny, black-haired girl, married and the mother of two. Why she'd opted to be a police officer was beyond Tim's comprehension. Scott often told him and Kathy stories of how perps mistakenly thought they could overtake the small woman. They learned the hard way she was a black belt in karate and a force to be reckoned with.

"Hi, Timmy!" she called out from the driver's seat. He'd prosecuted a couple of cases in which she'd been the arresting officer; they won both.

He waved and she drove away.

"Anna didn't want a burger. Did you order my double bacon with cheese?"

"Yep."

"So, what's up?"

"Do you still have that computer geek friend, Simon ... I forgot his last name."

"Sheridan. Police crime lab. Use him all the time, why?"

"Do you think he would look at this?" Tim handed him the thumb drive he'd stored in a plastic baggie. "Remember last night, when I told you Dani's so-called friend had come on to me?"

"Yes," Scott grimaced as if he knew what was coming next.

"She made good on her threat: *pictures*. This and printed copies were delivered to Dani this morning. Only they aren't what happened. They've been altered. These make it look like I wanted the tramp."

"Oh, crap."

"Yeah, 'Oh, crap.' Dani thinks I cheated on her. First woman I actually wouldn't even *consider* cheating on." Tim rubbed his brow, trying to ease the tension headache.

Scott was staring at him. "You never cheated on any of them. Just when it was over, you had someone new the next day. That's not cheating. You got it that bad for this girl?"

"Yes, I do." No further explanation was necessary.

"Boy, you do manage to bring out the worst in women," Scott laughed and then his expression melted to sympathy.

"Don't I, though? It's that McAndrews charm; gets 'em every time." Tim shook his head in disbelief, laughing at himself.

"So, what are we looking for?"

"How were the photos altered? How were the time stamps added on the security camera footage? Can we trace the flash drive to the originating computer? Can we figure out who, how, and why? I've got to salvage this with Dani."

"I thought you said it was Katrina."

"She isn't working alone. Who helped her? Why was it so important to break us up?"

"It's usually one of the big three," Scott said. "Love, money, revenge. Or a combination thereof. So, are you ready for what we found out?" Scott asked, lifting an eyebrow and taking a big bite out of his burger.

"On the poisoner case?" Tim asked.

Scott nodded.

"Absolutely."

"The week before she died Amber Brown withdrew $50,000 from various bank accounts in cash. Kathy and I were wondering if she was a hostage, trying to pay for her life. But when I viewed the bank's footage on the withdrawal dates, she was always alone. He could've been waiting just out of range. Smart."

Tim gasped. The thought was horrible. Immediately, he put Dani in Amber's place and felt angst in his chest. He set his burger on the plate, no longer hungry. Now that she'd booted him, how could he guard her?

"That's not all. Jillian Garner's sister said that she had a safe and a collection of about $250,000 in gold coins. We searched her house three times and never found it. My guess? The unsub took it," Scott said, gesturing with a French fry before popping it into his mouth. "She'd taken pictures of the coins for insurance purposes. We never found those, either. This guy is careful. Gold coins are hard to deal with, but if you do it slowly … we've started to check in all the pawn shops and coin brokers. Rare coin collectors are a small group; they tend know each other. So, I've asked brokers to call immediately if someone new starts trying to convert gold coins into cash. We're tracing all transactions we can on auction sites like eBay."

Dani was in danger. She was the killer's type: rich, vulnerable. Tim couldn't let her wander around unprotected. He swiped a fry though some ketchup and ate it absently. He was going to have to watch over her whether she wanted him to or not.

FORTY-FIVE

Sinking deep into her chair, Daniela knew she'd be useless for the rest of her day. She wasn't going to beat herself up any more for being a fool. Lying was a sin because humans were designed to trust and believe each other. And wasn't it just the other day that Tim had been in this very office, asking her to marry him not once, but three times? There was only one motive that she could think of for his behavior: money--hers.

She'd gone to great lengths to keep her financial affairs discreet. But her fortune wasn't hard to find if you were willing to do a little searching. She'd encountered gold diggers before; after her divorce, there'd been lots of them. They usually found her at charity events, hospital fundraisers and the like. Tim's story of falling for her as she walked down James Street, though sweet, was just that: a big, fat story. Not only should he get the Academy Award for Best Actor, now she was thinking he should get the award for Best Screenplay, too.

The tears were just behind her eyes. At any silly provocation, she knew she would cry. Because no matter what sarcastic, angry thoughts spilled out, she'd wanted to love him. And that made her madder yet.

"Karen?" she pressed the intercom for her trusted secretary and friend. "Yes?"

"Can you have Mitch ready the 340? I'm going to the ranch."

"Are you all right?"

"No," she answered softly. "I need a Bugsy fix." No matter how bad she felt, the stallion always made everything better. "At least *he* loves me."

"Dani, you have the Wright-Johnson meeting tomorrow. They want to sell us their grapes."

"Oh, no. Can you get Harold Grant on the phone for me? He can handle the purchase, can't he? He's our best vintner."

Daniela looked up and Karen was in the doorway. "Damn it, Karen. Don't pity me."

Karen came into the room and sat across the desk from her. "It's Katrina. She's in the lobby and she's been crying."

"Crap!" Daniela rolled her eyes "Which do you think it is? 'He assaulted me', or, 'I'm sorry, I didn't mean to, but I've stolen your lover.'"

"You don't believe Tim's story, do you?"

"No. But I want to--God knows, I want to," she groaned. "Tell Mitch no more than an hour and a half. I can work from the ranch for the next few days. Tell everyone I'm ill or something." Daniela ran her hand through her hair. "Oh, Karen, what's the matter with me? Am I not smart enough? Not pretty enough? Tell me how to stop wanting him? Oh, damn it. He warned me. He kept telling me he was selfish."

"You are beautiful. Just because the man's a slut doesn't change what you are," Karen counseled. Daniela shrugged her shoulders.

Daniela forced control over her emotions and directed her, "Send Katrina in." Briefly, she wondered if Tim and Katrina were lovers, if they were in it together and she was their prey, like in the movies. If that were true, she wanted to find the person who was her good Samaritan and thank them. They'd done her a favor by dropping off those ugly pictures.

"Katrina, what's the matter? You've been crying!" Daniela pretended sympathy. *Now who should get the Best Actor award,* she thought.

"That terrible boyfriend of yours came on to me last night at the club." Katrina wiped her eyes with a Kleenex from Daniela's desk. The smudges of black mascara there earlier had been rinsed away by tears.

"Yes. I received these this morning," Daniela said, as calmly as she could. She took the envelope from its drawer and passed it across the desk to Katrina. "Obviously, someone from the club was concerned and thought I should know."

Katrina leafed through them. Suddenly, the weeping stopped. "I told you he was bad news." She sniffed. But Daniela could swear her expression was one of guilt. For a moment, she studied her.

"I'm sorry I didn't listen to you."

"Where did you get these?" Katrina asked.

"I don't know; they were here on my desk when I arrived from Napa. I imagine whoever worked the front desk at the club last night felt sorry for me." Daniela brushed her long hair away from her face. Her eyes felt tired. She could only think of getting to the ranch and away from the city. But Katrina's demeanor was unsettling. Daniela got the impression she knew exactly who had taken the pictures and was hiding it.

"Felt sorry for you? They should've come to *help* me. It was just awful!"

"Did you call the police?"

Katrina stuttered. "Ah, um--ah, I didn't want to; he's your guy. I didn't want to hurt you with an arrest! Besides, he's big friends with the cops, being a district attorney. They wouldn't have done anything. Good old boy network, and all."

"If he assaulted you, we should call now." It was a test. Daniela knew it and she was afraid Katrina did, too.

"Dani, he's a member of the club. How would that look? They can tie him to you. I think we should just let it die and go away."

None of Katrina's rebuttals made sense. If Tim were truly guilty, Katrina would be the first one to call the police. *Just think of the television notoriety she's missing by not taking down a wayward D.A. Think of the delicious scandal!* Not like Katrina at all. It made Daniela skeptical, and made Tim's story seem more plausible. But that time stamp. The club's computer wouldn't screw that up; the computer had no agenda. Thinking about it all made her head hurt.

"Katrina, he could do it to someone else," she finally said.

"Well, no. I don't think he will. It was all because I tried to apologize for the way I acted at dinner at your house that Sunday--I was terrible. He suggested we have a drink. I refused, of course. I said we could all get together when you were back in town. But then he wanted to walk me to my car. I won't--can't press charges. It wasn't that serious." Katrina's eyes darted left. Was it a tell? A micro expression, like she'd read about online? Was Katrina lying to her? But Daniela's headache was worsening rapidly. If she didn't stop thinking about this mess, she was going to have a full-blown migraine.

"Okay. You're the victim and the only one who can press charges. So, we'll leave it at that."

"Daniela, what are you going to do?"

"What I'm going to do, I have already done: I broke it off with Tim earlier this morning. I'm not going to see him again. He's just another Carl. I can't live with any more cheaters."

"He didn't actually ... cheat--"

Daniela stared at Katrina. "Well, yes, but only because you wouldn't. What would've happened if you'd said yes?"

"Good. I'm glad. Now, Bill."

"Oh, good grief, Katrina! No more men! I can't even stand the thought of men--not any of them!"

FORTY-SIX

Up until now, he'd only been inside Daniela's house during daylight hours. Night sent excitement thrilling though him, energizing him. Before dark, she'd taken her dogs, the cat, a small suitcase, and the Cessna 340 out of King County Airport again. This time Gerard wasn't there, and the young woman behind the desk wouldn't give him any information. With strong muscled arms, he lifted his weight to the top of the concrete wall at the back of her property. Waited. Then sprang to the grass, pretending to be a leopard. The pale solar landscaping lights cast long shadows across the green lawn from the trees. He stayed tight to the darkness.

Before climbing in, he halted and listened: The neighbors to either side had already gone to bed. It was midnight and all lights were out. Quickly, he was over the chain-link fence of the dog run, dropping the last few feet to the ground. As he paused for the rattle to cease, he looked around to make sure the noise hadn't awakened anyone.

He traversed the concrete pad to the doggy door and squatted. With experienced hands he reached through, straining to find the lock in the center of the doorknob. Finding it, he twisted. Then he felt with his fingers until he found the latch to the dead bolt; done. He opened the door.

The familiar scent of oil lingered on the air in the garage. He waited until his eyes adjusted to the darkness and then silently edged his way to the interior door. The break-in was easy; months ago, when he'd first explored the house and grounds, he'd installed an electrical bypass to her alarm system. The operating light still gave its reassuring SYSTEM ARMED signal, even though it wasn't.

Preparing to enter the house, he adjusted his gloves. If he'd only known where Daniela was going before, he would've booked a flight and run into her. *What a coincidence, you're here, too? Let's have dinner! A nice wine?* He closed his eyes and braced himself against the doorjamb, letting the craving flood over him, like a river breaching a dam. With his left hand, he cupped the erection swelling in his jeans. Sex and death, purple and black, mixed in his mind like a witch's brew. He adeptly removed a small leather case from his jacket pocket. He inserted the small pick into the lock. In seconds both latches opened. He was in.

Since the dinner here he'd been in three times, each one more dizzying than the last. Tonight he was fevered; he'd delivered the pictures, and she had seen them. Tonight, the need was so acute ... so desperate he almost forgot to slip the hospital booties over his shoes. He forced calm over his runaway heart. "*Slow. Slow,*" he whispered on the air. Covering his shoes, he crept through the laundry room and into the hallway. He could smell her--roses--and lust pulsed once again. He sneaked down the corridor to her bedroom and waited, breathless in the open doorway.

The breeze from the house's central air ruffled the sheer curtains at the French doors like the memory of a dream. In the stillness, he heard the babble of water from a fountain on the patio outside. He crossed the bedroom to the doorway and twisted the blinds closed, shutting in the light as he switched it on.

Clean, white, fragrant, soft. Impressions shimmered through his thoughts like heat off a paved roadway. He had to keep these feelings alive. He retrieved the digital camera from his waist pack and snapped pictures of the room, of her bed. Replacing the camera in his pack, he lingered at her dresser, lifting perfume bottles, and exploring their scents. Carefully, he returned each precisely as he'd found it. All but one. One bottle he moved to the bedside table: a hint, a tiny clue that he'd been here. She would know he'd been here. And she'd be as excited as he.

He slipped into her bathroom, guardedly opening the drawers, noting the brands of toothpaste, deodorant, and cosmetics she used. He'd examined all this before. It was reassuring to see it there. It reminded him she was real. He wanted to know more about her than she knew about herself.

As he wandered back to the bedroom, he suddenly longed for something of hers. Something intimate. He searched through her dresser drawers. Rejecting the costume jewelry and silk scarves, he searched through her lingerie. At last, he lifted a pair of pale pink satin panties from the drawer. The fragrance of a rose sachet lingered in the smooth fabric. He took them, folding them, and placing them gingerly into his camera pack as if they were priceless.

The treasure almost made him forget to put things back in the drawers the way they'd been. He caught himself. Forcing measured control over each and every second, each and every movement, he replaced what he'd moved.

Finished, he crossed the room to the French doors, switched off the light, and opened the blinds. For a while, he stood in the darkness, dreaming of joining Daniela in her bed, making love to her—watching her die. A delirium shuddered through him.

FORTY-SEVEN

When Tim entered his office, Kathy was leaning back in his swivel chair with her feet on his desk. She looked cute this afternoon. There was a pink glow in her cheeks and her normally straight blonde hair was smoothly curled along her face to just under her chin. As usual, Scott was sitting on the front edge of the desk, long shirt sleeves rolled up, tie hanging loose to the left side of his unbuttoned collar, and the exposed shoulder holster perfectly positioned for a quick draw, if necessary. He chuckled to himself at how his best friends had taken over. Tim set his briefcase just inside the door and then loosened his tie. He'd had a hard day in court. The case was Fullerton's and with Fullerton out with a bad flu, he'd been obliged to try it. It was one Tim would've never considered for trial; he would've pled it out long ago, had he been in charge. The evidence was weak and could easily be countered by a good defense, and this particular scumbag had had the best. But Goddard was up for reelection and he needed a tough-on-crime record. The jury was out, so Tim still had a chance of winning, but it was slim at best.

"Impromptu meeting!" Kathy exclaimed, pulling her legs down from his desk and sitting forward. The front casters of his chair slammed down on the plastic carpet protector.

"Don't break it," Tim laughed. "Meeting about what?"

"Drinks at McTavish's," Scott teased.

Tim rolled his eyes at him. "Couldn't we have met there instead? Then Kathy wouldn't be screwing up my desk with her big feet."

Kathy ignored him. "I was able to get more pictures from the victims' families." She shoved some papers aside on Tim's cluttered desk and started to spread the photos out side by side.

"Hey, don't do that." Tim quickly rescued his messy filing system. "I know just where everything is, now...Damn it, Kath! Besides, how's that going to help?" Tim asked, scrunching his brow at her.

"She doesn't know. But she thinks we aren't working hard enough on the case. It's our only one, you know." Scott's tone was full of sarcasm and frustration.

"If you see the victims as people, with families that love them..."

"Scott can't manufacture evidence out of thin air," Tim defended his friend.

"I know; I just need to stop this guy before he kills again."

"We want the same thing, Kathy. You know that." Tim pulled up one of the extra chairs from the corner of the room and sat in front of his desk. He lifted each picture one at a time, staring briefly at the pretty faces looking back at him. He passed the photo on to Scott and picked up the next. "What a waste of life," he sighed.

"Beautiful girls in their prime. Somebody's daughter, girlfriend, wife, mother." Kathy was morose.

"He's going to slip up. They always do. And I'll be there waiting," Scott announced.

"But how many more women have to die first?" Kathy interjected.

Tim knew Scott would solve the puzzle if he could. He was a great detective; always had been. He could connect things faster than anyone he knew. His powers of observation were almost uncanny. But this case lacked puzzle pieces. Their adversary was cold, methodical, organized--but most of all, careful. Kathy had matched the DNA they'd recovered to the same perp, but he wasn't in CODIS. He had never been DNA-typed before. He'd left no fingerprints, so even if he was in the IAFIS system or anywhere, he'd left nothing to match. And since the victims had been transported to the emergency room by paramedics trying to save their lives, the prints on their clothes and belongings had been ruled out. But that alone would be a great cover--if the unsub was a paramedic. Man! Tim was instantly ashamed of himself. He needed to get his jealousy under control. He forced his mind back onto the case.

The lab had found the batch of antidepressant the killer used to poison his victims by its chemical markers, but until they found the murderer in possession it was just molecules. They had interviewed witnesses, followed all leads, and turned up zip. Vanishing at will, the unknown subject was a ghost.

"McTavish's!" Tim said, standing. They were at an impasse. Without more to go on, they were frustrated. "Let's go; it's well after six. First round's on me," he insisted. Kathy gathered her pictures and put them in her huge purse.

"I'm starving," Scott said as they left the office.

"Doesn't a big slab of McTavish's prime rib sound perfect?" Tim asked.

McTavish's was especially quiet this Wednesday evening. Tim walked over to and slid along the red leather seating in their regular booth. Kathy and Scott followed. Mic looked up from the bar and Tim made a circle in the air with his index finger. Mic soon appeared with a tray bearing two Jack Daniels neat, with beer chasers, and a white wine for Kathy.

"You having dinner tonight?" Mic asked.

"Prime rib," they all chimed in unison. McTavish's probably had the best prime rib in town. Tim thought about calling Dani. But he'd called her at least five times today and she was still refusing to take them. She'd stood him up three days ago, when they were supposed to talk. She'd chosen to believe the false story of the mysterious pictures. Tim knew if she wouldn't talk to him, there would be no working anything out. He felt constant pain, but life and work had to go on. He had been particularly dispirited when he tried today's case. The fact that it was a loser made him feel like a loser himself.

"I heard some news on your flash drive." Scott lifted his eyebrows as if Tim would be cheered.

Tim sat forward. "You made me wait until we got here? What?" He was anxious to know.

"Hey, I was hungry," Scott joked, then turned serious. "The pictures aren't from the parking garage cameras. First, the angle is all wrong. The parking garage cameras would've been pointing downward; these are almost level to the subject--meaning you. They were shot with a 1080p digital camera with a zoom lens. No way would anyone spend that kind of money for a surveillance camera in a parking garage. The date stamps were added. Sheridan was able to strip away the layers in Photoshop. These were clearly tampered with. Because the pictures were downloaded to a thumb drive, I can't trace it back to a computer. FBI probably could, but ... we aren't going there. Tampering, though--that I can prove," Scott said.

"Someone is intentionally trying to break you and Dani up," Kathy added.

"Trying? Succeeding. That raging bitch!" Tim growled.

Kathy sat back, glanced at Scott, and asked, "Who?"

"Katrina Collins. She said I'd be sorry." Tim's mind raced. "Can we get the parking garage film for comparison?"

"Without a warrant? How? Do you have friends working at the Sevens who would get that for us? Someone trashing your relationship, though tragic, isn't a crime. But check me on that: you're the one still practicing law," Scott chuckled.

Tim glowered at him.

"That's not logical, Tim," Kathy said quietly.

"What isn't?" Tim could clearly see Katrina behind his breakup.

"Katrina Collins is in the pictures; she couldn't take them. She would be risking her friendship with Dani, too. She could have had someone take them of course, but ... I think Katrina Collins isn't your only enemy. Does Dani have an ex who wants her back? Another suitor?"

"Once again, Kath, not every bad deed in the world is our guy," Scott said.

"What gave you the idea I was suggesting our poisoner took these pictures?" Kathy asked.

"Dani's the killer's type: rich, beautiful, long brown hair. He gains if he succeeds in getting rid of Tim." Scott took a drink of whiskey.

Tim felt his stomach squeeze. How could he protect Dani, now that she wouldn't let him anywhere near her?

Just as Kathy finished her thought, in walked Gary Warden, Katrina Collins, and Bill Fraser.

"Speak of the devil and her minions," Tim said as he glared at the three. At least Dani wasn't with Bill Fraser. He wasn't sure he'd be able to stomach that eventuality.

They took seats on stools at the bar, unaware that Tim, Kathy, and Scott were in the back booth. After a few minutes, Katrina swiveled in her stool, turning it around to survey the small crowd. Her gaze stopped short and she briefly stared at Tim. He could feel hot anger flashing from his eyes like lightning bolts. He wished they were real and he could zap her. She turned back to the bar, but Tim could tell by her expression he had intimidated her. Her body language had become fidgety, nervous. *Good; she should be scared.*

When she turned away, Tim swallowed his shot of whiskey, feeling the burn all the way down his throat.

"Did you bring those pictures with you, Kath?" Scott said suddenly.

"No, dummy. You just said Sheridan has them," Kathy snickered.

"No, Kathy--the victims." Scott wasn't joking. He focused on the three people at the bar. Tim tried to follow his gaze but couldn't tell what he was looking at.

"Right here." Quickly, Kathy handed over the envelope, glancing over at Tim and raising an eyebrow.

Scott didn't say anything, just rifled through them. When he found the one he wanted, he pulled it out, briefly looked at it, and handed it to Tim. Tim studied the picture but wasn't getting any connection.

Gary Warden stood and headed for the restroom, and Scott got up suddenly as if he'd been waiting for that moment as a cue.

"It's Warden who's dating Katrina, right? I'll be right back," Scott said, walking over to where Katrina and Bill remained at the bar.

"Looks like our favorite bloodhound's got the scent," Kathy said. Tim could tell she was proud of Scott.

Tim strained, but couldn't hear what they were saying. Scott was laughing and back-slappingly friendly with Bill and Katrina. Now, Scott was pointing to their table. After a few minutes, he shook hands with Bill and came back over.

He slid into the booth, a sly smile on his face. He took a sip of whiskey. "They always make a mistake. Always."

"Do tell?" Kathy smiled big.

"My dear Dr. Watson--or in this case, Dr. Hope. In the words of the famous Sherlock Holmes, the game is afoot." Scott grinned.

Tim stared down at the photo in his hand, studied it hard. Scott wasn't going to tell, or couldn't while they were here at McTavish's. He was ready to give up when the ah-ha moment hit him: sparkling around Katrina's throat in all its blue, green, and purple glory, was the beautiful natural gemstone necklace--or one very similar to it, belonging to victim number two--Amber Brown. Tim relaxed back into the comfortable booth.

Scott smiled at him. "Yep," he nodded.

Mic brought over their prime rib dinners.

"Do me a favor, Mic; a big favor."

"Anything for my regulars," he answered.

"Bring us some to-go bags," Scott said. "You have them, don't you?"

"You mean you're going to take this to go? You should've said and I would've--"

"No, we're eating here, just need three to-go bags."

Mic left and returned with the bags.

"Thanks. Now, be patient when you have an impulse to call the police. Just pretend to." Scott winked at Mic. "Just think of it this way: I am the police."

Mic shot Scott a confused look, but nodded; he'd play along.

Scott ran his hand down over his lips and chin, like he did when he and Tim were boys, and Scott was figuring out how to beat him with one last chess move.

"How long would it take for you to get DNA back if I got you some saliva samples?" Scott asked.

"Really...depends on how backed up the lab is. About two weeks." Kathy turned and cautiously looked at the three people at the bar, then back at Scott.

"If we can't get saliva DNA, can we get it from fingerprints?" he asked, smiling at Tim.

"Yes, sometimes," Kathy answered, her voice full of intrigue.

"Okay kids, here's what we're going to do ..." Scott said.

FORTY-EIGHT

"Hey, guys. Thanks for dinner," Tim said loudly, slurring his words. He walked away from the table, bumping into a chair as he left and laughing as any drunk would do.

Katrina turned on her barstool as if to watch the show.

"Hi, Katrina." Tim stumbled up to her. "You're looking good tonight. Want to finish what you started the other night?" he snickered, covering his mouth with his hand. "Do you, bay—bee?"

"Okay, that's enough," Gary Warden said, a threatening tone in his voice, whirling a half turn on his barstool to face Tim.

"Oh, that's right-- you don't know your woman is a slutty little tramp, do you?"

Now both Fraser and Warden were standing.

"That's enough, McAndrews. You've had too much to drink and you need to calm it down," Bill said, trying to push him back. The men were evenly matched in size.

Tim let Bill push him back. Tim looked around Fraser's body. "Katrina, I won't stop you this time." He lifted his hands in the air. "Come and get it, bay—bee!"

Scott and Kathy were on their feet.

Warden had pushed his way past Frasier and took a swing. Tim ducked it. Warden lost his balance, stumbling forward against an empty chair. It wasn't strong enough to hold his momentum and weight and it crumbled, wood splintering and pieces crashing to the floor. Warden went down with it. Katrina grabbed up her purse, jumped down from her barstool, and smacked Tim's arm with it as hard as she could as she passed by him to come to Gary's aid. Bill had positioned his body between the men to keep a fight from breaking out.

"You're an asshole, McAndrews," Katrina spat as she helped Warden up.

"That's me. But compared to you ... I'm a saint," Tim laughed.

Mic was holding the phone, as if prepared to dial for the police.

"There isn't going to be a fight; we're leaving," Fraser said to Mic, lifting his hands in a conciliatory gesture. "Let's get out of here." There was panic in his eyes; he shot Tim a confused look. "What the hell has gotten into you?" he asked, as he supported Gary. He shook his head as he helped Warden limp toward the door.

166

Katrina looked back just as they passed through. "Fuck you!" she yelled back as the door closed.

"Do you have what you need, Scott?" Tim asked.

Scott held up three doggie bags. "Got it."

"Sorry about that Mic. I'll pay for the damages and new glasses," Tim offered. "I didn't expect he'd take a swing at me, but I guess I should've."

"You're not drunk? What's this about?" Mic asked.

"Police biz," Scott answered, as he wrote a name on each to-go bag. He took out his cell phone and pressed numbers on the dial pad. "Calling the lab. I'll hand these over for DNA testing," Scott said.

Tim didn't know how all the science worked. But it amazed him that now the crime lab could get DNA from saliva on a bar glass, DNA from a fingerprint. And if any of the DNA matched what Kathy had found on the victims, they had their suspect.

Tim slowly shook his head and an amazed smile curved his lip. "A necklace." He remembered the pretty hand-crafted choker. "A necklace might've just broken this case wide open!"

FORTY-NINE

The dream once again took him back, back to the dark, filthy, apartment. The air was dense with the blue haze of cigarette smoke and the sweet-hot smell of heroin cooking in a spoon. Music promising love pulsed from the old brown plastic radio on the battered dresser almost drowning out the drunken whispers. Outside of life, he watched her; a voyeur looking through the small crack and the tattered wallpaper in his bedroom wall into hers. She was exquisite, her long brown hair flowing down her back in soft, shiny, curls against her pale, luminous skin. The curve of her breasts and hips were bathed in the golden light spilling in from the hallway. The little boy loved his mother.

Unbidden, the shadow fell across her skin like a storm cloud crossing the sun. He couldn't do anything--he was too little, too afraid. The monster had come to make love to her, to kidnap her and steal her soul away to the underworld where he reigned as king. He could still remember Death's magnificent face, even features, piercing ice-blue eyes, and brown hair--not like any monster in the books his mother had read to him. But a monster all the same. He turned to the boy, and the wall disappeared. Their eyes locked. There was no warmth. Unspoken words filled his mind with terror--*I took her soul--I took her soul.*

He startled awake, drenched in sweat. Needing. Hungry. He sat up, tossing back the damp sheets. He swept his hand through his wet hair, brushing it away from his forehead. He wanted a drink. He grabbed up the blue jeans and the hooded sweatshirt he'd carefully laid across the chair beside his bed and dressed. He packed his pockets. Switchblade knife, Lily's pills. Before he left his room, he studied the image he found there in the dresser mirror; resplendent face, even features, piercing ice-blue eyes, brown hair. Death. The little boy was grown up now. He had become the monster.

FIFTY

It was still dark outside his office window when Tim started work on his latest stack of cases that would go to trial this month. He needed the quiet of a Saturday to study the evidence, pore through existing case law, and gather his thoughts. It was his practice to create a written outline for each case, so he could present it for the prosecution with the greatest effect, especially if the case was going to a jury. He made certain that each category of evidence had a witness (or witnesses) to corroborate his premise of guilt. Juries these days expected DNA. That wasn't always possible. And the public somehow had gotten the very wrong impression from TV shows that circumstantial evidence wasn't good evidence. But if you really looked at it, a compilation of a bunch of unique circumstances could be just as damning as DNA. So Tim worked hard to make sure his juries understood everything very clearly.

Lately, he hadn't been able to sleep. He had been unprepared for the emotional consequences of his breakup with Dani. Before, he'd just shrugged girls off and waited for the next one. For some reason, Dani was irreplaceable; he didn't want anyone else. Since their breakup a week ago, she'd refused his calls. He'd even left her messages about the altered photos, in hopes she'd give him a chance. No matter how he tried, he couldn't make her want him back. He'd stopped calling. There was no need to be a jerk about it. How he'd managed to screw this up was beyond him. But he had. Eventually, he would feel better--or at the very least, the misery would become bearable. He threw himself into work.

He heard footsteps echoing in the empty building. He glanced at the clock in the corner of his computer screen. Was it already 7:30? He wasn't the only one who needed to get ahead of his caseload. He stretched; he'd been able to put in two hours without interruption.

Scott strolled in without knocking. Kathy's influence was clear: the detective was dressed in a clean pair of blue jeans and a neatly pressed shirt under his leather jacket. Before Kathy, on Saturdays he'd just show up in sweats. Taking his usual seat on the edge of Tim's desk, he asked, "Hey, bud; I've been looking all over for you. Have time for breakfast? How busy are you?"

"Very busy. What are you doing up this early on a day off?"

"Never really a day off, is there? Want to see how this detective thing is done?"

"Maybe. What are we detecting?"

"The necklace," Scott said. "If I link it to Amber and the DNA comes back a match, I have enough for arrest and search warrants. That's when things really get interesting." Scott paused. "That necklace looks one-of-a-kind to me. Handmade. The kind you get down at Pike's Market. I figure our unsub killed Amber and kept the necklace as a trophy."

"So, how'd Katrina come to be in possession of it?"

"That's my point. First, I need to nail down that it's one-of-a-kind. Then we proceed to the next question. How'd she get it? Maybe she bought it at a pawnshop, direct from the unsub—or was it a gift from Warden--maybe, just maybe, he's our guy. I trace the jewelry to Amber Brown, they are gonna have some 'splaining to do. Warden fits Elias Cain's profile to a T: handsome, easy going, seemingly trustworthy. The kind of guy the ladies like. Friendly. And interested in the case."

"Has he been asking about the case?"

"Both he and Fraser, just the other day. Ran into them at the hospital; I'd gone to see Kathy. They were bringing in an emergency. They were real curious about the investigation and what we had. Early on, I'd brought them both in for questioning, since they transported three of the victims to emergency. At the time, I thought it was just firefighter-cop camaraderie, casual curiosity. But after seeing that necklace … wow. Bells, whistles, chimes, bombs went off."

"Yeah, I'm in." Tim started to get up from his chair.

Jenny appeared at his door. "What are we in on?" she asked. "I'm in, too."

"Bachelor party. No women allowed," Scott said, flashing a quick grin in Tim's direction. Tim agreed; they didn't need Jenny tagging along. She knew nothing about the case and Tim didn't want to answer the endless barrage of questions she would ask. Jenny pouted.

"Before you go, Tim, do you have a minute?" She was hugging a file folder to her chest. He'd been replaced as her mentor but her new one, Sam Brunxton, wasn't in on Saturdays. He guessed he could help her. He did notice though that her visits to his office were becoming too frequent for his liking. Still he motioned for her to come in.

"I'll help Jenny and then we're on our way," Tim said to Scott. Jenny had never been one to work on weekends. But since his breakup with Dani, she seemed to be where he was all too often, even showing up—uninvited--at McTavish's after hours. He was trying his best to ignore it.

"What'cha got?" Tim asked. Jenny pulled up a chair next to him and sat down. She opened the file and spread its contents on the desk so they both could examine it. When she leaned forward, she intentionally pressed her leg against Tim's thigh. Surprised, he quickly adjusted himself in his seat, moving away from her. He looked up and caught the twinkle in Scott's eyes. Scott ran his hand over the dark mustache and bit his bottom lip, hiding his smirk. Tim discreetly shook his head, indicating Jenny was not a woman he was interested in. Scott countered with an assuring smile; he got Tim's drift.

"Hey Jenny, are you flirting with Tim? Because from here, it sure looks like you are." Scott leaned forward, eyeing where her leg had been. Scott had a quirky mean streak sometimes and clearly meant to embarrass her. Tim wished he hadn't started, but there was no stopping Scott when he got going.

Color raced into Jenny's cheeks. Scott's plan had succeeded. She stared wide-eyed at Tim, then at Scott. Tim was trying not to react, but he knew a grin wanted to break out and finally he let it. But maybe, just maybe, his best friend had successfully put a stop to Jenny's pursuit. Tim leaned back in his chair, raising his eyebrows, waiting for her response.

"I--no--wasn't!"

"I didn't think so, Jenny. But I have to say it made me wonder, 'cuz when a woman rubs up against me like you just did to Tim, I sure think she's flirting. But it couldn't be that, could it? With Goddard's no-fraternization policy and all."

Jenny suddenly stood. "We can talk about my case later." She grabbed the file and fled.

Scott got up and looked out Tim's office door, watching her walk briskly down to her office. He turned back, laughter in his eyes. "Oh, bud. If you'd seen the look of horror on your face when she touched you. Wow! That was priceless!"

"Yes, but did you have to torture her?"

"You into her?"

"Not even. Since Dani and I are no longer a couple, her come-ons have become almost unbearable. She's Judge Mattison's daughter and thinks that gives her license." Tim shook his head.

"Does it? Mattison's a hard-ass. Did I just piss off the wrong woman?"

"No."

"You could always sue for sexual harassment."

"Oh, sure. That would go over just great, with Goddard up for re-election and Mattison one of his biggest supporters. I figure if I ignore her, she'll knock it off."

"So, when she shows up at McTavish's, you aren't the one who's been inviting her?"

"Nope."

"She's a stalker."

"I'm sure she just wants to belong somewhere. Just out of college, all her friends gone on to their own grown-up lives. We—you, me, and Kath--we had each other. She has no one. She's smart, funny, and cute. She needs to figure out she doesn't need me to fit in. She'll get the picture."

"Be careful. You know women like that can get crazy and do real weird shit," Scott warned.

"Sure. I know."

Scott stared at the door. "And you seem to attract them--those possessive ones. I always worried about Ellen, too."

"Do I? Dani wasn't possessive enough!" Tim laughed out his complaint. Scott shrugged.

"Let's get out of here for a while. Where do we start?"

"I went on the computer last night and researched local places that specialize in handmade natural-stone jewelry. I thought we'd start with them," Scott said. The two men left Tim's office.

"Amber could've bought that necklace anywhere."

"I know, but I've got to start somewhere. Her mother said she loved to come down to the waterfront. Meet friends and have breakfast on Saturdays. Go to the aquarium, shop the unique stores." Scott pressed the call button for the elevator.

"Where's Kathy today?"

"With her mom and sisters shopping for a wedding gown."

"Umm, bet you hate like hell to be missing that," Tim chuckled.

"Bad luck, they say; groom isn't supposed to see his bride in her dress until she walks down the aisle."

Tim liked Scott's satisfied smile. Kathy completed him. "You scared? About getting married, I mean?" Tim asked.

"Sometimes. I keep wondering when Kathy's going to wake up. I hope we make it through the ceremony before she does." They both laughed.

FIFTY-ONE

The waterfront was unseasonably warm and humid for late summer. To the east, big billowing thunderstorms were building along the spine of the Cascade Mountains and the weatherman on SBC News reported that an unusual low pressure off California would spin their way in the afternoon. Tim wondered about Dani: where she was, if she was happy. He was miserable. Walking along the waterfront made him melancholic. He remembered strolling along hand in hand with her. Instinctively, he knew this outing was Scott's attempt to help relieve the pain. They'd always been there for each other, joking each other out of every kind of life's disappointments. Kathy was usually there mothering them. He'd tried his best not to let on, to hide the constant ache.

The first three shops they'd visited were for tourists: T-shirts, Space Needle mugs, and shot glasses. Little things, memorabilia that would be displayed in a prominent place at home to remind the purchasers of the adventure they'd had here. But deeper, further away from the main thoroughfare, they found what they were looking for: handmade quilts, crochet hats and scarves for the coming winter, and finally, specialized artisan sculptures and jewelry. Stunning pieces, Northwest icons like whales, dolphins, and orcas cast in gold. In each shop Scott introduced himself, showed the picture of Amber in her necklace, and left the proprietor a card in case they remembered anything. In their wanderings, they found a small courtyard with Red's Famous Seafood to the left and on the right, a shop simply named Emma's. In the display window, Tim noticed necklaces similar to Amber's, along with some unique numbered lithographs, etchings, bronzes, and stone sculptures. He motioned to Scott.

"I think this is the place," he said.

"Well, sure," Scott said. "It's the last one on my list."

"No, I'm serious. Look for yourself."

They went in.

"Huh, NATURAL GEMSTONES BY EMMA." He grinned. "Are you Emma?" When Scott smiled, any woman, no matter her age, was instantly smitten. Tim was witnessing the Renton charm in full swing.

Emma was a dainty woman. Mid-seventies, he assumed. Her silver hair was swept up into a ponytail and tied with a silk scarf. She wore one of the beautiful necklaces he guessed she'd painstakingly created. "I am, young man," she said. "How may I help you?"

"I'm Detective Scott Renton, Seattle P.D." Scott showed his badge and handed her a card.

"Did I do something wrong?" she teased.

"You didn't do anything wrong," Tim quickly tried to dismiss her fears.

"Ma'am, have you ever seen this necklace before?" Scott handed her the picture of Amber Brown wearing the piece.

"Why, yes. I made it. It's number forty-two in my jade, jasper, and amethyst collection. I sold it about two months ago to the beautiful young woman in the picture, Amber—yes, Amber, I believe that was her name. I remember because at the time I was starting a collection in amber."

"Would you happen to have a copy of the purchase receipt? We went through Amber's credit card statements and didn't find the purchase there."

"I do. I think she paid with cash," Emma said and then suddenly she halted and stared at Scott suspiciously. "Why would you be looking at Amber's credit card statements?"

Tim knew this was going to be hard. Scott took both of her frail hands in his, a kindness Tim had never expected from his tough-as-nails cop friend. "Ma'am—Emma--Amber is dead. Murdered."

"Oh, no. God, no." Emma gasped, and almost lost her balance. Scott supported her, putting his arm around her back.

"Do you need to sit down?" Tim asked, pulling over an antique chair. She sank down into it. "Can I get you anything? A glass of water?"

"What is this world coming to?" She searched their faces.

"Ma'am, can you remember any distinguishing marks or special things about this necklace that can help us? I know it will be hard."

"Here." She removed the necklace she was wearing. "I attach this little oval right by the clasp as a signature. It says EMMA on it." She handed Scott the piece so he could see it. He nodded. "But the oval could easily be forged, so I etch a number on the last bead next to the clasp as well. See, this is number seventy-five in my Amber & Ammonite collection. Like I said, Amber's necklace was number forty-two." When Emma turned to engage Tim in the conversation, Scott gave Tim two thumbs up.

"You're sure it was number forty-two?" Tim asked.

"Yes, son. Amber modelled it in a picture for my blog."

"You have a picture? You have a blog? Wow, that's great!" Tim exclaimed. "Emma, when we catch this guy, we may need you to testify in court. Would you be willing to do that?"

"You bet I will. Amber was the sweetest girl."

Scott left his card.

The two men walked toward the detective's car.

"You know something?"

"We've got to get a look at that necklace," Tim answered.

"Yes," Scott answered. "I'm going to get the Sevens Club's surveillance tape."

"I thought you said wrecking my relationship was sad but not a crime," Tim laughed.

"I have a hunch I'm going to find something on there that I need," Scott said. "But, hey--if nothing else, I can help you get Dani back."

"I'm with you. But she's not coming back. I need to get over it," Tim sighed. Scott set his hand on his shoulder. Usually Scott would've offered some wisecrack about all the other women there were in the world. But this time he didn't. "Let's go have a look," Tim grinned.

FIFTY-TWO

The evening was cool and refreshing after the hot dusty afternoon. Tonight's affair was formal and all the women were dressed in their expensive gowns of all colors and the men in their tuxedos. And here Daniela was again, at the annual Northwest Wine Gala, alone. Most of the time it was okay: no one to complain about her work schedule, no one to complain about the horses. But since Tim, the solitary life had lost its appeal. Maybe she *wanted* to hear someone complain about something--anything. She chuckled to herself. She walked along the deck railing at the Columbia Ridge hotel, looking out over the silver ribbon of the river. The ripples were painted in the shimmery pinks of the setting sun. Stars had started to appear, blinking on one by one as the pale blue sky retreated into night's blackness. The wine competition was one of the biggest of the season. Her vintners had entered a 2011 cabernet franc and 2012 petite syrah in this year's red category. In her opinion, the syrah was a good 98-point wine and the cab was even better. But she never really knew where they would end up in a competition. Her white wines were a surprise; the signature label pinot gris won the Gold Medal and was given a 99-point score. She was sure the vintner's decision to finish it in French oak barrels the last six months before bottling was the factor that had rocketed it to the top of the pack. The final oak aging mellowed and softened the flavor just enough to make the pinot gris easy on the palette without overwhelming the fruit with tannins. It was a lovely wine and one of her favorites. To Daniela, there was nothing like a delicious wine that could become a top-seller. She was a business woman, after all.

Her pilot Mitch and his wife Shannon were out on the dance floor the competition's organizers had set up in the middle of the large concrete deck. The live band played love songs and couples were in each other's arms under the stars. She sighed. *How lucky they were*, she thought. Shannon had waited for Mitch through all his tours in Iraq and Afghanistan before he'd retired from the military. They were so in love. And Mitch had never once cheated, though he'd had chances. These last few years flying Daniela around, she'd seen him turn away from several opportunities. Instead, he'd chosen to be true. Daniela wished she could find a man like that. If only Tim had been faithful, they might be dancing now. She couldn't help but remember when they'd first begun dating, just months ago, how he'd spun her into his arms. Mr. Smooth Operator! And she'd fallen for it.

"Daniela! Daniela St. Clair, is that you?"

Daniela turned and was surprised to see Gary Warden. "Gary? My goodness, what brings you here?"

"Oh, I'm meeting my former in-laws, Jorge and Anabella Caro. Do you know them? Caro Mio Wineries? I was married to Angelina before she ... well, you know," Gary explained.

"I didn't know. I'm so sorry for your loss." Daniela hadn't known that about Gary. She'd been casual friends with Angelina Caro, but since her wineries were in California and most of Daniela's were here in the Columbia Gorge, they weren't as close as they could've been. She'd heard Angelina had married several years ago, and then the sad news about her death. So, Gary Warden was the husband. *Small world!* He'd never hinted he was a widower. Well, life did have to go on. But he was always so cheerful when she'd seen him in Seattle.

"Would you like to dance?" Gary asked.

"Is Katrina here with you?"

"No, no. I wasn't ready to introduce her to Angie's family yet. You understand, don't you?" he answered quickly, leaning on the railing, looking out over the river. Gary seemed sad and that made him seem even more handsome, in his tuxedo. The formal attire fit nicely and showed off his exercise-hardened body. She hadn't notice the ice blue of his eyes before. No wonder Katrina was so enamored.

"Of course, I understand. But no, thank you on the dance. I'm not very good at it." She smiled. As she recalled, it had been at least two years since Angelina's death. That was an acceptable length of time to grieve. Surely the Caros couldn't expect a young, attractive man like Gary to stay single forever.

"I'm not good at it, either; thanks for turning me down. I probably would've been dancing all over your toes," he laughed.

Daniela couldn't help but laugh, too. She wasn't being honest about her reason for not wanting to dance. Truth be told, she wanted Tim--bad boy and cad though he might be. Before the pictures, she'd planned to invite Tim here. She'd even bought a lovely royal-blue beaded gown for tomorrow night's final ball. But that was before the photos and before she'd had the chance to ask him. Now, she wasn't sure she'd even take the gown out of the garment bag.

"Actually, I wasn't telling the truth," he said. His brow pinched together as if he were going to reveal something very troubling to him. "Katrina isn't with me--well, because I believe she's seeing someone else." He paused, as if struggling with the words. "Rumors at the club are that she's having an affair with your friend, Tim McAndrews."

Dani gasped. It was like a knife to her heart. Daniela let out a sad little laugh. "No, she's not, Gary. She came to me and told me what happened. She's not, trust me." Daniela set a sympathetic hand on his arm. He covered her hand with his. She'd said the words but she wasn't sure she believed them. She pulled her hand away.

"I wish I could. But Tim McAndrews, he's just that kind."

"What kind is that?" Daniela asked. There was an edge to her voice that surprised even her. Why was she defending Tim? Gary threw her a look that said you-should-know. "I'm sure you're right, Gary." She tried to repair the damage her harshness might have caused. She knew what kind of man Gary meant: gorgeous men like Tim had their choice of women. Why wouldn't he go after a pretty girl like Katrina? All the same, there was something very unsettling about the pictures and something even more unsettling about Katrina's behavior. Daniela hated that she kept thinking Katrina was lying and that she should've listened to Tim. Katrina had pursued men aggressively before. She knew it; she'd watched her. And Tim--she'd just wanted to believe him, even though experience had taught her it was a bad idea. Better a little pain now than the big expensive mess that comes later. She'd made the right decision, hadn't she?

"Shall we go get a glass of wine?" Gary asked. His stare was unsettling. Daniela felt as though he expected her to be with him out of empathy. The betrayed pair commiserating and then falling in love. It was a story she didn't want any part of.

"No, thank you. I think I've had enough with all the tastings today. Can l catch up with you tomorrow? I'm getting a headache. I think I'll turn in now. Nice to see you. And don't worry about Katrina, she's completely faithful." Daniela picked up the skirts of her evening gown and headed toward the elevators.

She pressed the elevator call button and turned to survey the hotel lobby as she waited. Gary was there, a glass of red wine in his hand, chatting with the Caros. He watched her and lifted the glass to acknowledge her. She returned a smile. And for an instant, far across the mingling crowd, she thought she saw Tim. But when she looked back again, he wasn't there. She'd definitely had too much to drink! Why would he be here? But just in case, after she entered the elevator car she pushed the button for the ninth floor. She got off and took the stairs down two floors to her seventh-floor suite, a trick she'd learned when first divorced and being followed by the supermarket tabloid press. The hotel staff had been instructed not to tell anyone which room she was in. She never thought she'd be using the trick to hide from men.

FIFTY-THREE

Tim didn't like the thought that he'd become a stalker, but that's what he was now, wasn't he? But if he didn't follow her, how could he keep his promise of safeguarding her? Captain Martin and Paul Goddard had refused protective custody, telling him and Scott they were crazy if they thought they were going to spend any more taxpayer money on their serial killer fantasy. It was bad enough they'd talked them into a profiler. It had been three weeks since they'd found Candy Johnson, the eighteen-year-old prostitute who'd been poisoned and viciously stabbed. Goddard wanted the killer caught. *Now.* If there was one. He'd told them plainly and with emphasis. As if they could do anything at this point; he didn't want even one word about their suspected serial killer to hit the press unless it was to say they'd caught him.

When Scott's computer guy had confirmed the truth about the pictures of Tim's horrible encounter with Katrina, Scott had gone to get the surveillance tape from the Sevens Club. Tim still remembered the shocked look on Scott's face when he watched what really happened unfold. But, Scott's focus was mainly on the man in the hoodie who'd preceded Tim and Katrina into the parking garage. He'd taken a copy of the tape back to Sheridan to see if he could enhance it. Scott kept asking why anyone would care to take pictures of Tim unless his intent was to break up Tim and Dani. The similarities between Dani and the killer's victims had them all worried for her safety. Waiting on DNA was grueling. The time ticked away and they hung on, hoping that the killer didn't strike again.

Tim had promised Dani he'd keep her safe. And the pictures she'd received and the club's surveillance tape told two different stories. He could present his evidence, protect her, and save his relationship at the same time. He prepared his defense following his own outline, as if he were presenting it to a jury. He even got to have a practice run: he'd given his argument and the evidence to Karen Muldoon. She'd cried, tears flowing like a river. He took advantage of the opportunity to wheedle Dani's room number out of her; Karen was a terrible romantic. He'd even convinced her to let him surprise Dani.

The old elevator at the Columbia had a meter at the top, a half-circle that displayed its movements in the lobby: which floor it had stopped on, whether it was on its way back down or up. Dani had gone to the ninth floor. But Karen told him she was staying in the Cascadia suite on the seventh floor. Tim remembered the trick Dani had told him she'd used after her divorce when she was trying to elude someone. He was sure she'd seen him before she took the elevator. The logical conclusion: he was the very person she was trying to escape. He climbed the stairs to the seventh floor. He pushed through the doorway. He found himself in a small lobby with lavishly carved doors leading to each of four suites around him; the Cascadia suite to the east, the Mount Jefferson to the south, the Mount Hood to the west, and the Mount Rainier to the north.

He knew she didn't want to see him, but he needed to present his case. He had to take a chance, but he hesitated. Which way would this go? *Only one way to find out.* He knocked on the door to the Cascadia. A few seconds passed and the door opened. Dani stood before him in a T-shirt and blue jeans, as relaxed and as comfortable as if she lived here. He could barely breathe.

"Mr. McAndrews, what are you doing here? Did you not understand me when I said I didn't want to see you?"

"Perfectly," he answered, his eyes drinking in her sweet sexiness. He felt a rush of desire hit him. "But don't I get the chance to offer a defense? That wouldn't be fair." He stood his ground in the doorway. She was contemplating his request, he could tell. What was his plan if she slammed the door in his face? She closed her eyes in a long slow blink and the corners of her mouth turned up slightly with a smile. The last few days without Dani had been agony. Seeing her now reminded him how much he loved her and that he would fight to keep her.

"It wouldn't be fair," she conceded. "Come in." He almost thought she was happy to see him. Almost.

"Thank you." He'd decided when he first planned this adventure to keep this on a business-like level. At least until she saw the evidence--then, depending on her response, all bets could be off. "Do you have a computer?"

"My laptop. Will that work?"

He nodded. Her hair was still damp and she smelled of the delicious, creamy soap she used. He remembered it from kissing her. She was washed clean of all make-up, though in Tim's opinion, her beauty didn't need enhancement. In his eyes ... she was perfect.

She brought the computer into the living room of the suite, which he had just started to observe. The space was appointed with graceful antiques. A pass-through fireplace designed to warm both the living room and the bedroom occupied the eastern wall. The ceilings were at least twelve feet high and big supporting timber beams enhanced the rustic elegance. She closed the door to the bedroom. He understood: she didn't want him getting any ideas. *Rest assured, I already have them,* he thought. She set the computer on the coffee table. He started it up and loaded his defense program, inserting a small thumb drive.

"Please be seated, Miss St. Clair." Tim grinned at her.

She was obviously intrigued, and smiled back, but hers was tentative and skeptical. She sat down on the small sofa.

Tim stood and walked behind her so he could both see and narrate. He cleared his throat and commenced his defense in his most lawyerly tone. "I intend to prove that the pictures delivered to your office on Tuesday were not from the Sevens Club's surveillance cameras but instead were taken with a digital camera and subsequently altered." He paused, gazing at her upturned face. Her lips were parted, but she wasn't exactly surprised. *Interesting,* he thought. "Detective Renton and I went to the Sevens Club and acquired a copy of the parking garage surveillance tape. I want to play that for you now." He clicked the PLAY button on computer mouse and the footage filled the computer screen. Dani watched, saying nothing. But he could see her physical response. If this were a deposition, he would have noted in his file that she was upset. When the tape concluded, she searched his face but didn't say anything. He guessed she didn't know what to say. He started sweating. Maybe his big plan wasn't so great after all. *Did it backfire?* He swallowed down his trepidation.

"As you can see," he continued, trying not to react to her and finding it almost impossible. "The footage in the video is from a higher angle, pointing downward. The club's surveillance cameras are mounted on the ceiling so they can take in as much of the garage as possible. Our forensic computer specialist says the pictures delivered to you were taken at level, which means the person taking the pictures was just about my height. Those pictures were taken by a 1080-pixel digital camera and were altered in Photoshop. The sequence was changed, the time and date stamp added. Sheridan was able to remove the layers of altered information." He clicked on a side-by-side comparison. "As you see, in the digital pictures the gym bag, suit coat, and briefcase have been deleted. Pictures number four and five are actually the same shot, but the human hands have been manipulated from an earlier shot." His presentation was flawless. He knew it. But Dani wasn't responding as he expected. She was looking at her hands, at the floor, anywhere but at him. He wondered if he'd pushed too far, if she was angry. Too late: he had to see it all the way through.

"If we rewind the Sevens videotape back further, we can see the suspected photographer--briefly, just there: the man in the hoodie," he said.

She hadn't said a word, hadn't countered any of his evidence with any argument, and hadn't asked a single question. She just sat, stoic. But as he watched, he saw a single tear glittering in the subtle light as it trickled down her cheek. Quickly, she wiped it away. He moved and sat beside her.

She sighed and stared into his eyes. He tried to read her but couldn't. All he had left was hope.

"Miss St. Clair, the defense will stipulate that Mr. McAndrews hasn't been ... isn't exactly empathetic to a woman's emotional needs, is even a well-known hound dog, if you will ... but only if you will acknowledge that he--loves you."

She turned to him, her eyes brimming now with tears she was obviously fighting to keep from falling. She pressed the back of her fingers against her lips. "I wanted so much to believe you ... I couldn't ... I was so wrong ... so mean ... so unfair ... Did I lose you?" she asked. This was a case he'd clearly won.

"I left messages, but you never returned my calls. Did *I* lose *you*?" he whispered.

She moaned. "I didn't know you'd called. I was so upset I forgot my cell phone in the office when I left to get everything set up here. Stupid, I know."

He shook his head. He thought he was so smart, but he sure played this one all wrong. He should've been on one knee with an engagement ring in hand! He stood, gently encouraging her to her feet with him. He took her into his arms, held her against him. "You didn't lose me. I'm here; I'm not going anywhere. Dani, can I come home?" he asked as his lips found hers, lingering tenderly there as he savored the heady desire rushing over him. He couldn't think, could only feel the delicious ache.

"Yes." He felt her body surrender against him, an invitation he had no power to resist. He didn't want to resist, but he had to.

"Dani, sit. When I'm holding you, I can't think of anything but holding you. And I can't lose my thought process now." He guided her back to the sofa and sat beside her. "First, the man in the hoodie: do you recognize him? Is it someone you know? Your ex-husband? Bill Fraser?" They sat together, looking at the computer screen.

"Why? I don't understand."

"Someone intended to break us up. We need to figure out why. Someone is after you, Dani. Stalking you. Is it harmless? I don't know."

"What if that someone is after you, not me?"

Tim blinked at her. For a moment, the thought gave him pause. He'd put a lot of bad people away in his four short years with the prosecutor's office. Goddard had often reminded all the ADAs to be careful. "I can't dismiss the possibility, but there are things—thing I know--"

"The serial killer?"

He leaned back into the sofa cushions and groaned. He didn't want to frighten her, but he couldn't let her go on blindly. Better forewarned and forearmed. "Dani, you're his type: beautiful; long, honey-brown hair; rich. He kills with antidepressants and alcohol. We believe he slithers into a woman's life, courts her, he might even marry her, if it suits his needs. We speculate he's after money, too. He got one girl to empty her bank account before she turned up dead. Another victim is missing a collection of gold coins."

She gasped.

"Except one: he killed a prostitute. Poisoned her and then viciously stabbed her. He's devolving. He's enjoying killing for the killing now." She shuddered and huddled up close to him, linking her arm through his and pressing her body against him. "We're honing in on a suspect. We have DNA. We're close. So, look again. Do you recognize him? Anything?"

"The other morning when you left there was a man in a hoodie. A jogger," Dani said.

A jogger. Tim's mind flashed back to the night they'd gone to the symphony, the runner that passed him on the sidewalk and disappeared from view. He couldn't remember the face. *He intentionally hid his face!* He stood.

"Hell, this guy has been stalking you at least since the night of symphony. Maybe longer." He turned and stared at her. "You can't be alone; you'll need to stay with me at my place. You can't go back to your house for a while. He knows where you live."

"He knows where you live, too. Think about it: If he's the one that took the pictures, he followed you when I went to Napa. I could go to one of the wineries or the ranch."

"You might be safe there, but … he might know about them, too. You'll be so far from me. I need … I need to keep you safe."

"I could see if Mitch has any friends I could hire as bodyguards."

"Who's Mitch?"

"My pilot, he's ex-military and surely…"

"You have a pilot and an airplane?"

"A pilot and two planes: a Cessna 340 and a Gulfstream. You really don't know anything about me, do you?"

Tim stared at her and shook his head. "Apparently not enough."

"Who is it you thought you were dating?"

"The beautiful girl I saw dancing down the steps at the James Street parking garage," he answered.

"Disappointed?"

"Not in the slightest." He joined her deep in the sofa pillows, resting his head against the back, losing himself in her eyes. "Are you?"

"No." They kissed. He held her against his chest for a long time.

"Miss St. Clair?"

"Yes." She stirred as if she'd almost fallen asleep.

"I was wondering if you'd be interested in earning another notch on my bed post?" he chuckled.

"Oohh," she frowned. "Am I ever going to be able to live that one down?" she asked, laughing too.

"It was too good a put-down. How could I ever let you?" He untangled from her, stood, and pulled her to her feet. He swept her up into his arms and carried her to the bedroom.

FIFTY-FOUR

The hotel was quiet. As he walked on the deck, he heard the music of the river. The hotel was built on a deep still-water stretch, but in the distance, he heard the muffled thunder of the rapids. The reflection of the half-moon danced on the continuous undulations of black water. He leaned against the deck railing. He had gotten closer to Daniela than he'd expected. He would make sure she kept her promise of joining him for the tastings tomorrow. But tonight, it wasn't enough. He was unsatisfied; hungry, hunting. He strolled to his car, got in, and drove up the road four miles, past the tourist stop to a small tavern he'd noticed earlier.

He entered the bar, took a seat, and ordered a glass of red wine.

It was a Friday night, and the young locals had congregated to meet and socialize. They were a different kind of folk than in the city, but night people all the same. The bar was alive with music and alcohol-induced happy talk. He twisted on his barstool, studying the crowd. Young girls in T-shirts and blue jeans flirted openly with the young men dressed as cowboys. What you would expect from a one-horse town? He turned back to the bar and ordered another drink.

He hadn't noticed her before; he hadn't expected her. But she was here. She'd tried to disguise herself, with blonde hair falling in touchable ringlets framing her pretty face. *See me. See me now,* his thoughts whispered. He stared at her briefly, willing her to come to him. Out of the corner of his eye, he saw she was standing, moving down the bar to sit next to him. He smiled.

"Hi. Are you new here?" she asked.

"Why, yes. I'm at the Columbia, here for the Wine Gala," he smiled. "And you, do you live here?"

"No, I'm just passing through. Had a flat and have to wait until morning to get it fixed."

"You're travelling alone? You don't know anyone here?" he asked. This was better than he could have hoped for. It was fate.

"I know you, that's it," she flirted. "Why don't you tell me all about wine, since that's why you're here."

He motioned to the bartender. "Do you have a wine list?" The bartender produced a slip of paper. "Red or white?" he asked, staring into her eyes, lingering there until she sighed.

"You tell me; you're the expert," she answered.

He could feel his breath quicken, his heart pounding. She was his, he knew it. "How about a bottle of this nice Walla Walla syrah? Lovely wine, you'll like it. Fruity, dark red, and thick--like blood." He smiled, briefly closing his eyes, and savoring the feeling racing though him.

"Like blood? What are you, a vampire?" Laughing, she tossed her head back and the light shimmered on her blonde curls.

"Maybe," he answered pouring the rich red wine from the bottle into her glass and then into his own. He lifted his glass as if to toast her. They clinked their glasses together, drank, and laughed.

FIFTY-FIVE

Morning streamed through the windows and tiny particles of dust danced on the light. Daniela woke and smiled at the realization she was here, with Tim. She glanced at the clock. It was nine, much later than she could ever have imagined. The competition would start in an hour! She had planned to be there, at least before Tim showed up last night. Now, she wasn't sure she cared. He was still asleep. *Let him sleep.*

She carefully untangled herself from his arms. But he stirred anyway.

"Good morning," he said sleepily.

"I'm sorry, I didn't mean to wake you." She sat next to him. He was a beautiful man: perfect, symmetrical … yet masculine in every sense. She knew men didn't want to be called beautiful, but she still thought it. She loved his dark blond hair with its sunshine highlights. He wore it cropped short, but slightly tousled. He'd called it a shower-and-go style, saying he didn't have time to fuss with it in the morning after his workouts, but still needed to be neat for court. His eyes were deep water blue, kind and tough all at the same time. His nose was straight, perfectly proportioned for his full lips and masculine jaw. He radiated confidence and strength. Like him or not, it didn't affect him. Tim knew Tim and liked him. He knew what he wanted and went for it. He was all man, and it was refreshing.

"What time is it?" He blinked and rubbed his eyes, trying to fight sleep.

"After nine."

He laughed. "Wow! I never sleep this late. I think you're a bad influence," he teased and propped himself up on her pillow.

"You're the bad influence. Such a bad, sexy boy, ummm."

"Happy?" he asked.

"Completely," she purred, turning so she could settle back against his shoulder. He wrapped his arms around her.

"What's on the schedule for today? Do we have to talk to people, or can we just stay here and make love?"

"I choose …"she paused, "make love. But I have two wines in the competition. So I guess we'll have to talk to people."

He grabbed her, turned her around, and pulled her on top of him. "No, let's stay here."

"Just think how fun it will be trying to keep our hands off each other. And then when we finally *are* alone …"

He sucked in a deep breath and slowly let it out as he untangled from her. "I get it, you want me to walk around all day frustrated."

"Tim!"

He chuckled. "You think I'm joking? I've never wanted a woman so much as I want you. All I have to do is look at you, catch the tiniest whiff of your perfume ... I love you. I love feeling this way."

"Mmm, me too."

"Marry me?"

"Oh God, this is crazy. Yes. Okay. Yes, I will marry you."

The teasing over, Tim's expression went serious. He hadn't expected she'd agree. She felt a sudden panic inside. He was probably sorry he'd asked now. He licked his lips and scrutinized her. She wanted to take her words back.

"You will? Really?"

"If you want me," she said, almost as a question.

"I want you. God, Dani, I want you." He sat up and took her into his arms. "I want you for the rest of my life."

"Okay." She knew she was dreamy-eyed. She felt giddy.

"Crap. I always do things backwards. I wanted to have a ring--like Scott, all prepared." He looked around. On the nightstand, there was a small blue satin ribbon that had bound up some chocolates the hotel staff left on the pillows. He picked it up and took hold of her hands. "Miss Daniela St. Clair, will you marry me?" He tied the blue ribbon in a bow around the third finger of her left hand. It was so sweet. He was precious, like a little boy; the man she loved.

"Mr. Timothy McAndrews, I will marry you."

"I adore you, Dani." They held each other for a blissful moment.

The phone rang. She pulled away and gazed at him, trying to decide whether to answer. She knew she must, or Mitch would be up here in a heartbeat, kicking in her door. And she had wines in the competition. Waiting until the fifth ring, she finally picked up.

"This is Dani," she said. "Oh hi, Mitch. I'm great. Perfect, actually ... what am I doing? Getting engaged ..." she watched Tim's face break open with a big grin. "Yes, we'll be down for breakfast. Don't wait, start without us ... No, I'm serious. You'll like him ... See you in a few." She hung up.

"Spending the day with people it is," Tim joked. "I mean, I need to be a sport, right? After all, you went to the morgue with me."

She laughed. "Okay, what did you bring to wear?"

"What I had on last night. Oops." He grimaced.

"That's fine for today. Go, get in the shower."

"Aren't you coming?"

"Umm, yes. I'll be in in a minute." When he disappeared into the bathroom, she grabbed his clothes and dialed the concierge. "Martin? Daniela St. Clair, Cascadia Suite. Can you help me? Here's what I need. Can you send up a selection? Here are the sizes."

FIFTY-SIX

Dani was in the shower finishing up. Tim was dressed. He took out his cell phone and stepped out onto the balcony off the living room of the suite. He called his father.

He wanted to know if this was the way it should feel. He remembered his dad telling him he'd know when he was truly in love. He knew, but a little reassurance would be nice. After a few rings his father answered the phone.

"Dad, it's Tim ... Yes. Everything is great. No, I don't need money ... Dad ... I wanted you to know, I'm engaged ... No, not Ellen ... Daniela ... Dani St. Clair ... I know you haven't met her ... of course I'll bring her home ... Yes. I'm sure ... I can't imagine my life without her ... no she's not pregnant ... I know I didn't tell you about breaking up with Ellen ... a year ago ... I wanted you to know about Dani ... okay ... I'll bring her around ... of course I know Mom will want to meet her ... soon ... yes ... got to go ... call you later. Bye, Dad." Tim stared at the phone. That didn't go as he'd expected. He looked up and Dani was standing in the doorway.

"Are you ready to face people?" she asked. But she looked at him with sympathy. "Your father not as supportive as you expected?"

"I thought he'd be happy for me when I told him we were engaged. They want to meet you." He was perplexed.

"Do you know how lucky we are? We only have to please one set of parents, that's the good news. The bad: I have busybody aunts and sisters. And Mark. He's overprotective."

"I remember Mark. He promised to kick my ass if I broke your heart. You look pretty," he said, taking her hand. She had it on, that silly blue ribbon tied around her finger. He laughed. "It's a place marker," he said. "We'll have to do something about it when we get back to Seattle."

"Let's go face the public and see if my wines win gold medals."

They rode the elevator to the lobby, holding hands. Tim couldn't stop admiring her. She took his breath away. He couldn't believe she was his. And she was reflecting his feelings back as if he were looking in a mirror.

The elevator doors opened. The first person he saw as they stepped out was Gary Warden. What the hell was he doing here?

"Wait, Dani," Tim grabbed her arm. She turned to face him. He hesitated to speak, but knew he must. "Dani, I have to tell you something."

Damn it! How on earth did he keep stepping in dog crap? He had to figure out a way to explain their trick to get Warden and Fraser's DNA without compromising the case. He pulled her back into the elevator and pressed the button for the seventh floor.

"What are you doing? Tim, I thought we were ready to face people!" She cocked her head to the side.

"What's Gary Warden doing here? Did you know he was here?" Tim asked.

"Yes, I saw him last night before you came."

The elevator door opened to the seventh floor. He took hold of her hands and encouraged her back to the room. He waited while she inserted the electronic key into the release. She was defensive now.

"Okay. I'm ready. What's going on?" she asked. They were inside and she let the door close behind her.

"Do you trust me?" Tim asked, staring at her.

Her expression was wary. "Yes," she answered tentatively.

"Do you know why Warden is here? It's weird that he's here."

"Why? He said he was meeting his in-laws, Angelina Caro's parents. They own Caro Mio Wineries out of Napa."

"He's married?"

"Was--was married. Angelina committed suicide a couple of years ago," Dani said, her expression a giant question mark.

"Suicide? Let me guess: desipramine and alcohol?" *Badabing!* Elias Cain's profile came screaming into his brain. *Look for a guy whose wife might have died of an apparent suicide.*

"I have no idea."

"Did he come on to you?"

"Not exactly. Sort of--maybe. But we've seen each other around. I didn't think anything of it." She was evaluating her experience now. Tim could see it in her eyes.

"All right. Dani. You're in this up to your eyeballs, so here goes." Tim encouraged her to sit and she obeyed. He sat next to her. She studied his face, looking for answers. "We think Gary Warden may have given Katrina Collins a necklace that Scott--that the police believe belonged to one of the victims of the serial killer--"

"Gary Warden is the serial killer?"

"Dani, don't. We can't jump to any conclusions just yet. He could've bought the necklace at a pawnshop, bought it from a friend or yes--he could be our guy."

She gasped.

"The other night, we tricked him into giving up DNA."

"You tricked him? I don't understand. Don't you just do a swab?"

"Damn it." Tim stood and paced in a circle. "You shouldn't know this shit!"

Dani narrowed her eyes at him. "Can *you* trust *me*, Tim? *Can* you?" She lifted a skeptical eyebrow. There was something to her he hadn't seen before: a toughness, a strength. "Tim, either we're partners or we're not."

"Okay." He nodded his head, and in that instant, they made a pact. "Partners. Lovers and partners." He smiled and she nodded. "We were at McTavish's, having drinks--Scott, Kathy, and I. We'd just pored over some pictures we'd received from the victims' families. In one, Amber Brown was wearing a necklace. One-of-kind, natural stone, hand-made, expensive."

"Emma's?"

He ran his tongue over his teeth. "How did you know?"

"Tim, there isn't a woman in the city that hasn't at least wanted to buy something from Emma's. Her creations are stunning."

"Yes, we think it's from Emma's." He was amazed and delighted at Dani's quick wit. "They came into the bar: Katrina, Gary, and Bill Fraser. Katrina was wearing the necklace. Scott spotted it immediately. We devised a plan to get their DNA. If one of the samples comes back a match to what we already have, we get a killer off the streets."

"Okay. Now, why didn't you want me to run into Gary before you told me this?"

"I created a diversion so Scott could collect their bar glasses." He winced. "It wasn't pretty. I was rude and mean. Ended up with a lot of cuss-words flying around and Warden taking a swing at me."

"Why do I always miss the good stuff!" she laughed.

"You wouldn't have liked this, or me."

"That bad? Must be why he believes you and Katrina were having an affair."

"He told you that?"

"He said that there were rumors going around at the club."

Tim was immediately suspicious: Was Warden the man in the hoodie, the photographer? Dani was in more peril than he'd imagined. "Dani, he can't know. He can't suspect you think he's a killer. He can't know we're on to him. Do you understand?"

"Why?"

"We think he'll run."

"I understand."

"You're one of the insiders now. Sworn to secrecy, not a word to anyone. Promise me?"

She nodded agreement. "I promise."

"Tell me about Angelina Caro."

"She was sweet, happy. Tim, she was lovely. Do you really think he killed her?"

"I don't know. Scott will have to take that up. I get the case later, when all evidence is in and we're ready to prosecute." He looked at her and she moved close to him. He wrapped his arms around her.

"But you seem so involved."

"I am involved--because of you, Dani. You're his type."

"I don't want to be his type. I'm scared."

"Scared is good. That way you'll be cautious. Dani, I'm here. I'm going to protect you."

FIFTY-SEVEN

Los Angeles Fire Station 205 was impeccable. Even the concrete floor under the main engine's wheels was polished and shiny. A bright stainless-steel pole connecting the garage with the sleeping quarters reflected the sunlight from outside. Scott had always wanted to slide down one of those, but wasn't going to ask to try it here.

He walked into the open garage with Detective Woodburn from the LAPD. After Tim and Scott had viewed the surveillance tape from the Seven's Club, they'd pooled some money together and decided to do some investigating on their own. They were going to look into both Warden and Fraser. They both knew neither Goddard nor Captain Martin would authorize what they were planning to do without a DNA match: too risky and too expensive. If anything panned out, they could get reimbursed after the fact. Scott insisted that Tim go protect Dani, hoping that once she saw the real surveillance video she'd take him back. Scott hated seeing him this way. Though Tim hadn't said much about it and had seemed to take their breakup in stride, Scott knew the signs of his pain: all Tim did these days was work.

Meanwhile, with Sheridan's help Scott found employment records on both men. He took the cheapest red-eye he could find to L.A. He'd do a check on Warden first. And next weekend he'd fly to Spokane and check on Fraser. Hopefully though, by next weekend the DNA results would be back and their theory would either be confirmed or a dead-end.

A uniformed firefighter greeted him: "Hi, can I help you?"

"Yes, I have an appointment with Captain Leford. Scott Renton, Seattle PD." He showed the man his badge. "This is Detective Woodburn from the LAPD."

"Sure, right this way."

They followed the man down a short hallway to a small office on the main floor.

"Cap, this Detective Renton, Seattle PD, and Detective Woodburn from LAPD. They say they have an appointment?"

"They do. Come in, gentlemen." Captain Ledford was a short man, fit, well-muscled, his face gruff like a bulldog. When he smiled, however, his whole demeanor changed. He was a friendly, helpful guy. "Good afternoon, detectives. What can I do for you?" he asked.

194

"Do you remember a firefighter who used to work here named Gary Warden?" Scott handed him a picture he'd gotten from the DMV.

"Yes, of course I remember Gary--great guy. But I don't think his name was Warden. Wardley, I think it was. Here, let me look." The captain booted up his computer. While they waited, Scott read the many award plaques decorating the office walls. The 205 had a heroic group of guys employed here. The captain said, "Yep, Wardley," and turned his computer screen, displaying the employment records.

Scott grinned at Detective Woodburn and lifted a skeptical eyebrow. Only one reason someone would change their name: hiding an unsavory past. "You're sure?" Scott asked.

"Yep."

"But he's the man in the picture?" Scott glanced over at Woodburn.

"Yes. That's Gary all right, great guy."

"So, you said," Scott confirmed. "Any idea why he left?"

"Oh, yeah. Sad story, really--very sad." The captain motioned for the detectives to sit. Scott and Woodburn obliged. Scott leaned forward, interested. "Poor Gary came home from work and found his wife had overdosed. Man, can you imagine! A paramedic and unable to save your own wife ... just awful."

"Overdosed?" Scott asked, knowing his mouth was agape. "Do you happen to know on what?" He hoped Woodburn would know and glanced his way. Woodburn only shrugged.

"Not sure. We all thought suicide, but as I remember there wasn't a note, so the coroner ruled it an accident. LAPD investigated after Gary found out Lily had a million-dollar life insurance policy. He was cleared. He was here, on-duty when it happened."

Scott sat back in his chair. An accidental overdose and a million-dollar insurance policy. That was a prescription for murder. Kathy's words reverberated in his mind. *Desipramine, insidious little drug in overdose ... there's a rebound effect ... Sure, he was at work when she died.* Woodburn obviously didn't know about the rebound. But all of this was speculation, the wildly spinning thoughts of a homicide detective. Until they had more, this could just be an eerie set of coincidences, nothing more. But man, Warden or Wardley or whatever-his-name-was sure fit the profile.

"Can you imagine? I know it was hard for him. He missed Lily. Anyway. He didn't need to work here anymore. He moved away. Couple of years ago, I got a call from Napa Fire for a reference. I guess he got bored and went back to work."

"Do you know where the autopsy was performed?" Scott asked.

"Woodburn would know," the captain offered.

Scott gave Woodburn a look of dismay; he hadn't offered up the old files. But Scott realized that with a big city case load, details would be forgotten. Hell, they were probably happy to get the coroner's report of an accident--one case off their plate and ten to take its place.

"Well, thanks for your time, captain. Woodburn and I will go pull the old files."

"So, is Gary in some sort of trouble?"

"No. Just a background check."

"Is Gary going to try his hand at being a police officer?" The captain winked at Scott and scooted his chair back, scraping against the tile floor. "Great guy."

Scott didn't answer, just grinned letting him believe whatever he wanted to. "We're checking some things. Got to be thorough and careful these days," Scott said quickly. "Oh, and captain, we'd prefer Gary didn't know we were down here. He's not in any trouble and we don't want him thinking he is," Scott said. *Wasn't in any trouble yet, anyway.* "So, Woodburn. Let's go down to the station and pull those files. I've got some reading to do this afternoon."

They slowly walked out of the station.

"So, you think Warden is your serial killer?" Woodburn asked as they climbed into his unmarked police car.

"He fits the profile. I also need to look at any unsolved cases from around the same time. Pretty girls, long brown hair. Our DA is up for reelection; we have to make sure it's a rock-solid case before we issue an arrest warrant."

FIFTY-EIGHT

The wine gala reminded Tim of a fair. Each of the wineries had a booth set up to provide tastings and allow visitors to purchase bottles of the wines they liked. The more successful the winery the fancier the display. Delight Valley's booth was amazing. They'd hired a landscape architect and spared no expense in making their area as elegant as their wines. They'd built a lovely raised pavilion with Victorian trimmings, painted white. The support posts were wrapped in wisteria vines and blue-and-purple flowers hung like clusters of grapes. It was stunning. Inside the pavilion were several tables where guests could sit, enjoy their wine, and watch the Columbia River roll by. She'd created a fantasy and the participants at the gala were enjoying it. As for Tim, he relished walking hand in hand with Dani. The cordial competitors were all greeting each other like long-lost friends. And he really liked Mitch and Shannon. Mitch's war stories fascinated him. Mitch could pilot any kind of flying machine. The foursome walked down the aisle between the booths.

"You're causing quite a stir, Mr. McAndrews," Dani said, linking her arm through his.

"Am I?"

"I can just imagine the speculation and gossip now: Daniela St. Clair has a new man!"

"Shall I kiss you and really stir it up?" He stopped and looked down at her. "No. I don't think I will. I think I'll keep them guessing. After all, part of our game is trying to keep our hands off each other."

"You are such a tease. Come on, let's go taste some wines. Nothing less than 92 points. Do our own competition," she beamed.

"I don't know anything about wine. Just like the buzz," he laughed.

"I'll teach you."

"Hello, Daniela." They turned to face Warden. "McAndrews." He scowled a greeting, squinting his eyes as if sizing him up.

"Gary," Tim acknowledged him.

"Been insulting any women lately?" Gary asked. Tim let a sardonic smile turn his lips. Dani tightened her grip on his arm as if keeping them from a fight.

"Not today," Tim countered.

"Do you mind if I join you? I seem to have lost my party." Gary stared at Dani as if disappointed he wasn't going to be her date for the tastings today.

Tim could feel Dani pressing her weight against his arm for security. He was worried she would give their secret away; he had to diffuse this. Until they had DNA back, it was like a game of chess. He wondered if Warden played--and if he did, was he any good at it?

"Not at all! Rules are we taste nothing under a 92--isn't that what you said, Dani?" Tim offered.

"Yes. That's the rule."

"So, have you two made up? Or do you even know about Katrina?" Gary sniped, staring at Dani.

"He's apologized for what happened with Katrina and I've decided to forgive them. Is that what you want to know, Gary?" She closed her eyes and opened them in a bewitchingly slow blink. Tim was surprised at her sudden control.

"Where is Katrina, by the way?" Tim asked.

"Why, you miss having someone to slur?"

"No, but I miss being called ... what was it again ... oh, yeah ... a smart-mouth, arrogant, pretty-boy big shot D.A."

Dani started laughing. "Come on, nothing less than a 92. Let's start our own club."

"What's with the candy ribbon around your finger?" Gary asked, giving Tim a dismissive look.

"It's a place-marker." Dani glanced at Tim, and let her gaze linger. They were momentarily lost in the secret and each other's gaze.

"A what?"

"It's a reminder that I made an important promise." She laughed.

"Well, shouldn't it be on your index finger?" Gary teased.

"Not this one."

In the distance, Tim heard screaming.

"Girl in the water! Help her! Help her!"

He looked at Dani. "Call 911. Get the hotel staff to bring towels and blankets. Let's go, Warden; you're search-and-rescue."

Tim ran, and as he did he shouted to some boaters picnicking on the grass beside the river: "Life vest!" A man tossed one at him and he caught it. He glanced to his left and noticed Mitch was right along his side. He peeled off his long-sleeved shirt and put the vest on at a full run. He pointed at a rescue ring with a long rope and the owner tossed it his way. As he ran he got eyes on the girl. He momentarily gaged the current and then he was in the water.

Even this late in the season it was shockingly cold. He pushed that thought aside. The girl wasn't too far out, but she was facedown and he felt the current begin to take him. He scanned the shore; Mitch was with two other men manning the rope on the ring. They would pull him in if he got into trouble. Tim swam to the girl, but didn't hold out much hope. He rolled her over onto her back and held her head above water, like he'd learned years ago in lifeguard training. He began to drift downstream and finally felt the tug on the ring, as those on the shore slowly pulled them in. The girl's skin was a bloodless white and icy. He felt his body begin to shiver and the cold was like daggers. Water temperature had a lot to do with survival; if she'd drowned in this cold water they still might be able to revive her.

The shore was only a few feet away. In the distance, he heard the wail of the approaching sirens. He touched the bottom of the river now. He momentarily stumbled on the rocks, then found his footing and turned and picked the lifeless girl up in his arms. Mitch and the two strangers kept steady pressure on the rescue ring, making certain they made it safely to shore. He rushed to the grass and gently positioned her for CPR. Where was Warden? He looked around, caught a glimpse of him on the hotel's deck. Stunned that Gary had slipped away, he dropped to his knees to start CPR. Mitch stopped him, placing a hand on his shoulder.

"Tim, she's gone. She's dead." Mitch was feeling for a pulse.

"No!" Tim heard the agony in his own voice.

"You did everything you could," Mitch comforted him.

If anyone would know death, it would be Mitch. Tim knew he'd seen plenty of it. Tim looked back for Warden. He saw him standing on the deck with a strange grin on his face. An eerie feeling shuddered through him; had Warden murdered her?

When Dani threw a blanket around Tim's shoulders, he realized he was shivering violently. When she hugged him, he was grateful for the warmth of her body against him.

Suddenly, police and medics surrounded them and pushed them back away from the body.

"Darling, you're shivering." Dani put another blanket around him.

"I'm okay." He pulled her close. "Police are going to want to talk to me."

"Can they come to our room? I should get you out of those wet clothes."

"Yes. I'll tell them to meet us there." He turned and a microphone was shoved in his face. Bright lights blinked on and blinded him. "What's your name, sir?" The sound of hundreds of pictures whirring from high-speed cameras filled his ears. He lifted a hand in front of his face.

"Tim McAndrews. His name is Tim McAndrews. Now, if you'll leave us alone, he's very cold." Dani put her arm around him and guided him away.

"Mr. McAndrews, can you tell us what happened?" The reporters followed.

He shook his head and kept walking.

"We heard calls for help," Dani said. "Mr. McAndrews helped. That's all." She kept the reporters at bay, hustling him into the lobby and pressing the call button for the elevator.

"And what's your name?" A male reporter smiled at her.

"Dani St. Clair. Now excuse us, please." The elevator doors opened and she pushed the control to close them. Tim watched as she depressed the square for the ninth floor three times. He started laughing.

"So, Miss St. Clair. Will you do this for me when they hound me after a win in court?"

"Anything for you."

Tim was finally comfortable after standing under the hot water in the shower for half an hour. He toweled off, wrapped himself in one of the hotel's signature terry-cloth robes. He joined Dani in the living room.

"What's all this?" he asked.

"Food first. Then, since you decided to ruin your clothes in the river, I thought you might need something dry. The men's shop from downstairs sent these up for you to try. Pick what you like and we'll send the rest back down."

"Dani, I can't let you--"

"Tim, let's get this straight right now. I'm rich. If I want to give you gifts, I will. My parents gave me and my sisters a leg up in life that most people don't get. You didn't pack anything. Why? I'm guessing because you thought I wasn't going to let you in last night. That you didn't know I love you. But now you do. We are lovers *and* partners, remember? The police will be up in a half hour to talk to you. So, eat and get dressed. Then I'm going to insist on a nap; that water was terribly cold."

He was grinning at her. She was mothering and he was going to let her. But now the weight of what he suspected was heavy.

"Dani, what did Warden do while this was going on?"

"I don't remember. I was calling 911 and getting blankets. Why?"

"He killed her."

She whirled around to face him. "I thought ... he was with us."

"Here's my theory: he killed her last night. He threw her in the river, and she finally drifted down to the still water in front of the hotel this afternoon. He's search-and-rescue; why wasn't he in there helping me? Why didn't he start CPR when I brought her out? He knew she was already dead, because he killed her." Tim sat at the small dining table but couldn't eat.

"What are you going to tell the police?"

"I'm going to tell them to look for desipramine. I'm going to tell them I suspect she was murdered."

"What if they think you did it?"

"The ME will be able to establish the time of death. I was with you. The hotel surveillance cameras will also be able to confirm it. I came to your room around eight-thirty last night. We first emerged together around ten-thirty this morning."

"Okay. Then eat now. Get dressed." She wrapped her arms over his shoulders and kissed the back of his neck. "How did you learn to do that rescue swimmer stuff?"

"Scott. We took swimming lessons in Boy Scouts, but Scott had to be the best and the best was rescue. Never have been able to let him outdo me." Tim laughed, remembering.

FIFTY-NINE

Dani slowly walked up the five steps to her office, juggling coffee for herself and Karen. She was still spinning from Tim's proposal, but also from his suspicions. She couldn't wait to tell Karen about her engagement. She'd said yes and she was confused by that decision. After all, she'd vowed to herself she would never marry again. She opened the door and stepped through. Brad Hollingsrow, her attorney, and Mark Settle, the ranch foreman, were waiting for her. This couldn't be good. She hoped someone wasn't suing her.

"Good morning." She set a coffee down in front of Karen. "Are you here for me?"

"May we see you for a minute?" Hollingsrow asked, as if she were going to have a choice. He stood and picked up his briefcase. Mark's expression was serious. This was bad, she knew it.

"Of course. Hold my calls, Karen." Dani sighed. Karen had discerned her worry and was reflecting it back to her. "Shall we?" Dani motioned for the men to join her in her office. When they passed through the opening, Brad closed the door behind him. Dani wheeled to face them. "Are the horses all right? Mark, what is it? Are we being sued?"

"Everything is good at the ranch."

"Okay? Why are you here? What is this about?"

"First Dani, you need to understand your father charged us with look-ing after you and your sisters before his death." Brad started, motioning for her to sit on the hunter-green plaid sofa.

"Yes." This she already knew. She sat, all the while trying her best to read their faces for a clue about the purpose of this meeting. "Yes, Mark reminds me all the time."

"And I want to remind you how much your family is worth," Mark added.

"I'm running the business; I know." She said, questioning their motives.

"Actually, you don't know everything," Brad informed her.

"Why don't I? I should know."

"Yes, I'll go over everything with you now, don't worry." Brad fiddled with the handle of his briefcase. "Any way, we need to get to the business we came to talk to you about." He paused--probably to give her time to gather her thoughts, but instead he scared her. "Dani, as you know, your wealth leaves you extremely vulnerable—to smooth operators and cads who would feign love for money and the lifestyle it brings. Do you understand?"

"Of course." Dread began to twist her stomach in knots and she scooted forward on the sofa, sitting on the very edge.

"Your father was none too happy with you and your sisters' choices of husbands. And after Carl, he asked that I check out any new prospects. He just wanted you to be happy. And you know how Liz and Rachel's marriages have turned out."

"They're happy," Dani argued. Her sisters had never complained--at least, not to her. But she knew the truth. Both their husbands were disappointments.

"But Rob and Mike don't work and have pretty much become parasites and pampered pains-in- the-ass," Mark grumbled. "Your father didn't want that for you, Dani. He was hoping for something better next time around."

They'd researched Tim and they were going to drop the bomb on her before she did something stupid. Well, too late. She already had. Were they going to tell her Tim was after her money? Did they think she didn't worry about that already? "Okay?" she said, bracing herself for the bad news.

"We understand that you're contemplating getting engaged to Tim McAndrews." Mark thrummed his fingers on the coffee table in front on him and the look on his face was clear. Mark didn't like him.

"How do you know that?" Dani asked, "Are you spying on me?" The two men briefly stared at each other. "Oh, uggh! You are! I should fire you both!" Of course, she wouldn't. They had her best interests at heart.

"No. Dani, Mitch mentioned it." Mark's voice was soft, as if preparing her for the worst.

"He just proposed Saturday. You haven't had enough time to find out anything about him," she reasoned.

"We've been checking on him since you first brought him around. You have to understand we had to, for your safety," Mark clarified.

Brad winced. "We felt it was time to intervene and let you know what we've found."

"For my safety? Oh, I see. You've come to make sure my feet are firmly planted on the ground. Or is it to rip the rug out from under me?" She laughed nervously. "What if I don't want to be firmly planted on the ground? What if I don't want to hear it?" She watched as Brad opened his briefcase, pulled out a file and set it on the small glass coffee table, tapping it twice with his hand. She stared at it but didn't pick it up.

"That's your choice, Daniela. But in any case, I'm here to see to it you know exactly what you're getting."

She sighed and sank back into the cushions on the sofa. Oh, well, it was fun while it lasted. She looked at her ring finger and the blue satin bow, remembering how sweet it had been to let go and surrender to the dream. She felt tears forming and fought them back. She wouldn't let them fall.

"Mark, would you leave us? I'd like to talk to Daniela alone for a moment," Hollingsrow requested. Mark rose and quietly left the room, only adding fuel to her fears.

"What's that old saying? If it seems too good to be true, it's because it is. That's what you're here to tell me isn't it?" Dani said. She steeled herself for the bad news.

"No," Brad said looking at her straight in the eyes. "No. I'm here to tell you what I know and let you decide what you want to do." He took in a deep breath. "McAndrews is a Seattle boy. Raised here. He is the youngest of three boys. His older brothers--Anthony 40 and Jeffrey 37--run the family business, a busy finish carpentry and cabinetry shop. They are very successful and have an untarnished reputation. Tim will inherit a third of the company when his father passes. Right now, he takes care of the company's legal work, in addition to his role as a King County prosecutor. The older boys are both are married. Anthony has six children, Jeffrey four. Irish Catholic, I'm assuming. Both Tim's parents are still alive."

Dani stared at Brad. She and Tim hadn't talked about family. *Oh, dear;* she realized she had agreed to marry a man she knew very little about.

He continued. "Tim was quite the scholar and football star in high school. Graduated cum laud from University of Washington, Law School. Went on to Harvard Law from there. He graduated early and at the top of his class. Right out of the gate he was on the recruitment list for the FBI, several New York City law firms, and one out of Chicago, but he wanted to be here in Seattle. I guess it was to be close to family. He applied with the District Attorney's office." Hollingsrow chuckled. "I remember Paul Goddard telling me about him. He said: 'You should see the application I received today. Top grades, glowing recommendations. I'm thinking this is my candidate, this is my new hire. And then he comes in for the personal interview. Tall, blond, blue-eyed, male, handsome as hell, and the absolute poster boy for white privilege. He's screwed," Brad laughed. "Goddard's chief deputy and department heads were against hiring him. They had diversity quotas to fill. But Goddard overrode them and took a chance. McAndrews was hired on probation. He had to prove himself. When Tim took his first case to trial, Goddard asked me to observe and help him evaluate. He was a courtroom natural: confident, clear, logical, and well prepared. Defense tried, but couldn't rattle him. And the jury ... he won them over with his opening statement. Goddard worked him harder than his other recruits that first year just to prove he wasn't a favorite. I often thought he would break, but he just took everything in stride and asked for more.

"It's hard for me to talk about this next part. But we should." Hollingsrow paused, seeming to want her full attention. "We found that since starting with the District Attorney's office, he dated only one woman for about a year. He's seeing you now and no others. If he has a fault it is that he might be a little too ambitious, but not ruthless. He likes to win. Works hard. But he would never try to convict the truly innocent. He's a true believer in real, honest justice." He let his evaluation sink in for a moment.

"I'm not exactly neutral, Dani. I know Tim, like him, still play racquetball with him and did a lot more before I was appointed to the bench. When we talked about being married he always commented: 'Career first, then when you can support them, you start your family.' He is very practical."

Hollingsrow remembered one particular talk about marriage that he wouldn't share with Dani. But he remembered it clearly. He and Tim were having an early morning coffee at Jake's after a great game of racquetball. Brad was complaining to Tim about his worthless son-in-law.

"You're not married, are you?"

"No. Goddard keeps me too busy." Tim had answered.

"Do you ever think about it?"

"Sure, but mostly on how to keep out that trap." Tim had laughed.

"Do you have a girl?"

"Sort of."

That comment had completely surprised Brad. "How do you 'sort of' have a girlfriend? Either you do or you don't."

"It's the modern woman, not like the old days, she doesn't want to be tied down to me, either." Tim had grinned.

"So, those two pretty girls in the coffee line looking at us, trying to flirt with you, don't make you think about marriage?"

"What a lawyer you are, Brad. They make me think—or stop thinking, as the case may be—just not about marriage." The two men had laughed.

"Ever see a girl that did?"

Tim had picked up his coffee and started to sip, but instead slowly set his mug back on the table. "That girl. The one coming down the steps of the parking garage, right now. She just--." Tim had caught his breath. "What a knock-out," Tim had said it quietly with a tone of seriousness and passion Brad had found unexpected. He remembered turning to see the object of Tim's fascination. It was Daniela.

He snapped back from reverie. "Dani, McAndrews is authentic. He's exactly who he says he is and I approve. Your father would too, if he were here, if that makes any difference. Mark has reservations. Some stupid bull about Tim not being a country boy. But whether or not he wears cowboy boots isn't criteria I value. I have no reservations and you have my blessing. He's a good man and a damned good prosecutor. Used to beat me all the time in court." Hollingsrow laughed, holding her hand as if to reassure her. "All the information we've gathered is there in the file. Read it, and then make your decision."

Dani stared at him, barely able to speak, her thoughts trying to form words that wouldn't come. Finally, she asked, "Brad, answer one question for me."

He nodded his consent.

"You've determined he's good enough for me. Brad, am I good enough for him?"

"You are." He smiled. "Shall I get a prenuptial ready?"

SIXTY

Another Monday morning and Tim opened his office door and wasn't surprised. It had become like the treehouse they used to have as kids. Almost every morning lately, he'd arrived to find Kathy and Scott waiting for him.

"Morning," he greeted them. "If you're going to be here every day, at least you could bring coffee," he chuckled. He closed the door behind him and set his briefcase on his desk.

Kathy rolled her eyes at him. This morning her pale blue eyes matched her clean scrubs and her cheeks had a blush to them that he was sure was from happiness.

"There's a holdup and we're another week out from getting the DNA off our bar glasses," Scott complained.

"That's not good." Tim scrubbed his hand through his hair. "But wait until you hear what I found out." He removed his case files from the satchel and organized them on his desk for the day's work.

"Me first," Scott interrupted. "I went to check on Gary Warden--formerly known as Gary Wardley--at his old fire station. As amazing as this is going to seem, his wife had a terrible accident. She took antidepressants with a big glass of wine and dang, she died and left him a fortune. A big, fat million-dollar insurance policy. I talked to the L.A. medical examiner and he said at the time he didn't suspect anything untoward; Warden was on duty at the time of her death. So, he didn't keep any frozen samples. Nada. He wanted us to have a lot more evidence before he'd agree to exhume her body."

"I heard about the suicide, antidepressants, and alcohol, but not the insurance," Tim said, fussing with his tie. He loosened it. "What was L.A. doing involved with this? I thought she died in Napa?"

"Lily Johansson? No. She died in L.A."

"Lily Johansson? Who's Lily Johansson? I'm talking about his wife, Angelina Caro, Caro Mio Wineries? She died in Napa," Tim said, locking stares with Scott.

"Angelina Caro?" Scott licked his lips and started laughing.

Tim joined him, remembering Elias Cain's profile. Tim grabbed Scott's file and started to read the information he had.

"Huh, two wives? Go figure. He's such a sad guy. Two wives, one accidentally died of drug-and- alcohol poisoning and the second committed suicide by drug-and-alcohol poisoning. Now that's shitty luck," Scott added, running his tongue across his teeth.

"Elias Cain said to look for a guy who has one or more wives die under similar circumstances." Kathy joined in.

"We've got him," Scott said. "Oh, baby, we've got our guy."

"We've got squat. Remember, it doesn't matter what we suspect, we've got to convince a jury our suspicions are true. We need all our evidence to be irrefutable. The L.A. wife's death was signed off by a medical examiner." Tim tapped his fingers on the L.A. medical examiner's report in the file. "At this point, we have to assume the second wife's was signed off, too. Ruled a suicide. I'll order up a copy today. I'll probably have it by afternoon. We need to get a look at that necklace. We need to link him to our current vics. At this point we don't even have enough for a warrant," Tim reminded them. "What else did you find out in L.A.?"

"Warden had a fucked-up childhood. His mostly absent father was convicted of negligent homicide. One night he and the little woman were shooting smack and she overdosed--had enough heroin in her system to kill ten grown men. He did nothing to help her, fled the scene, and left a six-year- old Gary to deal with it. He was alone with the body of his dead mother for three days--probably watched her die. They found him when a neighbor called police to check on a crying child. Gary told them death had taken his mother's soul to the underworld," Scott grimly reported.

Tim sat back, staring at his friends for a moment. He had no words. Warden's childhood wasn't an excuse; there was always a choice, a moment when right and wrong, good and evil took divergent paths. But circumstances like these unleashed twisted understandings of love, sex, and death. Could've blurred the lines, especially in a child that age--and certainly if he were left to watch his mother die. Tim exhaled.

"Growing up, he went from one foster home to another. There were indications he was the victim of sexual abuse, never proved," Scott continued. "Warden has all the unhealthy ingredients that, when combined could've turned him into a serial killer."

"We need the DNA." Kathy's brow was creased with thought and she rubbed her index finger against her thumb.

"He's our guy. We've got to get him off the street. We've *got* to stop him from killing anyone else," Scott growled. "We definitely need to get a look at that necklace."

"How do you suggest we do that? I was hoping for a warrant--then we could get a good look. All the time we'd ever need to look," Tim argued.

Scott rubbed his hand down his face, over his mustache, and along his chin. "Do you think we can get to Katrina?"

"Not through me! After the last go, she'd never buy it, let alone let me within a hundred miles." Tim toyed with a pencil on his desk.

"Well, we weren't exactly thinking of you when we were devising this new plan." Kathy squirmed in her chair.

Tim cocked his head slightly, opened his mouth to speak, but stopped and contemplated her. "Oh, no. Not Dani. I don't want her involved in this. No. Nope. No way. She's not a cop, she doesn't understand this stuff. Not a chance."

"I thought about Anna, but it would take too long to get her ingratiated, so ..." Scott suggested.

Kathy was grimacing like it was too late. "Um, well ..."

Tim groaned. "You already asked her? Tell me you didn't."

There was soft knock on his office door. He scowled at Kathy, then Scott, knowing full well when he opened the door what he would find.

Dani stood there in blue jeans and a gray T-shirt covered by a matching fleeced-lined hooded sweatshirt and gray fringe-covered boots, looking absolutely ravishing. Just seeing her lightened his mood. She held a molded paper tray with four cups of specialty coffee.

Tim opened the door all the way, stepped aside, and let her walk in.

"Some friends you are--without even asking me," he grumbled.

"Hi. Good morning." She gave Tim a confused look and nodded to Kathy and Scott. "I came as quickly as I could. How can I help?"

"You can't help. I can't let you," Tim said, matter-of-factly. "Too dangerous."

She grinned and set the tray on his desk. He knew instantly he was overruled. She handed each of them a cup of coffee. "First, tell me what you were planning for me to do. Then we can talk about the risk."

"Have you ever worn a wire?" Scott asked.

"No." Dani looked over at Tim. "Whom are we taping?"

"We think we know who our serial killer is. We think he's given a friend of yours a trophy. Do you know what that is?" Scott asked. Tim had never seen him so serious.

"I think I do. Isn't that when a killer takes something from the victim to keep, to remind him of his grisly deed?" Dani asked, shuddering.

Scott nodded.

"Will Warden be there when I do this for you?" Her lips were parted with anxiety. Tim knew she was scared.

"Warden? Who said anything about Warden?" Kathy scowled at Tim.

"Isn't that your suspect?" Dani asked.

"He is. But he won't be there." Scott was clear. Tim realized there was no point in being cagey. Dani was too smart. "What we want to do is get a look at a necklace he gave Katrina Collins. We need you to find out everything she might know about it: where he bought it, the usual stuff. We're just asking that you have lunch with Katrina. We'll be outfitting you with a pendant that is both a video camera and an audio recorder." Scott continued.

"Is this dangerous?"

"Could be. We don't know the extent of Katrina Collins' involvement," Kathy offered. "She could be a co-conspirator."

"No. I could never believe that. She's not a murderer." Dani shook her head, but there was a momentary hesitation, a second thought. Tim wondered, *What's with that?*

"What about for money? If something happens to you, does Katrina gain in any way?" Tim asked, making certain she understood that's why he thought Katrina might be involved.

"No. I can't see her doing that," Dani said, telegraphing her displeasure, and leaving Tim to wonder if they were going to fight over Katrina, now. *After all Katrina had done to break us up, that would be annoying!* he thought.

"She's guilty of using men as props, but she's never been after money," she stated. But, when Dani looked at him now, he could tell there was something she wasn't sharing. Secrets. She was protecting someone. Tim studied her and she flinched away from his skepticism. His first instinct was to press for an answer. He didn't.

"All right. Here's the plan: you don't have any obligation to do this, Dani. You must first understand that," Scott said.

She nodded, but Tim noticed she was seeking his approval. He wasn't going to give it. How could he? She was in danger. But they needed to catch a killer. A killer he believed was stalking her.

"We believe the necklace is a one-of-a-kind. Handmade. The artisan places a small oval near the clasp with her name on it," Scott continued.

"Emma's?" Dani asked.

Scott dipped his head with a quick affirmation. "And the one she sold our victim also had the number forty-two etched on the last bead. It's like a numbered print or lithograph," he explained. "That's the necklace Emma sold to Amber Brown, one of the victims. First, we need to confirm the necklace is Amber's, then we need to understand how Katrina came by it."

"Under ordinary circumstances we would just pick her up and bring her to the police station and ask. But we're sure if we tip this guy off, he'll vanish," Kathy added.

"So, I take her to lunch. That's pretty public and safe."

"We need to do this quickly. It would be best at an outdoor café. We'll be less than twenty yards away in a city maintenance vehicle, taping the wireless feed," Scott said. "And Tim will be there. In the van."

She glanced over at Tim, lovingly. She was braver and tougher than he expected.

"How will we know when she's going to wear the necklace?" Dani asked.

"We'll call you when she's wearing it and set it up," Scott said.

"Are you following her?" Dani asked, her mouth open in surprise.

"Oh, you bet. We've been keeping a casual eye on her since the day we spotted the necklace," Scott clarified.

"You mean like a tail?"

"Not exactly. Just making sure she's still in town. But that all changed when we learned Warden's two wives died under suspicious circumstances. They weren't suspicious at the times of their deaths, but now--well, let's put this way: when the DNA comes back, those deaths may be investigated in-depth." Scott ran his index finger over his mustache.

"Wow. This is scary, but such a rush!" Dani grinned, touching her hand to her heart.

"You aren't obligated to do anything, Dani," Tim reminded her. He worried, but catching this killer would be good all around. "I'll be right there. But better yet, Scott and several detectives will be there, too," he assured her.

"All right, here's how this is going down," Scott began.

SIXTY-ONE

It had been two days since they'd talked to her about wearing the wire. Dani had talked herself into and out of doing it on pretty much an hourly basis. Tim wouldn't blame her if she bailed. If he could replace her with a female detective, he would. But setting that up and gaining Katrina's confidence would take weeks. They didn't have weeks. If Warden was their unsub, they needed to stop him before he killed again.

Though Dani didn't share her agonizing with him he could sometimes see the dread in her eyes. She paced around his apartment, unable to relax. How did he ever expect that life would be peaceful until the killer was caught? The minute he finished his dinner, she'd cleared the dishes. They used to spend time talking. When he took a sip of wine, she'd fill his glass. She was as nervous as an expectant mother in the first few hours of labor.

"Dani, sit. You're wearing holes in the carpet." He puckered his brow at her. He'd brought files home and needed to work for a while yet. He had court in the morning. "You don't have to do this if you don't want to."

"Tim, how can we catch the killer if I don't?" She stood in front of him as he sat on the sofa and stared down at his face. He set his file on the coffee table. "He's been stalking me. Do you know how that feels?"

"I know. Makes me want to take care of business." He looked fiercely past her, imagining what he would do to Warden, given the chance. He stood and took her into his arms. "I'll take care of you. I'll keep you safe," he whispered against her neck, kissing her skin.

"Do you think he knows we're onto him?"

"No, I don't. I think he believes he's smarter than we are and that we'll never catch him."

"Do you think he knows I'm here?"

"He understands we're back together. Maybe. But we're on the third floor and there are two officers guarding the only way up and patrols driving by regularly all night. This isn't something he's likely to try." Just in case, Tim had made certain his Walther PPK .380 was loaded, a bullet already chambered, and within reach on the bedside table.

"I know you think I'm silly."

"Dani, caution is the first ingredient in safety. It's good you're wary; you'll be on the lookout." He held her against him for a while, until he felt her relax. "Why don't you go get ready for bed? I'll be in a few."

"Okay." She kissed his cheek.

When she left the room, he realized he wouldn't be able to concentrate on court cases now. He checked the front door lock. He closed the slider to the deck off the kitchen, locked it, and placed the round wood pole in the sliding tract for extra security. He locked the windows. In the bedroom, he closed the French doors to the balcony and locked them. He pulled the drapes shut. He could hear the water from the shower start to spurt. He closed and locked the bedroom door.

Quietly, Tim went into the bathroom. Through the misted glass of the shower, he could see the silhouette of Dani's lovely body. Desire surged with every heartbeat. He was in love, more than he ever thought he'd be. She was the one woman he could imagine being with for the rest of his life. Maybe tonight would be the right time to give her the bow-shaped sapphire ring he'd found online and had shipped to the office to replace the satin ribbon she still wore.

Briefly, he wished Scott and Kathy hadn't involved her in tracking down the killer. But she was involved and he couldn't change that. He could only keep her safe. And that he intended to do.

For a moment, he stood, eyes closed, and let passion break over him. He stripped. Gently, he opened the shower door and stood in the entry. She turned as if in slow motion. Her hair was wet-dark and her skin glistened and glittered in the water's spray. The clean fragrance of her creamy soap lingered deliciously on the air. She sighed, lips parted as if seeing him excited her. A smile barely turned the corners of her lush mouth. Her every move invited him to make love to her. Tim stepped into the shower stall and closed the door.

SIXTY-TWO

He stood in the garden staring up at the third-floor balcony off Tim McAndrews' apartment. The silver Mercedes was parked in its assigned spot. But if Daniela was there with him, he did not know. For a moment, he stood under the streetlamp, but when he noticed he was exposed, he retreated deeper into the shadows. She wasn't at her home outside the city; he'd been there. She'd flown away on Tuesday. She'd taken the Gulfstream and he hadn't seen her for days. The previously chatty crew at the private terminal had all clammed up. They would no longer share any information with him. And tonight--unlike other nights she'd stayed with McAndrews--the curtains were drawn shut. Was she there? Anxiety wrenched at his gut. Anger began to boil and with it came the cold, relentless hunger. He wanted to stay but needed to hunt. When he could no longer contain the emotion, he walked away.

When he was back in the city he stalked like a leopard down the side streets and alleyways. He wandered through Pioneer Square. The autumn chill in the air made him pull his hood up. He strolled to the waterfront. The salt air stung his nostrils. The fog-dampened streets glistened under streetlamps. Tonight, it was exceptionally quiet. The cold had chased most of the night people indoors.

He prowled up James Street, past Jake's Deli, and ducked into the doorway to the apartment building. When he opened the street door, he heard talk and laughter from his neighbors coming down the narrow stairway. He pulled his hood tighter around his face. When they met, he turned his back to them, willing himself to disappear. No one greeted him. He'd vanished like the tobacco smoke he smelled on the air. He felt invincible. He quickly made his way to his apartment, slipped through the door, and softly closed it behind him. He went to the cupboard, grabbed a new, unopened bottle of Lily's pills and slipped them into the pocket of his sweatshirt jacket. Amazingly, he'd filled her prescription six times after she'd died. The pharmacy didn't even realize Lily had died. He snorted a laugh.

For a moment, he stood in the darkness, looking out the window. Daniela's office was dark. He went to his special room and turned on the lights. The sconces along the wall colored the room with a mellow incandescent light, romantic like candles. And she was there, everywhere:

pictures of Daniela St. Clair covered the walls. She was smiling at him as he added another picture to his collection.

He sat in the center of the room, surrounded by her pictures. Breathing in a lungful of air, he sank down on to the floor in the middle of the room. He closed his eyes and the dream came unbidden.

His mother had read him their favorite story before she'd tucked him into bed. When she'd left him and turned out the light, he'd snuck from between the sheets, to his secret spot to watch through the torn and tattered wall paper. Drifting in the soft music, he watched her slip out of her clothes. The light from the hallway painted her skin a rosy gold. Daniela. He became the shadow surrounding her, loving her, taking her with him. He was Death, the king of the underworld.

SIXTY-THREE

"Hi, Dani, over here!" Katrina stood and waved. Dani made her way past the other tables on the patio. The October sunshine created the perfect temperature for an outdoor lunch. Rudolph's Restaurant had placed big pots of gold, orange, and red mums around the terrace's perimeter, matching the changing leaves on the trees. Dani slid into the chair across from Katrina. The white tablecloths were decorated with runners and napkins in corresponding autumn colors to celebrate the season. The breeze from the Sound passed through Rudolph's kitchen and brought the savory smells of herbs, garlic, and butter with it. Dani was hungry.

"You look great. How are you? I haven't seen you for weeks," Dani asked, glancing around until she spotted the city maintenance van parked nearby, just as Scott had promised. She sighed with relief. "Have you seen the waiter?" She gave herself cover. "I'm dying for a cup of coffee."

"Over there," Katrina tipped her head in the waiter's direction, opposite the van. "Not me, I'm having wine. It's afternoon, right?"

"I'd join you if I didn't have to work ... ugghh." Dani grinned. But she remembered Kathy Hope's warning. Under no circumstances drink any alcoholic beverages. None. The killer mixes antidepressants with alcohol. "That sweater is just stunning on you. I love the color," Dani said.

"Do you like it? I had to have it when I saw it the other day. Perfect with my new necklace, don't you think?" Katrina bragged and fingered the beautiful natural stone beads in the necklace. Dani knew she had more to tell her.

"Is it one of Emma's?" Dani made certain the tone in her voice was dripping with envy.

"Yes." Katrina giggled and squirmed in her chair. "Gary gave it to me."

"He did? Is this getting serious?"

"I hope so. He's my soulmate. I just know we were together in a past life," Katrina said.

Soulmate? Of all the people in the world to be soulmates with: a serial poisoner wasn't one of them. But then, Katrina didn't know her suspicions. And if Dani were being honest, she would admit she was racing to judgment and being unfair. She remembered Tim's words: *innocent until proven guilty.* Dani looked down at her own pendant and quickly brushed her hair away, hoping she hadn't blocked the camera. "I shouldn't ask, but could I see it?

You know how I feel about Emma's jewelry. I should just splurge and buy some myself."

Katrina unclasped the necklace and handed it to Dani. Dani let her gaze swiftly course over the stones. The tiny oval with EMMA engraved on it was exactly where Scott told her it should be. Carefully she held it in front of the camera, the way he'd instructed her. Now, she had to find the etched jade bead. She swallowed a gulp of air; she didn't want Katrina involved in this. Even knowing she'd tried to seduce Tim didn't change the fact that Dani didn't want any harm to come to her. She really couldn't blame any woman for wanting to seduce Tim. She sighed at the thought of him. When she lifted her gaze to engage Katrina in more conversation about the necklace, she saw her suddenly beaming a smile.

"Hi, darling," Katrina said. At that exact moment, Dani felt the weight of a man's hands on her shoulders. She twisted her head back. Gary Warden was behind her. He began to skim his hands slowly down her arms and deliberately covered her hands with his, coaxing her to put the necklace around her throat. He fastened the necklace and placed his hands on her shoulders. She was on the verge of panic. With ease, he could close his fingers around her neck and choke the life out of her. Dani's imagination was going wild. She was terrified, but to resist might give her subterfuge away. She tried her best to show no emotion, barely allowing herself to breathe.

"It looks beautiful on you," he said, lightly kissing her cheek. Dani fought the impulse to stand, to flee. "Don't you think it looks beautiful on her, Katrina?" he asked. She could still feel his fingers pressing, softly gripping the muscles on each side of her neck. She froze in fear. Slowly, he let go. Dani tried not to cringe. Was he warning her? Did he know? He moved back and then sat down in a chair between the two women. Dani felt her heart racing in her chest. He stared at her, searching her face for a reaction. She tried to smile, but wasn't sure she had.

"Beautiful on her, better on me," Katrina answered in a flirty tone.

Don't panic. Don't panic. Dani realized if she lost it now, she might not complete the task Tim, Scott, and Kathy needed her to do. She forced control, tightened her muscles so she would not tremble. She carefully unfastened the necklace. She needed to make sure the camera could record the image of the etched bead. She looked down. Tiny, gold numbers glittered in the sunlight. She read them: 4-2. She could barely contain the gasp she felt sticking in her throat. She looked across the table at him. Warden was the killer! This necklace belonged to a dead girl. Now she knew, she had to playact; it was up to her to let Tim and Scott know.

Warden was watching her every move. Her mind raced. She had to make sure the mini camera captured the image of the numbers. She lifted the necklace up slightly. Warden narrowed his eyes. Was he on to her? She forgot the word she was supposed to say if she felt she was in trouble, the cue that would send Tim to her rescue. She dropped the necklace on the table in front of her.

"Oh my! I'm so clumsy! I better give this back to you before I break it." She handed the necklace back to Katrina as if it were flaming hot.

Staring at her as if his thoughts were churning, Warden stood and helped Katrina fasten the beads around her neck. Katrina adjusted herself in her chair turned around and kissed his cheek. "Thank you," she smiled. He returned to his seat and sank into it, staring at Dani all the while.

Why hadn't she noticed how ice-blue and cold Warden's eyes were before? Dani ran her hand over her brow. Adrenaline had heightened all her senses. Katrina and Warden were etched in her mind like high-definition television. The waiter brought her coffee, but she was already trembling. She didn't dare drink it.

"Have you ordered?" Gary asked.

Dani realized he was joining them for lunch, invited or not. She swallowed hard.

"No, we haven't. But I see the waiter has disappeared again," Katrina complained.

Gary took up a menu, studied it for a moment, and then casually looked over the top. "Did you tell Katrina you reconciled with McAndrews?"

Katrina looked up from her menu and blinked in disbelief.

"We were just about to get to that, but I was so enchanted by Emma's necklace you gave her. She knows how much I love jewelry. Every time we go shopping I stop by Emma's and drool." Dani made even herself sick with that pathetic lie.

"Daniela! Tell me you didn't go back to McAndrews!" Katrina moaned. "Especially when there are other guys who would love to have a chance with you, like Bill Fraser!"

"Katrina, you know what a fool I am for a pretty face," Dani tried, but wasn't sure it would fly.

Katrina tipped her head from side to side. "Yes, I do. But McAndrews? Really?"

"That's what the attraction is about? He's good-looking? A pretty face? Daniela, that's shallow," Gary gruffly scolded her. "So girls, am I handsome enough for you?"

"Well, of course, Gary. Katrina is just as shallow as I am." Dani forced a laugh.

"Dani can do better. She knows it." Katrina was emphatic and sat forward, leaning her elbows on the table. "But she never could pick men. My God, I thought you'd never leave Carl--and he cheated on you almost every day."

After seeing the video of Katrina going after Tim, Dani wondered how Katrina knew Carl cheated on her every day. Now there would be a pair: Katrina and her cheating ex. But she knew she had to get the conversation back to the three things Scott told her to find out about the necklace: the oval, the numerical etching, and where and how Katrina had come to be in possession. Did he buy it? Was it a gift from a friend? One thing they knew for sure: if he said he bought it from Emma, he was lying.

"You know what impresses me more about you than looks?" Dani asked, regaining control. She answered for him. "It's your attention to detail. I'm impressed that you would know that sea tones are Katrina's favorite colors. Most guys don't pay that much attention."

"You give me too much credit, Daniela. Katrina and I were goofing around on the waterfront. We went to Emma's shop. Katrina said she admired the necklace and I went back and bought it for her. Simple."

Beep! Wrong answer! Her heart skipped a beat and she forced a wan smile.

"We did? I don't remember you ever going with me to Emma's. When was that?" Katrina asked, tipping her head and bouncing her curls around her face.

"Darling, it was months ago. It took me a while to save up the money," he answered, almost dismissively. Katrina frowned; she was no dummy. She was clearly rejecting his answer though she didn't say so. And there was a strange formality between them. Almost as if they suspected each other of betrayal.

Dani couldn't believe what was happening to her. A part of her was watching herself sitting at a table on a warm autumn afternoon, having lunch with a serial killer. She'd accomplished all the things Scott had asked of her. Now she wanted out of here in the worst way. She picked up her spoon to stir some sugar into her coffee, but noticed her hand tremble. Warden had ordered a bottle of wine and poured her a glass. Her insides were all balled up. She found herself missing Tim, wishing he'd come breezing through the patio in the charcoal suit and tie he'd worn this morning. Maybe he'd pretend to be having lunch with a colleague, anything to let her know he was protecting her. She glanced over at the maintenance truck. Would he see the desperation in her eyes? She turned back. Warden poured a glass of wine for Katrina. He'd lifted the glass and filled it. With an almost imperceptible flick of his thumb, Dani thought she saw him deposit something into the goblet. He swirled the wine in the glass.

"Ah, look Katrina, this wine definitely has legs," he said, and set it in front of Katrina's place.

Dani felt a panic. Yes, the wine had a beautiful red color and it formed a lovely cascading pattern on the side of the crystal as the alcohol evaporated into the air, but Dani was sure it was poison. She wasn't going to let Katrina drink it. Suddenly, she stood, intentionally bumping the table as hard as she could with her thigh. As she pretended to try to catch her balance, she knocked the wineglass over, making certain it emptied its contents all over the tablecloth. Dani looked up at him. He glowered at her. If he didn't know before, he knew now: she was onto him.

"Daniela! Oh, no!" Katrina cried. "You've spilled red wine all over my new sweater."

"I'm so sorry. I'll pay to have it dry cleaned--or I'll buy you a new one." She raced to Katrina's side and brushed at the wine spots with her napkin.

"It doesn't matter," Katrina pouted. "I've lost interest in lunch. I'm going to go get changed. I'll call you later, Gary." Hastily, Katrina left without even saying good-bye to Dani.

Dani motioned for the waiter. "I'm so sorry; I've ruined our lunch."

She retrieved several twenties from her billfold and tossed them onto the table. She dashed after Katrina. But unexpectedly, she felt Warden grip her arm.

"What are you trying to pull?" he scowled, his ice-blue eyes flashing with what she assumed was anger.

She wheeled to face him head on. "What are *you*?" She was confrontational. *Even a big dog hesitates to tangle with a hissing cat with her claws unsheathed,* she thought. Their eyes locked. Would he try to kill her here, in this public place?

"That was intentional. You were trying to get rid of Katrina." Gary held on to her, searching her face as if he thought she wanted to be alone with him. His lips were forming a slow, seductive, smile.

Dani choked back her fear. He'd given her the way out. She tried to compose herself, to draw down deep and come up with a ruse. Out of the corner of her eye, she saw Tim. He rushed toward them.

"Dani! Hi!" he called out cheerfully, as if this was a surprise meeting. The moment was diffused: Warden let go of her arm. Scott was right behind Tim, weaving through the tables.

There was an instant of electricity in the air as Warden and Tim sized each other up. Warden's face suddenly lit up. He made the connection. He knew, they knew. He turned, and with the agility of a leopard leaped over the small wall to the sidewalk and disappeared into the crowd on the street. Scott was on his heels. He reached the barrier and motioned—apparently, there were detectives on the street. Dani watched as they gave chase.

"Wait! Don't touch it!" Scott called to the waiter who was about to clear their table. He reached into his inside jacket pocket and retrieved a plastic bag. "Get me some plastic wrap--do you have that?"

The waiter stood speechless. Scott shook his head and rolled his eyes. He pulled out his badge. The waiter nodded and left to fetch the wrap.

"How did you know he was trying to poison Katrina? Did you see it?" Dani asked, leaning her weight into the crook of Tim's arm.

"No. You clued us in. Quick thinking, girl. When you stood and spilled the wine, I knew," Scott said. "Tim was already on his way. He said you looked scared and he was going in."

Tim petted her hair, looking at her with all the love in the world in his eyes. "I told you we'd be close."

Dani settled against his chest for support. Her heart was pounding and she took deep breaths to make it settle down. She looked around her. The other restaurant patrons stood, many with their napkins in hand, watching them, whispering amongst themselves. Dani was embarrassed. She'd saved Katrina's life; she knew that, they didn't. They thought she'd just made a scene.

SIXTY-FOUR

Tim had no intention of letting Dani out of his sight until Warden was behind bars. He took her hand and led her through the assistants' main workspace on the way to his office. The women stared but he just pushed on like this was ordinary behavior. When he reached his new office, Myra stood and Tim stopped at her desk. She gawked at Dani. Tim realized that though she may have seen Dani in the office before, she'd never seen him holding her hand like they were lovers. He didn't let go.

"Hi, I'm Daniela St. Clair." Dani reached out with her free hand to shake Myra's.

"This is my assistant, Myra," Tim said, watching a flush of color race into Myra's cheeks.

"Mr. McAndrews, Kittitas County Sheriff's office called. The test results came back positive for desipramine, whatever that means." Myra was being formal for some reason.

"Is Goddard in?"

"Yes." She looked from Tim's face to Dani's and back again.

"Can you tell him I'm on my way? And then get the Kittitas County Sheriff and prosecutor on a conference call, pronto. Put them through to Goddard's desk. And when Detective Renton and Captain Martin get here, send them to Goddard's office, too."

"Yes, sir!" Myra was impressed, but her brows nearly reached her hairline she was so curious. She and the other secretaries watched him as he kept a hold of Dani's hand and headed for Goddard's office.

"… Oh holy crap!" Goddard screamed at the phone. He motioned for Tim to come in. "We're doing everything we can." His angry face melted to a smile when he saw Dani. "Trust me, we are very interested in catching the perpetrator in this case … yes … we are doing everything we can … thank you, too." He hung up the phone. "Sorry, protesters are marching up the street and planning to block the entrance to the building. They don't think we're working hard enough on the Alan Sharp murder." Clearly annoyed, he continued. "Close the door. So, to what do I owe this pleasure?"

"Scott Renton will be here shortly. We need your help to get a warrant for the arrest of Gary Warden and a search warrant for his home, his car, anything, everything. We're specifically looking for desipramine. We suspect he's our poisoner and that he may be keeping trophies from his victims. Scott will be presenting his case for the warrant with some compelling evidence. Kittitas County Sherriff's office called and confirmed that the drowned girl at the Columbia Wine Gala was poisoned with alcohol and desipramine, too; that ties him to her and the others," Tim explained.

"Who do you want? Mattison? Simmerhorn?" Goddard asked.

"Judge Mattison; Judge Simmerhorn is in the hospital," Tim remembered aloud.

"And now, why are we discussing all of this in front of Miss St. Clair?" Goddard gestured by waving his hands in the air.

"Because I'm not letting her out of my sight. We believe Warden is stalking her. She's in danger; I need to keep her safe."

Goddard nodded. "Take Miss St. Clair to the conference room, please. I'm going to be making some important phone calls. I'll send Myra for you when Judge Mattison gets here."

Tim complied. He took Dani's hand and led her to the conference room and placed her in a chair. He sat on the edge of the table, facing her.

"I'm a lot of trouble, aren't I?" she asked.

"No. Not to me."

"I can call Mitch and he can get the Cessna ready. I can go to the ranch."

Tim knew he could let her. She would be safe there. Mitch would be there and so would Mark; they wouldn't let anything happen to Dani. But he didn't want to be away from her. In the end, he wouldn't let his selfishness get in the way of safety, but he wanted to try something else, so they could be together. After all, when Warden ran from the police, he'd tipped his hand. He wouldn't last long with the BOLO (be on the lookout) out over the radio.

"What about Katrina, will she be okay?" Dani asked.

Tim nodded. "Scott sent officers to pick her up. They want to get their hands on the necklace. And they need to interview her, eliminate her as a suspect."

"You don't believe she's a part of this, do you?" Dani's face was incredulous.

"After what Katrina tried to pull with me, I think she's capable. I guess the question is motive: What does she stand to gain if you die?"

"Nothing she doesn't already have." Dani looked at her hands. Tim knew there was more to this story, something Dani wasn't willing to share.

He scolded her with his stare. "You need to tell me everything. Even things you don't want to."

"You're surprised that she pursued you? You shouldn't be. Katrina talked about you before I met you. She was husband-shopping and had picked out several men at the club she said she wanted to date. You were one of her choices. But she's dating Gary and he was on the list too. She *is* bad, like I said before--naughty, but capable of murder? I can't make myself think that."

"Husband-shopping?" Tim snickered. "Were you?"

"No," Dani shook her head. "I'd already had my fill of husbands. You took me by surprise. I didn't want to fall for you." She closed her eyes and slowly opened them, taking his breath away. "But I did."

He took hold of her hand, looking at her fingers. He remembered last night, what he was going to do before he became distracted. He'd even put the ring in his pocket this morning, hoping to surprise her sometime during the day.

"You're still wearing this?" He toyed with the tattered satin ribbon.

"So I won't forget what I promised. Have you?" she lifted her chin, defiant. Her eyes, her lips dared him. Slowly, he untied the bow. She stared at him, stoically, as if she expected him to say he had second thoughts, changed his mind. She started to pull her hand away, but he wouldn't let her. He reached into his pocket, took out the ring, and slipped it on her finger. It was the same blue bow, immortalized in sparkling sapphires.

"It's still a place-marker, until we have time to pick out a diamond," he said, lifting her fingers to his lips and holding them there until she sighed with pleasure. When he let go, she looked at her hand.

"It's the most beautiful ring I've ever had. When did you find time?"

He grinned at her and shrugged. He hadn't found the time. When he decided to do this, he'd grabbed one of her rings out of her jewelry case and sized it. She didn't know it, but she had almost caught him. Then he'd had Myra look online while he was in court. He wasn't sure there would be such a ring, but industrious Myra found it. She found more than one, printed the selections, and left them on his desk. He'd dropped the picture of one he liked best on her desk the next morning with a credit card. In a few days the package had arrived. He'd decided not to tell Dani. He wasn't sure it would come across quite as romantic.

The radiant smile that crossed her lips made it all worthwhile. They were forging memories, working on that sweet life he'd seen his parents enjoy every day. Now he knew how it happened--that electricity, that passion, that harmony. Even in their middle-class life, working hard and living paycheck-to-paycheck, they'd had it all: the unspoken promise of complete love and acceptance was the magic between his parents. He and Dani were just starting their journey, working on their dream. He was full of hope.

Scott slammed through the door to the conference room, breaking the moment like glass.

"Oh! Hi, Dani. So, he eluded us--scum bucket vanished. We'll get him, but for now ... he's at large. But Katrina's in custody, cooling her heels in an interrogation room now. Captain Martin's in with Goddard and Mattison, working on our warrant. You'd better come."

SIXTY-FIVE

Goddard looked up from his computer. Scott and Tim stood before him, anxious and ready, like two football players up from the bench and itching to play in the championship game.

"I must say, Mr. McAndrews, you have outdone yourself. My Jenny is right about you," the judge said, looking over the top rim of his readers. Tim cringed inside without showing it. He didn't want to be Jenny's anything and he felt pressured. "I couldn't possibly turn you down after seeing this."

"Thank you, sir. But Detective Renton and Dr. Kathy Hope from the medical examiner's office have done all the work. She's the one who found the drug that links all our victims. Without her suspicion, it would've been missed." Tim held back a smile that wanted to explode all over his face. They were quite a team, Renton and Hope. His best friends were exceptional at their jobs. Now, after the arrest, it would be his job to see to it that Warden got justice.

"I see that. You are very impressive young men and women. Out of the ordinary, I'd say. I'll sign your warrants," the judge said. "Get them typed up and I'll sign. Now, go get this guy off the street."

"I want you there, Tim, when they serve the warrant. I want every item of evidence found thoroughly documented. Not one shred missed. You understand?" Goddard stood. He was beaming. "I knew you were the man for the job in major crimes."

"Thank you," Tim smiled.

"Now, why is Sheriff Randy Shore calling me?"

"The girl that died at the Northwest Wine Gala had traces of the antidepressant linked to our victims. We believe our killer poisoned her with desipramine and wine. When she was incapacitated, he tossed her in the river to drown," Tim said, remembering the anger he felt when he saw Warden on the hotel deck that day. "I asked the sheriff to check for desipramine and she was positive."

"Good God! This guy is horrible."

"Yes, sir. Evil without any concern whatsoever for human life." Tim shook his head slowly.

"We must stop him," Judge Mattison added.

"Detective Renton, we all agree that you should take charge of the warrant service. You have done a very impressive job so far, no reason to change quarterbacks mid-game, so to speak," Goddard insisted. Tim knew Goddard needed this arrest. They'd get a killer off the street. This would make Goddard a hero just before the election. Scott would get a commendation, Tim was getting a raise and major crimes. He guessed Kath would get a raise, too. Life was good.

"Yes, sir," Scott said. The two friends were almost pawing the ground like race horses at a starting gate. Even as little boys they had imagined being the good guys. Good guys in grown-up life was really something.

Tim knew this wasn't Scott's first warrant service; he'd talked about it. But it would be Tim's. He'd never done anything like this before. Didn't even expect to be asked. But Goddard was hands-on and wanted his attorneys to know what the police knew, see what the police saw, and translate that—with evidence--to the jury in court.

"Sir? We need to take care of Dani St. Clair. She's in our conference room and in need of protection," Tim reminded Goddard. "We're sure Warden is after her. He tried to poison her best friend. Had she not spilled her glass of wine, Miss Collins would be headed for the emergency room with heart problems tomorrow morning."

"Yes. All right, do what you need to do," Goddard gave permission. His concerned expression said it all. He couldn't afford to lose such a wealthy donor. "We need to move on this, quickly, get this one behind bars, because I need you two to take up the Christopher Alan Sharp murder. We've got to get these protestors off the steps--the sooner the better."

"Yes, sir," Tim answered.

"Oh, on this Warden case— when we get him, I'll want you, Detective Renton, and Dr. Hope with me for a press conference," Goddard said. "Will the DNA be back in a few days?"

"Not sure, sir, but I'll get with Dr. Hope." Tim felt his stomach flop over. He wasn't one for television cameras. But as time went on, he'd need to get used to it.

Tim and Scott walked briskly from the room, closed the door behind them. They took off for the conference room. They were going to have to get Dani situated in a safe place as long as Warden was at large. Now, not only was he a serial poisoner, he was desperate. As they passed the elevator the doors slid open and Kathy was standing there. She grinned at the sight of them. She stepped forward waving a piece of paper in the air.

"I have DNA results," she said, as Scott linked her arm through his. "But Tim's office is the other way," she resisted.

"Tell us *now*," Scott demanded and Kathy was taken aback. Tim wanted to know as badly as Scott did.

"And? It's?" Tim started her sentence for her.

"It's Warden. He's linked to the victims he had sex with by seminal DNA. He's linked to the others by the drug," she answered, as she walked along with them. "Why are we going to the conference room?"

"We need to hit him with a big surprise at 4:30 in the morning. I'll get CSI on board. I want them in there as soon as the house is cleared," Scott said. Tim nodded agreement. "All right, you take care of Daniela, I'll take care of this."

"Wait a minute, you already have a warrant? What did I miss?" Kathy was standing in front of them with hands on her hips. "And what's with all the protestors downstairs? It was like running a gauntlet to get to the front door."

"Christopher Alan Sharp. The young man we found in the alley the other morning was gay. They think we aren't doing enough," Scott stated and sighed.

"About that," Kathy grimaced. Tim stared at her and motioned for her to continue speaking. She didn't.

"Kathy, we can multitask," he chuckled. For some reason, Kathy was hesitating.

"I know what you're going to say Scott, so zip it! I found the knife wounds consistent with the knife wounds on Candy Johnson, our eighteen-year-old prostitute."

Scott and Tim stared at each other, momentarily speechless.

"Dani went to lunch with Katrina today. The necklace is Amber's. Warden showed up and--hey, Scott did you give that wineglass to the lab?" Tim asked.

"Yes. But I don't think the results are back."

"What results? Damn it. I *give* you this case and you leave me out?" Kathy shoved her wheat-blonde hair back away from her face in frustration.

Tim looked at Scott and flinched. "Everything happened so fast. Warden tried to poison Katrina at lunch. Dani caught him and he bolted. Scott's boys gave chase, but they lost him in the lunch crowd on the street. We rushed back here to get a search warrant. That's all you missed. And here you are with the most important piece of the puzzle: the DNA," Tim explained, putting his arm around her shoulders, so she'd feel included.

"Well, I'll be--so we really have him?"

"We catch him. He's finished." Tim hugged her. "You should be proud of yourself. And Goddard wants you at a press conference in few days."

"Was anyone going to tell me?" She stared at Scott, shaking her head as if perturbed.

"I just did," Tim smiled, and was ready when she softly punched his shoulder.

"I have a warrant to serve. I need to get it coordinated. Katrina Collins is cooling her heels in the interrogation room at the station. Got to go." Scott pecked Kathy's cheek and headed for the elevator. "See you tonight, hon," he said, as he entered the elevator. He waved as the doors closed.

"Sheesh!" Kathy sighed.

"Don't you have work to do?" Tim asked.

"No more, today."

"Want to do something for me?" Tim asked, tipping his head and peeking at her as if she wouldn't want to.

Kathy scowled at him. "What?" She narrowed her eyes.

"Stay with Dani this afternoon. Just until I get finished with all this."

"I thought you were going to ask me to do something hard. Of course. What's the plan?"

"Maybe a suite at the Four Seasons, police guard; Warden knows she's on to him," Tim answered.

"Did you ask Dani?"

"Just on my way."

"Let's go then." Kathy linked her arm in his.

Dani looked up as they entered the room. Tim was, as ever, amazed that in the middle of all this chaos, he could see Dani and would instantly think of love.

Tim went to her and pulled a chair around to face her. "I've got to get you somewhere safe until we have Warden in custody."

"I can call Mitch and have him fly me—us--to the ranch," she offered.

"Oh, no. Dani, protective custody means an armed guard at the door. You do understand? Right?" Kathy explained.

"I may not be able to see you for several days--unless Warden is rounded up," Tim said, disappointment coloring his voice. He didn't want to in-fluence her decision but, he'd gotten used to having her near him. Loved waking up in the morning with her in his arms. "I was hoping I could have you stay--maybe a hotel?"

"I have a place—in the city," Dani said, her expression hopeful, as if this would mean they could still be together.

"Okay?" Tim was surprised. How many of these revelations were there going to be? The ranch, the vineyards, the horses, the airplanes, the pilots, and now another place. He ran his fingers over his lips, trying to cover his concern. They were from such different worlds. Would they be able to mesh their lives together?

"The top floor of our building is a penthouse suite. Dad built it so we'd have a place to stay when in the city and a place to entertain. My sisters use it when they come to shop, keeps them from having to rent a hotel room. It's fully set up. A kitchen, bedrooms, all the amenities. Even a helipad." She sat forward and took hold of his hands. "I don't think I want to go anywhere without you."

Helipad? Was she going to tell him she had a helicopter, too? He stared. "I know I don't want to be without you." He lifted her fingers to his lips. "But it may not be safe for you to stay there." He glanced at Kathy.

"No. Dani, listen: protective custody means a safe house, where the police can protect you." Kathy added, trying her best to convince her.

"*Safe?* The penthouse is like a fortress. You must have a special key to get to the twenty-sixth floor. Without the key, the elevator will only take you to the twenty-fifth, the executive kitchen and dining room. The emergency stairways are locked from below. It only has one-way access unless you have the key and the code," she argued. Tim was moved and a little amazed. She wanted to stay with him as much as he wanted her to.

"Who has keys and the code?" Tim asked. If there was a compromise, he was ready for it.

"Only me." She fished her key chain out of her purse and pressed an interestingly shaped key into his hand. "And now you."

A smile ticked across his lips. He played with the key for a moment. "We'd have to get you there unseen."

"There's visitor parking underneath the building. It's open during the day. Cleared by security and locked at night around 6:00."

"So, we use a car he doesn't recognize just in case he is watching," Tim strategized aloud.

"We could send a decoy to the ranch with Mitch. If Warden is trying to follow me, he'll think I've gone to the ranch or one of the wineries," Dani offered.

"Warden has to be in hiding now. He knows we suspect him. He's sure to figure we'll test the residue in that wineglass from lunch. He knows when we have the results, we'll clearly have him on attempted murder. I'm just hoping we can get him before he disappears."

"And before he can kill another woman." Kathy added, scrunching her eyebrows together.

"I think he's going to run." Tim studied Dani's face. "All right. Let's do it. You and Kathy go to the penthouse. I'll trade cars with Myra. I'll have a police woman drive your car to the airport and leave it in front of the charter office. I'll finish what I have to do here and join you later."

"Before six," Dani smiled at him. But a shadow of worry crossed her face and was gone.

"Before six."

SIXTY-SIX

Tim joined Scott at the police station. Standing behind a two-way mirror with Anna, he watched as Scott interviewed Katrina. He listened as their voices crackled through the ancient intercom. They needed to upgrade it.

"You've kept me waiting for two hours," Katrina whined. "I have other things to do."

Humored by her haughtiness Scott retorted, "Well, ma'am, what you need to do right now is tell me how you came to be in possession of Amber Brown's necklace?" He sat across from her at the battered interview table and slid the picture of Amber wearing the necklace at her.

"Are you accusing me of stealing? I don't know any Amber Brown." She looked down at the photo. Tim noticed a look of surprise pass over her face like a cloud across the sun--and just as suddenly, it was gone. "I told another officer that my boyfriend gave it to me as a gift."

Katrina began to size Scott up. *Oh, boy!* Tim thought. Instantly, her demeanor changed; she was toying with a full-court seduction play. She shifted in her chair and let her jacket slip off her left shoulder. As usual, she was dressed in a low cut-blouse, tight jeans with sparkles all over the pockets and down the outer seams, and fancy black cowboy boots that had never seen the stirrup of a saddle.

"How long have they been in there?" Tim asked Anna. She sipped on some nasty cop-shop coffee in a paper cup, looking through the glass.

"About twenty minutes," she answered between sips. "Can I get you a cup?"

"Oh hell no. That stuff is undrinkable," Tim teased, though he also spoke his mind.

"Miss Collins, do you know where your boyfriend Gary Warden got the necklace?" Scott's voice crackled over the intercom.

Katrina leaned forward and Tim could see almost the entirety of her black lace bra. He knew Scott could, too. *Slut!* he thought.

"That girl is a tramp," Anna said to Tim. "She putting some heavy moves on Scott; I better go rescue him." She handed Tim the empty cup.

Tim chuckled. "Scott's been warned. He's seen what she can do. He knows what to expect."

"I hope so," Anna said.

"He'll be okay," Tim knew Scott could easily handle the likes of Katrina.

The intercom crackled to life. "Gary said he bought it for me from Emma's. That's a jewelry shop on the wharf. He said I admired it and he bought it for me," Katrina cooed, extending her arms across the well-used table. She slowly lifted her gaze as if determining if Scott was interested.

"All right. That's what Gary says, is that how *you* remember it?" Scott asked, making bold, disarming eye contact.

Tim shook his head. Scott could give it right back. Scott waited, held her gaze with his and then smiled at her with one of his woman-melting smiles. Uncomfortable, Katrina sat up.

"Not exactly. I don't remember Gary and I being at Emma's together. Am I in some kind of trouble?" She shook her head and the blond curls bounced around her face. Slowly—deliberately--she brushed them back.

"Miss Collins, do you take antidepressants?" Scott asked.

"No. Why would you ask that?" Katrina was perplexed--or was she? Tim noted a coldness to her eyes. Something had clicked for her. Had it just dawned on her that Warden had used her to get close to Dani? He wondered. Katrina raked her fingers through her curls. The jacket slipped down her shoulder again and she did nothing to replace it.

"Miss Collins, the necklace Warden gave you belonged to a woman who is now dead. Poisoned," Scott said coldly, abruptly changing from flirtation to reality. "Antidepressants and alcohol. Desipramine. You do know that Miss St. Clair believes that Warden slipped something into your wine glass at lunch, don't you?" Scott added.

"He would never do that." Katrina sat back in her chair. She blinked seductively and bit at the tip of her thumb. Clearly, she was doing the math, coming to some disconcerting conclusions.

"That's genuine," Anna said. She turned to Tim. "I don't think she had any idea."

Tim watched as Katrina's breathing rate increased. "If this were a deposition, I'd think she's acting."

"Yeah?" Anna turned and stared. "She's an actress, that's for sure."

Katrina unfastened the necklace and dropped it on the table. All the seduction in her body language was gone.

"You want me to believe he was going to kill me?" she asked Scott. "He would never do that. You're crazy; we love each other!" Katrina answered, but there was hesitation in her voice. *Two plus two equals four.*

For the first time Tim felt a twinge of empathy for Katrina. He could see a shudder rush through her shoulders. She pulled her jacket up around her and zipped it shut. Was she just realizing that her guy was ready to move on and he'd kill her to get free? That was likely a shock.

"Your friend Miss St. Clair saved your life today by spilling your wine," Scott said.

"She ruined my new cashmere sweater. You think she's so great—ha! She stole my life, took everything," Katrina complained.

"Stole your life? You're fine; you're alive. So, what does that mean, Miss Collins?" Scott asked.

"She has what rightfully belongs to me." She glared at him. Scott studied her--waited in case she elaborated. She didn't.

"I'm the police, you can file a complaint." Scott tendered.

She didn't answer, she only stared ahead as if he weren't there.

The comment didn't make sense to Tim, but he stored it away in his brain. If it had meaning it would be crystal when it needed to be.

"Miss Collins, do you have any idea where Gary Warden might be? Where he might go?"

"Why?"

"We'd like to talk to him about the necklace," Scott answered.

"He has a house. On Northeast Alder Street. 34784, I think."

Scott wrote the address down.

"I told you he bought it from Emma."

"Emma says no. I've talked to her; she sold the jewelry to Amber Brown," Scott said deliberately, watching for a reaction.

"She's mistaken. She's old, after all." Katrina defended Warden, but her cheeks flushed with color. Tim knew she was lying.

"Is there anywhere else Warden might go?"

"He might go to Bill's. Bill Fraser's--his friend's--house."

"And where's that?" Scott asked.

"I have no idea. I've never been."

Scott motioned to the mirror, stood, and met Anna at the door. "Run this address through the DMV and ID Warden's vehicles. See if you can get an address for Bill or William Fraser." Anna took the information he handed her.

"If I were you, I wouldn't go home. Do you have friends or family you can stay with? Best be with someone and somewhere Warden doesn't know," Scott informed her.

"I do. But you aren't going to leave me alone, are you?" she purred.

"No. ma'am, I'm going to see to it you're protected." Tim almost broke into laughter. Scott was handing the seduction right back to her. "Write down where you're going to be." He'd let Katrina believe he was going to watch over her personally.

"Thank you, lieutenant," she said in a breathy voice.

"Detective," Scott corrected her.

"De ... tect ... tive," she repeated, slowly fluttering her dark eyelashes, and pursing her lips, promising something she was never going to deliver.

"I'll assign extra patrols. Don't leave town."

"Thank you." She passed as close to Scott as she could. As if she'd pulled one over on him. Tim briefly wondered if she had; Scott was helping her with her coat and purse.

They left the interview room.

As they came out of the door, Katrina's gaze locked on Tim. Her lips suddenly tightened. She looked Tim up and down.

"You. What are you doing here? Is this *your* doing?" Katrina hissed like a coiled snake ready to strike. Tim had heard she'd been confronted by uniformed officers in her boutique and asked to come to the station in front of customers. She was clearly fuming.

"Nice to see you too, Miss Collins," Tim answered, letting sarcasm richly color his voice.

She flashed him a sassy smile. "Well, is it? Is this your way of getting back at me?"

"Katrina, I'm a part of law enforcement. I'm here to catch a murderer. The fact that you're involved is interesting, very interesting--but it has nothing to do with you coming on to me at the Seven's Club." He leaned against the counter between the viewing area and the interview room. He intended his smugness. "Oh, and by the way, Dani knows the truth. I showed her the Sevens Club's real surveillance video. Still, she saved your life, still calls you her friend."

"Fuck you," Katrina mouthed the words but didn't say them aloud. She spun on her heel and walked away. Scott looked back and raised his eyebrows at him. Tim wasn't sure why he kept the antagonism going. Maybe he liked seeing her squirm.

Scott passed Katrina to another detective to take her home. He returned to where Tim and Anna stood talking.

"Well McAndrews, you certainly do have a way with women," Scott laughed.

"I don't think she cared much for being picked up and interviewed," Tim said. "You aren't going to let her go, are you?"

Scott bit his lip. "I don't think she's involved, other than as the unwitting recipient of stolen property," he said. "I'm going to clear her for now."

"She was obviously lying. I don't trust her," Tim protested. "Doesn't it bother you that she wasn't scared when she learned Warden tried to poison her? If what Kathy said is true, had Katrina ingested that wine, she would have rebounded and coded in the wee hours. Warden would've been on duty, transported her to emergency, and would've had his usual alibi. Come on man, something is really wrong with this picture."

"I'm going to go round up Bill Fraser. I checked the fire stations duty roster and he's on at station 20 today. I confirmed Warden was off today, on tomorrow." Scott grinned at Tim. He knew more than he was telling.

"And she's complaining about her sweater!" Anna laughed.

Tim stood for a moment. The puzzle pieces weren't a right fit. Katrina just found out her boyfriend had tried to murder her and she'd defended him. She seemed more worried about a sweater. Everyone around him was dismissing her as if she were just a shallow bimbo. *That's exactly what she wants them to think.* Tim was certain.

SIXTY-SEVEN

Dani was safe with Kathy in the penthouse suite and Tim returned to his office for a little work. He didn't want to stay too long, but he needed to get organized for tomorrow. He slowly removed his suit coat and hung it over the back of his chair. Deep in thought, he loosened his tie. Katrina's interrogation had his mind reeling. Anna was right: she was a very strange woman. Why wasn't she repulsed by the fact that Warden had given her a dead woman's necklace? Why wasn't she disturbed by the fact Warden had tried to poison her? His only conclusion: Katrina was a liar.

To Tim's dismay and over his objections, Scott had dismissed Katrina as a suspect. He and Scott seldom disagreed. Scott had admonished her to stay in Seattle, but other than that, he'd cleared her. Tim couldn't. He wondered if his confrontations with her had colored everything? She'd practically ruined his chances with Dani. She was constantly intervening, throwing Bill Fraser's hat in the ring at every turn. Even today, at lunch. Katrina was a schemer. Tim found himself playing with a stack of Post-It notes, letting them fall, one pack at a time, through his fingers and onto his desk. Hell, he had work to do. He needed to leave the detective work to the detectives.

He booted up his computer. Goddard had installed some new technology and he decided to try it. He turned on the small digital camera at the top of his computer. The new program created a video. He could now leave personalized instructions to Myra while he was in court--or anywhere, for that matter. He could even access the program with his iPhone. If he needed anything from one of his case files, she could text or email the information. It was cool. And this afternoon was the perfect time to try it, since Goddard wanted him to go with the police when they served the warrant on Warden's premises in the morning.

He pulled a stack of files from his right-hand drawer.

"Good morning, Myra," he began. "I've set out the files I need you to work on this morning. You'll find them on the corner of my desk. The top four I need you to prepare for filing continuances. The next three I've decided we should prepare to plea-out: evidence is weak; we need more from the cops. The final one--the Jones case--defense wants discovery. We need to get everything ready for him. After he sees what we have, he's going to want to bargain. See what Goddard wants to do. I've told him as far as I'm concerned, no deal; let's go to court. But see what he thinks, and leave it for me."

He was fascinated. He played the video back and chuckled. It was working perfectly. He took a breath, smiled to himself and continued.

His office door flew open and slammed into the doorjamb. Tim stood in surprise. Jenny grabbed the knob and closed the door behind her.

"You have to talk to me!" she exclaimed.

"Don't you knock? Jenny, I'm sorry but I'm busy: I've got to go through my cases." He'd forgotten to tell Myra he didn't want to be interrupted.

"Tim, you have to listen to me. You have to!"

He was peeved. He had his own cases, for crying out loud! But he'd promised Goddard he'd help her. "All right, Jenny. What is it?"

"Goddard assigned me to vice! You're going to major crimes; I have to go with you!"

"Jenny, Goddard makes sure we have experience in all areas of the law. We all have to put in our time." She'd continued to advance into the small office and was standing too close to him. He could smell alcohol radiating from her skin. He backed up, but she closed the distance. "Goddard makes those decisions, not me. You know that."

"Why weren't you there in court with me today? I went to McTavish's but you weren't there, either. I needed you. Tim, we have to work together."

"Goddard wants you to do something new. That's how we learn." She approached him aggressively. He backed up until he was against the wall; she kept coming. He put his hands up to keep her at bay.

"Tim, we have to work together. I love you!"

"Whoa, Jenny! Time out! This is inappropriate! We aren't going there," he insisted. "This has to stop!"

"I love you! I have from the minute I first saw you."

He wanted to laugh, but her expression was so serious. "Jenny, quit joking around. This isn't funny. Never going to happen."

She stopped. "I love you. Don't I even get a chance?"

He shook his head. He looked down into her face. Was she kidding or just drunk? "I'm getting married," he said with kindness, expecting her to understand.

"Married! She doesn't love you; she's never going to marry you. You're just a toy!"

"Jenny, don't."

"Just kiss me. One kiss." He couldn't believe it, but she was looking at him as if she thought that would make a difference.

He pushed past her. "No. Time for you to go." He headed for the door. She grabbed his arm.

"Wait, Tim! Just--"

"This has to stop, Jenny. It stops right here and right now," Tim said, in as stern a voice as he could. "No more. You're drunk. Don't tell me you love me. No more. I don't want to hear it."

"Deep down you love me." She was close again.

"No, I don't. I don't want this." Her slap stung his cheek. He grabbed her wrist so she couldn't do it again. "What was that for?"

"You have to love me." She was defiant but there were tears in her eyes. He let her go. He hated it when women cried. He backed away, rubbing his face with the back of his hand. She was watching him, her mouth turned in an angry pout. He kept thinking of the judge's words: *What Jenny wants, Jenny gets. Not this time!*

"You led me on!" she accused him.

Shocked, he admonished her. "That's not true and you know it. How could you even suggest that?" He bit at his bottom lip.

"That's not all I'm going to suggest," she threatened.

"You'll only make trouble for yourself."

"I'll make trouble for you! You *have* to love me. Why did you have me transferred to vice?"

"You're delusional! I didn't transfer you anywhere. I told you, Goddard decides all that." Tim forced her to her sit in a chair. "You have to choose what you want. Do you want a career with the prosecutor's office? Do you want to use your law degree or not?"

"I want you," she said, just above a whisper, and popped back up.

"And I want Dani St. Clair. Now what?"

"Want me."

He chuckled. "Just like that? Is that how it works?"

"Don't make fun of me. Kiss me. Kiss me and you'll see how it works."

"You need to go. Go now and I'll forget this happened."

"You're not going to forget this happened. I won't let you."

"God Jenny, do you know how bad you're going to feel in the morning?"

"Take me home."

"No. I'll call you a taxi." Tim's office door opened and Amy Kent and Jill Oscar, two new Assistant D.A.'s appeared behind Myra.

"Take me home, Tim. I'll show you I love you."

He looked at the young women. "Miss Mattison seems to have had too much to drink. She's talking nonsense." *God! This looks really bad!* he thought, and rubbed his hand through his hair.

"I'm sorry, sir," Amy sputtered, staring at him as if wondering whether he and Jenny were romantically involved. "Jenny lost her case this afternoon. We were having shots at McTavish's when she disappeared. We came to look for her."

"Here? My office? *Why?*" He studied her. Jenny had obviously shared her feelings with her friends. "All right, I understand. Okay, it happens. Juries can be unpredictable."

"Is she in trouble?"

"We don't win every time," he assured her.

"This isn't over," Jenny wagged a finger at him.

"Amy, will you get her home?" he asked, truly concerned.

"Yes, sir. Are you going to say anything to Goddard? Please, Mr. McAndrews."

"Just get her safely home, okay?" He stepped into the lobby and watched as the young women made their way to the elevator.

"I love you, Tim. I love you!" Jenny called back.

Agony. That was the only word Tim could think of to describe today. He stared at Myra's shocked expression. He felt he'd moved from one disaster to another all day long, each problem more distressing than the one before. He was getting a headache.

"Myra, do you have any aspirin?" he asked, rubbing his forehead. She said nothing but squinted at him. "Well, do you?"

Quickly, she fetched a bottle from one of her desk drawers. But her perplexed expression didn't change. He poured two pills into his hand and swallowed them down without water. Myra handed him one of her new bottles. He twisted the lid open and took a swig.

"Thanks." He managed a smile. Still she glared at him. "I won't be here tomorrow. I've left the files that need our attention on my desk. All right, Myra, what? Do you have something you want to say?"

"Sir, Jenny Mattison isn't a very nice girl."

"She was drunk. We can all be idiots when we have too much to drink."

"You're being kind. But Mr. McAndrews, did you really want me to have this?" She asked sheepishly, but there was a sparkle to her eye that intrigued him.

"Have what?" He tried to be nice, but his headache was making him grumpy.

"This." She stood and rounded her desk, turning her computer monitor to face him. She sat on the edge of her desk, pushed the PLAY button on the screen, and crossed her arms, almost defiantly.

In full living color and with stereo sound his confrontation with Jenny played out.

"Oh!" He grimaced. "Actually, no. I forgot I was recording instructions for the morning when Jenny cornered me. You shouldn't have had to see that. Delete it, okay?" He started back to his office.

"Sir?"

He turned to face her.

"You shouldn't delete it. You may need it," she warned. For a moment, he stood quietly, looking down into his secretary's loyal face. He waivered back and forth before deciding what to do. With his luck, he should definitely keep it: Jenny had threatened him. Without a defense, an accusation of impropriety could end his career. But he wouldn't embarrass her if he didn't have to. Besides, he doubted she would remember the scene in the morning. As far as he was concerned, the whole confrontation could just go away.

"Okay. But no one else sees it--or hears about it. It doesn't exist unless I absolutely need it. Right? We agreed?"

"Yes," Myra nodded, then pressed her lips tightly together. "You're a gentleman. Jenny doesn't deserve your protection."

"If I *were* a gentleman, I would have you delete it altogether," he said.

"So, now you're a gentleman *and* smart," Myra laughed.

SIXTY-EIGHT

"Tim said you live just outside the city. Man alive! I'd stay here."

Dani understood that Kathy was trying to make conversation. She walked through the elevator doors into penthouse foyer and slowly turned a complete 360 before entering the main living room. Kathy seemed to be awed by its full floor-to-ceiling glass windows. The view looked out to the surrounding towers and over the street canyons to the Sound. Dani watched as Kathy ran her fingers along the edge of the antique cherry table covered with a gallery of ornate silver framed family photos. She stopped and picked one up for a closer look.

"My great grandmother," Dani explained.

"Pretty." Kathy set it back on the table and walked into the main living room.

"My mother loved antiques, oriental rugs, my father, first edition books."

"I can tell," Kathy mused. "Wow, what a view! So, why don't you stay here?" Kathy asked, walking to the windows.

"I don't have such good memories of this place. We stayed here when my mother was in the hospital before she died, and then when my father did, too. I caught my ex-husband cheating on me here," Dani said, with a sadness in her voice. "I really hated this place for a while--but it isn't the place's fault, is it?"

"That sucks."

"I knew he was cheating long before I actually caught him. Confronting him was a formality. We had a pre-nup, so I was being quite ruthless. He cheated and I wasn't going to give him money forever if I could help it."

"No kidding? I wouldn't want to, either," Kathy sympathized. She had a look of pity in her eyes, that Dani hadn't seen before. She always had the impression that Kathy could take her or leave her, as if both Tim and Scott belonged to just her. In a way, they did. Tim had told her they'd been friends--the three of them--all their lives.

"I ended up paying him alimony for a year out of guilt. Otherwise he would've been out on the street. Can I get you anything? I have, everything--anything you might want, and what I don't have, I can order up from the kitchen," Dani offered.

"Must be nice. What are you having?"

"Did you have lunch? I could call the chef and have them whip us up something," Dani answered. "Mine was ruined by that monster trying to poison my friend. Well, ex-friend. She hates Tim."

"How could anyone hate Tim?" Kathy asked.

"I don't know," Dani answered, thinking of him. She looked at the sapphire ring on her finger. "He's perfect."

"Perfect? Well, maybe not perfect. But then, I've known him forever. He was always the more sensitive of the two of them. Scott can be nice but it's buried deeper." Kathy sat down at the counter in the huge white-and-stainless kitchen. "This kitchen is bigger than my whole house!" She spun on her stool and surveyed the layout. Painted white cabinets with glass doors displaying expensive hand-thrown pottery. Everything was one of a kind.

Dani set a plate and silverware in front of her. "Tim says you were always in love with Scott." She poured her a glass of wine. "Oh, my. I'm sorry, I forgot to ask; is red okay? It's a very nice cabernet from the Horse Heaven Hills region."

"It's fine! No, I wasn't always in love with Scott. I'd say my crush fluctuated regularly over the years between the two of them. They were my boys-next-door. Like I said, Tim's the more sensitive of the two. Whenever Scott was being a creep, Tim would be so nice to me. But he was very clear and he never led me on, like Scott. Tim was protective; like he was my big brother. You should've seen them in high school. They *were* the football team! They'd played so long together growing up, they knew each other's moves with just a glance. Scott was quarterback and Tim, the running back. They were something else."

Dani enjoyed hearing about Tim's life. She set a plate of cold cuts and cheeses on the counter.

"Tim's excruciatingly handsome. More so than Scott, don't you think? But don't ever tell." Kathy filled her plate with snacks and nibbled at some cheese.

"My assistant and I used to call him 'Apollo.' Long before I met him. We'd see him sometimes on the street by the deli on James Street. And don't *you* tell," Dani laughed and took a stool across from Kathy.

"Apollo, the sun god--that fits," Kathy grinned. "They took me to our senior prom. Did Tim tell you?"

"No. You tell me."

"They were the big football stars, like I said. We all knew they were expected to take the popular girls to the prom. The cheerleaders. You know. I was nothing but a skinny dork. But we were all friends, had been forever. I don't think they saw me as a girl. Time came to ask your lady to the prom.

Tim found out I didn't have a date, so he fixed it: they both invited me. It was dinner, flowers, limo, the whole works. I remember Scott looking at me at the dance and saying, 'Goddamn Kath, you really are a pretty girl.' Like it was the first time he'd noticed. We had a ball. More fun than anyone else. From then on, I was one of the in-crowd." Kathy laughed at the memory. Her cheeks were flushed with color. Her pale skin was flawless and her eyes were a light shade of blue, her blonde lashes were long. Her hair was naturally the perfect wheat color that many women worked hard to get out of a bottle. With a little time and effort Kathy could be transformed into quite a beauty.

"Tim told me he was quite the cad … is that true? With what you just told me it doesn't sound right."

Kathy looked her square in the eyes and cringed. "They were bad their first couple of years in college. But Scott was the worst. Tim … he just had women falling all over themselves to get next to him. Who could blame them? I always chocked it up to survival of the fittest. Just think of the kids you'd have with a stud like Tim. You breed horses so you know what I mean, right?"

Kathy might as well have taken a dagger to her heart. Dani quickly grabbed up her glass of wine and sipped. "Yes, of course." She felt a sadness so deep and sharp, she could barely breathe. There would be no children between them. Kathy's words were just a reminder that the time would come that she and Tim would have to face that reality, but she didn't want to face it, not now.

"Did I say something wrong?"

"Oh? No. Yes, of course, I breed horses; I know what you mean."

"Well, I've got to say, I've never seen Tim so in love as he is with you." Kathy's directness was nice. She truly loved her friend; that was clear. "Before, he mostly just went along. Does that make sense? Just kind of went with the flow. But with you, he's making a serious effort. Riding horses? He's very wary of horses." Kathy laughed. "I think when Tim's in love, it's all the way."

"Has he been in love before?"

"There was one girl in high school. He had a big crush--but Tim's mother saw to it they never got together. Mom didn't believe she was good enough or some such rot. Scott always said Tim's mother didn't want him to date at all. Probably didn't want him to grow up. Sharon--that was her name--Sharon Radcliff. I heard she married her long-time boyfriend and has three kids and one on the way. I don't think she ever knew about his crush. Tim's so different with you. He's asked you to marry him, hasn't he?"

"Yes."

"Don't break his heart, Dani. He's one of the good guys." She sipped her wine. Lifted her eyebrows. "Never was one for red wine, but this is nice." Kathy took another sip. "Did you say yes?'

Dani smiled at her. "I did."

Kathy grinned at her, lifted her glass in toast. "Now, you tell me the story behind that ring." She pointed to the sapphires.

SIXTY-NINE

If he were a betting man, he'd bet Kathy and Dani were buzzed. That wasn't exactly the protection Tim had in mind when he'd asked Kathy to stay with her. He and Scott looked at each other and shook their heads.

"So, what have you ladies been up to this afternoon?" Scott asked.

"Drinking wine," Kathy giggled.

"I forgot to tell you, Kathy is an easy drunk. One glass and she's toast." Tim said, "Did she fill your head with lies?"

"Truths, I think," Dani answered. She stood, walked over to Tim, and kissed his cheek.

"If you want a kiss, you'll have to come here. I don't think I can stand up," Kathy explained to Scott, laughing. He went to her side. She kissed him.

"Don't look so desperate, Scott. There's a suite for you and Kathy here. You can stay, no problem," Dani said.

"Great. Can we pour her into it now?" Scott asked.

"After dinner. A little food is what she needs." Dani laughed. "We made a tray of cheese and other charcuterie. Steaks and potatoes to come." Dani rested against Tim's chest and kissed his throat. The rush of desire was instant and he kissed her lips. He loved the way she made him feel.

"This isn't exactly what I had in mind, Kathy," Tim scolded. "Being drunk isn't exactly safe." He thought of the what-ifs.

"You didn't say. So we had a bottle of wine with lunch," Kathy giggled.

"Okay. We need a quick dinner and then off to bed; 4:30 am warrant service," Scott reminded Tim.

Tim flopped into bed. He reached for Dani and she nestled against him.

"Did you have a hard day?" she asked.

"What a nightmare."

"What happened?"

"Nothing much. Katrina thinks I had her picked up by the police because of what happened at the Sevens garage, and Jenny's in love with me." He rolled his eyes and shook his head, remembering. "Warden is still on the loose and we have to deal with a hate crime. We're in the middle of

Goddard's campaign and he's at peak stress. I'm upside down on my case files and Goddard wants me to go when the police serve Warden's warrants." Tim put his arm behind his head.

"No wonder you're so restless; is there anything I can do?" Dani asked, tracing her finger along the outline of his pectoral muscles. He closed his eyes and enjoyed her touch.

"I'm keeping you awake. I'm sorry." He kissed her hair.

"Yes, but I can sleep all day if I want to. What can I do to help you?" She found his lips with hers.

"Can we talk a little?"

"Of course, yes."

"I'm a little keyed up about the warrant service. We usually don't go. It's run-of-the-mill for Scott, but I've never done it before."

"Are you afraid?"

"No," he chuckled. "I feel like I did the night before a big football game in high school. Not scared, just full of anticipation. I'm sure I'm going to like it. It's all part of the good guy fantasy: kicking in some scumbag's door and hauling his murdering ass off to face justice." He made it sound like a joke. But it really wasn't.

"Is it dangerous?"

"Naw. Police will have cleared the house before I go in. There's no assurance he'll even be home. I'm not sure why Goddard wants me there--we have a top-notch police force and the CSI guys are impeccable."

"He's the one who's scared. He wants you there as insurance, to make sure everything goes right. You're there to ensure his campaign doesn't get dirt on it. That's what I think, anyway," she said.

"Yeah, but you love me," he laughed. "You do, don't you?"

"I do." She seemed to know he needed to be reassured. But as always, he sensed a hesitation. He knew he loved her more than she loved him; it made him work that much harder.

"Remember when you asked me about Ellen?"

"Yes." He could hear an uncertain tone in her voice.

"I was wondering what happened with your marriage." He turned toward her, resting his elbow on the pillow and looking into her face.

She smiled and settled deep into the pillows. "Unvarnished truth?"

He laughed, remembering he'd asked that. "Yes."

"Carl and I were married right out high school. We went to college together as a couple. After school, he went to work for my father at the wineries. He cheated on me. I couldn't reconcile that with what I wanted out of life. He just couldn't keep his hands off other women. I'd heard the rumors during high school and college, but I didn't want to believe them. Maybe I thought once we were married he'd stop. Then, I thought when we had a baby he'd stop--but when we lost the baby, I knew he'd never stop. My father was furious. When he became ill, he hired the divorce lawyer to enforce the pre-nup. He said he wasn't going to have the family ruined by a philandering man."

"Did you love him?" Tim hoped she'd say no. But she *had* married him, after all.

"Sure. In high school I was head over heels, less so in college. And later, when I found out he was cheating--I became indifferent to him. I threw myself into the horses--*they* were my happy times. When Dad died, he left me to run the businesses. It was logical: my sisters were married and had families. Even if I married again, I wasn't going to have children. So, it was the ranch and the wineries for me. And now there's you."

"Happy?"

"With you, yes. I don't much care for this Gary Warden stuff. But you, I love."

"We'll get him. Tomorrow. We're going to get him," Tim said, full of confidence. "He's going to get the 4:30 am surprise of his life." He traced the curve of her cheek with the back of his fingers. He loved her, he had to make life safe for her.

Dani kissed him and he couldn't think. His body made all the decisions for him.

SEVENTY

Scott tossed Tim a bulletproof vest. "Put it on. Take one of the metal plates and stick in it the pocket over your heart," Scott directed. Tim complied. "Do you carry?"

"Yes. But no guns allowed in the courthouse," Tim answered. He had a concealed carry permit. Goddard insisted on it and wanted them to carry on their off-hours, too.

"What about after hours?"

"Sometimes."

"Start carrying all the time!" Scott scolded him with a withering glance. Tim knew how to handle firearms. He and Scott had learned at an early age from Tim's father. He was an avid hunter, but Tim had never taken up the sport. There was no need: his dad and brothers kept him supplied with all the meat he could use and then some. He'd tramped around in the woods with them from time to time in season, but never filled his tag.

He and Scott honed their pistol skills about once a month at the police range. Tim was a good shot, but never expected he'd need to use a gun in real life.

"You're basically an observer until we clear the premises. We'll go in, serve the warrant, and arrest Warden. But Goddard wants you there, so you need to be there. And if you need to be there you need to be armed." Scott started to remove his backup pistol from a holster strapped to his calf. Tim lifted his vest so Scott could see the pistol holstered at his hip. He nodded his approval.

The warrant team was dressed in full black body armor, with POLICE emblazoned in bright gold across their backs. His vest was the same, but he still felt out of place. He was a member of this team, but he'd never played this position before. They were prepared for the worst case and that had adrenaline pumping through his system. Warden had nothing to lose if he decided to fight them. Arrested, he was going to prison for the rest of his miserable life without any possibility of parole. Tim intended to see to it he was charged with at least four counts of first-degree murder and one count of attempted murder for Katrina, no matter how she said she felt about him. If California wanted in, there would be other charges. Tim couldn't wait to see Warden's face when Scott read him his rights.

Outside the station the sky was still pitch black. There was a chill on the air that announced the change in the seasons. The sodium streetlights cast a strange orange glow across the dark pavement. Scott pulled the team together. He was their commander and they were willing soldiers in the war against crime. They were the thin line between a civil society and chaos. Tim was amazed at their courage and sacrifice. Most of the guys with him today were married with families, willing to risk their lives for people they didn't even know. Tim was part of law enforcement, but his part played out from the safety of the courtroom. Goddard was surely teaching him a crucial lesson before he started in major crimes: the policeman's perspective would be important when he argued his cases in court from now on.

Scott assigned his detectives their parts in the raid. There were two entry teams; one would take the front door and the other the back. The third and fourth teams would secure the perimeter, in case Warden tried to flee from a window. They were going to hit hard, hit fast, arrest Warden, and clear the premises. Then the CSI team would go through the house, photograph the scene, and gather and catalogue every shred of evidence they could find. Tim was ready. He knew Scott was. Time to go.

"I don't want to just be an observer," Tim said to Scott as they entered the SWAT van. Scott grinned at him.

"All right, stick right behind me," Scott said. Tim remembered their teamwork from football. The van lurched forward and everyone was ready. They shared encouraging glances, hearts racing, but no words. Tim was riding down the road with a van full of adrenaline junkies, danger revving their senses to high alert.

The van pulled silently to a stop. Scott gave hand signals, and the men cautiously began to take up their positions.

"Right behind me," Scott ordered Tim. "We're front door entry." He nodded. They quietly headed for the door. Scott pulled his pistol and Tim did the same. The entry team set up and quickly brought in the battering ram. With force behind it, the small ram could take a door right off its hinges.

It was time. Scott fingered: *one, two, three*--and they hit the door. Splinters from the frame shattered and smashed to the entryway floor as men dressed in black poured through the open door. Tim heard the back door slam open against the kitchen wall as the rear entry team hit it.

"Seattle police with a warrant!" someone shouted.

And then the bark of, "Clear!" as they completed the room-by-room searches.

After what seemed like only seconds, Tim watched Scott holster his weapon. He cleared his own and slipped it into his holster.

"Warden isn't here," Scott grimaced. "I didn't really expect he would be." He motioned for CSI to enter. Tim was amazed at their efficiency. Entry team out, crime scene in.

"Hey, Tim," Scott said, getting Tim's attention. Tim walked over to where he stood. "This is Sheridan. The computer guy who helped you out with those photos."

"Oh, yeah--Sheridan. Thanks, man." Tim shook his hand. Sheridan was a small man, thin and slightly stoop-shouldered. His black eyes were alive with intelligence. Tim admired his skill. He used the computer every day, but he didn't know the secret world of how it really worked. Sometimes Tim was awed by the realization that everything, even what seemed to be solid matter, was all made up of tiny particles of energy.

"Looks like the computer's in here. Sheridan is going to take it down, set it back up at the station. He'll go through the whole thing and see what we can find." Scott was in his element. Just like the quarterback in high school ball, he was calling all the plays.

Tim felt like a fish out of water. He stood in the middle of Warden's white-walled living room, while what seemed like hundreds of police officers, crime scene techs, and detectives swarmed around him like bees. He'd been asked to go to scenes before, but it was always long after the police had done their part. He was used to receiving his evidence neatly packaged in a report after it had been poked, prodded, scanned, and viewed under a microscope. Now, though Goddard wanted him here, he felt he was just in the way. A crime scene tech walked by with a big box he'd gathered and taken from Warden's bedroom. Tim stepped aside, but the tech brushed against the wall in the living room. Tim needed to get out of their way. Even with the surgical gloves Scott had given him, he was worried he'd contaminate something. He moved tight to the wall, but as he did, he noticed a small corner of wallpaper was slightly detached next to the molding. He bent down and looked at it. To his surprise, it was reinforced, as though it were a tab.

"Scott, come look at this!" he called out. Scott appeared at his side. "What do you think Warden is hiding behind there?" He adjusted the surgical gloves that were now making his hands sweat.

Scott grinned at him. "You'd make a good detective after all," he chuckled. He motioned for the photographer. Tim watched as Scott carefully lifted the tab. Underneath there was a cutaway in the dry wall. He allowed the photographer to document the location on the wall, the tab, and the hole with pictures. The flash from the camera revealed a small, ornate gold box with a hinged lid hidden inside.

"You found it, want to open it?" Scott asked, looking up at Tim.

Tim slowly shook his head. "I don't do this part. Best leave this for the professionals; I don't want to be the jerk that screws up the evidence and lets this scumbag go free."

Carefully, making certain to leave intact any prints that might exist on the box, Scott lifted the lid. Tim knew serials kept trophies and sometimes they were gruesome, disgusting reminders of the murder. But instead, glittering in the lamplight was only one shiny brass door key. Tim felt a chill across his shoulders. He grabbed his keys out of his pocket. It was the same Schlage brand as the key to Dani's house. His stomach tightened. Scott straightened, holding the key up to the light. He clearly saw the keys in Tim's hand. Without a word, he took the key and held the teeth against the one to Dani's door. No match. Tim sighed with relief.

"When I first started to suspect Warden was our guy, I followed him to an apartment building at Second and James. I'm betting this opens the door to an apartment there," Scott said.

"Second and James? You mean the apartments above Jake's, across from Dani's building?" Tim asked but it was more a statement. "Damn it, Scott! Dani and Kathy are right across the street!"

Scott gave Tim a half-smile. "The very one." He didn't seem concerned.

"Let's go," Tim was emphatic. "He's there!"

Scott motioned to two SWAT officers. "We have another lead. You're coming with us."

Anna was just outside, parking the squad car. She'd come to the scene with CSI. Scott said she was a wizard at uncovering evidence, but she hadn't been part of the entry team. Tim suspected that was Scott's doing--after all, Anna had two little ones at home. And besides, the full body armor worn by the team weighed about as much as she did.

They raced back to town. Scott drove and Anna called in their plan. Two squad cars and another CSI team were ready. She called the apartment building management to confirm that Warden was a tenant and learn which unit he rented. As it turned out, Warden rented a one-bedroom facing James Street. Scott cut the siren as they approached the apartment building. If Warden was hiding there, surprise would work in their favor. They pulled up and parked a short distance away. Scott motioned for two officers to watch the alley and fire escape; Tim and Anna had become his entry team.

Carefully, they mounted the stairs in the dimly lit hallway. They found Warden's apartment. Scott motioned to Anna and Tim stand to the side. He and Anna drew their pistols and Tim did the same. Scott quietly tried the key. When he turned it, the door latch clicked and easily opened. They cautiously entered.

Inside, the apartment was strange. Eerie. In the center of the main room there was only one piece of furniture: a wooden chair set in front of a camera mounted on a tripod. A powerful telephoto lens jutted toward the open window. The sheer curtains at the window fluttered and billowed in the breeze. Separated from the main room by a white counter topped with a wooden butcher block was a small, neat kitchen. It was an old building, but immaculately clean. The hardwood floors were polished to a wet gleam. Still, they creaked underfoot. The place smelled empty; no one lived here. No one slept here. No one cooked here.

Down the short hallway were three doors. The first revealed a small coat closet with shelves to one side for linens. Empty. The next door was to a bathroom, also clear. They gathered in front of the third door. Scott motioned for Tim to stand to the side. He turned the knob and kicked the door open, ducking away in case someone was inside, ready to fire a weapon. Like the other rooms, it was empty.

Tim flipped the switch and bathed the room in pale light from the sconces along the wall. In amazement, he turned in a slow circle. The walls were covered, but not with wallpaper--instead there were hundreds, maybe thousands of pictures pinned to corkboard sheets pushed up against the drywall. Pictures of Dani. In several he appeared with her. Tim was flooded with memories. In one Dani laughed as he carried her in his arms across a huge puddle of water spreading halfway across a rain-soaked street. In another he twirled Dani, her skirts flowing up around her legs; it had been the night of the symphony and the night they first kissed. There were photos of Dani and him holding hands as they strolled along the waterfront. The next photo sent a chill like an icy finger down his spine. He and Dani sipped wine on the balcony off his apartment bedroom, watching a summer sunset. *Warden knows where I live!* Warden shared moments with them he was never meant to see, never meant to share. Every picture of Tim had been vandalized: his face was crossed out with black marker or mutilated as if sliced with a knife or razor.

"What the fuck?" Tim knew his mouth was gaping wide open in surprise and anguish.

"Wow!" Scott set a reassuring hand on his shoulder.

Warden was obsessed, a feeling Tim clearly understood. But his adoration would end in marriage, Warden's in murder. Dani was in more danger than he had ever imagined. Warden was stalking her, following her, wanting ... Tim couldn't let his mind go any further. He swiped his hand along his jaw, fighting back anger. At that moment, he made a resolution: he was going to catch this piece of garbage.

"Look what I found." Anna danced a cha-cha into the room, shaking two amber prescription bottles she'd placed in a plastic bag so the pills made a rhythmic rattle like maracas. "Oh. My. God," she said, making a slow turn round. "Hey, is that you, McAndrews?" She leaned forward, staring at a defaced picture. "Yikes!"

"Yeah," he grimaced, apprehension simmering beneath the surface. He grabbed his cell phone and pressed Dani's number. When she answered sleepily, he felt reassured. "Are you okay? Don't go anywhere. Stay put." He nodded as she answered in the affirmative. "Okay. Gotta go ... me, too." He disengaged.

"Now, *this* is creepy stuff. Doesn't much like you," Anna said.

"Understatement. But, you found?" he asked.

"Norpramin." She shook the bottles again. "Brand name for desipramine. Five full prescription bottles made out to one Lily Johansson."

"Wife number one," Scott said, nodding his head. "CSI here?"

"Busy as little beavers out in the front room as we speak," Anna answered.

"Send them in to get pictures of all this—crap," Tim directed, regaining his composure.

"Take it all. Tell them to carefully number the pictures; we'll reconstruct it down at the station," Scott directed.

Once again Tim turned around, taking it all in.

"Come on. CSI will take care of this," Scott said. They walked back into the living area.

"Is Dani still at the penthouse?" Scott asked. "I'm going to add two more officers."

Tim nodded. "Yes, and thanks."

"At least we know she's safe." Scott strolled over to the camera, sat down in the chair, and looked through. He sat back, scraping the chair noisily against the floor. "Oh-kay. You'd better look."

Dread and anger mixed in Tim's mind. He already knew what he was going to find. He looked through the lens. The camera was positioned so that Warden could watch Dani while she worked. Tim moved the camera and scanned up the side of the building. At least the apartment was too low and there was no view of the penthouse from here. It should've been reassuring; it wasn't.

"There's an APB out on Warden. We'll get him," Scott comforted, opening the drawers in the small kitchen one by one. "We've beefed up foot and bike patrols. I've put a uniformed officer at each entrance to her building."

"I know." Tim let a half smile tick up.

"Well, well, well, lookie here," Scott retrieved a switchblade from one of the drawers and held it between the very tips of his gloved thumb and forefinger. He left it closed and dropped it into an evidence bag.

Briefly, Tim wondered if he should send Dani to the ranch. Surely she'd be safer there than here in the city. He walked back to the bedroom and studied the pictures once more. There weren't any pictures of the ranch. He knew it could easily be found on the internet: and as obsessed as Warden was, he surely knew where the ranch was located. But how could Tim protect her if she were so far away from him? And where was Warden? They had found his house, his apartment, his car. He would never have left the desipramine had he had time to pack up. He was here. In Seattle. Hiding now--but when darkness fell across the city, would he be out stalking the streets?

SEVENTY-ONE

Warden slipped in through the thick plastic covering the open walls of the building under construction on Union Street. The sidewalk was cordoned off, and only workmen were allowed on the premises. Now it was evening, he had the whole first floor to himself.

Last night, he had made a place for himself in the centermost offices being built. Work crews had left a space heater there to keep it dry and he found working plumbing. He needed sleep. But his mind wouldn't let him. He was still free, at least. He wasn't sure how he'd accomplished that, except that the cops were stupid. At lunch yesterday, when he'd run from the police, he'd lost them in the crowd by turning his reversible jacket inside out. The police looked for a man in a blue jacket; he'd reversed it to green. He'd slipped up the alleys until he'd come to Union. There he'd almost run smack into a patrol car. Ducking under the scaffolding on the closed sidewalk, he'd found a hard hat left unattended by the construction crew. He grabbed it up and slid through the plastic barrier to a secluded part of the building. He'd waited there until well after dark. He had to get home. Salvage what he could, pack it up, and move on.

The detective had been ruthlessly clever: there wasn't even a word in the paper or in the news. He'd assumed they still hadn't connected the chain of murders. Obviously he was wrong. He wondered what they had that implicated him. Or was it McAndrews? Was he the competitor he'd not counted on? His hatred for McAndrews was seething and was ready to boil over.

Cautiously, this morning while it was still dark, he'd left the building. He took the least traveled streets and alleyways and made his way the thirty blocks to the head of his street. Once there, he stopped in horror as he discovered his house was under full assault by the police. He'd watched from his hiding place in his neighbor's hedgerow until he saw them carry out his computer and his escape bag. He knew then that he had to get to the James Street apartment. He wondered if they would find the key. He couldn't worry about that now; at James Street there was another escape bag, Lily's magic pills, and the knife he'd used to kill the prostitute and the gay boy. He fled. He could almost hear the clock ticking in his ears. He felt adrenaline flooding his system and his heart begin to race. He started back the way he'd come. James Street was a hike from here. He pulled up his hood and began his trek.

To his amazement, he arrived at James Street just as the CSI van pulled up. He watched from the street as the lights came on in his apartment. He panicked. His plans were defeated. It seemed wherever he turned a police officer on a bike or a foot patrol appeared, and his latest decision--where to go, where to hide--had to be scrapped and a new plan made.

He was pursued but not caught. He had to make his way back to the building on Union Street. Ducking through alleyways, always wary, he slipped down Second Avenue. He had to get to his hideaway and escape the city. He needed money. They'd be watching his bank. He snuck past the closed sidewalk, mindful of the police. He slipped under the plastic barrier and into the building. He sat down in a corner near the heater to think. Where did he go wrong? He had been so careful. He knew they would never match his fingerprints to those the fire department had asked for. He'd worn gloves, meticulously wiped each place he'd been, except his own home where his prints would be expected. He'd been vigilant about fiber.

Letting his mind wander back, back through the women, he closed his eyes. He really had loved each one. He relished watching his shadow fall across their skin, blocking the light from the hallway. He loved how their expressions melted from shyness to desire. Knowing the alcohol and Norpramin would soon flow with each heartbeat thrilled him. As if he were in the moment, he remembered their faces, one morphing into another. He recalled their desperate features relaxing when they realized he was the medic transporting them to the hospital when the heart fluttered wildly rather than beat. They trusted him. He was more than a paramedic--he was their lover. He remembered reassuring each one. He was there to help. And he let them slip slowly, painlessly, into his underworld and eternal sleep. Amber, though, had wanted to live. She'd grasped his hand at the last. Her blue eyes pleading for him to help her though she could no longer speak. He could've. Instead, he pretended to help, until she was past saving. When she passed on, he took her necklace. He'd never done that before. But Amber had touched him somehow.

Clearly, McAndrews was the one calculation he'd failed to make. Warden sat on the concrete floor, letting the warmth from the glowing coils of the electric heater chase the early morning chill from his body. He wondered, if he killed McAndrews, would it stop this spiraling chaos? He imagined pressing the blade of his switch blade into his throat, feeling the smooth slice and smelling the coppery scent of blood. He imagined the red, pooling and mixing with rain, and cascading in a pink-tinged waterfall from the sidewalk, over curb, and into the storm drain, like the gay boy's had done. Seeing Tim dead warmed him better than the heater. He already knew he'd lost his chance with Daniela St. Clair. Eliminating McAndrews wouldn't bring that back--or would it? He had to move on. If he stayed any longer he risked being caught. Tomorrow he'd have to venture out in the daylight. He'd get to his safety deposit box, fill his pockets with the cash he'd taken from Amber, and the credit cards he'd acquired in a new version of his name. He'd buy a train ticket to anyplace—anywhere, just so long as it was far away from Seattle.

SEVENTY-TWO

Tim stood in the conference room in the district attorney's offices, studying the pictures they'd pulled off Warden's walls and laid out on the table. CSI would reconstruct them as Warden had displayed them on the apartment walls and would search for any leads they could find in the collage. CSI kept several photos for analysis. They would fume for fingerprints and swab for DNA to match against the evidence they already had. They would irrefutably link Warden to all the murders.

Tim had developed a theory: Warden found Dani two years ago, while he was married to Angelina Caro, probably at a wine gala like the one last week. After talking to Angelina's parents, Tim surmised Warden realized he wasn't going to land in the clover he'd expected when he married her. Angelina's parents insisted on a prenuptial agreement, so he'd turned his attention toward a woman who had no parents to interfere. A vulnerable, lonely heiress was a perfect victim. That Dani was beautiful had to be a bonus. If he was going to have to marry for money, she might as well be someone he enjoyed looking at, at least for a little while. Warden killed Angelina, but not for money. He killed her because she'd become inconvenient. He was ready to move on to a bigger prize. So good-bye, Angelina. So long. Poof, you're dead.

Warden hadn't counted on Kathy. Alcohol and antidepressants were a favorite mix for suicide. The two California medical examiners hadn't even considered murder. But ever-curious, ever-scientific Kathy dug deeper. Warden hadn't counted on tenacious, observant Scott identifying a victim's necklace after seeing it only once in a photograph. And he hadn't counted on Tim stumbling into this steaming pile by falling in love with a lovely girl dancing down the steps at the James Street parking garage. Tim knew Warden had committed at least six murders, but he wondered: *what was the real body count? How many young women had he killed with his potion?* Unless they could get Warden to confess, they would probably never know.

"What the hell is a fucking serial killer doing with photos of one of my prosecutors on his computer?!" Tim heard Goddard long before he saw him charge into the conference room. Tim knew when he saw all the pictures in that windowless room, his hopes of being lead prosecutor on this case would disappear. He was compromised. A clever move on Warden's part--the defense could assert that it was all a set-up and the two men were merely

259

rivals for the same woman. He'd already imagined the defense's arguments in his mind. No jury in the world would believe that line of reasoning. Not with all the forensic evidence they had. But Goddard would do whatever the hell he needed to do to make sure the defense had no chance to use it.

"McAndrews?"

Tim looked up at Goddard. "Sir." Tim acknowledged. The older man stared down at the photographs.

"I just got back from the police station. There are pictures of you all over Warden's computer. Goddard yanked out a chair, spun it around, and sat across from Tim.

"Yes, he's obsessed with Miss St. Clair," Tim answered.

"And you?" Goddard was angry. Bad news.

"Obsessed with me? No. Dani--Miss St. Clair--and I are engaged. I'm with her, so I'm in the pictures."

Goddard lifted both eyebrows in surprise. "Engaged? Well, congratulations!" Goddard stood. "You know this disqualifies you from prosecuting Warden when we get him?"

Tim felt the muscles in his jaw tighten. He had known this was coming the moment he'd entered the room wallpapered with pictures of Dani. "I suspected. Defense could say I manufactured the case to get rid of a rival."

"Did you?" Goddard asked, staring into Tim's face before pressing his large hands onto the table and leaning forward as if to review each photo.

"No."

"I know you would never do that, but I wouldn't put any man in the position where there could be an accusation of impropriety or where the temptation would be so great. Hell, he was after you and your girl--you understand?"

"I do." Tim nodded. "It's the right thing to do. I'd still like to help prepare for court, even though I won't be able to be at the table."

"Hell, you may end up being a witness!" Goddard exclaimed, rubbing his beefy hand along his brow. "If so, you may have to take a leave of absence."

The statement hit him like he'd been run over by a bulldozer. "Sir, I can't. I have—I have to work." Tim felt his heart sink. Anxiety twisted his stomach. Dani was in love with a successful prosecutor, not an unemployed lawyer floundering around without work. He didn't even know what he'd do without a job to go to. Work was every part of him.

"I can loan you to another county for a while. Jack Reardon owes me a favor in Kittitas County. Tim, you didn't ask to be stalked by this sick fuck. But the way some of these judges are these days, always taking up for murdering scum--I can't take any chances. I could always use you on my campaign. That pays as much as you make now." Goddard's eyes sparked as if almost hoping Tim would take the offer.

Tim sank into his chair. Goddard was right. Had he been the district attorney, he'd have done the same thing. Their job was to keep murderers off the street, not give them a way out. "I'm not much into politics. Wouldn't have a clue as to what to do. I don't think I'd be much help on your campaign."

"We could always make the argument that when the police served the warrants, you discovered Warden was obsessed with Miss St. Clair. Then you could recuse yourself publicly. Voters would see you as noble."

"Make the argument? You mean, tell the truth? I had no idea he was obsessed with her!" Tim responded, surprised Goddard didn't realize that was exactly the way it happened. "And voters? I don't understand." He wasn't running for office, what the hell did he care what the voters thought?

Goddard chuckled. "Don't tell me you haven't thought about being district attorney? I always thought that's why you worked so hard. I've been grooming you to take over when I retire."

Tim's mouth dropped open. He was only twenty-eight. Had he thought about being D.A.? Sure. But for now, he was just enjoying being a good guy keeping the bad guys from harming the rest of humanity. When he thought about it, he really enjoyed convincing a jury that a perp deserved to be removed from society and put behind bars.

"You think it over. You're like a son to me. You're my best and I don't want your chances for the future ruined by an accusation of impropriety."

Tim nodded. "I'll think about it." He hadn't realized the extent of Goddard's esteem. The man was formidable; could Tim ever match up? Goddard stood, rounded the table, and patted Tim on the shoulder as he left.

But that didn't change the fact that not only had Warden tried to mess with Dani, he was messing with Tim's career. He shoved a chair hard against the conference table. He picked up one of the photos that slid off the table to the floor. It was the one where he'd carried Dani across the rain flooded street. He groaned. Tim was being forced into the role of spectator in the case of the decade.

SEVENTY-THREE

Warden slowly climbed the stairs in the Union Street building. He had to do something to keep his mind and body active. Most of his avenues of escape were cut off. Everywhere he looked the police were there. Even the train station. He had to think. He reached the 26th floor and pushed into a hallway. Business suites lined each side of the hallway. The workers must be entering the building from Sixth Avenue. He realized that more than half the tower building was still operating; only the ground floor was under reconstruction.

As he walked along the hallway, he tested doors to see if any were left unlocked. He turned the corner at the end of the corridor and ducked back immediately. A janitor working the floor almost saw him. An idea hit: he would follow the man into the next office he opened. He was desperate to get on a computer and find out the latest news. He and Fraser used to chat up their friends in the police department. But Warden was sure Fraser would turn him in without hesitation. And his friends in the police department were now enemies.

Staying close to the wall, he managed to peek around the corner. The janitor had left his cart bracing the door open to "Chin Chung Export and Imports." He slipped up the corridor. Carefully, he looked inside. The janitor was in a far office along the window, headphones in his ears. Warden snickered. He wouldn't hear him. Warden slipped past him, ducked into the office he'd just cleaned, and carefully, quietly closed the door behind him and twisted the lock. He realized he could kill the man, and he would never see it coming. He savored the thought. But that would give away his hiding place here in the building. There was such power in murder. Watching a person's life ebb away, a life he controlled--was tremendous.

Warden sat in the plush chair in front of the desk. He twisted back and forth, wondering what imports and exports this company handled? He would have to wait until the janitor moved on to find out. He turned the chair to look out the large window. He saw the other towers in the area and started to orient himself. There was the huge Ferris wheel outlined by its florescent lights, the ferry terminal, the St. Clair building. He stopped short; he couldn't believe his eyes. *Lights* illuminated the top floor. In all the times he'd looked at the building, he'd never seen lights on the twenty-sixth floor. *Daniela was there!* He didn't know how, but he knew it. And he knew exactly what he needed to do. He needed to get in. He started to make a plan.

SEVENTY-FOUR

It was five in the morning and still dark when Tim pulled his gray sweats over his gym shorts. He straightened, drew back the drapes to the bedroom window, and looked out over the sleeping city below. There wasn't a room in the penthouse that didn't have a spectacular view. He and Scott had decided to meet for a workout this morning. He packed his charcoal suit; a royal-blue long-sleeve shirt; and the gray, black, and royal-blue tie Dani had picked out for him into a garment bag. He would change for court at the club. He was looking forward to a tough game of racquetball. Vigorous exercise always seemed to revive him and supercharge his mind. Nobody challenged him like Scott. They were well-matched and read each other's moves so easily they often had to quit because their time was up on the court before either of them scored a point on the other. A couple of times they'd tried to join a tournament, but it always seemed work interfered.

Tim thought about Warden. Scott was making it impossible for Warden to operate at all. The police were tracking his credit cards, his bank accounts. Scott had closed off access to his house and the James Street apartment. The Seattle detectives and the FBI Behavioral Science Unit had a bead on other names he'd used from the information they'd recovered in his go-bags. Warden had a strange quirk: he always kept the same initials: G. W.--at least for now. They had put out a statewide BOLO (be on the lookout) to all police and sheriff's departments. They had officers watching the airlines, buses, train stations, ferry terminals, and rental car companies. Scott had contacted the shelters and warming centers, and had provided pictures and descriptions in case Warden turned up needing help. With some relish, Tim wondered if Warden liked his new life on the streets. It was only a matter of time; they would get him.

All the same, Tim was pissed off that Warden had made him a vagabond, living out of a suitcase. After seeing the pictures on the wall and the other files on Warden's computer, he and Dani weren't safe at her house on the outskirts of the city, and they weren't safe at his loft. And each day as he left the penthouse, he worried he would give their safe place away.

Dani brought him a cup of coffee and sat on the bed watching him pack. He could see her reflection in the dresser mirror as he pulled on his sweatshirt. Even in her fuzzy robe, without makeup, she was stunning.

What he loved most, though, was the expression on her face. Sometimes she made him believe she loved him as much as he loved her. Other times there was a hint of hesitation, a holding back he had to acknowledge. He turned, walked to her, took the cup of coffee she'd brought him, and kissed her cheek. He took a sip and continued to get ready to go. He ran his hand over the scruff of a beard he'd grown overnight. He'd shave later; he had a full kit at the club that he left in his locker. He picked up the belt he intended to wear and added a small conceal carry holster to it. He retrieved his Walther PK 380 from the bottom of his suitcase. He'd chosen the Walther for its concealable size and ease of use. The clip had plenty of rounds for personal defense and chambering a bullet was easy: one smooth pull and you were good to go. He slipped the seven-round clip in the handle of the gun until it clicked in place. He checked the safety. When he looked at Dani, her expression had changed. Her full, kissable lips were softly parted and her brow was creased with worry. He didn't usually wear his pistol until he got to the office. And now Dani's face said it all. He'd been asking her to trust the police but it was obvious he didn't.

"You look so handsome. Do I have to let you go?" She tried a laugh, but he could still see the apprehension in her blue eyes.

"You aren't going to say anything about the gun?" *Might as well get it out there and over with*, he thought.

"Okay, sure. Adds an air of daring to your whole gorgeous mix. How's that?" She teased, but it wasn't working. She was worried.

"That's it? No nagging?"

She sighed and concern creased her brow. "The pistol is a new, unhappy addition. I liked it better when you didn't feel you needed it. I am assuming Warden's far more dangerous than you've let on. I deserve to know; don't you think?"

He walked over to her, took her coffee cup out of her hands and set it on the bedside table. He sat down beside her. "Dani, do you trust me?"

"Yes," she whispered. "Tell me. I'm not a child and I need to know."

Tim took hold of her hand. "Warden had a room wallpapered with pictures of you. I was in some of them, and my face was either blacked out with a marker or sliced up with a razor or a knife. Both Scott and I believe Warden would kill me to get to you."

She closed her eyes and let out a tiny whimper.

"Scott has posted police officers at both entrances to your building, in addition to your own building security. There are extra patrols in the area. Everyone in the police department is looking for Warden. Getting him off the street is our number-one priority. Scott's partner Anna will be staying with you today." He brushed the back of his fingers along her cheek.

"Don't go to work. Goddard will understand."

"The courthouse is a fortress, Dani. I'll be fine." He kissed her. As always it was delicious, exciting. He savored the rush, like letting dark chocolate slowly melt in his mouth. It would be easy to stay. He had to work, though, and forced reality to take charge.

"I'm going to the ranch," she said with resolve.

"Dani, don't go. This will be over soon. We're making it hard for Warden to stay in hiding. He'll make a mistake and Scott will have him. Trust me." Tim knew he couldn't keep her locked up. He knew the ranch and all its ex-military employees was far safer than anywhere in the city. Dani was used to her freedom and used to flying wherever she wanted to at will. He had to face reality. The real reason he didn't want her to go to the ranch was simple. "I don't want to be without you," he stated.

"I could have Mitch get the Cessna ready--we could be at the airport in an hour," she offered.

"Dani, I have to work." He watched her face. She didn't have to say anything. He guessed what she was thinking. If he wanted, he never had to work again. She could and would provide their living in a manner he would never be able to match no matter how he tried. After all, it was the family tradition. Her sisters' husbands had eased right into the life of leisure: neither worked. Tim considered it a trap. Would she ask him to be a kept man? Could he do it? Moments ticked by and the silence was excruciating. They were searching each other's eyes as if trying to decide on a compromise. Tim waited for her to pull out the irksome *if you really loved me* argument like other women had when things hadn't gone their way. She didn't.

"I understand," she conceded. It surprised him. Once again, she was unexpected. No angry pouts, no nagging. "Tim, I don't want to be without you, either."

"If you're here, I'll know where you are and that you're safe." He touched her hand. "I know I can't keep you locked up forever. Mitch and Shannon are here; why don't we all meet at McTavish's after work? Around five?"

"Okay. You'll win your case and we can all go to dinner. Then on Saturday morning we can go to the ranch; it's the weekend and we can have two whole days to not think about Warden," she presented her case.

"It's a deal!" Tim exclaimed. He still worried that Warden could find the ranch. It was advertised all over the internet. If he were Warden, he'd head for the other side of the world and quick, but if a man could murder indiscriminately rational thought wasn't part of his make-up.

"Go win your case." She squeezed his hand. "I'll take care of packing."

He shook his head. "You can't go out. Not until Warden is in custody."

"Okay. I won't go out. See you tonight." Dani was beaming. He couldn't deny her this weekend at the ranch now, even if he wanted to. He kissed her.

"Gotta go," he said, already planning to talk with Anna about how they weren't to leave the security of the penthouse. He had compromised about dinner only because Mitch would be escorting her.

It had been a long time since Scott and Tim played such a ripping good racquetball game. They usually were too busy and ended up playing with other partners to keep their skills honed. Tim enjoyed the challenge. This morning Scott was just slightly off his game and Tim beat him handily. They'd long ago made the deal that the winner would buy breakfast.

"Jake's okay?" Tim asked, slipping his arms into his clean blue shirt.

"I guess." Scott was less than enthused and scowled at him as he pressed the Velcro straps closed on the body armor he wore over his shirt.

"Not the best, but I'm due in court in two hours and I want to do a quick review before we start the case. It's one of your favs: Racie James," Tim informed him with a grin. He knew Scott would be annoyed. He'd arrested Racie about six times for some petty crime or another over the last couple of years. Racie would go to jail, get out, and pull another robbery, having learned absolutely nothing.

"Put him away for good this time, will you?" Scott scolded. "At least I won't have to deal with his thieving ass now that I'm in homicide."

"I'll do my best, but it's up to the jury," Tim laughed.

After they both finished dressing, they walked to Jake's and ordered coffee and breakfast sandwiches. They took a seat by the window and watched darkness melt into a gray morning. Tim sat deep in his chair, remembering how he'd often sat in this very spot, waiting for Dani to come down the James Street garage stairs.

Across James, walking briskly along the sidewalk, Tim noticed a man in a black hoodie. In this weather, a hoodie was standard gear. But his gait, the way he swung his arms as he moved, put Tim's senses on high alert. He said nothing but Scott followed his gaze.

"Warden!" They both said in unison.

Scott immediately picked up his radio and called it in. Tim noticed a big smile spreading across Scott's face. "The race is on, buddy!" He pointed to one exit. Tim acknowledged him and took the other. Scott would approach Warden head on and Tim would cut off his escape to the rear. Hopefully patrol officers would arrive just as they were prepared to take Warden down on the sidewalk in front of Jake's.

"Hey, Gary--Gary Warden, right? That's you, isn't it?" Scott said, smiling big as if he were greeting a long-lost friend. Warden returned the grin, but it quickly collapsed. Tim thought he was going to take the bait and let Scott in close enough to arrest him, but he turned--and when he spotted Tim, he panicked and dashed into oncoming traffic on James Street. Tim flinched as a car clipped Warden. The street was suddenly filled with the noise of squealing tires, honking horns, and the smell of burnt rubber. Warden managed to roll off the hood of the car like a Hollywood stuntman, barely missing a stride. He'd succeeded in momentarily stopping traffic; Tim and Scott took advantage and sprinted after him. Warden dashed up Third Avenue, weaving through pedestrians, knocking them roughly out of the way, creating a clear path for his pursuers to gain on him. Warden turned right on Columbia. Tim saw it was a mistake. Warden tried to backtrack, but realized he was blocked. Tim was less than fifteen yards behind him and squared his body for a tackle. Once again Warden zipped into traffic, dodging cars like a running back. Tim was amazed he managed to get through unscathed, but kept the pressure on. Scott reported each of Warden's moves on the radio. *Cops had to be closing in all around*, Tim thought. He kept Warden in sight on the other side of the street and noted his desperation. Warden tried to open the doors of businesses along Second Avenue, but it was too early. They were all still closed and locked tight. With each try, he lost some of the distance. Tim poured on the speed, finally closing within yards of Warden as he turned right up Union. When Tim reached the corner, Warden was gone, as if he'd vanished. Tim stopped. Slowly, he spun in a circle, letting his mind absorb every movement, watching every passerby. Patrol cars appeared in the intersections.

"Damn! I lost him!" Tim yelled as Scott caught up, bending forward to catch his wind. Tim kept repeating, "Damn it! Damn it!" Both he and Scott began measured turns, searching faces, examining doorways, looking in shop windows. Tim saw it; the plastic covering on the building on Union under construction was undulating as if a breeze had hit it.

"There!" he pointed to Scott. He worked his way under the plastic and entered the building. Tim momentarily let his eyes adjust. Darkness and shadows merged into a flat gray light. Tim stopped and listened. In the distance, across the clear expanse, he could hear heavy footfalls clamoring up concrete stairs. He dashed off in the direction of the sound. He started up the stairs, taking them two at a time, stopping only for a few seconds to listen again. At the eighth-floor landing, the door leading to the interior of the building was only a second from closing. He grabbed it to keep it open and from locking them in the stairwell. Tim leaned against the wall, waiting for Scott to catch up to him. He rubbed his thigh muscles, which were burning from the blast up the stairs.

Tim gestured that Warden had gone through the eighth-floor door into the offices beyond.

"All right. You need to go. We'll take care of this," Scott whispered. He reached for his pistol and jerked it from the shoulder holster, smoothly releasing the safety.

Tim started to move forward but Scott blocked him. "Get out of here, man! You have no body armor, no training. If he ambushes you, you're dead. Now go." Scott motioned for two uniformed officers who had just arrived to move into place.

Tim wanted to argue, but Scott was right. He watched with envy as Scott and the two officers positioned themselves to breach the doorway. "Told you--you should've gone to the police academy with me," Scott teased. "Get out of here! Go on."

Adrenaline made Tim wish he could stay in the hunt. He waited long enough to watch Scott and the others pull the door open and charge through. Consoling himself with the knowledge that Warden was cornered and would soon be arrested, he descended the stairs. He walked out of the building, under the plastic, and strolled up Union. When he hit Fourth Avenue, Tim headed south, briskly making his way back toward the courthouse. Patrol cars suddenly raced up the street and turned broadside, blocking traffic. The officers waved him through. He watched as two K-9 units unloaded their dogs. A whole three-block area was cordoned off. Tim jogged and cleared the blockade. A crowd of spectators gathered behind the barriers. Quickly, he glanced at his watch. He'd lost track of time and was due in court in fifteen minutes. He had just enough time to make it. No matter how much he wanted to remain for the inevitable arrest, he had to take care of his part of the business of crime and punishment. He'd call Scott at recess to learn the eventual outcome of this morning's romp. But for now, he was sure Dani's ordeal was over. She'd never complained about being a prisoner in her own home, but now they would be able to resume a normal life. That made him happy.

He turned to look once more, hoping to catch a glimpse of the arrest.

Instead, he noticed Detectives O'Malley and Rodriquez emerge from the onlookers behind him. O'Malley almost ducked back into the crowd. *Odd*, Tim thought. But he assumed they'd heard something over the radio that made them pause. Tim acknowledged them with a nod and continued to the courthouse.

SEVENTY-FIVE

"Guilty," the bailiff announced the verdict. Tim couldn't keep the smile down, but he tried-- the jury might not appreciate him dancing in the end zone. He picked up his briefcase, set it on the prosecutor's table, and packed it.

"Good job, Rudolf," Tim congratulated his companion. He knew his decision to ask that Rudolf be his assistant had been the right one. The young man was a fast learner and his research was impeccable. The other ADAs were starting to call him "Tim, Jr." behind his back. Tim hoped it was a compliment, but sometimes he wasn't sure. Unfortunately, not everyone was happy: he noticed two women in the back of the courtroom--Racie's girlfriend and his mother--were wailing. *Unintended consequences.* Racie's decision to continue in his life of crime had shattered his life and theirs, too.

"You owned Don Markum. What a putz!" Rudolf said, obviously pleased with their victory.

Tim just bowed his head in agreement. Rudolf was right: the defense didn't have a chance. The evidence was complete and compelling; Tim didn't go before a jury if it wasn't. His job was to make certain a recidivist thief was out of society for at least fifteen years.

Tim couldn't wait to meet Scott. He hadn't been able to reach him at lunch recess. He looked at his watch. The jury had only taken forty-five minutes to decide the case; it was only three in the afternoon. He had time to call Scott for an update on Warden's arrest and then use these two hours to finish some work before heading to McTavish's to meet Dani. If this went the way he hoped, he would have the whole weekend to devote to her. She deserved some fun after being locked away in the penthouse all week. He was looking forward to it.

Tim closed the door to his office and called Scott once again. He didn't answer; his phone again sent him to voice mail. He left a message that he'd like to meet for a quick drink before they went their separate ways for the weekend. Tim couldn't wait to hear all about Warden's arrest and he wanted to talk about Katrina Collin's interview. He was still bothered that Scott had so easily dismissed her as a suspect. He hoped the walk to McTavish's would clear his thoughts.

As he left the building, the November cold hit him and he buttoned up his overcoat. Winter was on its way. Steel gray clouds banked to the west and darkness settled over the city and it was only 4:30. In the shops and businesses along the street, lights flickered on. Tim passed by the Alaskan Club and briskly walked up Third Avenue.

Suddenly, a shiver raced through his shoulders and he felt the hair on the back of his neck stand on end. He had the creepy feeling he was being followed. *Warden,* he thought. But that was unrealistic. There was no way Scott hadn't caught the man this morning. Still, he unbuttoned his overcoat, making certain he could reach his firearm, should he need it. If by chance Warden was still at large, he'd love nothing better than to take him out and save taxpayers the cost of a trial. To make sure it was only his overactive imagination, he ducked into a candle shop at Third and Cherry.

As the door closed behind him, the spicy mixture of scents on the air overpowered him. He pretended to shop, all the while carefully watching out the window. Two men stopped and lingered in the entryway of the Grand Mason Hotel across the street. No doubt about it--he was being followed and none too discreetly. But it wasn't Warden. They were obviously looking in the direction of the candle shop. For a second he wondered if they were detectives or private security. Was Scott having him followed? Was Dani? He shook it off. *Friend or foe?* It was time to find out.

"Do you have a back door?" he asked the clerk behind the counter.

The man stared at him, blinking. "Are you going to rob me?"

"No. Oh. No," Tim laughed. "I think I'm being followed."

"Are you a spy?" The young man engaged him in a brief stare down.

Tim offered up a big grin. "So. Do you have a back door?"

"Yes. Around there. What do I do if they come in looking for you?"

"Call the police," Tim said as he headed for the back.

"Oh, mister! They're coming! They're crossing the street!"

Tim bolted. He heard the delivery bell ring as he hit the touch bar on the back door. He ran through the opening and made a dash for McTavish's. He blasted through the big wooden double doors to the tavern, slowing only briefly to let his eyes adjust to the darkness. Scott was waiting at their regular booth.

"Oh hey, Tim. You're finally here," Scott greeted him, lifting his hand to indicate he was on a phone call.

Tim slid into the booth, forcing Scott to slide around so he could keep an eye on the door.

"Did you get Warden?" he asked, ignoring the fact that Scott was on the phone.

Scott shook his head.

"Shit!" Tim stared at his friend.

Scott put the phone down. "He vanished. Fucker just vanished. K-9 had his trail for a while, lost him in the underground. I've got to finish this call."

"Are you having me followed?" Tim demanded, anyway.

"Uh, nope. Why would I do that?" Scott evaded his gaze. They were too close to not know when one of them was lying. Tim narrowed his eyes.

"Why? Why are you having me followed?" he asked.

"Call you back." Scott disengaged the call and shot Tim an annoyed glance.

"Why?"

Scott glared at him, then ran his hand over his mustache.

"Are you tailing me?" Tim pressed, gesturing with an open palm it was time for Scott to explain.

"Okay, it's Branson Holt," Scott confessed.

"Branson Holt?"

"You know. *Seattle News at 6:00*." Scott took a sip of his beer, peering over the rim of the mug as if he hoped Tim would be satisfied.

"And you know that how?"

"Because O'Malley, the detective who *is* tailing you, just called and told me you lost Holt and his cameraman by ducking out the back door of the candle shop on Third and Cherry."

Tim looked Scott square in the eyes. "Why am I being followed--by O'Malley?" He suspected his friend would evade the answer if he didn't clarify the question.

"Goddard. After he saw the pictures on Warden's computer and from the apartment walls, he wanted you to have help if you needed it. Hell, I knew you'd never agree. So, I assigned an inconspicuous security detail."

Tim tapped his fingers on the table. "Inconspicuous? O'Malley?" Tim remembered him from the morning, trying to duck back into the crowd when Tim had inadvertently made him. "You assigned O'Malley to be inconspicuous! That's rich. The man's as big as a house!" Tim noticed bar patrons were glancing his way and realized he was talking too loud.

"O'Malley *and* Rodriquez, but who's counting?" Scott grinned. "As for Holt, apparently, he was trying to get the scoop on the Alan Sharp hate-crime case. Some shmuck from your office leaked that you might be the lead prosecutor."

Tim squinted at his friend. He wondered who would leak that information. His mind sprinted through the list of usual leakers, but landed square on the boss. *Goddard*. If they had a lead prosecutor assigned, the media would assume they had more information on the case than they did.

Goddard could shift the heat off himself and his campaign and onto Tim. He knew he had the reputation with the press of being a stone wall. Tim didn't believe in trying cases in the media. When cornered, he'd be forced to say, "No comment." It would be better politically coming from Tim than Goddard.

"I don't need your damn tail." Tim shook his head.

"Don't you? Holt has been following you all day."

"Good, then he's reported on my guilty verdict this afternoon," Tim laughed, covering the fact that he hadn't noticed Holt. He was embarrassed he hadn't been more aware.

"And you never made O'Malley and Rodriquez. They've been on you for two days. Hell, Warden could be here right now and you'd never know it," Scott joked.

"I made them this morning. I just didn't realize it," Tim commented.

"I heard." Scott chuckled and motioned to the waitress. When she looked his way, he lifted two fingers. Scott peeled off his tweed suitcoat and carefully laid it across the back of the booth. His shirt was pressed, a side effect of his engagement with Kathy. His blue eyes showed fatigue from lost sleep despite his jolly front. Tim chuckled inside when he thought about how happy his friends were.

Tim looked up as the waitress brought him a beer and a whiskey shot. "Thanks, Lindy." He smiled at her and he turned his attention back to Scott. "So, you really cleared Katrina Collins?"

"Is that still eating you?" Scott tossed his head back and laughed. "No. All that was a ruse. I wanted *her* to believe I'd cleared her. I assigned Durkans and Reid to see where she led. And you'll never guess where- -William Robert Fraser's house, that's where. Funny thing, she told me she had no idea where he lived. But she drove right there after we released her."

Tim sipped his whiskey, swallowed, and said, "She's a lying skank."

"But damn, there's no physical evidence to link either her or Bill Fraser to the murders. At this point, all we could charge her with is receiving stolen goods. And that can be easily explained away. Hell, your lover gives you a present, how do you know if he bought it or murdered someone to get it for you?"

"She's in it." Tim was emphatic.

"I don't know, but it is getting interesting. Very interesting, indeed."

"What does Kathy think?"

"Ask her yourself, she should be here in a few minutes."

Tim looked at his watch. "Dani should be here soon, too."

"Dani? You invited Dani? You aren't letting her come by herself, are you?"

"No. Her pilot and his wife are bringing her."

"I don't like it. Dangerous." Scott frowned and ran a finger over his dark mustache.

"I figure if Warden wants to walk into the local police hangout with a BOLO out on him, he should roll the dice and take his chances."

"Good point!" Scott looked around as if searching for Kathy. When he turned back, he had an expression of pure dread. "Uh-oh! Incoming." He snickered and ran his hand over his mustache.

Tim glanced up and his breath caught in his throat. Ellen Mason was approaching their table. He hadn't seen her in so long--over a year. He was surprised.

"Hi Tim," she greeted him. Ellen had a look in her eyes—predatory, like a lioness deciding if he were her next meal. She was casually dressed: blue jeans and a green tank top covered by a checkered long- sleeved shirt in a matching green and blue like Seahawks colors. Her short blonde hair had been curled so it framed her face.

"Oh hi, Ellen. How are you?" Scrambling, Tim attempted to stand, but the booth made it unwieldy and he almost spilled his beer. He sank back down, trapped. *Oh, crap!*

"Hello, Scott." Ellen gave Scott a dirty look. She had always accused Scott of being a bad influence. He was, of course--but no more than Tim had been.

"Ellen," Scott nodded a tentative greeting. She returned a scowl.

Ouch. Scott mouthed the word to Tim and shook his hand as if he'd touched something hot. Tim forced himself not to laugh. Ellen wasn't pleased. She'd always asserted that when they were together they acted like little boys; Tim supposed they did.

"I'm good, Tim and you?" Ellen smiled but all the hurt of their last month together was still there in her eyes. Tim cringed inside; he'd never meant to hurt her.

"Good, too."

She shifted her weight with uncertainty. "Nice to see you."

Tim wasn't sure this was going to be *nice*. Ellen was one of those women that seemed to like public drama. He hated it. "Yes, it's been over a year."

"That long? So, you're still with the prosecutor's office; how's that going?"

"Yes, still there. Going good. How about you? Still teaching?" Ellen hadn't changed. She was still pretty in a sweet, homemade sort of way. He was instantly reminded of his original assessment of her: Ellen deserved to be married to a nice guy who loved her. And Tim knew he was 'Mr. Wrong!'

She nodded, looked at the floor for a second, and then back into his eyes. "I see your name in the paper from time to time when you put some bad guy in prison."

"One of the perks of the job," he briefly smiled. He had never been good with encounters with girlfriends after they'd broken up. He shifted his weight uncomfortably.

She twittered nervously, then was serious. "May I sit?"

Tim started to make an excuse, "Well, we're expecting--"

"Yeah, sure. Join us," Scott interrupted--to Tim's chagrin. Without hesitation, she scooted into the booth next to Tim. "Can we get you something to drink?" Scott offered.

"A beer would be nice. Light, if they have it."

"Ah, the waitress is busy, why don't I just go get that for you," Scott volunteered. He slid along the booth and got up, chuckling to himself as he headed for the bar. He was obviously enjoying Tim's misfortune.

Tim was at a loss for words. He picked up his glass and drained the rest of his whiskey shot. He could face Ellen better if he had a little buzz. He looked toward the front door, hoping to see Dani.

"So, are you really doing okay?" She rested her elbow on the table and leaned her chin onto her hand, levelling her gaze at him.

"Good. And you?" He wondered; was she flirting? *Do I really care?* He glanced at the front door again.

"You're as handsome as ever," she purred.

He intentionally ignored the compliment and slid a few more inches away from her. Ellen uneasily twisted the ends of her hair. He remembered that she used to do that when she was going to confront him. A storm was coming, he felt it. "When the girls wanted to come here tonight, I wondered if you still did. And here you are, just like the old days."

"It's still the hangout."

She looked around as if searching for her friends, then back. "Tim, I came a little early in case you were here. I wanted to talk to you."

He was hesitant and studied her. Maybe she wanted free legal advice. He could only hope. "Okay?"

"I heard through the rumor mill at the Sevens Club that you were unattached."

"Who told you that?"

"A friend."

Tim was betting on Katrina Collins. If Ellen said her name it would confirm that she was still trying to break him and Dani up. There was some motive to that desire, he just hadn't figured it out yet.

"Who?"

"Katrina Collins, do you know her?"

Tim lifted his gaze and studied Ellen. "I know her."

Tim could see Ellen was slightly confused by his tone, but dismissed it. "I was thinking--Tim, I miss you so much. I think of you all the time and wish ..."

His expression was pained, he knew it by Ellen's sudden defensive shift in the booth. "Ellen, Ellen." He shook his head. He had to stop her. "We were miserable. You said you hated me. You never wanted to see me again, don't you remember? You were so unhappy."

"We say a lot of things we don't mean when we're angry. I wasn't *that* unhappy." She let out a small sigh and then looked at him with a wistful smile.

"You gave me the boot. Usually, that's a sure sign a girl's unhappy," he grinned, hoping it would be infectious. It wasn't.

"I never thought you'd go away for good. We'd had fights before. Come back. We could try again."

He was speechless. What Ellen was asking for was impossible, would've been impossible even if he wasn't involved with Dani. She might not have been that unhappy, but he sure had been. He needed a way out of this situation, but knew it was best to just get it all out in the open. He was going to hurt her, knew it--and couldn't do anything about it. "The rumor mill is wrong. I'm seeing someone," he said, with as much empathy as he could for the pain it would cause.

"Of course you are. I should've known you wouldn't be a single for long." She laughed, but it was false. She was covering up hurt; he'd seen it too many times before not to know it. Her shoulders dropped. "Is it that girl from Jake's Deli, the one you were cheating with before we broke up?" she sniped.

He gaped at her in disbelief. "After all this time, are you going to try to suck me into that old fight?" Tim asked.

"I'm sorry, I shouldn't have said that." Ellen quickly tried to make amends.

"You tell me. You said no strings attached. What did that mean? I thought it meant no strings attached." He knew it didn't. He knew it back then. His defense was shameful, but he was still going to use it.

"That changed."

"Don't you think both of us needed to agree to a change?"

"Are you going to go all lawyer on me? It changed when I told you I loved you."

Tim contemplated her with a frown. The day she'd said she loved him was the day he'd started to leave. "I found out the hard way. There I was, trying to be a big-time prosecutor, all full of myself, having coffee with Judge Mattison and Brad Hollingsrow. You confronted me at morning rush at Jake's. Very loudly, as I recall. You embarrassed the crap out of me." Tim chuckled. Once again, he tried to bring levity into their conversation. But her lips were tight, she wouldn't even smile. "You need to lighten up. Ellen, it was funny! Brought me down a notch--several notches, actually."

"You were cheating. You know it. You deserved it. That girl--"

"What constitutes cheating, by your rules? She was beautiful. I looked. I wasn't the only one. She had a fan club. We used to stand at the window bar facing the parking garage and watch her come down the steps, cross at the light, and disappear into the city. If we'd been construction workers rather than suits, there would've been whistles and cat calls."

"You are so gross! You talked about her?"

"Of course not," He laughed because he had to. "You do know when you yelled at me at Jake's, I'd never even spoken to her? I didn't even know her name."

"You do now, though." She tipped her head sideways as if that would make him tell the truth.

Tim smiled at her and nodded. "I do now."

"I hate you."

"See, less than a minute and I've already made you unhappy," Tim pointed out. *Dani should be here by now.* He stared ahead at the doorway.

"So, is it serious?" Ellen searched his face as if she stared hard enough, long enough she could read his mind--and maybe even change it.

"You cut me loose, Ellen." To dodge this answer would only prolong their mutual misery. "Yes. It's serious."

Ellen gasped, but recovered quickly. "Congratulations."

Tim wondered: was she considering why he was serious now, when he hadn't been serious about her? To be honest, he had no answer. He hoped she wouldn't ask. "Thanks. So, you're meeting friends?" Tim wanted to change the direction this was going in worst way. He found himself watching the tavern door and hoping Dani would come through. When she finally did, he felt relieved. The cool wind from outside tousled her hair and she brushed it away. Dani was lovely and he delighted in looking at her.

Shannon and Mitch came into the pub behind her. He noticed Ellen had followed his gaze and turned to see what had so engrossed him.

"Is that her?" Ellen turned back to him, desperation coloring her voice. "She's pretty." She looked again. "She's the one. She is! The one you were cheating with!" Ellen's voice had a sharp edge to it.

"Ellen, I wasn't with her then. I already told you."

"I don't believe you."

"Believe what you want." Tim knew it sounded cold.

"It doesn't matter to you?"

He stifled himself from saying the obvious: *How could it possibly matter, now?* He could feel his brows pinch together with incredulity. "It matters. I'd like you to think of me as a great guy. But you think I'm a rake. I got wind of all the things you said about me to your friends at The Sevens Club. Truth is, I'll never be the man you want me to be. I wasn't then, I'm not now."

"You know I didn't mean any of it." Ellen's eyes were tearing up. Dani was weaving her way through the crowd to their booth. The collision was eminent. Bad was just about to get worse--he had to do something. Suddenly, Scott intervened. Tim watched as he slipped his arm around Dani's shoulders and guided her to the bar, where he introduced Shannon and Mitch to Kathy. Scott said something to Dani and she looked over at Tim. *Sorry,* she mouthed sympathetically.

"Listen, Ellen. My fiancée is here."

"You're getting married?" Ellen squared her body, shocked.

"Yes."

"She doesn't know about me, does she?" Ellen's face was full of hate.

"She knows about you." He stared hard, felt annoyance rising up. She noticed and was pushing for a fight.

"I could tell her a thing or two."

"I'd appreciated it if you kept things civil."

"Or?"

"We say good-bye. You meet your friends. I meet mine." Ellen stared at him and wouldn't budge from the booth.

"Does she know you cheat?"

He glared at her, biting back the harsh things he was tempted to say. "I'm not going to fight with you, Ellen. Go meet your friends."

"Can we get together later? Talk?"

"I think its best we just put an end to this now, don't you?"

"You never loved me."

"If we'd loved each other, we'd be together, now."

"God, you are so brutal. I loved you. I still do." Her voice trailed away.

"Please, Ellen; I told you I'm sorry for what happened between us. I hate these fights."

"You liked making up, though."

Tim chuckled. Ellen had just used trick number 92 from Scott Renton's guide to surviving an encounter with an ex: She'll bring up sex. Women know men can't resist when reminded of sex.

"Did I?" He instantly wanted to take it back. His tone was cruel and he hadn't wanted to be mean. But at best, their lovemaking had been unremarkable and completely forgettable.

"You haven't changed. You're still a jerk!" Ellen raised her voice.

"No contest," Tim acknowledged his agreement by lifting both hands in surrender.

"I hate you!"

"So, you said. More than once. I think we're done here, don't you?" He slid along the booth to get away from her. She reached for him and touched his arm. "What do you want from me, Ellen?"

"I want you back," she whispered.

For a few moments he stared at her, wishing she wasn't going to force him to be harsh. But her expression was clear. There was not going to be any way out other than straight through. "Ellen, I'm trying to be as diplomatic as I can be. We don't want the same thing," he said softly, inwardly cringing, knowing he was going to hurt her. "You're a sweet girl, a pretty girl. But I'm involved with someone and we're getting married."

"I hate you." She stood but lingered beside the table, glaring at him.

"I know," he said.

She wheeled around in a huff and headed for the bar. Tim held back. He'd really botched that. Dani moved his way. A wave of relief made him unclench his fist. She was the quiet, the peace of home.

As Ellen passed by Dani, Tim heard her say, "I feel sorry for you. He's a cheating prick!" Dani turned in a circle watching her as she went by. She quickly made her way to the booth and slid in next to Tim. She kissed his cheek.

"Scott said you were blindsided by Ellen. That looked like fun," she teased him, with a look of pure pity.

"A real party, if you like torture." He put his arm over her shoulders and hugged her to him.

"Are you okay?"

He nodded. "How was your day?"

"Busy. A whole container of Lodi Malbec was misplaced at the freight dock for a few hours. A Marchant Farms grape truck rolled over and turned Highway 90 into a winepress. Oh, and my nephew has the measles. My sister was afraid to vaccinate him because of autism and now they're quarantined--two weeks. And what can I do? I'm trapped in the penthouse? A regular day." She set her head on his shoulder. "Did you win your case?"

"I did." He remembered how pleased he'd been just a few hours ago.

"Perfect. I made reservations for all of us at Alexander's. I thought about eating here, but Ellen is still shooting daggers at you from the bar. So I thought we'd better move on." Dani traced a line down his cheek.

"Can we set a wedding date?" he asked. He knew it was unexpected.

"You're just trying to get rid of ex-girlfriends!" Dani laughed. He joined her.

"Yep."

"How many more are there?"

"No more, thank God." He leaned back into the booth. "Dani, wouldn't it be good to be settled? It would be so sweet to know I have you to come home to."

She matched his posture and turned to face him. "Shall we elope?"

"Yes."

"My family would freak." She pulled her hair up and away from her face. He loved that, especially when it fell back, shiny and soft around her shoulders. He gently took hold of one of her long curls. The fragrance lingering in her clean hair was heady and he pressed it to his lips.

Dani watched him and Tim was sure she wanted him a much as he wanted her.

"My mother would be brokenhearted, too," Tim said. "I'm the baby." Tim's mother had never accepted any of his girlfriends. He remembered her scowls of disapproval whenever he brought a girl home to meet the family. He wasn't sure being the youngest had anything to do with it. To him it was just a mystery.

"Wedding it is," she laughed, but it was tinged with disappointment.

"Or both? We could elope, tell no one, and have a wedding later for the benefit of family."

"Perfect. I love that idea," she whispered. "But it would really have to be secret. I mean double, triple-x secret. The tabloid press still follows me from time to time. They'd love nothing more than to turn it into some sort of scandal."

He took hold of her hand and kissed her fingertips. "I love you, Dani."

"And I, you." Dani swallowed, looked down. When she met his eyes again, he stared at her.

"Are you worried about something? Not Ellen."

"No." She shook her head. "Not Ellen."

"Good, because I don't want you to even give her a second thought. I don't."

"What did she want, anyway?"

"She wanted to re-litigate our old fights. I haven't seen her for over a year and she's the same broken record. So, what is it? Warden? Dani, we'll get him. I know it doesn't seem like we're making progress, but we are. We almost had him today." He tenderly touched her hair. He looked up and noticed the rest of their group making their way to the booth. He straightened his tie.

"So, what's the plan, lovebirds?" Scott asked, scooting into the booth and pulling Kathy with him, making room for Mitch and Shannon.

"Dani made reservations for Alexander's." Tim sat tall.

"Ooh, yum." Kathy winked at him. "When are the reservations?"

"Seven-thirty," Dani said. "We'd better go."

"Ready for the nasty remarks? We have to walk past Ellen and her friends to get out." Tim took hold of Dani's hand.

"Yes." She stood and straightened defensively. Tim couldn't help but grin. "Maybe they won't say anything." She crossed her fingers, kissed them, and touched Tim's lips with the kiss.

SEVENTY-SIX

Tim stumbled, still half asleep, from the bedroom to the penthouse kitchen. He pulled his crumpled T-shirt down over his jeans. It was a good morning. He was one satisfied man, he thought. Dani had agreed to set a date for their wedding--and icing on the cake, it was the weekend! He didn't have to worry about work today. When he rounded the corner, he noticed that Shannon was already making coffee.

"Morning. I was just coming to do that. Glad I don't have to." He grinned and scrubbed a hand over his hair.

"Morning!" Mitch called out from behind the paper.

"Anything good, or is it all bad news?" Tim asked.

"You're on the front page! Below the fold, though," Mitch laughed.

"Me?"

"You won a guilty verdict yesterday, right?"

Tim moved behind the counter and read the front page Mitch held out for him. "At least they spelled my name right," Tim chuckled.

"Makes you sound pretty big-time."

"Good. Do you think Dani will be impressed?"

"*I'm* impressed," Shannon said, setting a cup of coffee in front of her husband and then one for Tim.

"The secret is: don't go to a jury trial unless you know you can win," Tim joked, even though it was true.

"I smell coffee." Tim turned. Dani stood at the edge of the kitchen.

"Tim's in the paper," Shannon said, handing her a cup.

Dani padded over, a terrycloth robe wrapped over PJs she didn't actually wear to bed, her fuzzy slippers scuffing against the kitchen floor. "Let me see." She read the story, turned, and hugged him.

"What's the plan for today?" Mitch asked. "I drank last night, so it's four more hours before I can fly."

"Then, we're going diamond shopping," Tim announced. "Time I bought this beautiful woman a proper engagement ring."

"What about Warden?" Mitch immediately took the glow out of the room.

"Time to get back to living," Dani said emphatically, looking at Tim with contentment.

Tim heard the elevator doors open and footsteps in the penthouse hallway. He knew it was Scott. He was the only other person who had the elevator key. When he appeared with Anna and Sheridan at the kitchen doorway, Scott was dressed in full suit and tie, like he was on duty.

Surprised, Tim asked, "Isn't this your day off?" He'd told Tim of his plans to take Kathy to a surprise breakfast. Anna's uncomfortable shuffle unsettled him. But most disconcerting was the frown on Scott's face. "What's up?"

Scott looked as if deciding whether to answer. He seemed to steel himself. *Bad news,* Tim thought.

"Ellen Mason is dead."

Tim groaned. The shock wave was palpable. Dani sat down. Mitch crumpled the newspaper in his hands. Tim swallowed hard. He didn't love Ellen, hadn't wanted to marry her, but he didn't want her dead. He looked over at Dani and her eyes were filled with fear and sadness.

"How?" Tim asked, moving to where Dani sat, putting his hands on her shoulders.

"The emergency room doctor said heart attack. But Kathy's working on that now. She'll call when she has preliminary results. You know I have to ask you some questions." Scott was stern; clearly, he didn't want to do this.

"Are you thinking she was murdered?" Tim stumbled through the words though he couldn't imagine someone their age having a heart attack.

"Yes," Scott said, without flinching.

"You can't possibly think Tim had anything to do with it?" Dani stood and defensively linked her arm through his.

"Tim is her former--friend. He was seen arguing with her last night. I'd be remiss if I didn't ask some questions," Scott was apologetic. It was obvious: Scott was being forced by his superiors.

"You've got to be kidding!" Dani griped. "You were with us last night."

"Scott's right." Tim looked at his friend. "Here, or down at the station?"

"Here. I can interview everyone." Scott motioned and Anna entered.

"Everyone?" Dani asked, as they moved into the living room and took seats around the coffee table.

"Someone may remember something—may have seen something," Scott explained. "All right, let's get started." Scott was somber. "We were all together at dinner, so we can rule out that time period. At about 10:30 Tim McAndrews, Dani St. Clair, and Mitch and Shannon Barkley arrived at the twenty-sixth-floor penthouse belonging to Dani St. Clair," Scott said into the recorder he'd set on the coffee table.

"You can get the exact time from the alarm system, it's logged on my computer," Dani offered helpfully.

"Did anyone leave the penthouse last night?" Scott continued.

"Not that I know of," Tim answered, trying to get a read from Scott's expression.

"You can check that, too. The alarm system logs all departures from the penthouse." Dani was starting to get annoyed. Tim put his hand on her arm. He knew they had to be formally removed from the suspect list or Scott would be accused of not doing a thorough job.

"Can it be overridden?" Scott asked.

"Yes. But I had my I.T. department disable the override. We wanted to make sure no one who shouldn't be here, could be," Dani stated. "You recommended that, don't you remember?"

Scott stared at her. Obviously, he remembered and didn't appreciate the confrontation. "Tim, you are stating for the record that you didn't leave the penthouse at all last night?" Scott continued.

"Yes. I didn't leave the penthouse," Tim answered.

"Miss St. Clair, are you absolutely sure Mr. McAndrews didn't leave?"

"Yes. Absolutely sure." She covered Tim's hand with hers.

"Is it possible to get a copy of the computer log?"

"Yes, of course."

"Do I have your permission to have a forensic computer analyst recover that information?"

"Yes, you do," Dani said, looking at Tim's face.

Scott motioned and Sheridan came into the living room.

"Is now a good time to get the log?" Scott asked.

"Yes." She was becoming defiant. "Do I need my lawyer?"

"I don't think so," Tim said. "But if you would feel better, call him."

Scott's cell phone rang; he paused the recorder and he excused himself. Everyone waited in silence. Scott came back into the room. "That was Kathy. Tim, we need to go to the morgue."

Tim stood. "Does this mean I'm no longer a suspect?"

"Never were," Scott answered, scowling. Tim knew Scott had just been doing what he had to.

"We're going through McTavish's surveillance tape right now," Scott said and clicked on his recorder. "One more question, Tim. Did you put desipramine in Miss Mason's beer last night while she was at the table with you?"

Tim shook his head. "No. I didn't. Buddy, you never brought her beer back to the table. Ellen didn't have anything to drink with me."

Scott groaned and then laughed. "You're right, I didn't. I didn't even order it." He clicked off the recorder. "That was rude. We're rounding up Ellen's friends. We'll interview them, find out where they were *besides* McTavish's last night," Scott informed them. "I need you, Tim. Can you help me out?"

"Yeah." Tim glanced around the room. "Mitch, as soon as you can fly, I want you to take Dani and go to the ranch. I'll drive over when I can."

"I can pick you up. Ranch is just an hour from King County Airport: it'll take you four to drive," Mitch replied. "Call about an hour before you're ready to wrap it up and I'll fly in."

"Sounds good. I'll take you up on that." Tim started for the bedroom to grab a jacket from the closet. "Are you all right with this, Dani?"

"Whatever you say, I'll do," she said. The tears were still there in her eyes. He wanted to hold her and have her hold him. There was a tightness in his chest he couldn't explain. He placed his hand across his forehead, rubbed his fingers down past the outside corners of his eyes, and pinched the bridge of his nose to fight the headache that was brewing. He'd never wanted anything bad to happen to Ellen, regardless of their bickering and hard feelings.

"Let's go, Scott," he said.

Tim slid into the passenger's side of Scott's unmarked cruiser. "Where are we headed first?" Tim asked. "Is Anna coming?"

"She came with Sheridan."

Scott sat still. Didn't turn the ignition key.

"What's bothering you?" Tim asked.

Scott turned square to face him. "First, promise not to get mad, no matter what I ask you."

"Depends on what you ask. But go ahead."

"Was Dani there with you the whole night?"

Tim nodded. "Are you crazy? Of course she was."

"I told you not to get mad. She's the only one that could've overridden the security system." Scott replied.

"I can't believe you. She was there all night." Tim glared at his friend.

"She didn't get up, disappear for a while?"

"No. She didn't."

"You're sure."

"Scott! I can't sleep anymore if I'm not holding her, all right? She moves, I reach for her. Is that what you want to know?"

Scott fussed with his mustache. "Would you lie to me? For her? Would you lie for her?"

Tim sucked in a breath. "You might as well punch me in the gut. You have evidence she's done something wrong, show me! She was with me all last night. That's what I know."

"I don't have anything."

Tim stared, baffled. "Why would you--?"

"Goddard wants you both cleared. He's taken donations from Miss St. Clair, can't have that connection if she's murdered someone--end of his career. Captain Martin wants me to get your cell phone records."

"You can have them. You won't find any calls to Ellen. I hadn't seen Ellen for over a year before last night."

"I know. It's crazy. Everyone is going nuts," Scott sighed. "You need to call Goddard."

Tim took the cell phone out of the pocket of his leather jacket. "I only have this--" he began, asking Scott's permission to use it. Scott nodded. Tim dialed his boss' number.

"I'm going to drop you at the morgue. Anna is going to start interviewing Ellen's friends. I want to see where that leads. I'll meet up with you and Kathy later."

"All right. My Saturday with Dani is out the window," Tim acknowledged.

"Criminals never quit. They never take a day off," Scott answered.

SEVENTY-SEVEN

The morgue was, as usual, cold and uninviting. Goddard had once again asked Tim to take charge. He'd asked him to meet Ellen's family for the identification. He needed to prepare himself, and asked Kathy if he could see the body. Kathy pulled the green surgical sheet back. Ellen looked completely at peace, as though she were only sleeping. He wanted to wake her and take back the mean things he'd said to her last night. Tim ran his hand though his hair and sighed.

"It's Ellen," he said quietly to Kathy.

"I'm sorry, Tim." She replaced the sheet. He closed his eyes, briefly.

"She deserved better." He shook his head. "Do you have a cause of death?" he asked.

"Antidepressants and alcohol. It was Warden," Kathy announced.

Tim groaned and paced in a small circle in frustration. "Fuck! Wait, she's not his type. Can't be." He swiped his hand over his chin.

Kathy set her hand on his shoulder and continued. "The chemical markers of the antidepressant in her blood are identical to drug he used to kill the others. The semen matches his blood type. We'll need the DNA back to confirm, but that's just a formality. It was Warden," she said. When he looked at her face she continued, "There's more."

"Okay?" Tim steeled himself.

"The knife Scott found at the James Street apartment, remember?"

Tim nodded.

"I told you the shape and depth of the knife wounds on Candy Johnson were consistent with those found on Alan Sharp. We found three sources of DNA on that knife: Warden's, Candy's, and Alan's. He killed that boy, too."

Tim stared at her, almost incredulous. "The M.O. doesn't match--does Scott know?"

"My conclusion: Warden's lost it. He's killing for killing's sake now. Scott doesn't know; Lab report just came back."

"All right. I'll call Goddard and see if we can round up a judge. Scott will want another arrest warrant when you tell him. Warden's really escalating. We're going to need FBI help on this one."

"Scott called Elias Cain this morning."

Tim and Kathy turned when they heard footsteps echoing down the hallway. Scott was walking briskly to meet them.

"Hi, kids." Scott was in a cheery mood. Tim knew his interviews had gone well.

"Kathy just connected Warden to the murder of Alan Sharp," Tim announced.

"Wow!" Scott stopped short. "How?"

"DNA on the knife you found at Warden's apartment," Tim answered and watched Kathy turn to Scott as a smart-ass grin crept across her face.

"Well, you're going to love this: Ellen and her three friends left McTavish's about 9:00 p.m. They headed north on First and went to Top of the Crown. They had a drink there, but nothing was shaking so they moved on. They hit The Crow's Nest about 10:30. While there, they met a guy. They think his name was Geoffrey Watson. I'm thinking aka *Gary Warden*. Apparently, he took a liking to Janine, but she's married. So Ellen's friends coaxed him to flirt it up with Ellen to make her feel better. While she was powdering her nose, they told him she'd had a sad encounter with her ex-boyfriend. She was still madly in love with this guy, a D.A., and he just broke her heart. Watson-Warden agreed to do his part to cheer her up."

"Great. You could've left that madly-in-love and D.A. part out," Tim frowned; he felt bad enough, no need to rub salt in the wound.

"Then you're really going to like this part," Scott was somber. He set a reassuring hand on Tim's shoulder. "The girls said Ellen had gone to a whole lot of trouble hoping to get this guy back. She'd lost weight, fifteen pounds. She'd been working out, got her hair and nails done. She'd been going to McTavish's with the girls the last three Friday nights, hoping to run into this special guy."

Tim groaned.

"Knock it off, Scott. This isn't Tim's fault. She's the one that broke up with him. What'd she expect, he'd be pining his life away?" Kathy was angry.

"She expected me to come back. Katrina Collins told her I was unattached," Tim considered Katrina's roll in this. He looked past Scott, deep in thought.

Scott was frowning, "So, if Katrina gets you and Ellen back together, she can move Bill Fraser in for the kill with Dani, is that it?"

"Something like that," Tim said coldly.

"What? Why am I not in on this loop?" Kathy muscled her way past Scott and stood directly in front of Tim, hands on her hips.

"It's just a theory of mine that Scott has thoroughly impeached," Tim sighed.

"I want to hear it," Kathy insisted.

"I think it goes like this--correct me if I'm wrong. Katrina Collins, Bill Fraser, and Gary Warden meet each other at the Sevens Club. They're working out and start hanging out together. They start grousing about their unfortunate lots in life, drinking, maybe doing drugs. But Warden cashed in on a million-dollar insurance policy with wife number one. He tells them he knows how to pull off a murder- for-money scheme that's easy and the perfect crime. And he's already set his sights on a victim. He learned his lesson on the last heiress; she had meddling parents. But this new girl doesn't. Both mother and father are gone. And she's so rich there's plenty to set them all up for the rest of their lives." Scott looked over at Tim. "Right so far?"

Tim shrugged, "So far." There were holes in his theory, he knew it. But wasn't that what detectives were supposed to do, fill in the obscure?

"Being unhappy with their lives isn't a very logical motive. I mean, who *is* completely happy? Sheesh." Kathy said, shaking her head at Tim; clearly she thought his idea was stupid.

"Kath, are you putting humans and logic in the same sentence? If humans were always logical, the world would be at peace," Tim retorted. Kathy and Scott both mumbled in agreement.

Scott started the story again: "Katrina pretends to be or is actually involved with Warden. They decide they'll set Dani up with Bill Fraser. He's good-looking, has a good job--perfect guy for her, right?"

"But, Tim. Tim is in the way. Katrina tries to seduce him to break them up," Kathy joined in.

Tim listened, then added, "I was in the way--or a dupe. I haven't decided on this part of their scheme."

"Back to the main story. They set Dani up with Bill Fraser, the relationship proceeds, and they marry. Then when they've waited long enough, they kill her and take the money," Scott finished.

"But, wait. Doesn't Dani have sisters? Wouldn't they inherit first, before a husband?" Kathy asked.

"Boom!" Scott said, looking at Tim.

Tim lifted his hands in defeat. "So, I hadn't worked out every detail. If they're doing this, they have."

"Insurance," Kathy said, and both men turned. "Fraser gets Dani to buy a big fat insurance policy. She flies a lot, travels here and there. She needs one, right?"

"Keep going," Scott encouraged her.

"They plan to kill her and split up the insurance money. But things are starting to go wrong. Warden likes killing," Kathy mused.

"No. He *needs* to kill. He gets off on it. It's become sexual," Tim mused aloud.

"Good one." Scott drummed his fingers on his mustache.

"That, and he needs pocket change. He ripped off fifty thousand from Amber Brown, but that may be long gone, especially split three ways. He took Jillian Garner's coin stash of two-hundred-fifty thousand, but gold coins are risky to cash right now. Especially here in Seattle. He's got to believe we know about them," Tim speculated. "He's tired of this chump change, he wants some real wealth."

Kathy narrowed her eyes. "Warden makes a mistake: he takes Amber's necklace and gives it to Katrina. When she wears it, she gets the attention of a remarkable detective." She grinned at Scott.

"Why did Warden try to kill Katrina, then?" Scott asked.

"He's decided he doesn't want to share the booty with the others anymore. Or how about this: his chums are getting cold feet. And they know the plan: he has to get rid of them. He's going rogue," Tim answered.

"That works!" Kathy grinned and got them to laugh briefly, then they fell silent.

"There's only one glitch," Tim interjected.

"What's that?" Kathy asked.

"We don't have a shred of evidence connecting Katrina and Fraser to the crimes. Only Warden." Tim decided he needed to review all the evidence again, knowing he'd missed something.

"Except the necklace. Which can be explained away as a gift," Scott said. "And a comment from Katrina that Dani had stolen her life. Whatever that meant."

"The most we could charge Katrina with is receipt of stolen property. And I doubt I could even get a judge to go along with that." Tim brushed his fingers along the stubble on his chin.

"Katrina lied to me," Scott said. "If they're in it, Warden might roll for a deal when we catch him."

"No deal." Tim was unequivocal. "He killed people without any remorse, snuffed out their lives as if they meant nothing. He's a monster."

"I agree." Kathy rubbed her brow. "Why did he kill Ellen? You don't think he's attacking you personally do you, Tim?"

"I don't know. Maybe," Tim answered. Ellen's death was all his fault.

"I reviewed the surveillance tapes of McTavish's from last night, he wasn't on them. I figure it was one of those freaky, ugly coincidences. Ellen stumbled into the wrong bar at the wrong time and her friends, thinking they were doing her a favor, sent her into the arms of a serial killer. Nice, huh?" Scott said.

"Everything and everyone involved is connected. No coincidence--Katrina set it up. She told Ellen I was unattached, when she knew Dani and I were back together. What if she told Warden where Ellen was going to be last night? Ellen's friends told him about her ex being a D.A. and Warden could've put that together."

"I didn't see Katrina on the surveillance tapes, either," Scott countered. "We could get her cell phone records."

"I'll need to run that by Goddard. With Ellen's death, though, we might be able to convince a judge you have probable cause," Tim stated. "Safer if we get a warrant."

"I agree," Scott nodded. "Katrina's going to scream; she'll say we're harassing her."

"I know. Too bad." Tim tapped his palm against his forehead. "What aren't we seeing? What aren't we getting?"

The three stood in a tight circle staring at each other. No answers came.

"Kathy, when are Ellen's parents coming to identify her body? I need to be here, offer my condolences, do what I can for them." Tim couldn't keep the guilt from bubbling up. He let his mind wander back through their argument last night. Could he have been kinder?

"Any minute now," Kathy said, looking at her watch.

Tim turned to face the corridor when he heard footsteps. The echo always added to the creepiness of the morgue. He braced himself. A parent's grief for the loss of a child was hard to watch. Tim knew there were no words that could console them. The one thing he could do for them: put the perpetrator behind bars. He walked down the hallway to meet them.

"Mr. and Mrs. Mason?" he asked.

"Yes," Mr. Mason answered.

Tim could tell Mrs. Mason was in shock. She moved as though she were walking in a nightmare she couldn't escape. He couldn't avoid noticing she was an older version of her daughter. Ellen had always wanted him to meet her parents. He'd made excuses. This wasn't the way to meet them now.

"I'm Tim McAndrews, with the district attorney's office. This is Detective Renton, Seattle P.D. and the medical examiner, Dr. Katherine Hope. We know this is going to be difficult, but we need you to identify your daughter."

Mr. Mason had steeled himself, but Mrs. Mason was lost, confused, unwilling to accept the news. Tim took hold of her arm. Instinctively, he knew her reaction would be extreme. He led them to the body draped in the green surgical sheet. Kathy pulled it back.

Mrs. Mason looked and immediately lost her balance. Tim was there to brace her. He helped her out of the room and to a chair in the hallway. He took a seat beside her. She sat for a moment, staring into his face.

"You don't know how wonderful she was. She was such a sweet girl. So caring." She shuddered with a sob. Mr. Mason joined them, sitting next to his wife. He nodded to Tim and put his arm around his wife's shoulders.

"It's Ellen," he choked on the words. Tim studied them. They hadn't connected him with Ellen. Maybe they didn't know. For all her protestations of love, Ellen had never told her parents about him. *Good.* Tim couldn't help thinking *he* was the reason Ellen was dead. If only he hadn't made her so angry, maybe she wouldn't have been so vulnerable.

"Do you know who did this?" Ellen's father asked.

"We're pretty sure we do. The police are searching for him now," Tim reported. "We're going to get him."

"How did--? She looks like she's just sleeping." Mr. Mason observed.

"He poisoned her," Tim stated. "I'm so sorry."

"Did you know Ellen?" Mrs. Mason asked.

"I did," he answered honestly.

"Were you friends?"

Tim remembered how many times last night Ellen had told him she hated him. What difference could that make now? He took Mrs. Mason's hand. "Yes. We were friends." Mrs. Mason's eyes lit up and she squeezed his hand.

"Will you be the prosecutor on her case?" she asked.

"No. I'm sure Mr. Goddard will want to take this one personally. He's the best," Tim assured her.

"What happens now? Will you notify us when you catch her killer?" Mr. Mason asked.

"Yes. We will. Until then, if you have questions or want updates, you can contact Detective Renton. He's in charge of your daughter's case. Scott, could you give Mr. and Mrs. Mason one of your cards? And here's mine. Though I won't know the day-to-day progress like the detectives, I will be happy to get any information I can to keep you updated." Tim knew he was trying to assuage his guilt. But even now, as he looked at Ellen's parents' distressed faces he knew he couldn't do anything to make this better. He realized also that, no matter what, if he had a do-over with Ellen, he'd still choose Dani.

"Are you going to catch this guy?" Ellen's father stared in his eyes begging for an answer.

"Sir," Scott said emphatically, "I'm going to take him down personally."

Tim watched the Masons leave. He ground his teeth together as a cold, controlled anger roiled beneath the surface.

"Hey, what's going on?" Scott asked. "You have that look in your eyes. Did you think of something? Something I should know?"

Tim wheeled to face him and shook his head slowly. "Nothing--there's just something I need to do."

SEVENTY-EIGHT

"Thank you for seeing me. I know it's Saturday, and I hate to interrupt you, Sir." Tim explained as he followed Brad Hollingsrow through the white, marble-tiled foyer of his home. Before entering the home office, Brad peeled off his gray-striped gardening gloves, and removed the white Seahawks baseball cap revealing his full head of silver hair. He dropped his gloves into the hat and set them on the small mahogany table outside the door. Hollingsrow's home was exactly what Tim expected for a man of his position.

"No problem. When Dani called and told me to help you, it seemed so urgent. Is it?" Brad motioned for Tim to sit in one of the dark leather wingback chairs stationed in front of the massive mahogany desk. "Can I get you a drink? I'm parched."

"Yes, urgent." Tim sat down. Behind the desk, a wall of wood-paned windows revealed a view of a red brick deck and beyond, a manicured lawn and neatly trimmed rose garden. Inside the office, the whole left wall was floor-to-ceiling bookcases, filled with expensive leather-bound volumes of Washington State and Federal Law. The hardwood floors were covered by imported oriental rugs in red tones. The room smelled of leather, pine, orange and cinnamon. The right wall had a cozy gas fireplace surrounded by an antique mantel, probably rescued from an old Victorian era home--or at least, built to look like it had come from one.

"I have an unopened bottle of Maker's Mark Reserve I've been wanting to try," Brad tempted him.

"Sure, I'll join you," Tim said. Brad pressed a button on the wall and the bookcases slid away and revealed a fully stocked bar. *Slick!* But Hollingsrow's had always been the preferred law firm for Seattle's rich and powerful. Why *wouldn't* he have something like that? Brad poured them each a glass of whiskey, handed one to Tim, and moved behind his desk and sat.

"What is so urgent?" he asked, his even features and sparkling blue eyes revealing his kindness. "Are there terms of the pre-nup you'd like to negotiate?"

Stunned, Tim temporarily lost his train of thought. Of course, there would be a pre-nup, Dani would be a fool not to have one. They just hadn't discussed it with each other. Obviously though, Dani had--with Brad. At least Dani was serious enough about marrying him to have one prepared.

"No. Not about that." Tim recovered and dismissed the matter. "It's about Katrina Collins."

Now Brad was the one with surprise on his face. He set his whiskey on the desk and sat back in his chair. "Katrina Collins? Why on earth would you ask about Katrina Collins?"

"Does she have a reason to dislike—hate--Dani? Does she stand to gain—financially--if something happens to Dani?" Tim held the whiskey glass, looked down into the amber liquid, but didn't drink it. He clearly remembered Dani's dodge when he asked her that question in the office conference room.

Brad was instantly uncomfortable. He stared hard at Tim, as if trying to discern his motives for asking. He quickly blinked. If this had been a deposition, Tim would assume there was something to Katrina's complaint.

"You've been the St. Clair's lawyer for years. I won't ask you to compromise attorney-client privilege—but can you tell me anything?"

"I'm not Katrina's attorney. I'm Dani's. Is this official? Part of an investigation? Or personal?"

"Official. Part of an investigation," Tim said straight. "*And* personal." He left it there. "Katrina Collins told the police when they interviewed her that Dani had stolen her life. Is there any reason she would say something like that?"

Brad sat forward, picked up his whiskey glass and drained it. "Want another?" he lifted the glass.

Tim shook his head. Brad got up and walked to the bar, poured another shot in his own glass. It worried Tim. *This story needed two shots of whiskey?*

"Where to begin--not sure where to begin," Brad said as he moved back behind his desk and sat down. He took a sip of whiskey and savored it. "Simon St. Clair and Robert 'Bert' Collins, Katrina's father, met during the Vietnam War. Simon was severely wounded in the battle for Khe Sanh. Collins saved his life. When the war was over the two men bought two-hundred acre parcels, side-by-side. Simon started Delight Valley Winery. He offered Bert a partnership, but Bert didn't want the risk. He'd sell Simon his grapes, but he didn't want the rest of the hassle that goes along with the wine business. I drew up the contract."

"Okay. They had a business deal."

"They had a friendship, Tim. Forged in blood. Collins saved Simon's life. When Bert was diagnosed with lung cancer and was written off as hopeless by the VA, Simon paid for his care in a private cancer hospital. Collins was proud and wouldn't take a handout. He deeded his land over to

St. Clair as payment for the overwhelming medical expenses. Dani hasn't told you any of this?"

"No," Tim answered. "Only that she and Katrina were friends."

"Friends? Tim, growing up they were like sisters."

The thought of Katrina Collins being his *like-a-sister-in-law* was puke-worthy. The fact that he suspected her of conspiracy to commit murder might not go over so well with Dani. He needed to tread carefully. "Does Katrina blame Dani for taking her land?"

"If she does, she's all wrong. Simon St. Clair set up a trust for the Collins children. It was his wish to give the land back when they were old enough to appreciate it. When Simon passed, Dani became trustee of the Trust--she's doubled its value. The Collins children have been provided for all their lives, they've been sent to the colleges of their choice. Dani set the boys up with their own winery business and bottles their label for them. Sure, she gets some of the profit, but she takes all the risk. She financed Katrina's boutique and hasn't asked for repayment—against my advice, I might add."

"Dani is in control of Katrina's purse strings? What happens if Dani dies?" Tim asked, confident he wasn't going to like the answer.

"If Dani dies the assets of the trust are to be distributed to the Collins children in three years. But that will happen no matter what. Simon believed the kids would be mature enough to handle their fortune at that point in their lives. Michael, the oldest, will be thirty-five."

"How much money are we talking about?" Tim took a swallow of the Maker's then leaned back into his chair and crossed his legs, setting his right ankle on his left knee.

Brad hesitated. "Is this necessary?"

"Yes."

"Do you want to elaborate or are you fishing?"

Tim knew a grin of admiration had broken out on his face. Brad was connecting the dots and deserved to know the truth. "Fishing."

"What are you fishing for?"

"A motive for conspiracy to commit murder," Tim answered coolly. He sipped his whiskey and watched Brad's smile faded into consternation.

"Around six million now--but in three years, who knows," Brad speculated, worry creasing his brow.

"Do they know? Do the Collins children know about the trust—about the money?"

Brad slowly shook his head. "Just after he--Simon set up the trust, there were problems. Simon decided it was best that they didn't know about the money until it was time to distribute it. There were rumors. Loretta

Collins was reported to have kept a tell-all diary, with some very unsavory information in it." Brad squinted; this was distasteful and he wasn't enjoying the telling.

Tim frowned. "What kind of troubles? What kind of rumors?"

"Rumors that Simon St. Clair and Loretta Collins had an affair while Bert was dying. And that Katrina was the result--Katrina was the love-child of that union."

Tim tried not to react. He forced calm like he did when he was blind-sided in court by a well-prepared defense attorney. "Is she? Is Katrina Simon St. Clair's daughter--Dani's sister?" Tim uncrossed his legs and leaned forward in his chair. It was an unwelcome thought. Especially considering the come-on in the Sevens Club parking garage. But suddenly, Tim understood the motive for murder: if Dani was keeping Katrina from her share of the St. Clair fortune, it could've inspired Katrina to hook up with Warden and plan her murder.

Brad stared, his teeth clenched together. For a few moments, the two men faced each other in silence. Brad opened the middle drawer of his desk and retrieved a small key. He unlocked the right-hand drawer, removed a letter-sized file, and slid it across the desk to Tim.

"What's this? Just tell me, Brad." Tim didn't reach for the folder.

"Do you have any idea what the family you're marrying into is worth? Do you, Tim?" Brad asked, sipping from his whiskey glass, watching Tim's face.

Tim slowly moved his head side to side. "No. I'm not sure I want to know."

Brad sat deep into his leather chair. "If Katrina Collins is contending she's Simon St. Clair's daughter and that proved to be true, she'd be entitled to a quarter interest in a fortune that makes her six-million-dollar trust look like pocket change."

Tim breathed in and let it out. "Is she? Is she Dani's sister? Did Dani steal her life? These days with DNA profiling, it would be really easy to prove."

"Do you know how many people covet that kind of money, and want a part of it--*any* part of it?"

"Of course I do. I put people away who've murdered another for as little as twenty dollars."

"Katrina's paternity has already been litigated. Pick up the folder, Tim. The court records are sealed, but the case numbers are in there. As a prosecutor, you know you can get everything: testimony, the forensics science, the truth. I'm not at liberty to say anything more. Take the folder. If Katrina is contending she's Simon St. Clair's daughter, you'll need it." Brad drained his whiskey glass and set the empty down on his desk.

Tim reached for the folder and slowly slid it to the edge of the desk. He wanted answers, but he wasn't sure he'd like them. He looked up at Brad. "Since I'm here—I should sign that pre-nup," he said.

Brad lifted an eyebrow as if he knew Tim had been caught unaware by the news of the agreement. Tim didn't allow his expression to change. He wanted Brad to understand he didn't want Dani's money. He just wanted her.

SEVENTY-NINE

Early mornings at the ranch refreshed Dani. She loved going to the barn before sunrise on crystal-clear days. November was her favorite month for stargazing at 5:30 in the morning. Sunrise this time of year was almost 8:00 am. As she walked to the barn, she took in a lungful of crisp, cold air. She looked up and watched the Milky Way twinkle against the blackness. Picking out familiar constellations was a game she'd played with her father when he was still alive. She turned in a slow circle, looking for her favorites. Ursa Major was directly overhead, Cassiopeia on her upside-down throne just above the mountains to her northeast. She looked for Orion but remembered he'd already be set behind the southeastern hills at this time in the morning. She slid open the big barn door and closed it to keep out the cold. The horses greeted her with soft nickers, anxious for an early breakfast.

"Good morning, Phil and Ryan!" she called out. Mark had assigned his two boys morning duty on the weekends. They were busy cleaning stalls and filling water buckets.

"Morning," they acknowledged her in a sleepy chorus. Dani knew the boys didn't dare cross their father. He was a great dad, but he believed hard work and responsibility at an early age made for good men in later life. The boys were only eight and ten. Mark expected them to do the chores for free, but Dani insisted on paying them. She argued that, that way they would learn that hard work brought rewards.

The boys were particularly happy Tim had arrived last night. He knew so much about football and as it was the season, and he'd talked to them about the game.

The boys knew they had help this morning: Dani liked to feed and it lightened their load.

She walked to the grain room and filled buckets, adding the specific ingredients for each horse's unique needs. Grandma, her thirty-three-year old matriarch, needed a scoop of a soybean meal mix to keep her weight up. And Princess Petrina needed a special mineral supplement to help process insulin. She organized each preparation in order by stall on her cart and wheeled over to the hay room.

Dani weighed the flakes of hay, making certain each horse received the exact amount needed to keep them in peak condition, but added a little extra this morning to counter the cold. It was mornings like this that made her wish the ranch could be her only life, especially now that Tim was in it. She contemplated Tim for a moment. She hated that she was still hesitant. Once burned, twice shy. If Tim left her now, she knew she wouldn't die from it; she would just wish she could.

Maybe that was why her father had chosen to put her in charge of the businesses on his deathbed. She'd always had a good head for business, he'd told her. She was divorced, she didn't have a husband to care for, and she was childless. Her sisters were not. Besides, he'd told her, her sisters were too darn romantic. Was that her problem? She wasn't romantic? She wondered as she cut through the twine on a new bale of hay and loaded an armful on her cart, but before she could get more, she heard a rustle. Darn it! The flakes were falling to the floor. Now they wouldn't be as easy to handle. She turned to fix it but the bale was still intact. In the darkness, she thought she saw a shadow huddled against the last row of bales in the bay. A shudder raced along her shoulder blades as if she'd been touched by an icy finger. It couldn't be--could it? *Warden*! Her first impulse was to run, but instead she froze. *The boys*! She forced herself not to react. She fought the trembling inside. If she panicked she couldn't make a plan, and she had to devise a way to get herself and the boys to safety. Slowly, she continued her task. She had to pretend she hadn't seen him. She had to get a weapon. She thought she remembered seeing a metal pitchfork just outside the entry to the bay, leaning against the wall.

Before he made his move, she had to get the kids out of here. Would he hurt the boys? They were only children, but Warden hadn't cared about all those other lives, so why would he care about theirs? She positioned the cart in the doorway to create a barrier.

She grabbed for the pitchfork. It wasn't there! Her heart sank. *Of all the days for the boys to put things where they belonged!* She searched for the boys but only saw Ryan. Maybe Phil had already gone down to the house. Breakfast was waiting and he could've finished early. She had to hope for that. So far, Warden had not made his presence known. But he would; *What was he waiting for?*

Dani thought if only she could get one of the boys down to the house, they could get Tim, Mark, and Mitch. Warden wouldn't have a chance against three men. If only she could see Phil! If only she knew he was safe!

"Oh! Ryan--Dang it!" she called out. "Ariah has pooped in her paddock! Can you come clean it?" Ryan appeared with a plastic WonderFork and a perplexed look on his face. He'd just cleaned her paddock. Dani met him at the door to the mare's stall. When he discovered the paddock was clean, he started to say something, but Dani had a finger to her lips and shook her head.

"Pick up the pitchfork, go out to the paddock, then over the fence, and get help," she whispered." Tell Mr. McAndrews it's Warden. He'll know what you mean. Do it calmly. Go out like you are going to clean. When you're over the fence, run," she whispered.

The boy's face echoed her terror. He nodded, and did exactly as he was told.

EIGHTY

Tim woke to the delicious smell of coffee on the air. He felt for Dani and then remembered she'd gotten up earlier to go help in the barn. He stumbled out of bed. Sleep lingered heavily over his mind. Last night had been the first good, hard sleep he'd had in a long time. Dani claimed it was all the oxygen in the air from the trees on the ranch. Tim didn't know about that; he thought maybe it was the quiet and the fact that the ranch seemed to be the one place he wasn't worried about Warden.

He pulled on the blue jeans he'd strewn across the nightstand beside the bed last night. He made his way to the bathroom and splashed cold water on his face, hoping to chase some of the grogginess away. He scrubbed some water through his hair, brushed his teeth, and then finished dressing. As he made his way through the bedroom for the stairs, he noticed his sidearm on the bed stand. He'd left it there last night. He doubted he'd need it here and started to leave, but then had second thoughts. He picked up the Walther and threaded his belt through the holster. He grabbed his sweatshirt from the armchair where he'd thrown it last night and slipped it on, covering over the pistol--no need to alarm everyone. Tim headed down the stairs to breakfast. There were voices in the dining room.

"Well, I don't like him," Tim heard Mark say. He stopped short outside the door and listened.

"He's a good guy, Mark," Mitch chimed in. "Dani adores him."

"She adored Carl, too."

"If it were up to you, Mark, she'd have to stay single for the rest of her life. Besides, he's really handsome," Shannon laughed.

"Go ahead. Make fun all you want. Her father charged me with looking after her. I don't like him. She needs a good country man, not some helpless, slick city lawyer. Good-looking or not."

Tim could imagine the scowl on Mark's face from the grumble in his voice. It was some consolation at least that Mitch and Shannon were defending him. He stood tall and moved into the doorway to face the enemy.

"Good morning," Tim said as cheerfully as he could under the circumstances. The buffet at the north wall of the dining room was loaded with silver chafing dishes on warmers. He assumed he was supposed to help himself, but waited for direction so as not to offend Mark any further. The scowl he'd imagined while still in the hallway was only half as bad as the one he saw on Mark's face.

"Hi," Shannon chimed in. "We're rather informal in the morning. Coffee and breakfast are on the buffet; help yourself."

"Thank you." He headed for the food. He was hungry and wanted a good, strong cup of coffee.

"Do you know how to work the latte machine?" Shannon asked, rising from her chair.

"No. Usually get mine from the deli across from my office." He looked over at Mark and saw his pursed lips; he was nodding his head.

"Helpless," Mark mumbled under his breath.

Tim couldn't help but chuckle. Getting Mark to warm up to him was going to be a challenge. "Dani not back from the barn?"

"Do you see her?" Mark retorted.

"Just wondering. Does it usually take this long to feed?" Tim asked, sliding into a chair at the end of the dining table.

"Oh, one of her friends from high school stopped by to see her. Said he wanted to see the gelding she has for sale," Mark answered, taking a sip of his coffee.

"At six-thirty in the morning? Awfully early," Tim commented. He felt an unease race through his body. His senses were coming alert; he shook it off.

"We don't laze around all day in the country."

"Mark!" Shannon scolded.

This was the first day in a long time that Tim had slept in until six-thirty. But he wasn't going to bother defending himself to Mark. Shannon brought over the latte she'd made for him and set it down. "Thank you," he smiled at her. He couldn't wait to take a sip.

"It was a bit of a surprise. Dani usually has me clean up a horse she's preparing to show to a customer. Bath, clipping, polishing the hooves, and such. Greg Walker, he said his name was. He knew me, but I didn't remember him. Hope he buys that gelding. I must be getting old. Yep, Greg Walker. I just don't remember him," Mark rambled on.

Tim stared at Mark for a moment. "Greg Walker? Did you say Greg Walker?" he repeated. He stood. "Mitch, it's Warden." Tim pulled his pistol from the holster. Mark 's chair screeched against the hardwood floor as he shot back from the table. "Shannon, call 9-1-1. Tell them no lights or sirens, but get here fast. Then call Detective Renton; his card is by the phone in the entry. Tell him Warden is here at the St. Clair Ranch. There may be hostages."

Everyone at the dining table looked at Tim as if he were insane.

"Well, do it!" Tim shouted.

EIGHTY-ONE

"Is this who you're looking for?"

Dani gasped. Gary Warden emerged from the hay bay with Ryan in front of him like a shield, a knife at his throat. He hadn't made it to the house. Help wasn't coming. And now she knew Phil wasn't safe, either. The boy was coming from the shavings bin with a wheelbarrow full of fresh bedding for the last stall. "No, no, no,' she whispered as a prayer.

Phil looked at her and then at his brother. "Hey, what's going on? Let go of my brother!" He started to run toward Warden.

Dani quickly interceded. "No! Don't!" She grabbed the boy before he could get any closer. She hugged him to her. He fought for a second, but then stopped. Dani knew he'd seen it too, the glint of a knife blade in the barn lights.

"If I were you, kid, I'd knock it off right now. Unless you'd like to trade places with your brother," Warden laughed. Dani hugged Phil tighter; Warden seemed to feed off their fear.

"What do you want? I'll give you anything you want, just let the boys go!" she pleaded.

"Yes. You. Will." Warden was cold. "But shouldn't we have some fun first?" The twist of his grin made him look demented.

"Please, Gary; they're just children."

"Children grow up and become you." He glared as if she were disgusting. Ryan struggled and Warden tightened his grip. Dani saw a thin line of red trace the boy's throat.

"Don't struggle, Ryan! Don't! Please, Gary. I'll trade--me for the boys. My life for theirs."

He snorted. "No deal! I don't want you, you used-up whore. I want your money. Their lives for your money."

"Yes. I'll give you anything you want." She was looking beyond him now, her eyes searching every inch, every corner for something she could use to turn the tables and save their lives. Her mind raced through every scenario: she could stab him with a WonderFork, but it was plastic, the metal one was too far away. She didn't know if a plastic fork would hold up or break. Would he kill Ryan before she could get there? There were scissors in the hay room, but from here it looked miles away.

"Dani, let me go. Dani, let me go!" Phil whispered tugging on her jacket. She couldn't listen, not now.

"Their lives for money. As much as you want. All of it." She needed to buy time. He had to know he would never get a dime. But it was worth a try.

"Dani, let me go. *Bugsy. Bugsy,*" Phil whispered again.

Bugsy? Why was Phil talking about the stallion? She tried to look past Warden to the stallion's stall behind him. The horse was standing in front of his closed stall door and bobbing with his head out the window like he always did when he was impatient for breakfast. As each second passed, he was becoming increasingly agitated. He started to buck in place. His ears were flicking back, front, back again. But for the life of her, she couldn't imagine what Phil could do. He couldn't get past Warden to open the stall door. As soon as he ran, Warden would kill his brother. Dani knew that; Phil didn't.

"I can get you the money. Just tell me how we're going to do this," Dani offered. Bugsy started to paw the ground. She could hear his hoof hitting the metal bar on the door. Did she see it? The stallion's antics had opened the stall door, just a tiny crack. He'd opened his door before when the boys had forgotten to latch it. He was working it now. Would he be distraction enough to help them get to safety?

The vision came to her: the horse would work the door to a point where he could slide it open. It would happen fast. Once open, he would bolt from the stall like a racehorse from the starting gate. To an inexperienced person, it would look like Bugsy was going to run him down. There might be enough time for her to grab the cleaning fork. In her imagination, she gauged the distance from her location to the wheelbarrow where it rested. She wasn't sure it would penetrate his skin, but with all her weight behind it, it would surely hurt like hell. Gary would let go of Ryan and the boys could escape and get help from the house. The pawing was like a steady drumbeat. Each strike opened the door one more inch.

EIGHTY-TWO

Mitch leapt from the table, knocking his chair over. Tim knew Mitch's military training would be the key in this situation, since the sheriff was at least a half hour away.

Mark was on his way to the front door. "Wait! Mark, wait!" Mitch called to him. "Don't go rushing up to the barn. If he has hostages and you bolt into the barn, he'll kill them!"

Mark stopped and spun to face them. "They're my boys!" Mark's expression was desperate. Tim set his hand on Mark's shoulder.

"We need to get a look and see what we're up against," Tim said. "I'll go."

"There's a camera system. Dani had it installed so we could watch the foalings," Mark offered. "One at each foaling stall, and a master to look at the barn aisle."

"Can we see the feed?" Tim asked.

"On any of the televisions. The closest one is in the living room," Mitch said.

"Quick. Let's go!" Tim urged them on. They went into the living room and turned on the television. Mitch clicked through the images until he came to one that sent Tim's heart into his throat. Warden had one of Mark's boys with a knife to his throat. "God!" he exclaimed.

"I'm going." Mark was resolute, his face rigid with a stony rage.

"No, Mark. You barge in, you'll be killing Ryan," Tim warned. "This fuck has already killed six people that we know of. We need to think this through." Tim could see Mark was on the verge of panic. He understood--Dani was in there, too. It was their duty to protect them. "Let's listen to Mitch. He has tactical experience. We'll get your boys--and Dani--alive and unharmed," he said, in as calm a voice as he could manage. He wasn't sure he believed it.

"Mark, go down to the road. Make sure that stupid sheriff turns in the right driveway." Mitch commanded.

"Send the city boy," Mark growled.

"No. You do it," Mitch demanded. "You lose your head, you lose Ryan. Don't grumble; just do it!"

Mark scowled, but Tim could tell he would comply.

Mitch turned to Tim. "Can you shoot that thing?" he asked, pointing to the pistol on Tim's left side.

"Yes," Tim answered.

"Are you any good?"

"Yes."

"I figured since you were packing you'd know how to use it. Here's the plan."

Tim was in motion, out the door of the house, keeping to the fence line that would obscure him just as Mitch had instructed. It was nearly seven, but sunrise was still forty minutes away. Light from the windows and stall openings in the barn made a pattern of ribbons on the lawn. Tim was advancing on the barn from the left and Mitch from the right. As he approached, he could hear the *bang, bang, bang* of a horse pawing his stall door. The commotion was good cover; it'd prevent Warden from hearing their assault. Tim reached the first paddock. Quietly, quickly, he climbed the wood rails of the fence and dropped inside the paddock. He inched against the stall's outer wall, staying low. He hoped Mitch had rounded the other side of the barn and was progressing through the back of the stallion's stall, directly behind Warden. Tim would enter in front and slightly to the right of Warden. He was the only one who knew what Warden was capable of. The photos of Alan Sharp and Candy Johnson, Warden's victims, raced unbidden through his mind. He feared Warden would kill Ryan without hesitation if he felt threatened. Hell, maybe even if he didn't. He was one sick man.

Tim ducked into the stall opening. The steady pounding of the pawing horse grew louder. He crept forward until he reached the corner post. He stood slowly. He could see Warden holding the boy with his left arm, the knife in his right hand against the boy's neck. Dani was directly opposite him. Phil was behind her, hugging her leg, eyes squeezed shut. But Ryan was stoic and stone faced with resolve; he was not going to die today. Tim wasn't sure, but for a second he thought Ryan saw him. There was an instantaneous connection, unspoken words; Ryan seemed to know Tim had come to save him.

Tim removed the Walther from its holster and pulled back the slide, chambering a bullet. He clicked off the safety. He aimed. His thoughts raced. What kind of man took a child as a hostage? No real man. Only a coward. His stomach twisted with disgust and anger. Slowly, he raised the pistol and aimed between Warden's eyes. It was a clean shot, like a paper target at the gun range. Tim was surprised to realize he felt no pangs of mercy. He expected them, but they never came. He forced himself to focus instead on Warden's right shoulder and lowered his aim. It took every ounce of control he could find. In the background, the noise of the stallion's pawing matched the beat of his own heart. In the distance, he heard the faint wail of sirens. *Oh God, no!* He'd told them no sirens! Once Warden heard them, he'd know he was cornered and would kill the boy.

The stallion's pawing stopped. The sirens wailed and Warden's eyes widened with panic.

"Stop! Drop the knife! Let the boy go! Now!" Tim yelled. Time slowed. Warden turned to see why the stallion had stopped his fray, just as Mitch had predicted. His grip on Ryan tightened; a strange manic smile twisted his lips. He blinked and started to move as if he would slit Ryan's throat. Tim squeezed the trigger, saw the muzzle flash, and felt the pistol recoil. Warden's upper body jerked hard right. Tim could hear the bullet tear flesh and bone. A red mist of blood spattered the stall wall behind him. Warden's arm flailed in the air and the knife fell from his hand. Ryan slipped to the ground as if his bones had turned to water. Tim felt sick; had Warden cut the boy? Had *he* shot him? Warden reached for Ryan and Tim fired again. Warden plunged to his knees. Ryan was on the ground, wriggling toward Dani as fast as he could. A red stain began to spread from Warden's shoulder down the sleeve of his shirt. He looked at Tim with shock and pain. Outside the barn doors, Tim heard the unmistakable sound of car tires skidding to a stop and gravel spray pelting the barn door. Mitch rushed from the stallion's stall and kicked Warden in the back shoving him to the ground. He placed the barrel of his rifle against Warden's head.

"Make one move and I'll blow your brains all over the floor--and enjoy doing it!" Mitch growled.

Tim holstered his pistol and scrambled to get to Dani. She collapsed against him and tears formed in her eyes.

"It's over, baby." Tim helped stabilize her. "Ryan! Ryan, are you okay?" He grabbed the boy and looked him over. "It's over. You're safe." Ryan had an angry scratch on his neck from Warden's knife, but it was only a scratch. Tim hugged the boy. One tear trickled down Ryan's cheek; he quickly wiped it away, standing straight and strong like he wasn't afraid. "You're going to be okay," Tim smiled at him. Both boys were surprisingly calm for their ordeal. But when Tim started to walk toward the barn door they huddled against him for protection.

"Let's get out of here," he said.

The barn door slid open and two uniformed officers rushed through with guns drawn.

Tim raised his hands, "We're not a threat!" The deputy saw his pistol. "Drop it! Drop your weapon!"

Tim complied, carefully pulling the pistol from his holster and slowly dropping it to the ground. The deputy kicked the Walther away from Tim's reach. Dani grabbed the boys.

"Get on your knees, hands on top of your head."

"No. Not Tim. Don't arrest Tim, Sam," He heard her say, but he knew that until the officers assessed the situation, the only weapons they wanted to see were the ones in *their* hands. Tim did as he was asked.

The other deputy shouted at Mitch. "Put the rifle down! Now!"

"Come get this piece of shit and you can have my rifle, not before!" Mitch answered.

Tim was impressed by his bravado. He watched as the deputy took charge of Warden and Mitch handed his rifle over. The deputy signaled for the medics. One medic took charge of Warden's care. A second tended to Ryan.

"My ID is in my right jacket pocket," Tim calmly told the deputy Dani had called Sam. He nodded to the right, leaving his hands on top of his head. "The man who's been shot is Gary Warden. Call it in. There's a BOLO out on him." The deputy cuffed Tim's hands behind his back.

Sam! Sam! Stop--you're making a mistake!" Dani hated that she was begging. But Sam Johnson wouldn't listen. "Mr. McAndrews isn't the bad guy!" She followed the deputy as he took Tim to the police car.

'Daniela, we go way back, but don't interfere or I'll have to arrest you," Sam replied sternly.

"Go ahead! Arrest me! Listen to me! Sam, he was defending us."

"Daniela, I need you to get back now."

"Dani, it's okay. They don't know what's happening. The officer has to sort it out. I'm fine." Tim explained.

"You can't do this," Dani reasserted. "You can't arrest him for protecting us."

"Have a seat. Watch your head." Sam looked at Tim's driver's license, concealed carry permit, and Department of Justice ID.

"Sam, please."

"Now Daniela, back up. I've already warned you."

"Dani, it's okay. I'm okay. Far less goes wrong if we do as they ask," Tim said, trying to calm her.

Now Dani noticed the other deputy was putting Mitch in the cruiser, too.

"Stupid idiots!" she complained, kneeling beside the open car door. "I'm calling my lawyer!"

"Is Warden being attended to?" Tim asked.

"Yes. The medics are with him," she answered.

"He can't hurt anyone now," Tim said, as if relieved.

Suddenly, she thought she heard something. She looked toward the west. She recognized the engine noise and *whip, whip, whip* of helicopter blades against the air.

"Scott," Tim said. She nodded and he smiled at her.

"Scott will fix this!" Dani ran to the pasture where the aircraft was sure to land. Dust and noise filled the air. Scott emerged from under the rotating blades.

"Scott, they've arrested Tim. Fix this, please!" she shouted over the whine as the helicopter's engine shut down. She ran to Scott's side, but he seemed to ignore her, briskly making his way to the deputies.

"Detective Renton, Seattle P.D." He showed the deputies his badge. "You got Gary Warden? Good Job!" Sam Johnson and Randy Peel looked at each other.

"In the ambulance. He's been shot-up, pretty bad." Sam handed Scott back his badge.

"Life-threatening?"

"Blew his right shoulder all to hell."

"Did you read him his rights?" Scott asked.

"His rights?"

"Warden is wanted in King County on suspicion of murder. Get in that ambulance and read him his rights," Scott demanded. "Oh, and Warden's a flight risk. "You!" he pointed to Deputy Peel. "Go to the hospital with him. I want a twenty-four-hour guard. Which one of you shot him?"

"Some guy named McAndrews shot him. He's in the back of the cruiser. Admits it," Sam reported. "Warden says they were in some sort of dispute, claims McAndrews was trying to kill him."

Scott laughed. "I guess stopping a guy from poisoning women when he doesn't want to is a dispute of sorts. But know this: if Tim McAndrews wanted to kill him, he'd be dead. Good work. Nice collar," Scott said, patting the deputy on the shoulder. Sam seemed to be second-guessing himself. He hustled over to his car and logged Warden's name into his computer.

The arrest warrant information flashed on the screen. Deputy Peel ran for the ambulance.

"Are you the sheriff?" Scott asked.

"She's pulling up now." Sam pointed to the direction of the car turning into the driveway.

"Help me, Scott; Tim's over here," Dani pleaded. Finally, she grabbed his hand and dragged him to the cruiser where Tim was seated.

Scott chuckled and opened the back door. "Nice, McAndrews. I have to say, as much as I enjoy seeing you in handcuffs in the back of a police car, I think I'll go ahead and get you out of this." Scott approached the sheriff as she climbed out of the front seat of her car. Dani raced to meet her.

"Rosa, Sam's arrested ..." Dani was desperate. No one was listening to her.

"Hold on, Daniela. Let me get my bearings." Rosa Gonzales looked Scott Renton up and down. "And you are?"

"Scott Renton, Seattle P.D. Looks like your deputies captured a wanted serial killer. Congratulations. But in the confusion, they've put a King County D.A. in cuffs. Can we let him go?"

"Now, slow down--they did what?" She squared her stance and put her hands on her hips.

"And Mitch Bradley, my pilot. Can we release them both?" Dani asked hopefully. "They rescued us."

"Sam!" The deputy rushed to Rosa. "Did you cuff a King County district attorney?"

"Well, ma'am."

"Let him go. Now. And Mitch Bradley, too," she insisted. The deputy nodded.

"Now Scott Renton, Seattle P.D., do you want to tell me what's going on?" Rosa lifted an eyebrow and delivered a smile that looked to Dani like a flirt.

Tim climbed out of the police car and turned his back to the deputy so he could unlock the cuffs. "Thanks," he said, rubbing his wrist. Dani was immediately there, hugging him. "I'm okay." He held her to him. "No harm done. At least you and the boys are safe." Tim looked around and saw that Mark was holding on to both boys. He smiled. Mark nodded back. For the first time, there was a small crack in Mark's disapproval.

Sheriff Gonzales made a beeline to Tim. "You're being released conditionally," she warned.

"I'm going to the hospital. Check on my prisoner," Scott announced.

"Your prisoner? Not just yet, Mr. Seattle P.D.," Rosa said.

On cue, just as Tim expected, Scott sent the pretty Sheriff one of his lady-killer grins.

"So, you're the King County D.A.?" she asked Tim. If Scott had managed to melt her, she wasn't showing it.

"Tim McAndrews." He offered her his hand. She shook it.

"How is it Mr. Warden ended up getting shot?" She didn't mince words.

"As you know, there's an arrest warrant out for Warden," Tim started, but waited for her acknowledgement.

"Yes."

"He had taken ten-year-old Ryan Settle hostage. Had a knife at his throat. He was demanding money from Miss St. Clair. Mitch Bradley and I assessed the situation. We had Mitch's wife call you. We went to the barn to wait. But from what I knew about Warden, if he made one wrong move, Mitch and I agreed that whichever one of us had the best shot would take it to save Ryan. When Warden heard your sirens, he made a move to harm the boy and I neutralized him."

"Neutralized him? You practically shot his arm off." Rosa looked at him skeptically.

"My second choice," Tim held her gaze until she understood he would've killed Warden had he needed to.

"Got it," she said.

"We've linked Warden to the murders of five women and one man here in Washington, two women--at least two--in California," Scott said.

"So, Warden's on the run and ends up hiding out here in Miss St. Clair's barn. When the kids go out to clean in the morning, he takes a child hostage for some travelling money," Rosa surmised.

"Something like that," Tim offered.

"Something like that? I guess you'd better give me the whole story," Rosa retorted.

"Come inside. I'll make coffee and Mr. McAndrews and Detective Renton can fill in all the details. Would that be okay?"

Rosa frowned, "Deputy Peel radioed that Warden was the victim, said that McAndrews set him up. Said that you intended to kill him and that this is personal. Want to explain?"

"He's a liar!" Dani exclaimed. "We have proof: this is a breeding facility, I have a digital video system."

Rosa smiled. "Coffee and movies sounds like a perfect idea," she said.

EIGHTY-THREE

The house was suddenly quiet. All the commotion was over. Only the occasional crackle of the flames in the huge stone fireplace, the centerpiece of Dani's large living room, interrupted the stillness. Tim sat forward and stared at Dani across the coffee table. She was relaxed all the way back into the cushions of her chair with her eyes closed. Tim guessed she was asleep.

He was now on administrative leave until the sheriff could determine if he was justified in shooting Warden, and whether there would be any charges. Tim had time--and lots of it. He knew his shot was defensible and felt no remorse. His choice had been clear: he could've let Warden kill Ryan or he could save the boy. Maybe his only mistake was letting Warden live.

Tim was looking forward to a few days off. Scott was escorting Warden to Seattle in an ambulance--and handcuffs. Mark had taken the boys to town for a movie and treats, grateful they were safe. Mitch and Shannon had saddled up a couple of horses, taking advantage of the break in the rain to ride up to the little cottage overlooking the ranch.

Tim and Dani were alone. It had only been hours but seemed like days since he'd had a moment to look at her. Her honey hair fell in curls that framed her peaceful face. He studied her lips, searching for the familiar and beloved freckle at the top curve. It reminded him how much he loved to kiss her. Her olive-green T-shirt hugged her body, accentuating the full rounds of her breasts, and tapering down to her slender waist where it tucked into her jeans. Her legs were stretched out in front of her, crossed and resting on the leather ottoman. She'd kicked off her cowboy boots earlier; they were drying next to his on the hearth.

To him, Dani was the loveliest woman in the world. *How did I ever win her?* She was exactly the woman he'd always dreamed he'd marry but never thought he'd actually get. She seemed to accept him, never asking him to be anything other than who he was. She didn't mind when he spread his case files all over the bed and reviewed evidence at night. When he needed to polish up a presentation, she helped. She never nagged when he and Scott spent Sunday afternoons obsessing over the Seahawks. And making love to her was as near to heaven as he would get on earth. Tim was never going to be one of the men who called his wife "the old lady," or "the ball and chain." He was lucky to have her. There was only one thing that bothered him: even though she'd agreed to marry him and they were talking about a date, he knew he loved her more than she loved him. There was always an unspoken uncertainty in her eyes. The past intruded and he didn't know how to change it.

Tim decided he wanted a cup of coffee. He left Dani to sleep; she needed quiet to process the nightmare of this morning. When she was ready, he'd help her reason it out. He slipped from his chair and padded quietly in sock feet to the dining room. He studied the coffee machine for a second to figure out how it worked, then brewed two cups. When he turned to bring them back to the living room, Dani was in the doorway.

"May I have one of those?" she asked, her pretty mouth turned in a smile.

"Yes." He started to hand her one. But she took both cups and set them on the dining table. Her invitation was clear and irresistible. The hesitation he'd usually seen in her eyes was no longer there. Something had changed. She was sure of him, and it was heady. Was he reading her right? They hadn't even touched, and he was already intoxicated. She turned and started toward the stairs, looking back only to reach for his hand. He wanted to pick her up and carry her up the stairs, but instinctively he knew to let her lead. Had she decided to love him? The thought was exciting, exquisite, and longing raced through him, leaving him breathless. When she reached the top of the stairs, she turned.

They stood face to face. She held his gaze for a moment then looked from his eyes to his lips and back again. She kissed him. The touch was so light, so tender; his every sense strained for more. He wanted her, wanted to be inside her. He knew he had to wait. He fought against his need and as he did it became more urgent. She led him into the bedroom and quietly closed the door by leaning her weight against it. He sat on the edge of the bed. She came to him and stood between his legs. She pulled his T-shirt loose from his jeans. He lifted his arms, helping her easily remove it. She unbuckled his belt, then stepped back. Teasing him, she slowly stripped away her T-shirt and unhooked her bra. He watched as she slipped the straps down her arms and let the bra fall away. Swamped with desire, he gazed at her. She was so beautiful.

Her skin was smooth and firm, her curves the promise of pleasure, completeness, and home. He was entirely and utterly in love. He wanted her but knew he must wait. He fought the very thing his body demanded of him, and it made it more thrilling. She wriggled out of her jeans and left them in a pile on the floor. Need hit him hard, and he closed his eyes trying to keep lust reined in. She slipped down between his legs and kissed the denim fabric over his erection. She started to unzip his jeans. He needed to slow this down.

"Let me." He tried to get control. He knew her touch would push him too far. He wouldn't be able to think anymore.

"No. Me," she whispered. He eased back onto the bed, closing his eyes. If he looked at her he knew he wouldn't be able to keep desire in check. He could feel the warmth of her hands on his skin as she slid his jeans down and off his body. He tried to think of anything else to keep control, but when she lay next to him, touching her body to his it was too late. Want overrode reason. He rolled her onto her back and was over her. He gently pressed her legs apart and pushed into her. Warm, wet, tight, she felt so good, so incredibly good. Her perfume and his sweat mixed on the air, delicious and intoxicating. She yielded to him, and he took her.

Tim sighed and settled back against the pillows. He reached for Dani and pulled her close. He closed his eyes and savored the sheer pleasure of his intense state of bliss. Slowly, as reason returned, he realized that, without a ceremony, he and Dani had just married. For the first time, their spirits had merged together, intertwining, and wrapping each other in a bond deeper than he'd ever imagined possible. She had given herself to him completely, holding nothing back. He knew she was finally his. The feeling was unique and wonderful. When he'd rescued them from Warden, he'd let her know he was going to be there to love and protect her. For the first time she believed him, he knew it.

EIGHTY-FOUR

"Where's Tim this morning?" Jenny demanded of Myra, standing in front of her desk, hugging a file folder to her chest. Myra disliked Jenny. Especially since she'd cornered Tim and threatened him. Myra had never had a better boss and she'd been with the D.A.'s office for twenty years.

"Haven't you heard?" Myra answered dismissively. "He's on administrative leave." Jenny narrowed her eyes at Myra. There was no love lost between them.

"No, I hadn't heard. What did he do?"

"He was the man who shot Gary Warden, the serial killer. It's all over the news," Myra announced.

"Then he was at Daniela St. Clair's ranch this weekend?" Jenny mused coldly, her lips forming a distinct pout. But Myra also saw the anger bubbling just below the surface. Jenny's left eyelid twitched as if she were scheming. This was something Myra had feared; she knew what Jenny was capable of.

"Leave him alone, Jenny. He has enough to worry about," Myra stated firmly.

"Whatever do you mean?" Jenny countered, her voice suddenly sugary sweet.

"You know what I mean. Don't you go throwing yourself at him."

Jenny glared. Myra knew she would probably be reprimanded for that comment. She really didn't care. They could fire her! She wasn't going to let Jenny ruin Tim's career. "The sheriff will need to determine if he was justified in shooting Warden. There will be a hearing. In this anti-gun climate, it could go wrong for him," Myra added.

"So, he *was* at the St. Clair ranch this weekend," Jenny repeated. Her eyes flashed with a kind of wicked anger Myra easily recognized. "Is Goddard in?"

"You'll have to check with his secretary. I haven't seen him yet this morning." Jenny was up to something and it wasn't going to be good. As she walked back to her cubicle, Myra unlocked her desk drawer. She looked down to confirm the small blue thumb drive was still where she'd hidden it, under some new envelopes.

EIGHTY-FIVE

Tim was happy. He poured Scott and himself a drink of sipping whiskey. This was the first time Scott would get to see the ranch without the arrest of Warden coloring the view. And this was Kathy's first time ever. Tim was looking forward to having them here, to enjoy the country and his impromptu wedding.

Next week, he'd have to go back to Seattle and face the review board about the shooting. And Goddard had sent him an email asking him to review all the evidence they had on Warden and to recommend charges. The real world was still spinning and orbiting the sun. Next week he'd find out if he still had a job. But for now, he just wanted to be here, where life was at peace and love was everything.

"Kathy's not coming down. She's pouting about something," Scott apologized. Tim handed him a glass and they each took a sip. Tim knew Kathy was mad. When she first arrived, she'd blasted him with a wicked glance as she passed through the front door to the ranch house, and had continued the dirty looks all the way up the hewn log stairs to the guest room Dani showed her.

Tim didn't want to think about that now. Tomorrow he and Dani were making it official. They had a minister arranged at the little white church at the corner intersection for 1:00 in the afternoon. He didn't want his happy mood spoiled by Kathy's moodiness. Tim set his glass on the hand-carved log mantel surrounding the stone fireplace in Dani's living room.

"Go up and talk to her Tim," Dani encouraged, linking her arm through his.

"What can I do?" Tim asked. He was frustrated with Kathy. She was supposed to be one of his best friends and she was acting like a big baby. All he'd asked was that she and Scott stand up for him tomorrow when he married Dani. He would do it for them without question. Kathy really had him confused.

Dani shot him a scowl that surprised him. He'd only seen her annoyed with him once before, when the infamous pictures were presented. "Woah. Okay, I think I'll go up and talk to Kathy," he laughed. Dani smiled, letting him know he'd made the right decision.

Tim took the stairs two at a time. He rapped on the door to the guest room, and turned the knob to see if it was locked. When it turned in his grasp, he pressed the door open. Kathy was lying across the bed, still wearing her blue jeans, boots, and overcoat--as if she intended to leave any minute.

Tim walked over to the bed and plopped down, stretching out so that his head touched hers. "You mad at me?" he asked.

"Yes. Who do you think you are, summoning me, sending your damned airplane to pick me up like I'm some peasant at your beck and call," she exhaled. He knew she'd been crying.

"What? That's what you're mad about? You'd still be driving if we hadn't sent the plane. Now we have more time to spend together. Besides, it's supposed to start snowing tonight and you'd be stuck driving in that," Tim explained.

"Agghh! You just don't get it, do you?"

"Apparently not. So, what? Kath. What did I do to make you mad?"

"You didn't call and tell me you were getting married."

"We just decided to sort of elope. I called Scott. He told you, didn't he?" Tim turned so he could look at her.

"You told Scott, not me," she said huffily.

"Oh? So, that's it? Okay. I'm sorry, Kath. Will you stand up for me? Tell me you'll be there tomorrow, when I marry Dani? I want you there--I need you there," he said quietly.

"Oh, God! Tim, I'm losing you!"

"What are you talking about, losing me? What does that mean?"

"Dani's going to take you away and I'll never see you again."

"After all these years--grade school, high school, college, starting our careers--we've all been together. How can you think I'd let you out of my life now?" he asked. He reached over and stroked her cheek, drying her tears with his touch.

She sobbed and he was confused by his usually practical friend. Scott had shared some of their battles with him, but it had been a whole lot of years since Tim had seen Kathy all girly-emotional. They stared at each other for several moments. Tim turned onto his back, putting his hands behind his head.

"Lying here reminds me of when we were kids. Remember when we used to throw blankets in the backyard on warm summer nights? In a circle, heads touching, looking up at the stars. You, me, Scott, the fearless threesome--"

"Yeah." She let at out a little laugh, then sniffed. "I remember. I used to pretend it gave us extra brain power," she whispered.

"Well, we were superheroes then, so it probably did," Tim chuckled.

"Where did it all go, Tim? It was so easy then, so magical. Now, you're getting married, I'm getting married, and we have to be grown-ups."

"Kathy, we already *are* being grown-ups. You scared about getting married?"

"Yes."

"Being grown-up and getting married has its rewards, too," Tim assured her.

"Is Dani good to you? Does she love you? Tim, we don't talk like we used to."

"She's all in, Kath. And I love her so much."

"All in--do you think Scott is?"

"Of course. Do you think he'd ask you to marry him if he wasn't? Come on, Kath, you know he loves you."

"Remember when Scott told me he was going to go steady with Shelly Garth?"

"We were fourteen--what has that got to do with anything?" he asked, rolling onto his side so he could look at her.

"You held me, up in the treehouse, all night while I cried."

"I remember," he nodded. Oh, yeah, he remembered. "And next morning when our parents found us, my dad kicked my ass and grounded me for two months. And as I recall, your parents made you go to the doctor and get a pregnancy test even though we assured them absolutely nothing happened. Not one of my more golden memories, Kath." He laughed, and she started to giggle, too.

"Yes, but if I'd been pregnant, it wouldn't have been your baby."

"You have to do the deed for that to happen."

"It would've been Scott's."

"You little vixen!" Tim grinned at her. "Scott never told me! We were kids--and you were having sex? Sheesh!"

"Dummy, why do you think I was crying?"

"Because you were a girl? What did I know? Like I said, I was fourteen."

"Do you remember what you promised me?"

He remembered. At the time, he hadn't known what else to say to make her stop crying. "I only remember how much trouble I was in," he teased.

"You told me you'd always be there for me, if Scott broke my heart again."

Tim once again stroked her cheek with the back of his fingers. She'd always been his friend, so close--like a sister. "That hasn't changed. But that's never going to happen, Kath--Scott loves you. Dani and I will always be here for you, too, if you need us," he comforted.

"Do you think Scott will leave me for another Shelly Garth?" she whimpered, sniffing back a full-blown cry. "I'm so scared. I'll marry him and he'll leave me."

"Is that what this whole thing is about? Kath, Scott loves you. You're his girl. I think you always have been," he said with gentleness.

"You're my best friend," Her eyes were brimming. "You'll jet off with Dani, she'll take you away, and I won't see you anymore." She gazed into his eyes. "We've always been friends. Always."

"Dani has never even hinted that she wanted that to end." Tim was tender.

"I love you, Tim." Kathy reached for him. She traced her fingers over his lips.

"I love you, too, Kath."

She kissed him. It was unexpected and sweet.

"Okay. Promise me we'll always be friends, that I'll never lose you, even when we're both old married people," she pleaded.

"Always. I promise." He sat up and encouraged her to sit too. "Now, will you come down and have dinner?"

She nodded and he grinned.

EIGHTY-SIX

The elevator doors opened and Tim stepped out. He'd walked from the elevator to his office a thousand times before, but he'd never drawn this much attention. The whole office seemed to be looking at him. He nodded his greeting, but the stares were unsettling. Today the ethics committee would announce their ruling on whether he was justified in shooting Warden. Had they ruled against him? By saving Ryan's life had he ruined his own? *Too bad.* There wasn't a thing he would change about that day.

He stopped at Myra's desk, but even she seemed changed toward him. She averted her glance almost as if his bold secretary had somehow become shy. He wasn't sure if that was a good or bad thing. Finally she smiled, breaking the tension.

"What's going on? Did I forget to wear pants?" he asked her, laughing.

She giggled, "No, you have them on. But don't you know?"

"Not a clue." He bit at his bottom lip.

"You're a hero! You're getting a commendation from the Kittitas Sheriff's Department for saving Ryan Settle ... oh, darn! I wasn't supposed to tell you!" She grimaced.

"For a moment, there I thought maybe they'd ruled against me."

"No," Myra said. "Goddard wants to see you."

"Of course--now, I suppose?"

"He said to as soon as you get here," Myra answered. "But I need to talk to you first--privately."

"You're not giving notice, are you? I wouldn't be able to do this job without you." He slowly turned, noting that the whole office was still looking at him. Even other ADAs had come to their office doors to stare. He and Myra went to his office and he closed the door.

"You're sure I didn't forget my pants?" he laughed. "So, what did you need to talk to me about?"

"Jenny Mattison."

"Jenny?" He felt a sense of dread coming over him. "What did she do now?"

"She's resigned."

"And? I feel an 'and' in there? Is there an 'and'?"

"And Jenny accused you of--you know--harassing her."

"Great." *From one shit storm to another,* he thought.

"I know you didn't want me to, but I showed Goddard the video message from the other day." Myra looked at him as if he was going to yell at her. She should know better; he'd never yelled at her.

"Okay," he said tentatively.

"Jenny was asked to resign or Goddard was going to fire her, bring her up on charges, and have her disbarred," Myra reported.

"Does everyone in the office know?" That would explain why they were all staring at him.

"No, only me. Now you. Goddard wanted her resignation to look voluntary, but asked her to be gone before you came back. And he wants to tell you himself--so act surprised, okay?"

Tim nodded and peeled off his leather gloves. He removed his overcoat and hung it on the rack by the door. "Anything else I should know?"

Myra was staring at him, her mouth agape. "Oh my God!" She grabbed his left hand and gestured at the beautiful gold band on his finger. "You? You? What's this?"

"Just taking your advice: married men live longer and all that. Dani and I made it official last week," he grinned.

"Hearts are going to be breaking all over the office today! Okay. Go now, before Goddard comes looking for you." Myra was almost giddy.

Tim straightened his tie. He walked down to Goddard's office and tapped on the closed door.

"Come."

Tim entered the room. It looked as if Goddard was just finishing a political meeting. "Should I come back?"

"No. We're finished," Goddard said. It was a dismissal. The operatives scrambled to get their belongings together and quickly retired from the room. "How was your--vacation?"

"Nice." Tim motioned to one of the chairs in front of Goddard's desk.

"Yes, sit. Sit down, son," Goddard smiled. "So first of all, I want you to know that Jenny Mattison resigned. She decided she didn't really like being a prosecutor."

"Oh?" Tim tried to act surprised, but found he didn't know what to say. He thought he'd wait to see what Goddard brought up.

"We need to pick a replacement. I have a folder full of applicants. Go through it for me, will you, Tim? I'm so busy with the campaign. You can leave your recommendations with my secretary."

"Okay." This was a new request. Goddard had never asked him to review resumes before.

"Are you ready for the press conference about Warden?"

Tim nodded.

"We'll have the family members of the victims around the podium with us. I've asked Daniela St. Clair to be there too, as his intended victim. You'll take care of her for me, won't you Tim? It'll make for good press. There'll be questions about the shooting. You can explain why you shot him. I'll let the press know you were cleared of any wrongdoing. Warden's been screaming prosecutorial malfeasance. Claims you were trying to kill him because of a dispute over Daniela St. Clair. He claims you, with the help of the cops, manufactured all the evidence in the case."

"Bull crap ... but that's the tack I'd take too, if I were the defense."

"So, Tim. Did you ever discuss the Warden case with Jenny Mattison?"

"No. I didn't discuss Warden with anyone but Detective Renton, you, Kathy Hope, and Judge ... Judge Mattison signed our warrants."

Goddard stared at Tim. He had raised an eyebrow. "But you didn't discuss the case with Jenny?"

"No. We only discussed her cases. Never mine," Tim answered.

"Just so you know, Jenny accused you of sexual misconduct."

Tim slowly nodded. "I heard from Myra."

"I blame myself. I saw the way she looked at you, even on her first day. But I was so caught up in the campaign that when Judge Mattison came to me and asked that you mentor her, I just gave in. Why didn't you come to me?" Goddard complained. "Well, amazingly enough, Myra saved your bacon. She showed me the video of Jenny's advances. I asked Jenny to quietly resign. She's working for her father now."

"Judge Mattison asked that I mentor Jenny?"

"You know Broussard is usually our training guy."

"I do. Let me ask you something: were you and the judge hoping I'd get together with Jenny—romantically?" Tim was sure this was the plot. Goddard didn't respond for a few seconds. A sly smile turned the corners of his meaty lips. "Is that what Mattison meant when he said, '*What Jenny wants, Jenny gets.*' Was Jenny intended to be the keys to the kingdom?" They'd promised her something they had no right to and no chance of delivering. He remembered Goddard's lecture about men marrying to advance their careers. Had they set him up from the beginning--and were they disappointed? He wondered where he'd be now save for Dani. Probably in a loveless marriage that only advanced his career. Was that even something he was capable of? *Scary thought.* Thank God he wasn't going to ever have to find out.

"I won't lie to you, I didn't care one way or the other--but yes, Judge Mattison wanted the best for his daughter." He chuckled, then dropped his gaze to Tim's face. "He's been asking about you since he met you one day with Bradley Hollingsrow and realized you were one of mine. He said his daughter was graduating law school soon and was looking for a career and a husband. But you," Goddard wagged an index finger at him, "you brought your own keys to the kingdom, didn't you? I must say you really set the judge back on his heels with that one. Daniela St. Clair: beauty, brains, and money. And did I say money? What more could a man with smarts, a near-perfect conviction record, and a future political career want?"

Tim felt disgust rising into his throat. He tried to think what he'd done to lead anyone to the conclusion that he wanted a political career. He'd just wanted to be self-sufficient, a good guy, and a contributing member of society. *Is this how it happened, influential men offering the elixir of power to ambitious young protégés?* Goddard had been clear: he was grooming Tim for higher things. Would he be able to resist? Should he even try?

"Myra said you didn't want to ruin Jenny's reputation or her career, even though you were aware she might try to ruin yours. Called you a gentleman. Judge Mattison knows had Jenny not pressed her case with me, she would still be here and the whole thing would've just been forgotten. He's seen the video. No hard feelings on his part. How is Miss St. Clair holding up, now that we've got Warden?"

"Good. Great," Tim said, knowing a grin was breaking out on his face. He twisted the new wedding band around on his finger.

Goddard was studying him. "You'll take care of her at the news conference. It'll play well to the public to have the victim or their families ... well, you know."

"Of course. I'll take care of her."

"Now, about Warden. We need to talk about the charges. You know he's lawyered up?"

"I suspected he would."

"How do you think we should counter his accusation of misconduct?" Goddard asked.

"The truth. We present the evidence just as we would if he weren't accusing me of impropriety. There's DNA linking him and no one else to the victims. The antidepressant he used belonged to one of his dead wives. It was found in the systems of all his victims except Alan Sharp. Forensics has evidence of that down to the molecules. Then there's the knife--with his, Alan Sharp, and Candy Johnson's DNA on it. We found his girlfriend in possession of Amber Brown's necklace. We present a timeline. Up until we served the search warrants and found the pictures, we had no idea he had set his sights on Daniela St. Clair. She can testify as to their relationship.

We state he was at Dani's ranch because he was stalking her and I shot him because he was going to kill her ranch manager's ten-year-old son. If I were trying to rid myself of a rival I would've killed him, not aimed for a shoulder. But I'm not going to be able to work on this case--I'm recusing myself, right? Isn't that what we decided?"

Goddard didn't say anything for a moment. He just held Tim's gaze. Finally he said, "I need you to help me on this."

"Sir, if I recuse myself, it had better be on the up and up. If I say I'm out and then help—if the press finds out, they'll crucify you. The media will spin it."

"Who do you think should prosecute this case, then?" Goddard asked, worry coloring his voice.

"You." Goddard's lack of confidence surprised Tim. "This is one of those once-in-a lifetime cases. And it's a slam-dunk. With the election coming up, it's over for Raney Marsh; he'll never get the vote. What makes you think Warden is going for a not-guilty plea?"

"His attorney said so."

"Has his attorney seen what we have on him? It's so damning, you'd think he'd recommend a confession."

"His attorney offered twenty years in exchange for a full confession."

"Twenty years? For six first-degree murders, two attempted and a kidnapping charge? Hell, I'd tell them to pound sand. We're going for the death penalty for each murder and the max for the kidnapping. Have you countered?"

"Not yet. That's why I need you. I would've countered with life and no possibility of parole for each case. But she's already said if I offer that, it's no deal. No confession."

"She? Who's the idiot representing Warden?" Tim asked.

"Jenny Mattison."

Tim didn't know what to say. A smile of incredulity swept across his face.

EIGHTY-SEVEN

Tim headed for his office and sat down heavily in the chair behind his desk. It irked him that Goddard--and for that matter, everyone else in the damned office--assumed he was with Dani for her money. It was a surprising slam to his character. He laughed to himself. If he were completely honest he'd have to admit his original attraction to her was based on her beauty. That was shallow, but it had never been about money. Now that he knew her, she was his best friend, his only lover, and made his whole world better.

It also worried him that Goddard was relying on him so heavily these days. He didn't have the experience to hire people. He guessed he had to learn if he was going to be promoted to chief deputy one day. But was he ready now? Nope. He tossed the folder of new candidates to the edge of his desk.

Right now, he wanted to get ready for the press conference. It was coming up in about two hours and he should review the evidence they had on Warden so he'd be well prepared for questions. Goddard had him confused there, too. Recuse yourself because Dani was one of Warden's intended victims and because you participated in the arrest, but help prepare for court? The campaign had Goddard afraid of his own shadow!

He picked up the case file and several letter-sized manila envelopes fell onto his lap. Each one was labeled with a victim's name. These hadn't been sent to him earlier, at the ranch. If it was exculpatory he'd be furious. Sometimes Goddard could be frustrating. He opened the first one and spilled the contents on his desk. He looked through the different-sized slips of paper and realized they were credit-card receipts, banking statements, and cell-phone records. Same for the other envelopes. Even the one marked with Dani's name had the same contents. He set it aside, hesitant to read it; they'd never discussed finances--he'd never asked Dani about hers and she'd never asked about his. It was probably a mistake, but they were doing fine without knowing, why change what was working? Besides, Brad Hollingsrow had told him more than enough the day he'd gone to see him about Katrina Collins. Eventually he would have to look, but he felt like he was snooping where he didn't belong, even though they were married now. Scott had gathered all this information and Tim knew instinctively what he was looking for: Scott had been looking for a connection that would reveal Warden's hunting grounds. He'd wanted to prevent another murder. Tim thumbed back to the outline in the front of the case file. If Scott had found a solid link, it would be noted there—but there was nothing. Tim dialed Scott's cell phone. He'd just ask. But the phone directed him to voice mail.

"It's Tim. Call me." He sat back deep in his chair for a second and then leaned forward and started back through the receipts. He began to jot notes on a yellow legal pad. At first, he thought the victims were all connected through the Sevens Club, but only Dani and Ellen were members—Christine, Jillian, Candy, and Amber were not. Besides, Scott would never have missed that. He went back through the receipts, carefully writing down each vendor in a column under the victim's name. He found it! The one thing the women had in common practically jumped off the page: it was the Backstreet Boutique, Katrina's boutique! Every one of the victims except Alan Sharp had shopped there--even Candy, the eighteen-year-old prostitute. Then he went back through the cell-phone logs. He made a list of all the phone numbers the women had in common. Christine, Jillian, Amber, Ellen, and Dani had all called the Boutique. Dani had once told him Katrina was good with fashion and advised a lot of young professional women on dressing for success. Katrina Collins, whether intentionally or inadvertently, had supplied Warden with his victims.

Scott peeked through his door and Tim motioned for him to come in. He was excited to discuss his discoveries with Scott.

"You rang? I tried to call back, but I was almost here so I thought I'd just pop in. How's married life?" Scott pulled up a chair from the corner and sat down in front of Tim's desk.

"Great, so far. I keep worrying she's going to wake up and figure out I'm a shmuck," Tim laughed.

"Guess who's begging me for a conference?" Scott asked, grinning like he was the guy who drank your last ice-cold beer on a hot summer day.

"Um, let's see ... Warden?"

"Yep. Says he won't talk unless you're there."

"Me? He's accused me of prosecutorial misconduct. Why would he want me there? And why would he think I'd hear him out?" Tim noted sarcastically.

"They all claim police brutality or prosecutorial misconduct, don't they? Ah, who knows? We sent our recommendation for charges to Goddard last week. I'm betting Warden doesn't like 'em. Wants to negotiate."

"Goddard sent them to me last Monday. Wanted me to go over the evidence and make my suggestions. I said we charge him with first-degree murder. Ask for the death penalty. Why should he get less than he gave?" Tim knew that wasn't a very politically correct point of view, but what was wrong with saving the rest of society from a monster? "I expected Dani and I would be subpoenaed for the grand jury."

"You would've been. But after Kathy presented the forensics, they were done. Didn't need anything else for indictment," Scott commented. "Warden's lawyered up."

"I heard. Jenny Mattison." Tim shook his head. "Still having a hard time getting my head around that one. She hasn't tried anything but a few DUIIs. This is a little out of her realm of experience. Wonder what the strategy is? Maybe he thinks he'll be able to do an after-conviction appeal alleging his defense was incompetent? Or maybe he thinks Judge Mattison will pull some strings."

"Is Goddard going to let you be on the team?"

"Can't. I was directly involved in the arrest, I shot Warden. Goddard thinks I'll be better as a witness; I can't be both. Now I regret not saving the taxpayers the expense of his trial."

"LAPD sent up everything they could find on Warden. There wasn't much. We already knew his father killed his mother with an overdose of heroine when he was six. Police believed he may have watched her die."

Tim stared at Scott. No words were even possible.

"No wonder he's so fucked up, right? Bad things get all twisted up in a child's mind. But Gary was a functioning adult. He was a firefighter, a paramedic. A hero. He snapped. He unraveled. When he stood on the precipice, he made the wrong choice. There's always that moment of choice. Did he know the difference between right and wrong? He did." Scott paused. "Didn't get to ask you, are you okay? I mean, about Ellen." Scott looked at him with empathy.

"No. She didn't deserve to die. Scott, I used her."

"That's just guilt talking. Don't kid yourself. She used you, too," Scott said.

"I guess. We were never really a couple. When she broke it off, I was already slithering, anyway."

"Slithering? Like in our college days, love 'em and leave 'em?" A smile crossed Scott's lips for a moment and was gone.

With a slight gesture of his hand, Tim acknowledged the truth. He bowed his head and rubbed his hand across his brow. The guilt felt like a tight band around his chest and he took in a big breath, trying to relieve it. "She came looking for me that night because Katrina Collins told her I was available. But Katrina knew Dani and I were together. We have her on tape whining about it at the lunch." Tim tapped his fingers against the edge of his phone console. "I keep going back to that stupid conspiracy theory of mine. And then I found these bank statements, receipts, and cell-phone records. Goddard hadn't sent them to me earlier."

"I pulled those to see if I could figure out how Warden was finding his victims. Then we saw the necklace and it was off to the races," Scott reported.

"There *is* a connection: it's Katrina Collins. They all shopped at her boutique. They all called her and she called them." Tim announced looking straight into Scott's face. "If money was Warden's motive, who would know better than Katrina who was or wasn't rich? Or at least, who seemed to be?" Tim set his elbow on his desk and rubbed his index finger back and forth over his lips.

Scott nodded, studying Tim's face with renewed interest. "Do you think Katrina was feeding Gary his victims and sharing in the money?"

"You know I do," Tim answered. "There's another thing. Each woman, except Candy and Dani, called another number consistently up until the time they died. That particular number, different for each girl, was to a prepaid cell phone."

"I suspect Warden was using untraceable devices to cover his tracks. After he killed his current mark, he tossed the prepaid phone and bought another. He paid with cash, because I couldn't find a cell phone purchase on any of his credit cards," Scott added.

Tim bit at his bottom lip. "Well, there's our evidence of premeditation. He courted them at least long enough to figure out what they were worth and if he could get his hands on it. What about Katrina? Was she calling a prepaid phone number?"

"Yes."

"Any overlap? Was she calling a prepaid at the same time as any of the others?" Tim sat forward, hoping Scott had done his homework.

Scott briefly laughed. "I didn't look at that. Should've. But, wow, that would be quite the juggle."

"Maybe he color coded them--the blue phone was Katrina, the black Jillian and so on."

"You think if Katrina was calling at the same time as one of the victims, she's in on it?" Scott questioned his logic.

"I don't know. It really bothered me that she said Dani had stolen her life. I went to see Dani's family lawyer. I need to get down to archives. There are some sealed court records that might shed some light--or lead nowhere. Dani and Katrina's fathers were friends, business partners."

Scott lifted his index finger and pointed at Tim. "Yeah? What happened there? So, is your conspiracy theory becoming more plausible?"

"Maybe. I guess we'll find out," Tim answered.

"We know Katrina is hooked up with Warden. Is it for love--or is it for money?" Scott mused, lifting both eyebrows with intrigue. "Let's say—just for fun--it's for money. Warden has the resume. He's already done this. He killed Lily for insurance, Amber for cash, Jillian for gold coins. He probably stole from Candy, but drug and sex profits can't really be traced. What do you think he got from Angelina?"

"Nothing. Her parents thwarted Warden from getting her fortune. I figure he killed Angelina just to get rid of her," Tim said, deep in thought.

"Sure. He'd already set his sights on Dani," Scott speculated.

"Joining forces with Katrina is a natural—until it isn't," Tim added. "Warden was ready to kill Katrina at lunch the other day."

"Of course he was. Dani was the ultimate prize." Scott sat back into his chair, spreading his arms across the back. "He used Katrina to meet up with Dani." Tim stared at his friend and thought about the other cases they had solved with just this kind of brainstorming. Usually, though, Kathy was there too, adding pieces to the puzzle.

"There's just no direct evidence that Katrina's involved consciously or willingly. She could've been duped like the rest of them. Warden is a good-looking guy, has a great job--what smart young woman wouldn't want him, right? I'm still bothered by Katrina's big seduction play the night Dani was out of town. Who does that to their best friend?"

"Maybe you're just irresistible."

"That's got to be it!" Tim chuckled. "No, she was sure I was going to go for it. Then what? Was she planning on recruiting me into her con?"

"Dani was already involved with you. If Katrina's part of this, then she turns you, she wins. Can you believe it? Looks like both Warden and Katrina planned to cut each other out. She turns you, she has that poor, little underpaid government lawyer thinking he's going to get a big, fat payday. She counted on you being swayed by sex and money."

"Well, this poor, little underpaid government lawyer didn't want money, he wanted Dani. Don't laugh, but I didn't know about Dani's money back then. I thought Dani was just a secretary working for S.C. Enterprises and Delight Valley Wineries. I had no idea she *was* S.C. Enterprises and Delight Valley Wineries. Besides, what narcissism! Katrina thinks she's the world's best lover and once I had her I was supposed to be hooked for good?" Tim slowly shook his head in dismay.

"Hey, what do you know--maybe she is."

"Maybe. If you could get past the sleaze and conniving." Tim laughed. Then he set the joking aside and was completely serious. "So Scott, is it enough? Are a few receipts and cell-phone records that could be pure co-incidence enough to convince a judge to sign a search warrant for Katrina's home and the boutique? It's thin. Really, really, thin."

"Buddy, you just gave me reason to take another look." Scott sat forward set his left elbow on the desk and ran his index finger over his mustache.

"I'm just surprised after we brought her in for questioning about the necklace she didn't lay low. She has to realize we suspect her." Tim furrowed his brow as if it could help clarify his thinking.

"She doesn't realize anything. She's sure she's been cleared. I told her she was cleared." Scott's eyes sparkled with mischief. "I've been feeding her rope, waiting for her to hang herself. I've never pulled surveillance. When she lied to me about not knowing where Fraser lived, I had a feeling she knew more than she was telling. We're still tailing her. I say we try to get Warden to roll on his bud."

"I don't think I can stomach making a deal with Warden. His victims got the death penalty without a trial. They had no chance to plead for their lives. If there's a deal to be made, Goddard's going to have to do it."

"Makes me sick, too," Scott swallowed.

Tim's intercom buzzed. "Yes, Myra?"

"Mr. McAndrews, there's a Sheryl Garner here to see you."

"Okay?"

"She says it's important." Myra paused. "It's about her sister?"

Tim wasn't making a connection. He looked at Scott, hoping he could help. But Scott's face was as blank as Tim's memory. "Send her in."

When Sheryl Garner stepped into Tim's office, he could see Scott recognized her immediately.

"Sheryl, how are you?" Scott stood, offering the woman his chair. Sheryl looked very familiar. She was a tall, thin woman in her forties. Her honey-brown hair was cut in a short bob that curled just under her chin. She was casually dressed in blue jeans and a big sweatshirt embellished with embroidery and beadwork. She clutched a binder in her hands and shyly looked around Tim's office.

"Tim McAndrews." Tim introduced himself, standing and reaching out to shake her hand. He hadn't met her and wasn't sure why she was here in his office now. But it was clear to Scott. "How may I help you?"

"You don't know me," she started. "I'm Jillian Garner's sister."

"Oh, yes." Tim nodded. He didn't smile. He remembered her now. He didn't want her to think he didn't take her sister's murder seriously. Scott grabbed another chair and pulled it up to the desk.

"I found this book, we've been searching for it since ..." she choked back tears as she set the binder on his desk. Tim felt his jaw tighten. The grief of a victim's family always moved him. It inspired him to work harder. He couldn't imagine her pain.

She took a moment to compose herself before speaking again. "It's a picture record of her coin collection. It has the date each coin was minted, a copy of each certificate of authenticity, and a picture of each coin. You remember, Detective Renton, you said if I found it I should bring it to you or Mr. McAndrews? You said it might help solve her murder. This is the copy she gave to her insurance agent."

"I do remember," Scott said, softly. "Thank you, Sheryl."

"I can't believe she's gone, that I'll never see her again. We were so close," Sheryl said, her voice wavering. "Thank you for catching him." She glanced across the desk at Tim. He didn't know what to say. There was nothing he could say that would bring back her sister or ease her grief. "You'll put him away forever?"

"Yes, ma'am," Tim affirmed.

There was a tear tricking down her cheek and she was slow to wipe it away. "Do you think this book will help?" Sheryl lightly touched her fingers to her lips.

"Yes, ma'am. I'm sure of it," Tim said. It would help immensely if they were able to recover any of the lost coins.

"Thank you. Thank you so much," Sheryl said. "Well, I should go; a Mr. Goddard requested that he meet with me before a press conference. Do you know where ...?

"My secretary Myra will show you," Tim said, and buzzed Myra with instructions.

Tim and Scott sat silently for a moment.

"You haven't recovered any of Jillian's coins, have you? Any of the pawn shops or gold dealers report anything?" Tim asked.

"Not yet."

"What if we let the public believe Warden acted alone? What if we let any accomplice get nice and comfortable with life?"

"Get so relaxed--"

"Can you put financial pressure on Katrina?" Tim asked.

"You mean like have her bank accounts frozen, credit cards declined, bank deposits lost, that kind of thing?" Scott picked up a pen from Tim' desk and was twirling it through his fingers.

"Yes."

"Fuck no, we're not the IRS." He tossed the pen at Tim and Tim caught it in midair. He set the pen up in his fingers like it was a football and tossed it back. "But we won't have to worry about that—Katrina's always on her last dime by the end of each month, I've seen her bank statements. If she thinks we're not looking at her as a suspect and she has the coins, she'll start cashing them in," Scott nodded.

"I think I owe Branson Holt a favor. I did ditch him the other day when he wanted an interview." Tim remembered how delighted he was when he found out he'd confounded the press.

"But you didn't know it was him."

"He doesn't know that. I can lead him to think otherwise. Let's plant a couple of questions with him that imply we're certain Warden acted alone. Goddard will be good with it."

"And if Katrina is innocent?"

"If she doesn't have the coins, she doesn't. No harm, no foul. As a bonus, it might just piss Warden off enough to roll on his playmates if he thinks they're going to get off without a scratch."

"I like it. Let's do it," Scott agreed.

"You sure are a crappy foil! You're supposed to give me the reasons why this is a bad idea, not go along with my hair-brained plans," Tim teased.

EIGHTY-EIGHT

"Hubba, hubba! Who's that handsome man?" Beebe Knoll teased Branson Holt as he posed for his cameraman for a lighting adjustment. Branson wanted to look the best he could for his TV audience. Beebe was with a rival network and had moved up from the newspaper ranks--if you wanted to call the *National Globe* a newspaper, that is. Really, it was nothing more than a supermarket tabloid, a gossip rag, reporting on movie star-sleaze, Bigfoot encounters, and alien abductions. Branson resented her. He was an actual journalist with a Master's degree. Beebe had been one of the most outrageous reporters in the *Globe's* stable of hacks before she'd landed her current position with SBC News. He knew she got her position just because she was a pretty, perky blonde, and looked good on TV. But Branson had heard from an unnamed source that she had credit-card debt up the wazoo. He worked hard for his place in the city's TV news market, and competing with Beebe was almost more than he could stand. But what she didn't know--and he wasn't going to tell her--was that he and he alone had earned the confidence of the district attorney's favorite boy.

Just a few minutes ago, as they were setting up, he'd been invited to the D.A.'s office where McAndrews had apologized profusely about ditching him weeks ago. He'd said if he'd known it was Branson, he'd gladly have given the interview. And then Goddard, McAndrews, and Detective Renton had pressed him to ask a couple of planted questions during the interview, with the promise that if what they were hoping and expecting to achieve happened, he'd be given the breaking news at least two hours before his competitors..

Branson glanced over his shoulder. "You mean the tall, fit, striking blond?" He forced a laugh. He'd been here before. Beebe would bat her big brown eyes at McAndrews and think she could land an interview. He wished her luck on that one. McAndrews had already explained in no uncertain terms that he wasn't going to try any of his cases in the media. Period.

"Yes, the one that seems to be protecting Daniela St. Clair. Is he private security? If so, which company?"

"You mean you don't know who he is?" Branson scolded her, making certain she understood he thought she was stupidly ignorant.

"Would I be asking you if I did, cupcake?" she toyed with him openly.

More than once, Branson had considered taking her up on her flirts, just to see what would happen. But she had a reputation for ruthlessness that scared even him. She was known to land you in a one-nighter, ply you with alcohol, and then to scoop you on the very story *you* were working on!

"That's Tim McAndrews. The D.A.'s guy."

Branson watched her look McAndrews up and down. "*That's* our shooter? Well, well, and another well!" She grinned at Branson. "Is he married?"

"Don't think so. You interested? Want to meet him?" Branson winked at her.

"I want to meet him. Can you arrange it?"

"Anything for you," Branson lied. He knew McAndrews wouldn't give her jack. He was like talking to a brick wall. In fact, it bothered him a little. McAndrews' suddenly, cooperative attitude and the planted questions made him suspect the cops and the prosecutor didn't believe Warden acted alone and that they were trying to draw an accomplice out from the shadows. It was kind of a scary thought. But Branson was no idiot; he knew if he played ball with them today, they'd come to trust him and he'd get other leads in the future. A real win-win.

"Looks like the press conference is going to get started. Catch up with you later?" Beebe was sugar sweet.

"Sure." *This is going to be fun,* Branson thought.

Paul Goddard was a big man. His size matched with his reputation in the court room. His brown hair was neatly cut and a trim mustache accented the curve of his upper lip. His brown eyes were fierce, a trait Branson had heard Goddard had acquired after trying so many criminals. Holt had heard that as a younger man Goddard had been quite the dashing prosecutor and a favorite with the ladies. But the years and good home cooking had distorted those looks with too many pounds. The set-up crew had placed the podium on an upper level and it gave Goddard the appearance of a giant looking down on Lilliputians.

Goddard gave a prepared statement. They had caught Gary Warden. In King County, he had allegedly killed four women by poison and murdered one man, Alan Sharp, by slitting his throat. Branson knew all of this already from the police reports. Warden was captured during an attempted kidnapping. He'd been shot in the shoulder by McAndrews when he'd acted like he might kill the child he'd taken hostage. Nothing new there, either; Branson had heard there was a compelling video. He wanted to get his hands on it; he'd even chatted up one of the new ADAs in hopes they'd leak it. But so far, no go.

McAndrews had been cleared of any wrongdoing by a review committee. But really, who would convict a hero saving a child! The big surprise had been the part about McAndrews recusing himself from being lead prosecutor on the case. He hadn't wanted any question of impropriety since he'd participated in the arrest. He wondered what McAndrews must be feeling about that decision: sidelined in the case of the decade. Branson was taping the speech so he could pore through it before the evening news and glean out the good parts for his show.

Beebe slipped alongside Branson. "So, what do you think is going on between Miss St. Clair and the handsome D.A.?"

"Nothing. What are you talking about?" Branson was annoyed.

"This whole conference he's had his hand on her back. And occasionally, she reaches across and rests her left hand on his arm. Like now." She grinned. It was one of those I-know-something-you-don't-know grins. "And what was Mr. Gorgeous doing at the St. Clair Ranch in the first place?"

Branson studied the couple. "So? Wouldn't you want to cozy up to a handsome D.A. if you were an intended victim of a serial killer? She feels safe around him."

"Me? I'd like to 'cozy' up to that D.A. even if there was no more crime on earth ever! So, are you thinking Mr. Up-and-Coming *doesn't* have political aspirations? Trust me; he does. Now, I haven't followed Daniela St. Clair since her nasty divorce, but from that three-carat diamond and the matching wedding band on her ring finger, I'm betting she's married again. Married and huddling up with a single and very attractive prosecutor who will someday soon need all of the St. Clair fortune he can get his hands on, if he wants to get off home plate and into the office of his dreams. Scandalous, isn't it?" Beebe observed with glee. She was checking to see if Branson was on board. He was annoyed instead. She was talking like this nonsense was the news story, not the fact that they'd caught a prolific serial killer. Branson shot her a half smile. His station's management team was discussing hiring her as a co-anchor and she was nothing more than a gossip-rag idiot.

"Beebe, do you ever wonder why your mind is always in the gutter? I guess you can take the girl out of the tabloid, but you can't take the tabloid out of the girl! *Who cares*?!" If Beebe wasn't so sexy in her tight blue suit, she wouldn't have a job.

"Branson, did you ever wonder why most people live in the trash heap with me? Scandal is delicious and diverting for people with ordinary, humdrum lives! It's our job to give it to them. Besides, I can make a quick five-to-twenty-five-thou on a story like this." *Cha-Ching!* There might as well have been dollar signs in her brown eyes.

"You don't still write for the *Globe,* do you?"

"You bet. I write under a pen name. Everyone loves gossip about the rich and beautiful, even you. Besides I haven't written anything about our favorite socialite and philanthropist in years. Do you know who she's married to?"

"No idea. But you go for it, girl. Count me out." But he knew this was just the kind of story that would kill it for Beebe with his network. A big grin crept across his face despite himself. "So, what's your pen name--or am I going to have to buy that piece of garbage just to find your story?"

"Alice Carroll."

"That's an odd name."

"*Alice in Wonderland,* baby. Because the stuff I uncover is just that strange!"

EIGHTY-NINE

Tim was grateful to be away from all the questions and back in his office. He'd explained why he shot Warden three times. But he was delighted Goddard had been able to say unequivocally–in answer to Branson's planted question–that Warden had acted alone in all the murders. If his hunch paid off and Katrina and Fraser were in on it, they might be emboldened to start cashing in some of Jillian's gold coins.

When Tim saw no one was looking, he took hold of Dani's hand and quickly hustled her though the door to his office and closed it behind them. He engaged her in his arms as he leaned back against the edge of his desk.

"Mrs. McAndrews, what are you going to do for the rest of the day?" he asked between kisses. As usual he wondered how he'd ever been so lucky to marry this wonderful woman.

"When I called Karen she said our second shipment of Lodi malbec is at the freight dock. I think I should make sure they don't lose it this time. And I guess the vintner at our Walla Walla location is in negotiations with a wine distributor. He wants to put our cabernet franc in the supermarkets. Which means the thousand-acre parcel I've been eyeing next to our vineyards for the past six months is now a priority. I'd better go make an offer. How about you? What are you doing this afternoon?"

"Nothing that exciting. Warden wants a pre-trial conference. Said he won't talk unless I'm there. Scott's setting it up. Other than that, I guess I'll be working my other cases." Tim held her gently around the waist. "Did I tell you yet today how beautiful you are?"

"A hundred times so far. Did I tell you yet how much I adore you?" Dani countered.

"A hundred times, but I never get tired of hearing it."

"I adore you." She hadn't hesitated a second.

"Do you want me to take you out for dinner?" he asked. "I will, anywhere." He was amazed by how he would do anything for her, just to have her say she loved him.

"No. Dinner is planned. Can you be at the penthouse by six, or do you need more time?"

"Six. Does that mean I have to let you go now?"

"Yes."

"Six works."

"Tim, please be careful. I don't like you even talking to Warden. He's evil."

"I'll be careful." He kissed her again, savoring the feelings she inspired. He let her go. He opened the door for her and walked with her partly into the lobby. He watched her walk the rest of the way to the elevator.

"Mr. McAndrews?" Tim turned and saw an attractive blonde approaching him from his right side. He didn't recognize her and suddenly wondered if she were one of the new applicants wanting an update on the status of her job application. Myra was on break and so he had no one to run interference. *Crap!* With all he had going on he hadn't had a spare minute to open the candidates file, let alone make any recommendations.

"Daniela St. Clair is a beautiful woman, isn't she?" the blonde commented.

"Yes, very," he agreed and turned back to watch Dani walk into the elevator. He didn't engage with the woman until after the elevators doors closed. "How can I help you?"

"I'm Beebe Knoll from SBC News. I wondered if I could ask you a few questions."

"Sorry, no. I gave my statement at the press conference." Tim smiled graciously, but he wanted no part of this. He'd given the reporters all they were getting out of him until the trial.

"Yes. I was there for your statement."

"Okay. You got it then, I don't have anything more to say. If you'd like, my assistant can send you a transcript. Just leave your card on her desk and I'll let her know." Once again, he gave her his formal smile and turned to head back to his office.

"Mr. McAndrews--are you having an affair with Daniela St. Clair?" She had raised her voice loud enough so several of the secretaries in the main lobby were now looking in his direction.

"Excuse me?" Shocked at first, he momentarily stood looking at her. Tim felt a flush of anger bubbling up. He frowned to indicate her question was out of line. Now he realized who she was: Dani had told him about a female reporter who had hounded her during her divorce and published trash about her in a grocery-store tabloid. Dani had warned him that the rags would be all over their wedding, and if they caught wind of their secret one it would send them into a high-speed spin.

"Are you having an affair with Daniela St. Clair?" She was bold. The expression on her face said it all. She thought she had him. She shoved a small microphone at him from a recording device she held in her hand.

He blocked it with his forearm. "I have no intention of discussing my personal life with a reporter from the *National Globe*. That's who you are, isn't it?" He walked away, putting an end to it.

"During the press conference, you shared glances, and you had your hand on her back the whole time!" Beebe called after him. He wheeled to face her. She was narrowing her eyes as if she'd discovered a big, juicy secret.

"Did I?"

"So, Mr. McAndrews, are you having an affair?"

He studied her. She wasn't going to drop it. "The answer to your question is no. Not an *affair.*"

"Do you know she's married?" Clearly, Beebe knew men didn't readily confess their affairs and she obviously wasn't buying his answer. He and Dani hadn't told their families yet about their marriage, and he could just imagine the flap if they found out by reading a tabloid headline in the grocery check-out line. Once Beebe did her research--if she did any at all--she'd learn they were married, but by then they'd have had time to tell their families.

"Yes, I know she's married." He was very annoyed and took pains to show it. She was prying where she didn't belong.

For a few seconds, Beebe was speechless. "Mr. McAndrews, do you think her husband is aware of what's going on?"

Tim stared at her surprised, then laughed. He briefly wondered why she hadn't connected the dots and put him in that role. Wasn't *he* husband material? *Oh, who cares what a reporter thinks.* It was what Dani thought that mattered.

"Her husband? Yes. He knows. Are we all good now, Ms. Knoll?" Tim started for his office.

"So, if it's not an affair, what is it? It sure looks like an affair. And don't give me that 'we're just friends' crap!" she blurted, squaring her stance and glaring at him. Again, he laughed.

"Ma'am, it's none of your business. *Affair* is your word, not mine," he stated. Now it was a game. "If you'll excuse me, I have work to do." This time Tim went into his office and sat behind his desk. He realized he'd better call Dani; he was certain Beebe Knoll was going to pay her a visit. When he looked up, he saw that Beebe had followed him in.

"What's your term for your relationship, then?" she demanded.

"Ms. Knoll, your manners need work. You don't get to barge into my office." He leaned forward in his chair.

"Your secretary isn't at her desk."

"And that gave you license?"

"You can easily get rid of me. Just tell me what's going on and I'm outta here." She was grinning as if she could make a deal.

He stood and pointed to the door. "Did you not understand me when I told you I wasn't sharing my private life with you?"

"Mr. McAndrews, come on. I'm just trying to make a living."

"Make it somewhere else," he insisted as he rounded his desk. Beebe saw the gold band on his left hand. She looked at his face, his eyes, as if she could read his thoughts. He was sure she understood now.

"Oh. My. God! No wonder you're being such an ass! You're married, too! You're stonewalling me to protect your own marriage! Oh, this is great stuff!"

Tim was amazed by her outrageous conclusion. Had it never crossed her mind that he and Dani might just be married? It was his fault. He could've just answered her straight, but he was having too much fun at her expense to stop, now. "Ma'am, you need to leave. Let me show you the way out." Tim took hold of her arm just above the elbow and began to firmly guide her to the elevator. "This is a workplace and it's completely inappropriate for you to cause problems here."

"Then meet me later. Otherwise I'll just have to write about my speculations."

This had probably worked before. He could imagine a politician or businessman who was actually having an affair panicking about now and agreeing to meet with her. "Ms. Knoll, you do realize this is the district attorney's office and that I'm one of the attorneys? I suggest you not write a single word of *speculation.*"

"Daniela St. Clair is a rich, beautiful heiress. She's fair game. The public is interested in her."

"Fair game? So, you think you can make up trash about her? Don't you dare." The elevator doors opened, and Tim urged her to move into the car. He pressed the button for the lobby floor and withdrew his hand. "No speculation. Am I clear?" He held her gaze long enough to make sure she was sufficiently warned.

Beebe just glared at him as the doors closed.

Beebe stomped off the elevator in the ground-floor lobby. McAndrews was so difficult! She knew what she'd seen. He and Miss St. Clair were lovers if she'd ever seen lovers--and she'd seen lovers! No doubt in her mind. She had him, dead to rights. But he'd admitted absolutely nothing. He was angry, even threatening. She'd heard the I'm-an-attorney-thing a million times--what politician wasn't? Didn't stop them from screwing around! But what if he was just protecting a victim, like Branson Holt had said? What if she were mistaken? She'd better watch her step! Oh, hell! She could see an affair a mile away! She'd never doubted her instincts before. She reviewed their conversation in her mind. Wait! He'd all but admitted it. He had said not once but twice he wasn't going to discuss his private life with her. Which meant he had a private life to hide. And he didn't tell her not to write anything; he told her not to write speculation. *All right, Mr. McAndrews,* she thought, *I'm not going to write speculation! I'm going to catch you with your hand in the cookie jar. Then I'm going to write the cold, stark truth!*

NINETY

Tim stood next to Anna in the viewing area outside of the interrogation room behind the two-way mirror, absently watching Scott set up the recording equipment. He was deep in thought. Both Warden and Goddard had wanted him here today, for different reasons. Goddard seemed to be running scared because of the election. According to the media, his poll numbers were fine, but Goddard had lost confidence somewhere along the way and was leaning heavily on Tim. Goddard's opponent for district attorney, Raney Marsh, was no competition. Tim had beaten him in court consistently, even when he was just out of college.

Then there was Warden. Tim wasn't sure what his request was about. The grand jury had taken all Goddard's recommendations for charges verbatim when issuing the indictments against Warden and that hardly ever happened--they usually amended something. Tim was certain Warden didn't like his prospects. Too bad! Maybe he'd decided to confess. At this point, with the evidence they had, confession was a smart option. Otherwise, Warden just might face a jury of single women terrified that their next date might poison them for their money, or parents horrified by the thought of a ten-year-old child being held hostage at knifepoint. If it went that far, those were the very kind of jurists Tim was going recommend Goddard choose.

Goddard arrived and entered the interrogation room. Jenny followed, avoiding eye contact with Tim. Tim chuckled to himself. At some point, if they both remained in the law, they were going to have to talk. Hell, he hadn't started this war.

With everything ready, two officers brought Warden into the room. The usually dashing Warden looked bedraggled. The orange jumpsuit accentuated the dark circles ringing his eyes and he had at least a two-day growth of beard. Tim noted that his arm was still cradled in a sling. He'd heard Warden was going to have to undergo a long haul of physical therapy. The good news: It would be a long time before Warden would be able to wield a knife again. Scott reminded Warden of his rights and obtained his consent to be recorded.

"You wanted a conference, Warden. What is it you want to talk about?" Goddard started.

"Is he here?" Warden asked, studying the two-way mirror as if he could see McAndrews if he looked at it a certain way. "I'm not talking unless he's here."

"He's here," Jenny assured him. "But Gary, as your attorney, I'm advising you not to say anything."

"Ms. Mattison, they have enough evidence to put me away forever. Isn't that right, McAndrews?" He raised his voice and directed his comments to the mirror. "Bring him in here. I want to see his face."

"He's not prosecuting your case. *I'm* the one you need to talk to," Goddard said harshly.

"No. This is personal. He *made* it personal."

Scott was surprised. "Just how do you figure he did that, Gary?"

"She was supposed to be mine. I found her first. I'm not talking unless he's in here."

"Who? *Who* was supposed to be yours?" Scott asked.

Was Warden playing at insanity? Tim wondered as he watched through the two-way glass.

Warden glared at the mirror and crossed his good arm across his chest, over his arm in the sling.

Goddard motioned and Scott rose from his chair. The decision was made: Tim was coming in. They had tried to avoid it. Warden was going to try to get to him, that was a given. As Tim entered the room Warden looked up at him and a strange, bizarre smile twisted his lips. Tim had always considered himself a decent judge of character, but months ago, when they had first met at Dani's, he'd not even seen a small glimmer of this side of Warden. That was before his more gruesome murders. Tim believed Warden had surrendered his mind to thoughts so dark he'd lost his soul.

Jenny had no choice now. She was going to have to look at him. Tim acknowledged her with a nod. "Miss Mattison," he said cordially. She lifted her chin haughtily and didn't return the greeting. Tim surmised she'd taken Warden on with the hope that she could defeat him in court. Now instead, she found herself up against Goddard. That was likely a rude awakening. Still, Tim didn't know how to feel about her false claim of harassment. He was more confused by it than angry. Warden was looking from Jenny to Tim and back again. Tim guessed he was trying to interpret the animosity that sparked like electricity on the air. Warden would use it if he could.

Tim sat down. "You wanted to talk to me."

"Did you get my present?" Warden taunted, the grin on his face making his eyes look coal-black and evil.

"No." Tim stared back. Then shook his head. "No present."

"Sure you did." Warden leaned back in his chair.

Tim knew that whatever Warden was referring to, wasn't going to be good. He knew the next exchange would reveal something irrational. He was determined not to give Warden the reaction he wanted. "Sorry, no."

"Ellen Mason?" Warden said, watching Tim for a response.

It took everything Tim could muster to keep his cool. If he responded in the way he wanted to, the defense could use it as evidence that his case against Warden was part of a personal feud. Warden was egging him on, but Tim knew this game and considered himself the better player. Scott set a hand on his shoulder making sure he was calm. "You admit then, that you murdered Ellen Mason?"

"Don't admit to anything!" Jenny was on the verge of panic. Tim glanced her way, letting her know it was already too late.

"Oh, Miss Mattison, like I said before, you know they have enough evidence to put me away for good and throw away the key. You know it. I know it. They certainly know it." Warden stared across the table at Tim. "They want something. That's why they're here. What is it, boys? You want to clear all your missing-person cases?"

"You asked for the meeting, Gary," Goddard reminded him coldly.

"I asked for a meeting with McAndrews." Warden shut him down with a vicious glare.

"What did you want to tell me, Gary? That you murdered Ellen Mason?" Tim kept the pressure on.

"You already know I did. By now your crime lab has confirmed she took an overdose of Norpramin with alcohol--a lovely Delight Valley syrah, by the way."

It would've been a cruel dig if Dani were here. *But any wine would've done the trick,* Tim thought. Warden had just confirmed their suspicions about his M.O. on tape, linking himself to most of the victims.

Warden continued. "And the DNA has to be back showing I'm one in 135 billion with that profile. Since there are only 7.3 billion people on earth, you'll argue, who else could have had sex with her?"

"We know you killed her," Tim answered. The sex comment was meant for him. But he and Ellen had been apart for over a year. What claim could he possibly have on her sexual fidelity? Still, the tight feeling of guilt was back and Tim wrestled it down. Was there something he could've done that night to protect her? Warden wanted to get to him, that was clear. Though he was succeeding, Tim wasn't going to give him satisfaction by showing it.

"Aren't you in least bit curious about how I found Ellen?"

"Sure, Gary. How'd you find her?" Goddard asked, and Warden whipped his gaze at the older man as if annoyed he was even in the room.

"I was speaking to McAndrews," he snapped, settling his dark glare on Tim.

"I think I have a pretty good idea. Katrina Collins and Ellen were acquaintances. Ellen shopped at her boutique. Katrina, being your girlfriend and all, gave you the names of your victims by design or by mistake--either way, that's how you found them." Tim felt his jaw muscle tighten. Just looking at Warden was making anger roil up to the surface. He imagined killing Warden with his bare hands and enjoying every second of it. He pushed the thought away.

"Aren't you the clever one? But you're wrong. Ellen came looking for me." Warden's voice dripped with wickedness. Tim felt disbelief surging through him. Warden wasn't Ellen's type. But he'd been in this job long enough to understand anything was possible.

"Sure, she did." Tim was dismissive. "You found your marks at Katrina's shop." He reiterated. "Almost all of them."

"I figure you found Dani at a wine gala like the one this summer."

"Dani, is that what you call her? Isn't that sweet."

"You found Dani just about the same time you realized Angelina Caro's parents had intervened and you weren't getting a dime of her money. What happened there, Gary? Angelina's parents threaten to cut her off? Or did you just need to move on to a bigger prize?" Tim paused. waiting for Warden to respond. He did only smirked.

Tim continued. "Killing Angelina was risky business. What if the Napa detectives contacted LAPD and connected you with your other dead wife? You'd be under a big black cloud of suspicion. Husbands always are. But you like that risk, don't you, Gary. Gives you a rush of adrenaline?"

Warden was surprised. He obviously hadn't expected they knew about Lily and Angelina. "Don't even pretend to know me. You'll never know me."

Tim let a smile tick up. "I don't want to know you."

Warden glowered at him. Suddenly, Tim realized it. Warden knew all the evidence they had against him was irrefutable and he was angling to go down in history as a famous serial killer. Another Bundy. *Sick!*

"Husbands are always under suspicion, so you decided to lay low. You followed Dani to Seattle. You rented the apartment on James Street. You watched her though that high-powered telephoto lens on your camera. You took pictures of her over and over again. You pasted them all over your bedroom walls. After a while you decided you'd waited long enough. Time to move in, right? You probably put yourself in her path, but she didn't notice you. Or if she did, she rejected you." Tim wondered if Warden's ego would be able to take that blow.

"She never rejected me! Never! I didn't want her to see me. *I* decide when it's time for them to see me!"

"Them?" Tim sat back in his chair. The shock in the room was palatable. There was always that unfathomable color of madness to every serial killer. Jenny started to say something but Warden silenced her with a wave of his palm. Tim knew she should stop him from saying another word. She should put an end to this interview right now, but she was too inexperienced to know she had that power. He felt sorry for her in a way, but he wasn't going to help her. It was already too late; Warden had confessed to murdering Ellen and was on the verge of confessing to all.

Tim started again, "You followed Dani to Katrina's dress shop. You saw they were friends. You planned to get to her through Katrina. You joined the Sevens Club and--"

"And there you were. Bringing her roses, taking her to fancy lunches at Marche, escorting her to the symphony, carrying her across rain puddles, staying all night," Warden chuckled. "We had to make a plan to get rid of you."

"We?"

"Oh come on, McAndrews. Do you really think I'm going to tell you anything more?"

"Was Bill Fraser in on this?" Tim calmly asked.

"That idiot? Not a chance," Warden growled.

"Wasn't the plan to get Dani to marry him? Kill her and cash in on the insurance? That was Katrina Collins' scheme, wasn't it?"

"You really are a fool, aren't you? My plan was to get Daniela to marry *me!* But she took you back at the wine gala. And why wouldn't she? Such a hero. I really enjoyed watching you charge into that freezing river after that girl. You should've seen the look on your face when you realized she was dead. How priceless."

"You mean Rachel Burk? You killed her, didn't you, Gary?"

"Why do you keep bringing up their names?" Warden was dismissive.

"They were people. Living, breathing human beings. How about these names: Christine Murdock, Amber Brown, Jillian Garner, Candy Johnson, Alan Sharp? People have names, Gary. They were someone's daughter, lover, sister, brother, friend. They had life and value."

"Value? Not to me. But Daniela St. Clair, now she has value. Real, tangible value."

"Did you kill them?" Tim pressed.

Warden just sneered.

"Did you?"

"I want a deal. I'll give you what you want for a deal."

Tim looked over at Goddard. "He wants a fricking deal." Tim stood, he leaned across the table pressing his palms down on the surface. "If it were up to me this would be your deal: the death penalty on every count of murder. Six counts."

"There's no death penalty in this state," Warden laughed.

"But there is. There's a moratorium on execution, but the death penalty is the law. You're one election away from all of this getting reversed. Click of a ballpoint pen, signature of a new governor, and you're going to hell where you belong."

"But it's not up to you, is it?"

"No. Mr. Goddard will be prosecuting your case."

"Ha!" Warden glowered.

Tim sat down, picked up one of the bottles of water Scott had set on the edge of the interrogation room table, twisted off the cap, and took a drink. He slowly set the bottle back on the table and smiled. "You think that's funny? Think again. Goddard is more of a hard-ass than I ever dreamed of being."

For a moment, Tim thought he read panic in Warden's eyes. He'd assumed Tim was lead prosecutor, not Goddard. "You killed Ellen, that's what you wanted to tell me?"

"I'm recanting my confession; you forced me to say that."

Tim chuckled. "We'll just play the tape and let the jury decide."

"I'm not saying another word."

"So, we're done here?" Tim stood, turned, and started for the interrogation room door.

"One more thing, McAndrews," Warden snarled.

Tim stopped, but didn't face him.

"I hid cameras all over Daniela's house."

"Did you?" Tim turned back. "Good to know. We'll add another count; invasion of privacy, felony voyeurism to your charges."

"She's one delicious woman. I watched you. I watched you make love to her."

Tim froze, his jaw tight fighting the anger. The thought made him feel sick.

"All right, that's enough," he heard Goddard say. Tim looked over at Scott, who discreetly shook his head. Instantly, Tim knew Scott and CSI hadn't found any cameras. Didn't mean there weren't any.

Tim slowly returned to the table, leaned across it menacingly, "Did you enjoy it? I hope you did, because I do. Every. Single. Night. You know, right now, I'm going home to that sweet, delicious woman. But you? The way I understand it, where you're going, you never know if tonight's your lucky night and you get to play the woman."

Tim wheeled and walked out of the interview room. He heard the door close, but also the footsteps of someone following him out. He knew it was Jenny, but he didn't want to talk to her, not now.

Jenny called out to him. "Tim! Tim, stop!" She reached for his arm.

"What? What do you want?" He faced her. His anger was barely checked.

"Warden's sorry he said that to you. It wasn't true. He wants a deal. He'll give you everything you want." There was true alarm in her eyes. She had an out-of-control client and was out of her depth.

"Goddard will be negotiating this case. Not me. He intended to kill Dani. I'm really biased here. Besides, aren't you afraid I'll sexually harass you?" He rebuffed her, his barb a reminder she'd unfairly accused him.

Jenny jerked her chin up and Tim realized she'd thought he would never find out. She tried to reason with him: "You and I know that Goddard relies on you. If there are any bargains, you make them." Jenny was trying to yank his chain with flattery. She was standing before him, attempting her most professional appearance. She even wore those fake glasses she'd bought for effect. He caught himself before he laughed at her.

He knew Goddard relied on him. He knew that Goddard would do whatever he recommended this time, too--despite his protests. "Warden's victims didn't get a trial before he killed them. He didn't give them a chance to beg for their lives. Unless he pleads guilty, this goes to court. With the evidence we have—take your chances. Goddard is going to ask for the death penalty and he'll get it."

"What about me?"

"What *about* you? Is this about *you*? Where are you going with this? You accepted the client. You need to defend your client or ask to be replaced. That's a matter for the court."

"I thought I could redeem myself with Dad on this case. I don't know what to do. Warden disregards my advice. He won't listen to me. You need to help me," she pleaded.

Tim stared at her. "Little girl, you're in way over your head. I'm not your friend; I stand with the victims."

"But Tim, we were a great team," Jenny said, just above a whisper.

Tim scowled at her. "We were nothing of the sort. I helped you as I would have any of the ADAs I was assigned." He shook his head. "Wrong argument, Jenny. Do you have something better? I really hope you have something better."

"What can I say to make you work with me? I know you hate me."

"I try not to waste my time on hate. I don't hate you; I don't *understand* you." He assessed her expression. She had realized that in her hubris she'd jumped into the deep end of the pool without knowing how to swim. Now she wanted him to throw her a life vest. But with Jenny there were always other motives underneath the surface. She wasn't trustworthy--at least, not where he was concerned. "There are experienced lawyers in your father's firm. Talk to them. Crack the books. Then go to Goddard. That's the only help I can give you."

NINETY-ONE

Tim rode the elevator up to his office alone. He and Scott had played their 5:30 am game of racquetball and he felt refreshed and ready for his day. Dani had promised to stop by with coffee around eight and he was looking forward to getting some work done in the quiet before the business day began in earnest. With Warden in jail, the regular morning meeting of friends was taking a more pleasant turn. Dani had suggested they plan a ski trip and made it sound like great fun. They would spend the Christmas holiday in a cabin nestled in the snow-covered mountains. Dani didn't say so, but Tim imagined it was another one of her properties. Instead of worrying about it, he was looking forward to relaxation time with Dani, Scott, and Kathy. Kathy didn't ski, but said she'd love the time to catch up on reading her medical journals and maybe a juicy murder mystery--as if living them wasn't enough.

When the elevator doors opened to the ninth floor, Tim noticed that only two of the many assistants had chosen to work this early. He nodded a morning greeting to them.

He passed by Myra's darkened corner, flipping on a light switch as he went. He was surprised to see Beebe Knoll sitting patiently in a chair in the waiting area outside his office, dressed in a gray business suit. He glanced around for the camera crew he worried might be there to ambush him.

"Miss Knoll, what are you doing sitting here in the dark?" As if he didn't know.

"Waiting for you." She stood, but no cameraman appeared.

"Still chasing down that fictional love affair you're so keen to write about?" Tim set his briefcase inside the door to his office, chuckling to himself. He figured by now she'd found out he and Dani were married and was going to confront him. He stripped off his overcoat and hung it on the rack. He walked past her, rounded the end of his desk, and sat in his chair, booting up his computer.

"Your jackassery is in rare form this morning," she quipped, dragging one of his office chairs to the front edge of his desk. He had intentionally not grabbed it for her. She wasn't welcome.

"I've been sharpening my skills overnight, just for you. Jackassery? Great word." He grinned. It's not that he disliked her for her accusations alone. It was his job to defend Dani and he did so fiercely. When she'd told him of the mean things Beebe had written about her during her divorce, it had gotten his back up.

"Yes. I admit I added the e-r-y, but, you can find the rest in *Webster's* under definitions for 'Tim McAndrews.'"

"Ouch," Tim laughed. Beebe was sharp. He didn't like her but he had to admire her wit.

"I thought I'd give you a chance for an editorial review before I sent my article for publication today." She passed some typed pages his way.

"Huh? Do Bigfoot and the gray aliens get the same courtesy, or am I special?"

She scowled at him. "Maybe you might be able to help me out with captions for these." She stood and emptied her briefcase of some computer-generated-photos that drifted and scattered across his desk. She sat down with a big so-there smile flashing from her eyes. Her whole demeanor was a dare.

He assessed her for a few moments before picking up her typed pages. He quickly cruised through the words. He didn't get very far. "I see research isn't your strong suit, Miss Knoll. Maybe you could look up the definitions for these words: unsubstantiated and speculation. I thought we were clear on that point." He tossed the pages back at her and they fluttered in the air before settling down. Some papers landed on his desk and some on the floor. He met her dare with his own. She didn't bother to gather up her story.

"Speculation! You're having an affair and I have pictures to prove it." She shoved a few of the photos toward him. He picked up one. He and Dani were walking hand in hand along the waterfront. It was Saturday morning and they'd been on their way to meet Scott and Kathy for breakfast.

"Hey, I like this one, can I get a copy?"

"Sure, buy a *National Globe* tomorrow." She narrowed her eyes at him.

"I'd rather you didn't print this," he said in a strong tone that he hoped let her know she was in for trouble if she did. "Beebe, did it ever cross your mind that my relationship might be something less scandalous and more conventional?"

"No."

"I didn't think so." Tim eased-up on the sarcasm a little. "Why not?" He really wanted to know.

She rolled her eyes at him as if he should know. He didn't. "Don't give me any B.S. I'm not buying the we're-just-friends crap. I told you that already. An affair is an affair. It's not speculation. You're so big on words, what do you want to call it?"

"I was thinking more along the lines of sacred and holy. At least that's what the minister said at the ceremony and I tend to believe him."

Beebe dropped the picture she had in her hand. She stared at him, her mouth forming a big round O. She groaned. "Crap! You and Daniela St. Clair are *married*?" She looked at him with an expression of disappointment he wasn't sure he understood. So she wasn't going to get to publish her trash. It was a lie, after all.

"Before God and to each other. Research, research, research," he teased. "We had a very small service at the little church about a mile from her ranch. I'd appreciate it--"

"You let me believe you were having an affair and now you want me to keep quiet?"

"I don't remember it that way. I remember telling you it wasn't an affair. All the same, you did accuse me of it in front of a whole office of gossipy secretaries. I don't like that. Sucks big time." Tim laughed again.

"Sorry." She shifted in her chair and her demeanor was more contrite. "Back to the drawing board. But with just a few changes--"

"I'd prefer you didn't publish anything about us."

"Yeah, well, so do ninety-nine-percent of the people I write about. Join the club."

"I really don't want my poor little mom reading about my marriage in the grocery check-out line before I have a chance to tell her. It's her heart, you know." Tim teased, hoping it would work.

"As in: you didn't think this through and you're about to break it?"

"And then--there's that!" Tim grimaced. "I was wrong; you really are a perceptive reporter. Besides, when she said yes, I couldn't give Dani any time to think! How else would I get her to marry me?"

"Oh, I see. You think a girl wouldn't jump at the chance? Ha! You're so cute McAndrews. The article is all blown to hell anyway. Even I have *some* ethics. But could I do a little teaser? Just an eensie-weensie one?"

"No."

"That's not fair. What do I get?"

"The reward of knowing you did something right?" he offered tentatively.

"Give a girl a break! How about some juicy goodies on Goddard's campaign?"

"Not a chance," Tim shook his head.

She shot him an exaggerated pout. "Please?"

"All right. Something comes up I promise I'll give you a lead."

"You'd do that?"

"Begrudgingly, but yes."

Scott popped into Tim's office doorway. Tim sat forward and Beebe turned.

"It's go-time. Guess who was caught trying to exchange gold coins into cash?" Scott asked, grinning with intrigue. "I was just driving up when the call came over the radio. Uniforms are holding her for me as we speak."

Tim shot out of his chair. "Gotta go. Thanks, Beebe." He hit the hallway at a sprint, heading for Goddard's office. "I'll get the search warrants started. Meet you at interrogation," he called back to Scott.

"I'll be in number three!" Scott exclaimed.

Tim knocked on Goddard's door and peeked in. Goddard looked up from his desk. Tim entered when he received the DA's nod and closed the door.

"It's a go." He couldn't keep the satisfied smile from creeping across his face. Catching Katrina Collins was like getting an expensive gift for no reason!

"I'll get Judge Carlson to sign your warrants, but does Detective Renton have probable cause? I don't want him to have to wait."

"Yes. She's trying to sell some gold coins. We believe they're Jillian Garner's." Tim reported. "The coin dealer called it in to the police. Our ruse worked: dealer says one of the Certificates of Authenticity matches Jillian's book, down to some pencil writing on the upper-left corner. If we find the rest of her coins, we may have a case for conspiracy."

Goddard was grinning. "This breaks and just think what it will do for the campaign!"

Tim stood quietly, trying not to react. But he was sure shock was carved all over his face. Since when did everything come down to politics? This was about getting two wicked criminals off the street. "Do you want to call Branson Holt, or should I? We promised him a two-hour advantage." Tim really didn't give a rip about the press, but he did keep his promises. "You could grab some media time."

"I'll call. You sure you don't want to work for the campaign?" Goddard asked.

"Don't think campaigning is for me." Tim did realize he had a personal stake in keeping Goddard in office. If a new boss were elected--especially if it was Raney Marsh--he might not be able to keep his job, good conviction record or not. "I don't have court today so would you mind if I observed the interview? I'd also like to visit CSI after they do their search and see what they find."

"Go, yes. Go--but keep me in the loop," Goddard ordered.

"Yes, of course." Tim backed out of the office and closed Goddard's door. As he turned to head back to his own he spun right into Beebe. It was almost as if she'd been listening at the door. "Oh, sorry!" he stepped back. "Are you still here?"

"McAndrews, I've changed my mind about our negotiations. I want to know what this whole flurry is about!" She lifted an eyebrow as if she had bargaining power.

"What is it you think we do here, Miss Knoll? This is a busy district attorney's office. We're prosecuting bad guys. We're always in a so-called *flurry!*"

She pursed her lips. "So, we're back to jackassery, are we?"

"The definition of my name, remember?" Tim had to admit he got a kick out of her outrageous boldness. But he owed her competitor a two-hour lead on this story and a promise was a promise.

"McAndrews, this flurry is a blizzard and I know it. I'll trade," she offered. "No press about you and Daniela St. Clair for the goods on this story." She lifted her eyebrows, hopeful, as if she believed he might consider it.

He tipped his head slightly pretending he was contemplating it. "Tempting--but no." Tim briskly walked to his office, grabbed his overcoat, and headed for the elevator. She followed. "I don't have the goods on this story. Listen, Carly Knights is our community liaison--you could get some information on upcoming cases from her, and Lieutenant Lynne Stuart is the PR officer with the police," Tim pointed out.

"And you?"

"I'm just a lowly lawyer."

"Un-huh; that's not what I hear. I'm going with you," she announced.

"No, you're not. This is serious, Beebe." He pressed the elevator's DOWN button. He retrieved his cell phone from his pocket and did a quick contact search, turning his back to Beebe.

"Hi. Change of plans. Where are you? Grab a table I'll meet you there in a minute." He disengaged. When he turned back he could tell Beebe had been eavesdropping.

"And that was ... Mrs. McAndrews?"

Tim just smiled and shook his head. "None of your business," he said.

"Jackass," Beebe said under her breath. She was pouting now; she was definitely going to follow him. "Will you see to it I get a couple of questions at the press conference? When is it, by the way?" she asked. He was meeting Dani for a quick cup of coffee, giving Scott a chance to get set up, and then heading straight to the police station. He decided he'd better lose Beebe. She wanted this story; she'd figured it was big and she wasn't going to make it easy. Tim wasn't going to let her taint the arrest with one of her despicable fictions or tramp through the evidence they might find at Katrina's home or business.

"Not sure. But questions—that, I can do," he conceded just as the elevator doors opened. He motioned for her to go first. She smiled as if she believed he was being a gentleman. He hesitated. "I forgot something," he said backing up and waiting until the doors closed. The surprised look on her face let him know she'd read this as a ditch. Quickly, Tim took the stairs down to the seventh floor, where he caught another elevator and rode down to the third. He'd take the stairs from here. If Beebe was waiting for him in the lobby, he hoped he'd mixed his trail enough to lose her. At the lobby level, he saw Beebe standing in front of the bank of elevators waiting for him. *Perfect.* He slipped out the side door to escape to the street. He walked down Fourth to James Street and crossed at Third Avenue to Jake's Deli where he met Dani for coffee.

NINETY-TWO

Tim called Goddard to meet him at the police station after reviewing evidence at the CSI lab. For some reason, he'd expected to be wrong about Katrina Collins. Maybe he wanted to be wrong for Dani's sake. Now, as he stood next to Goddard watching through the two-way mirror as Scott began interrogating, he was anxious to hear what she had to say. Anna was there, waiting.

"This is becoming a habit, McAndrews," she grinned. As always, Tim was amazed this tiny woman was a police officer. "Katrina's still denying she was at Samuel's Gold and Collectibles to exchange the coins. Even when confronted with the shop's security video, she lies," Anna filled him in.

"Miss Collins." Scott's patience was clearly at an end. Tim heard the annoyed tone in his voice over the intercom. "The Crime Scene Investigation Unit found Jillian Garner's gold coin collection under your bed. Can you explain that?"

Tim had learned that each coin had been carefully stored in a zippered plastic sheet with its certificate of authenticity. CSI meticulously matched each coin to those in the book Jillian had given her insurance agent and that her sister had brought to them only days ago.

It would've been harder to prove the theft had Jillian not been so meticulous. On each certificate she had written a date in light pencil. Tim was sure it was the date Jillian had purchased the coin. When the CSI tech created an overlay, they aligned perfectly with the hand-written date: the originals and the insurance copies were an exact match. CSI techs had also done a cyanoacrylate fuming on the plastic sheets for fingerprints. They found three people had handled the book and coin pages: Jillian Garner, Gary Warden, and Katrina Collins.

The intercom crackled with the next exchange.

"You keep accusing me of being a thief, Detective Renton. I don't appreciate it," Katrina scowled.

"Ma'am, trust me, I'm not accusing you of being a thief." Scott glared back. Tim knew Scott was going to accuse her of being a murderess. "But it's difficult to think otherwise when I find you have both Amber Brown's necklace and Jillian Garner's coin collection at your home. I just want you to explain why her property was found under your bed." He let his comment hang in the air. Katrina's expression was closed off.

"It was a gift from Gary."

"Gary Warden. Is that who gave you the coins?"

"Yes. I've told you that. I don't know any person named Amber Brown or Jillian Garner."

Scott motioned and Tim picked up two folders and a small journal with a quilted cover and handed them to Anna. Scott's partner shrugged and grinned at Tim.

"Looks like I'm on," she said, as she headed for the interrogation room door with the evidence and two cups of coffee. Tim turned back to the two-way to watch this part of the confrontation unfold.

"Here's your coffee, ma'am," Anna said. "Two creams, two sugars, right?" She took a seat across the table from Katrina and handed Scott the evidence.

Katrina took the gesture of coffee as kindness and relaxed a little. She took a sip and swallowed. Scott's accommodating smile changed as she set her cup on the table. He passed one of the folders across the table to her.

"Would you mind taking a look at these?" She opened the folder. "Now, read the heading at the top of the first receipt," he demanded.

"The Backstreet Boutique." Katrina shot him an angry stare.

"That's your boutique, isn't it Miss Collins?"

"You know it is."

"Yes or no, ma'am."

"Yes." Katrina scooted back into her chair defiantly. This afternoon she hadn't even tried a seduction; Tim was a little amazed.

"Can you please read the dates on the top of the receipts for me?"

She leaned forward, opened the folder, and started reading the dates. "March 21, 2016; March 23, 2016; March 26, 2016 …" She thumbed through the pages.

"Would you say this customer was a regular, from these receipts?" Scott asked.

"Yes. What does this have to do with anything? Why am I here?"

"These receipts match Jillian Garner's credit-card statements. Ma'am, she was at your boutique about three times a week. Her cell-phone records show she called your store and your store called her about two to three times a week. And you're sitting here stating you don't know her? That doesn't ring true to me. Ma'am, you really need to start telling me the truth."

"Maybe I remember her. I'm just not sure," she countered.

Scott let her know he wasn't buying it. "Do you have an employee named Holly Sutton?"

"Yes. You know I do; you have my business records."

"Miss Sutton told us you and Jillian were friends. Said you had lunch together about every two weeks or so."

"She was a stupid girl and a liar. That's why I fired her." Tim was amazed she'd tried that one on. Katrina hadn't fired Holly; as far as he could tell, she was still employed full-time. Tim noticed Katrina was starting to grasp the scope of what the police had on her and the kind of trouble she was in. Right about now, she must be realizing she needed a lawyer. He expected her to demand one. She didn't.

"Do you know Daniela St. Clair?" Scott asked.

"Yes. She's a good customer."

"Is she a friend of yours?"

"Yes. A friend. My best friend," Katrina answered snottily.

Scott handed her the quilted flower-covered journal. "Now before you say anything, I need you to know we've matched the fingerprints and handwriting in this book to you. Turn to page 60. I believe you wrote, and I quote: 'I hate Daniela St. Clair and I can't wait until she's dead.' That's not a very friendly thing to say, now is it?" Katrina didn't answer but shifted nervously in her chair. "Did you really want her dead, Miss Collins?"

"And from all these newspaper and magazine articles you cut out and saved, I'm inclined to believe you were stalking her."

"No. You—can't believe--" Katrina sat up straight and her countenance had completely changed.

Scott continued, "Do you know who else was stalking her? Your boy-friend, Gary Warden. Did you know he had pictures of Miss St. Clair all over the walls of his apartment? You see, Miss Collins, I'm not accusing you of being a thief--not at all."

Katrina froze for a moment. She'd made the connection. Scott was go-ing to charge her with conspiracy to commit murder. Katrina was alarmed; Tim could see it in her eyes.

"From what I have here, Miss Collins, I've concluded that you and Mr. Warden were stalking Miss St. Clair, just like you stalked Miss Garner and Miss Brown. You were stalking her and you intended to kill her, didn't you Miss Collins?"

Katrina gasped. Tim wasn't sure if it was because she understood she was caught, or the realization she'd been trapped by circumstances she didn't control.

"I'm placing you under arrest. I'm charging you with conspiracy to commit murder." Scott motioned with his hand and two uniformed female officers entered the interrogation room as he read her her rights.

"I want my lawyer. I get to have a lawyer!" she demanded, weakly.

Tim knew she was going to confess. He'd been doing this long enough to see the signs.

"Yes. ma'am. Do you understand your rights as I've just explained them to you?"

"Yes. Damn it! I want my lawyer."

"Anna, my partner, will take down his name and get him here for you. Until he gets here, I suggest you just relax and enjoy your coffee." Scott left the room and walked over to Tim. Through the two-way mirror, they watched Katrina begin to pace.

"You nailed this one, buddy. Except for Fraser. I picked him up yesterday. Interviewed him. He's not involved. He said he thought something was up the night we grabbed their DNA. Scared him. He stopped hanging with them and even put in for a different schedule at the fire station. I checked--he'd gone as far as asking to be transferred to a different station. When Katrina went to him the other day, it was to ask him for bail money for Warden. He refused. Said he couldn't help her, didn't have the money." Scott set his right hand on Tim's left shoulder. Tim wasn't sure he believed Scott, but there was nothing to tie Fraser to the victims. Tim nodded, but it wasn't agreement, simply to indicate he understood Scott's position.

Goddard looked at Tim, his head tipped with a question. "You had this figured out before now? How?" he asked.

"Just … a hunch. Because of Dani, I was sucked right into the middle of it," Tim answered.

"Do you think they were after money?" Goddard asked.

"Oh, it was all about money. The plan was to get Dani to marry Warden, get her to buy a big, fat insurance policy, then kill her and make it look like an accident, grab the money, and move on to the next mark. They probably even had their next target in sight. Warden had already done it twice before, why shouldn't he get away with it this time?"

"But didn't he try to kill Miss Collins?" Goddard reminded Tim.

"I think he changed his mind about her. Turns out he really didn't want to share," Tim mused.

"Oh, hey—Anna's motioning . I guess Miss Collins' lawyer has arrived," Scott said. "Are you staying for the rest?"

"He's gonna shut you down. But yes, I'll watch the show for a while." Tim felt a weight on his shoulders. He would have to tell Dani the woman she'd considered a friend wanted her dead and had intended to murder her. He knew Dani was no stranger to sadness. She would accept this bad news with her usual grace, but she didn't deserve it. He slowly walked away from the two-way mirror. He heard the door to the interrogation room open and he turned. As he looked inside, he and Katrina made eye contact. He froze, incredulous. He wanted to ask her, "Why?" But he already knew why. Ironically, in her haste and greed, Katrina had cost herself her own fortune. She was going to jail.

The boisterous and showy entry of Raney Marsh broke Tim's reverie. He was a big man and he was making certain with his loud voice that the whole police department knew he was here. Raney Marsh, Goddard's rival for district attorney, was Katrina's lawyer. *Of course, he is.* Tim bet Marsh wanted to cash in on the free publicity this trial would generate. News cycle after news cycle of free face time was like winning the lottery for a politician. Tim glanced over at Goddard who returned a disgusted roll of the eyes. Now, not only were Goddard and Marsh rivals in a heated election, they were going to be rivals in court in what could end up being the trial of the decade. Tim had no doubt it was going to be sensational. With Raney in it, a clown show immediately came to mind.

"Remember your first case up against Marsh?" Goddard grinned.

Tim remembered. "I was pretty green. He really intimidated me." Raney had marched into the district attorney's office, demanded a meeting, and in front of all the assistants and secretaries had dismissively asked Goddard why he was sending in the "little leaguer." Tim had only been twenty-four, newly out of college, and in way over his head. Luckily, he knew from sports that a bigger opponent wasn't always stronger or better at the game.

"When the jury handed down the guilty verdict on all counts, I had Sweet Stuff Bakery make a cake shaped like a crow and iced with black frosting, and sent it to him. Did I ever tell you this?" Goddard asked, chuckling.

"No, you didn't!" Tim couldn't help but see Goddard in a different light.

"Marsh was such a pompous ass. Still is. But he never called you 'little leaguer' again."

The surprise Tim read on Marsh's face as he realized they were going up against each other again was priceless. Marsh wasn't doing himself any favors representing Katrina Collins, but he didn't know that--not yet, anyway.

"Goddard, McAndrews." Raney's greeting was loud but icy.

"Raney, nice to see you." Goddard sounded cheery. It was false.

"Afternoon." Tim nodded politely.

When the interrogation room door closed, Tim looked over at Goddard and grinned.

"Hello, Titanic: meet iceberg." He patted Goddard on the shoulder.

"You think so?" Tim picked up a hint of insecurity in his voice.

"Katrina Collins is a gold-plated liar. She's lied to Scott so many times on tape, you'll be able to impeach her right away. I'll bet money he won't take her case. When he sees what we have, he'll dump her and send in one of his firm's 'little leaguers.'"

Goddard snorted, "He's going to play the big-mean-prosecutor-versus-the-sweet-little-woman card."

"He is. And we're going to counter with the scheming-jealous-black-widow right off the top of the deck," Tim answered.

"You're sounding ruthless, Tim," Goddard chuckled.

"Me? Why, sir?" Tim pretended shock.

"So, are you going to be on my team on this one?" Goddard asked.

Tim nodded. "And I'm going to enjoy every minute of it."

NINETY-THREE

Ever since his conference with McAndrews, Warden had seethed with anger. He'd gotten nothing for his trouble. Not even one word in the newspapers or on television like he'd expected. He was furious that his taped interview with Branson Holt hadn't aired either. It was McAndrews' doing, he knew it. He planned a dozen ways to murder McAndrews as he stewed alone in his jail cell. Every time he moved wrong and pain shot through his bandaged shoulder, he envisioned a new way to kill him.

Tonight, his shoulder was unbearable. When he lifted the bandage to look, the bullet wound was angry, red, swollen, and a stinking yellow-green pus oozed from the center. The toxins from the bacterial infection were making him feverish and phantoms and illusions from the past haunted his dreams each time he drifted off to sleep. Within a few seconds, he would startle awake in terror, hating McAndrews even more. He had to endure. The prison guards wouldn't check on him again until morning. He needed a doctor and shivered against the cold as his fever spiked.

He tried to stay awake, but his eyelids were heavy and he lost the struggle to keep them open. He began to drift--weightless, swirling down into a blue spiral--still aware of pain. He wanted to stop the spin but he whirled faster and faster as if he were in the maniacal grip of a tornado. His heart was thundering in his ears. *Am I dying?*

Abruptly, the spinning stopped, the pain faded away. He was there again: a child, watching through the tattered wallpaper, watching his mother. The shadow appeared, falling across her body, blocking out the golden light from the hallway. Suddenly, he was swept up and fused with shadow; he became shadow. His mother's face slowly faded and morphed into a new face: soft; symmetrical; loving blue eyes; full parted lips. Daniela St. Clair was bewitching, enticing, luring him to be her lover.

The sharp smell of sterile alcohol bit his nostrils and tried to wake him. He fought it. He wanted to stay with Daniela. Blurred visions and voices were all around him, but he couldn't make sense of what they whispered. The prick of a needle in his vein startled him awake. He tried to fight but his will vanished, and he quickly succumbed to the tingling rush of morphine. The dream faded away, and he surrendered to a deep and painless sleep.

Slowly, he rose to consciousness. He was aware of pain creeping over him, increasing in intensity as the morphine wore off. There was a scent of hospital cleaners in the air. He tried to move, but he had an I.V. tube running from his left arm to a clear bag of saline solution and a clean new bandage and sling on his right. There was a smaller bag connected to the large one filled with yellow liquid. Antibiotics, he assumed. He could hear the soft rhythmic beep of the electronic equipment that monitored his heart rate and oxygen saturation levels. He was in a hospital bed, but not at the prison clinic. How he'd gotten here and how long he'd been here, he couldn't recall.

In a few minutes a nurse came to check on him. She was young; her dark brown hair was pulled back tight into a small bun at the nape of her neck. She wore pink printed hospital scrubs that reminded him of a child's pajamas. At first, she was all business, checking the monitors, the flow of the liquids. She was an everyday woman, nothing spectacular, ordinary. Instantly, he knew she would be vulnerable, putty in his hands if he poured on the charm. He had always had that gift. He read the clues in her brown puppy-dog eyes.

"You're awake. How are you feeling this morning?" She was cheerful, but a bit shy.

"How long have I been here?" he asked. His mouth was dry, and he reached for a glass of water. But it was a struggle, with his right arm in a sling and the I.V. in the left. She rushed over to help him, holding the glass and the straw steady so he could take a drink, confirming what he already knew about her. He discreetly checked her left hand for a wedding ring. None.

"Two days. You were delirious with fever and pain. But it looks like the antibiotics are working, now. Is there anyone I can call for you?" She checked the saline bag and carefully replaced it with a new one. She glanced down at his face. She didn't want there to be anyone. He knew what his good looks could get him and he intended to use them.

"No. No one," he answered, realizing he was completing her fantasy. He would use her to help him fulfill his.

"Do you need anything for pain?"

Warden didn't want to go back to sleep. He wanted to find a way out. "Where am I?" He was in a room by himself, and there was a window without bars. He wasn't handcuffed to the hospital bed. He wondered if there was a police guard outside his door.

"Seattle North Hospital."

Warden closed his eyes and quickly drew a map in his mind. He calculated how far he was from Daniela St. Clair's building and the penthouse suite. That's where he would find them. He was sure of it. The desire for revenge ate at him like acid. Before his encounter with McAndrews at the ranch, when he'd last been in the St. Clair building, he found that the fire exit stairway was locked on the twenty-fifth floor just below the penthouse. It allowed the penthouse occupants a way out in case of fire, but no way in for an intruder. The door was steel, and without C-4 or detcord, he wasn't getting in. Also, he'd discovered that the elevator required a unique key, to access the twenty-sixth-floor penthouse. The suite would be impenetrable for a lesser man. But, he knew where the keys were and just how to get them. His old fire station had keys and entry cards to every high-rise in the city, just in case they were forced to fight a fire in the upper floors.

"The kitchen will be sending breakfast trays soon. Do you have any special requests?"

Warden opened his eyes, and a wan smile crossed his lips as he looked at the nurse. "Just that you help me," he said softly, slightly lifting his compromised arms. He waited until she glanced his way and then he locked his gaze with hers, promising a world of love, passion, and acceptance.

She sighed, "Yes, of course."

She stared into his eyes. Briefly, he wondered if she knew he was *allegedly* a serial killer. He knew some women were turned on by that. She wasn't the type. Instead, she was more likely to believe he'd been set up by a jealous and vindictive prosecutor. It didn't matter: when the time came to escape, he'd use this girl to help him. Because he knew she was his.

NINETY-FOUR

It was a crystal-clear morning and icy cold. The sky was deep blue and the winter sun was bright but brought no warmth. Tim held Dani's hand as they strolled down James Street from the penthouse to Jake's. The city was bustling. The weatherman on channel two was predicting snow overnight--and not in inches, but feet. People were getting prepared. In the afternoon, traffic would snarl to a stop as city workers raced home to beat the storm. It had been several years since it had snowed in the city. Usually that forecast instead turned into slush or worse--freezing rain, one of nature's most miserable tantrums, in Tim's opinion. He and Dani planned to escape to the ranch in the early afternoon, long before the storm was due. Goddard had already suggested the office close early, and no one argued against starting the weekend before five.

As they made their way to Jake's, they stopped momentarily to ogle the latest skis at the Little Ole Sport Shoppe on the corner of Second and James.

Tim felt the warmth of contentment in every cell. Dani had changed everything for him. He slid his arm around her shoulders and hugged her. When she looked up into his face, he knew he'd changed life for her, too. They didn't need to say anything; it was understood. They walked on to the deli.

It was busy at Jake's, so Tim sent Dani to grab a table for them while he waited in line for coffee.

"Hey, Tim—congratulations!" Tim turned and saw Brad Hollingsrow grinning at him.

"Thanks," he said, wondering why he was being congratulated. He took both cups of coffee and headed to the table where Dani waited.

"Congrats, buddy!" came from Martin Worth and then another, similar greeting from Walt Hartford, both defense attorneys he'd recently defeated in court. *Odd*, he thought. But he acknowledged them with a tentative smile.

He made his way to the table, set a coffee in front of Dani and slid into the chair opposite her.

"Congratulations, McAndrews!" Tim looked up and Judge Mattison was offering him a handshake. Tim stood and shook his hand.

"Thank you?" As the judge left, he toyed with the black lid on his coffee cup. What was going on? Too late for this to be about Warden. He decided to shrug it off and enjoy his coffee with Dani before starting his day.

He walked Dani to her office, and they planned to meet in a couple of hours for their escape to the ranch.

Tim briskly made his way to his office and started to organize his day. Court had been postponed due to the storm, so he had time to put his cases in order--a luxury he seldom enjoyed. He had jury selection starting next week on a home invasion robbery where the victim, a single mother of two, shot the perpetrator in the leg, putting a justified end to Devon Lee Keyes' illustrious burglary career. Devon's mother had done him no favors when she'd asked an SBC news reporter during an interview, "Just how else was he supposed to get money?" As if gainful employment wasn't a consideration!

Also on next week's agenda was the plea bargain conference for John Harder, a Seattle City Councilman, who had developed a drinking problem and kept forgetting about Uber or the city's many taxi services. Tim knew his attorney would negotiate for driving classes and rehab. One more DUII, though, and this guy was toast, buying himself jail time. Tim mused, reviewing his file.

Myra buzzed him.

"You still here? Goddard said you could go. You should before the storm hits."

"I will, but there are two Mr. McAndrews here to see you," she said. "Your brothers look a lot like you!" she giggled.

Peas in a pod; he remembered his high school teachers saying that when he'd ended up in a class with a teacher that had also instructed one of his brothers. Tim was a little bit taller, but the family resemblance was strong.

His brothers had come downtown to see him. This couldn't be good. He wondered if something had happened to his parents. He quickly made his way to his door and opened it.

"Jeff, Tony--what are you doing down here?" He was grinning ear-to-ear. It had been months since he'd seen his brothers. He'd missed the annual summer barbeque while trying to salvage his relationship with Dani. But his brothers' stern expressions weren't exactly showing him brotherly affection. Both were angry, and they strong-armed him backward into his office and closed the door behind them.

"What. The. Hell. Tim?" Tony, the oldest, confronted him, smacking a folded newspaper down hard on his desk. Tim took the opportunity to retreat to behind his desk.

"Mom's been crying all morning. She's sure you're ashamed of her," Jeff added. "What. The. Hell?"

Tim was surprised, but shouldn't have been. Beebe Knoll. He realized negotiating with her had been a rookie's mistake. He sank into his chair and unfolded the *National Globe* and groaned.

THE SECRET IS OUT! The headline screamed in bold print. Just beneath it was a picture of Dani and him walking along the waterfront, the very one he'd sarcastically told Beebe he wanted a copy of during their last confrontation. The story below asked: "What handsome young man has snagged up Seattle's beautiful philanthropist and heiress Daniela St. Clair? Paul Goddard's up-and-coming prosecuting attorney, Timothy McAndrews, that's who! The couple made it official last Saturday in a small ceremony attended by a few friends." The piece went on to describe Dani's charitable gifts to Seattle's Children's Hospital. It finished with Warden's arrest, woven into an outrageously embellished fiction about how Tim, the superhero, had rescued ten-year-old Ryan Settle from the grip of a crazed serial killer.

"Wow. The only thing this Alice Carroll woman forgot to mention was that I can leap tall buildings in a single bound," Tim laughed, staring straight at his brothers and trying to defuse their anger. "You can't possibly believe anything you read in the *National Globe*," he continued glibly, hoping it would fly.

Jeff's stern expression cracked briefly with a smile. "See, I told you it was all a lie. I told Mom, too." Jeff had always been the brother to stand up for Tim, but today his loyalty was misplaced. Tim realized he had just made things worse. However, Tony wasn't buying it, not one word.

Now he understood all the congratulatory wishes this morning at Jake's. The *National Globe's* circulation was far wider than he initially thought. He didn't care about the others--how was he going to salvage this with his family?

Tim glanced back down at the paper and continued reading. Beebe asked her readers to check back in nine months for an update. He hoped Dani never saw this birdcage liner.

"Mom was grocery shopping with Carol, and she has to see this! You didn't even bring your girl around to meet the parents. Are you ashamed of Mom?" Tony demanded.

"Of course not," Tim defended himself. He should've introduced Dani and knew it.

"She never liked any of your girlfriends--is that why you didn't bring her home? That's what she thinks," Jeff added.

"It has nothing to do with old girlfriends or Mom. That's crazy." He knew he'd avoided bringing Dani home to meet his parents, but he'd excused himself by thinking of his case load and the pursuit of Warden. It was the truth; his mother had never accepted any of his girlfriends. In a flash, the one fight he remembered seeing his parents have surfaced in his mind. Ten years old and terrified, he'd crouched down on the bottom stair and listened. It was the only time he'd ever heard his father argue with his mother. In a booming voice, laced at the edges with the remnants of an Irish brogue, his father had declared no son of his was going to be forced into being a Catholic priest, no matter family tradition. Especially, not his Timmy! Why was he even thinking of this, now?

"Answer this, Tim: Are you married? Is she pregnant?" Tony leaned across Tim's desk, pressing his weight into his palms and bringing Tim back to the present.

"What the hell is this family's obsession with pregnancy?" Tim asked, remembering his dad asking the same question when he'd called to tell him he was engaged. Tony and Jeff looked at each other for a moment without speaking, and Tim understood immediately and chuckled. "Oh--Okay, I get it. You both *had* to get married--didn't you?" he teased. Jeff shrugged his shoulders, giving the truth away. Tim couldn't keep a laugh down.

"Well, are you?" Tony asked, his eyes a little less angry now, a suppressed grin creasing the skin at corners of his eyes.

Tim stared at his brothers for as long as he could without saying a word. The one thing forbidden in his family was hurting Mom; and he'd just done the unforgivable. It wasn't the first time. She'd wanted something else from him though, and she'd never said so. "Married, yes. Pregnant, no," he answered.

Jeff was shocked. "*Now* what do I tell Mom?"

"I'll talk to her. I made the mess; I'll clean it up," Tim breathed out. He hadn't seen this pile coming and had stepped right in it. Beebe Knoll. If she'd left well enough alone, he could've softened his mother's disappointment. If Beebe thought she would ever get one word out of him again about anything, she was dreaming!

There was a soft knock on his office door. The brothers wheeled around. Dani opened it and peeked around, another copy of the *National Globe* in her hands.

"Oh, I'm sorry. I didn't realize you were in a meeting," she said, looking at Tim, then his brothers, a conciliatory smile on her lips and radiating from her eyes.

Tim stood. "Come in. This isn't a meeting. Dani, this is Jeff and Tony, my older brothers." He gestured to indicate who was who. "Guys, meet your new sister-in-law, Dani McAndrews." Tim noticed his brothers immediately stood straight, wide-eyed, smitten--buried under the same tsunami of awestruck emotion he'd felt when he'd first seen Dani. *To fall head over heels for her must be genetic,* he thought.

"Hello." She reached out and shook their hands. They practically melted into puddles on the floor.

"My brothers are here to berate me about getting married without telling family." Tim pointed to the front page spread out on his desk. "My mother saw this in the grocery store."

"That's why I'm here. I came to apologize for this awful article. This is all my fault. This Alice Carroll woman has been hounding me since my father died. And I'm the one who suggested we elope," she explained. Tim was surprised she took the blame so easily and covered for him. In that instant, he knew she would be forgiven for the social breach; he would not.

"Oh no problem," Jeff quickly pulled a chair up to Tim's desk for her.

"It couldn't possibly be your fault," Tony added, his anger and aggression vanished. Tim wanted to laugh at them.

"Do you think there's anything I can do to make it up to your mom? I know Tim's the youngest and this must be a shock. We didn't want to hurt anyone; we just wanted to be together--you understand?" She didn't sit.

Tim was watching a master adeptly handle his brothers. Would his mother be as simple? He doubted it.

He heard the insistent buzzing of his intercom. "Yes?"

"Tim, it's me," Goddard said in hushed tones. Tim picked up the receiver. "Raney Marsh's on his way up. Katrina Collins has agreed to tell all for a deal. Grab your files and meet me in the conference room."

"Be right there." He hung up. "You'll have to excuse me; I have a meeting."

"You'll come soon and straighten this out with Mom, right?" Jeff asked. Tim nodded.

"Jeff, Tony, why don't we go get a cup of coffee? Get better acquainted?" Dani offered. "Then you need to get home, before this storm breaks. Tim, I'll meet you at the penthouse in a couple of hours, if you think you can make it. We need to get out before the storm." She winked at him. "I'll catch up with you two at the elevator, is that okay?" she continued. His brothers nodded and headed for the elevator.

"So, that's how it's done?" Tim chuckled, pulling her into his arms. "You little flirt." He kissed her. "You amaze me."

"Do you think it worked? Myra called me. Said your brothers were here and not happy. She'd gone to get coffee and saw the *Globe*. She thought you might need help." Dani nestled against his shoulder. "I thought I'd rescue you, since it was my fault. I suggested we elope. Tim, I'm so sorry. I know you weren't prepared for these tabloid hounds. It can be … awful, intrusive."

"It worked. My brothers are both in love with you," Tim whispered and kissed her. The pleasure was wonderful, overpowering. He pulled back from her. "I've got to go."

"See you in a couple of hours?"

"Penthouse in two." He took her hand and walked with her into the lobby. He stood watching until she got into the elevator. He turned and headed back to his office. Once there he grabbed the files he needed. He was looking forward to hearing what Marsh was going to offer. He started for the conference room.

"Once again I catch you staring at beautiful women, right Mr. Jackass." Beebe Knoll said, laughter in her voice. She stood from the lobby chair. Tim was stunned she had the nerve to show up here after breaking their agreement. Myra looked up from her work, horror and surprise on her face. Obviously, she hadn't heard Beebe's endearing name for him, and Tim admitted to himself the joke was wearing thin. Real thin. He decided to ignore her. "Myra I'll be in with Goddard. You should go before the storm breaks. By the way, thanks for calling Dani; saved me again. See you on Monday," he said and frowned at Beebe as he started to walk away. He chose to act like she wasn't there.

"McAndrews. I'm speaking to you." Beebe's tone was demanding.

"Not now, Miss Knoll. I have a meeting," Tim said with a controlled and sarcastic politeness that wasn't masking his anger very well.

"A little birdie told me Katrina Collins is trying to work out a plea deal. You owe me. Any chance I might get--"

"Owe you? Screw you and screw your little birdie." He was ice cold and serious.

"Ahh, does this mean you didn't like Alice Carroll's front-page story?"

"It sucked stagnant pond water." Tim knew she wasn't here about the front-page story. He was sure Marsh had called her to help him get his face on television for free.

"McAndrews," she followed him down the hallway. "I didn't mean to embarrass you."

"Sure you did. But there's nothing embarrassing about being married to Dani. So, it was an all-around fail."

"You're mad."

"Yep. I thought we had a deal. I was mistaken. Now if you will excuse me, I have work to do." Tim stood at the conference room door.

"Can I make it up to you?" Beebe asked. Was she sorry? He was skeptical.

"I really don't have time for your nonsense. I have criminals to prosecute. Listen, Dani and I are just a regular newly married couple. We don't need the added stress of you following us and writing about our every move. I liked my life much better when you weren't here in the morning to ambush me. Let's go back to that. You want news, make arrangements with our community liaison. I gave you her information the other day."

"No. No deal. McAndrews. I've been assigned the crime beat."

"When did my being married to Dani become a crime?"

She pursed her lips in a pout, "You gave Branson Holt two hours' lead time on the Katrina Collins arrest. He bragged about it. Do you know what two hours means in my business? You should've given it to me. We're friends." She gestured, indicating she thought she and Tim were friends.

"So, that's why you did it. Friends? I sure didn't mean to give you that impression." Tim glared at her.

"Ooh, you *are* mad. Would you rather be enemies?" she issued her challenge.

"And the difference is?"

"I get it--with friends like me, who needs enemies, right?" she countered.

Tim shrugged.

She laughed. "Ooh. That's mean. Did you really hate the article?" she asked as if she hadn't caused him trouble.

"Beebe, you shredded my relationship with my family and you act like it's nothing."

"But didn't I see your brothers leave with Dani? So it's all fixed. Besides, I had to pay my rent." She grinned at him.

Tim was amazed at her callousness. But this was just a story, just rent to her. "I hate the trouble I'm in with family. The superhero stuff was way over the top."

"So, which is it going to be, friends or enemies?" she dared him. She was flirting outrageously. That too was a game with her.

Tim ground his teeth together trying to imagining the despicable things she would write about him and Dani, one way or the other. "I want none of the above."

"That choice left the station a long time ago," Beebe said, her lips parted into a big toothy grin. "Like I said, I've been assigned the crime beat."

"Fuck, lucky me."

"And Raney Marsh asked me to be here this morning." She shifted her body as if that gave her permission to annoy him.

Tim chuckled. "So, is Raney already taking over as D.A.? I thought the citizens had to vote first." Tim knew Goddard's internal polling had him up 12 points over Marsh.

"He's asked me to cover everything he does." She had to be aware of the polls.

"No press allowed in plea bargain meetings," Tim informed her, standing in the doorway.

"Afterwards, will you talk to me? I'll wait."

"Not me. Talk to your boss, Raney Marsh." Tim shot her a dismissive grin and closed her out of the meeting.

"You called the press?" Goddard confronted Raney as Tim turned and took his seat at the conference table. "That's unprecedented. Against the rules, I believe."

Raney ignored his protest and stood staring out of the bank of windows on the west wall of the conference room, watching the ominous approach of the snowstorm. He was nervous.

"Katrina Collins has agreed to turn state's against Warden for a lighter sentence," Marsh announced.

Tim looked over at Goddard. Raney wanted out. That was evident. He tried to keep his smile down.

"Warden confessed. We don't need her to say anything," Goddard retorted.

"She says she'll tell the whole thing, the whole story. There's just one condition."

"Raney, Miss Collins doesn't have any bargaining chips. She's an accessory to murder--four counts, and a co-conspirator." This was the Goddard from whom Tim had learned the trade: strong, cool, and self-assured. The man was back, the cowering candidate thankfully gone.

"In any case, she wants to talk to McAndrews."

Tim was taken aback. He wondered what her strategy could possibly be. Shaking his head, he said, "I've recused myself from this case."

"Privately." Raney glanced at Tim.

"No. I'm not her father confessor," he quipped. Whatever Katrina wanted, he didn't.

Goddard studied him with a skeptic's eye. *Damn!* He was calculating what he could get out of it. Goddard wanted him to talk to her.

"We'll give her the same deal we gave Warden. She can meet with

McAndrews, but not privately. Detective Renton and I will need to be there and it will be taped," Goddard offered.

"She wants McAndrews alone."

"No," Tim said again.

"Take it or leave it: Detective Renton, me, and a video tape. You have one hour." Goddard was firm.

"I'll need to consult with my client." Raney seemed to understand he had no leverage. "May I?" He motioned toward Goddard's office. It was a request for privacy.

"Of course," Goddard consented and Raney hustled from the room. Goddard turned to Tim. "What's going on, Tim?"

"I don't know. I don't get it. I can't make sense of it." He tried to fit the pieces together like a jigsaw puzzle, but he was distracted by the looming storm, and wanted to get Dani to safety before it broke.

Marsh came back to the conference room. His face creased with a stern frown. Tim could tell he wasn't happy. Katrina's agenda and his duty to defend her weren't meshing. Tim hadn't been able to conceive of Katrina's scheme, and he studied Marsh for a clue.

Raney sat heavily in the leather chair at the head of the conference table. Goddard raised his eyebrows, expecting a compromise. Even though he'd bluffed, any testimony Katrina offered up against Warden would strengthen Goddard's case and ensure a conviction. Tim expected Jenny would opt for a trial; she was scared, but with her dad behind her, she'd snap out of it. Either way, Warden was going to get the maximum sentence--with or without any evidence Katrina offered up.

"Katrina insists she talks to Tim. Today."

"Raney, there's a big storm on the way. Not today." Goddard was adamant.

"Today or not at all, Goddard."

Tim knew how much Goddard wanted this. After a few moments, he gave a quick nod of consent.

NINETY-FIVE

"Tim, you came," Katrina said, her lower lip trembling, her body language relaxing almost as if he were rescuing her. Tim was surprised. He wasn't help; he was the enemy. He closed the door to the interrogation room and set his file on the battered table. He looked over at Raney Marsh sitting at the table next to Katrina, stroking her hand as if consoling her.

"What do you want, Katrina? Why did you ask for me?" Tim was skeptical, wary. He glanced at the seat across from her but remained standing. He noticed the small red light glowing on the video camera recording the interview.

A sly smile crossed her lips, setting his senses on high alert. "Raney, could you leave us for a while?" she asked.

"We're taping this, and we *will* use it against you. Detective Renton and Paul Goddard are just outside, beyond the two-way mirror. You need Marsh to stay," Tim admonished her. Being alone with Katrina Collins was like being in a small closet with a coiled rattlesnake.

A distracted smile crossed her lips, but no recognition of the importance of his warning showed in her eyes. "No. Raney, please," she begged. "I need to talk to Tim alone."

Tim carefully considered her as he watched Marsh finally slide his chair back and stand. "Katrina, you need me to stay."

"Please."

"I'll be right outside," he offered.

Katrina didn't speak again until Raney left the interrogation room.

Quickly and breathlessly, she began: "I didn't kill those women. Tim, you have to believe me." She leaned forward across the interview table, but jail had stripped her of her usual tools. No makeup, no low-cut blouses, no black lace bra, no red lipstick, no blonde curls. They hadn't worked on him the first time--they would be useless now. But still, she tried.

"You set them up. You gave Warden their names. He hunted them down and killed them for you. Isn't that the way it worked?" Tim was cold.

"No. Tim, no. I need to see Daniela. Will you arrange a meeting for me? I need to see her. To talk to her."

Tim narrowed his eyes at her. "What do you think that will do for you? She's not going to bail you out. Not this time."

"I had nothing to do with killing those women." She reached across the table, set her head on an outstretched arm and looked up at him, attempting a seductive smile.

"You can stop flirting; I'm not interested. Understand?"

"You're so self-righteous. You wanted me that night in the parking garage. What happened? At the last second you remembered Daniela's money, didn't you?" She sat up, leaned back in her chair, and laughed.

Tim felt his jaw tighten; he ground his teeth together. He didn't think he hated anyone, but what he felt for Katrina was bordering on it. "You flatter yourself, Katrina."

"You hesitated--don't you remember?"

Tim kept his thoughts cornered, his mouth shut. If he let emotion in he'd lose control of the interview and he wasn't about to do that. He swallowed back the anger that wanted to boil over and then chuckled. "You confuse hesitation with surprise. You caught me off guard. I'm not used to having women grab me in the Seven's parking garage." She'd been lucky he hadn't punched her lights out. At the time that thought—and others—had crossed his mind.

Her smile was sassy. "You think I don't know when a man wants me?" She jerked her chin up defiantly.

"I'm not here to listen to your crazy fantasy. You have something useful to say, tell it to Raney Marsh." He picked up the folder from the table and turned to leave the interrogation room. It was a bluff.

"No. Wait, no." There was desperation in her voice. "I need out of here. I can't be in jail. I'll tell you everything if you get me out of here."

He slowly reversed. "You're not in a position to make deals, Katrina. Do you understand? This conversation is being taped and will be used against you. You were instrumental in getting a lot of people killed. You set up Ellen, and she died. Why would I want to do anything for you?"

"You want to nail Gary, don't you?" She gazed up into his face; a coy smile curved the corners of her mouth. She was right. He did. But Gary wasn't the only one he intended to capture.

Tim slowly took hold of the chair opposite Katrina, turned it around, and straddled it, resting his left elbow on the back. He kept the file folder he'd brought with him in his right hand and rested it against his thigh. "I'm listening."

"Gary wanted Daniela. He told us he knew how to get her money."

"Us? Who else was involved in this? Fraser?"

She smirked. "Don't you know?"

He didn't. He slowly shook his head. "You tell me."

"Like I said, Gary wanted Daniela. I wanted what was mine. Your precious, sainted Ellen wanted you back—at any cost." Katrina lowered her chin and leveled an icy stare at him as if she'd won a small victory.

He was shaken but forced himself not to show it. He pressed his index finger against his bottom lip. "Ellen? Ellen was involved?" he asked calmly, even though he found it incredible—unbelievable. His mind raced back through Ellen's cell phone records. She had called a prepaid cell phone over and over. Warden had even told him she'd sought him out and still he hadn't allowed himself to make the connection. If for no other reason, it was because he couldn't. "Her friends have been interviewed, Katrina. They said they only met Warden once. The night he killed her. They didn't know him."

Katrina raked her hand through her hair and snickered at him. "They didn't know him, but Ellen did. You men are so naïve. You have no idea the lengths a woman will go for a man she loves. Whatever you did to that girl--must've been something else! You were everything to Ellen—all she talked about—all she thought about. Was she involved? Up to her big baby blues." The innuendo in Katrina's voice disgusted him. Katrina was expecting a reaction, wanted one. He glared at her, not looking away for even a blink. Was she lying? Ellen couldn't refute her claims, Katrina could say anything she wanted. She was one devious woman. "We all had something to gain," she added.

Tim remembered when he'd first seen Dani, how his life had changed and taken off in a new direction. That day Ellen had followed him and accused him of having an affair; had her life gone in a new direction, too? Dark and dangerous.

Tim nodded as if he understood. "So, your plan was--"

"I was supposed to break you and Daniela up. Once I did, Gary planned to make his move. He would marry Daniela, kill her, and no one would be the wiser. When she died, everyone would think it was suicide or an accident. He said he'd done it before. Gary and I would share the money. And Ellen—she was supposed to get you back."

Katrina's confession was stunning. He'd suspected Katrina, but never Ellen. It took him a second to regain his composure. "How was Gary going to kill Miss St. Clair?" Tim asked. He already knew the answer, but it was crucial to get Katrina to say it on tape.

"He told me he had these special pills—he could put a few in a glass of wine. She would never taste it. She wouldn't hurt. She would just slip away." Katrina's eyes seemed to glaze over. "That's what he was going to do to me—what he did to Ellen. He was never going to share the money with me."

Tim swallowed and dipped his head signaling that he understood. He scrutinized her for a moment. "You weren't going to share the money with him, either. You'd already decided you were going to cut him out. That's why you kept trying to fix Dani up with Bill Fraser. What happened there, did Fraser refuse to play?"

She laughed, but her eyes said he'd hit the bullseye.

"Bill wouldn't play—so, that's what that come-on in the parking garage was all about, wasn't it? You realized Dani wasn't interested in Fraser, so you tried to enlist me in your con. Warden gave you the idea, and you were going to run the game without him, weren't you?"

"At first I was supposed to break you and Dani up. Yes. But you see, all Ellen ever talked about was how great you were. How sweet—how good. I changed my mind." She lifted her gaze and shifted her body forward. "Do you know how good it would've been with us, Tim?" she asked. "Do you?"

Repulsed, Tim transferred his weight in his chair away from her. "Did Fraser know your plan for him?"

"Mr. Goody-two-shoes? No. He started to suspect Gary was up to no good when they transported Jillian Garner to the hospital. He told me he thought they could save her, give her a shot of Narcan, but Gary wouldn't. They fought about it. But Gary had seniority. After that Bill asked to be transferred to a different shift. But you already know that, don't you? He had a panic attack that night you tried to start a fight with Gary at McTavish's bar. Don't you remember? You told me then you wanted me." She grinned as if that was proof.

He rubbed his hand over his chin and shook his head. "Narcan is for opioid overdose. The pills Gary used were Tricyclics not opioids. Gary knew that, Fraser didn't. And that night at McTavish's was a distraction. We were collecting DNA from your bar glasses."

Katrina blinked at him. "You suspected me back then?"

"You were wearing Amber Brown's necklace. That necklace broke the case wide open."

"Gary said you and the cops were stupid. No one would ever know--" Her words drifted off. Reality was gone. Her stare was vacant. Then she smiled. "You see, you have to understand: Daniela took everything from me. I wanted to hurt her." When she looked up into his face, he could see she was breaking. Guilt was a harsh master and a pampered woman like Katrina wouldn't be able to hold up to jail.

"What did Dani take from you?" Tim softened his voice, tried to infuse it with sympathy. It was hard to do.

"I told you. Everything. When we were ten years old, Daniela and

I found my mother's diary in an old wooden chest in the attic. It was all there--in her diary. Simon St. Clair had an affair with my mother. Did you know that? He was my father. Daniela is my sister. My. Sister. And she saw to it I was cut out of his will."

Tim could feel his frown. In his mind's eye, he could picture two ten-year-old girls playing dress-up in an attic, stumbling upon Loretta's hope chest, and finding a diary they were never meant to see. They'd read it, and this downward spiral was set in motion. Tim leaned forward against the back of the chair. Last week Tim had taken Hollingrow's advice and had issued a subpoena for the sealed court records. Two days ago, he'd spent the day in the court archives building reviewing the files. Whether from grief or greed, Loretta Collins had accused Dani's father of infidelity and claimed Simon St. Clair was Katrina's father. Tim guessed that way she could insure she'd have what she needed to save her family from destitution. Obviously, she hadn't really known Simon St. Clair. Hollingsrow, as the St. Clair's attorney, had counter sued for proof. The DNA results had exonerated St. Clair from paternity. Was there an affair? Maybe. There was no proof of that one way or the other. Simon was gone now and couldn't defend himself. But Katrina Collins wasn't Simon's daughter.

"Daniela has always been jealous of me. She hates me. She saw to it I was cut out of the will. You must believe me. You need to know what kind of woman she is," Katrina pleaded.

"All these years you believed you were a St. Clair?" Tim let his breath out as a sigh. He could imagine it. Katrina envied Dani and her sisters, wanted to be a part of their family. She was instead on the outside, looking in. Bitterness and jealousy combined until her mind was poisoned with it.

"I am her sister. She kept me from what is mine. I loved her and she betrayed me."

"Did you want to kill her?"

"Yes. I wanted to kill her. Wouldn't you?" Katrina asked.

Tim knew his expression telegraphed his disapproval. "Did you make a plan to kill her with Gary Warden?"

"Yes. But you must help me, Tim. I didn't kill those other women. I didn't know about the other women. You believe me, don't you?" She closed her eyes and then lifted her eyelids slowly. She still lacked any recognition that what she had wanted to do was wrong. Katrina was clearly a sociopath. But for the first time, Tim did believe she had nothing to do with the others. She was an opportunist instead. She'd taken the trophies as gifts, as tokens of love from Gary.

"I don't have to decide if what you tell me is true. Raney Marsh will need to convince a judge it is." Tim's anger had transformed into pity. He glanced up as Raney Marsh burst into the interrogation room.

Tim stood. Marsh didn't need to say anything. He recognized his interview with Katrina was over. Goddard would need to take it from here and negotiate the plea deal. "Dani doesn't hate you, Katrina--never has. She watched out for you, instead." He dropped the file folder containing the results of the long ago paternity test on the interrogation table and pushed it toward her. "You're not Simon St. Clair's daughter. DNA test says no."

"That's enough, Katrina; don't say anything more. She's done talking to you, McAndrews."

Katrina's face was stone. Had she known the truth, but convinced herself otherwise to justify murder? Tim could see the tears welling up in her eyes.

"I found my mother's diary. It was all there in her diary--" Katrina called after Tim. He slowly backed out of the room and watched as the door closed.

"Wow. Good job," Scott said, patting Tim on the back. "You made that look easy."

"Did I?" He was momentarily haunted by the insane, broken look in Katrina's eyes.

"You were right about her." Scott smiled as if apologizing for not believing him sooner.

Tim felt no satisfaction. Only pity. Dani's friend had slipped into ruin. Dani had known about the diary and when he'd asked if Katrina had a reason to hate her, she'd said nothing. Protecting her father, he surmised. Had her father told her the truth before he died?

"Do you believe all that about Ellen Mason being involved?" Scott asked. His expression was tentative as if he thought Tim would want him to let it go.

Tim shrugged. "Her cell-phone records showed she called a prepaid phone a lot. We know Warden used prepaids. We'll have to be ready for Warden to use her in his defense."

"We may be digging up things—things you won't want--" Scott grimaced.

"I know." Tim acquiesced. "I chose to get involved with Ellen. I get to face the consequences of that decision." Tim rubbed his brow. "Doesn't change the fact that Warden needs to face the consequences of his. He can't get away with what he's done because I was once involved with Ellen."

"All right. I'll look into it. But, whatever I find I'll run by you first if that's okay." Scott addressed the District Attorney and waited until Goddard consented with a single affirmative nod.

"Love sure can make people crazy," Goddard breathed out. He stared at Tim, but his eyes held no condemnation. "What do you recommend for Katrina Collins?"

"I believe her when she says she wasn't involved with the other women. She was, however, part of the conspiracy to kill Dani. She's going to have to serve time for that." Tim leveled his gaze on Goddard.

The older man grinned in agreement.

NINETY-SIX

Tim walked to the penthouse; he was deep in thought. The snow had started to fall an hour ago, and the streets were empty of cars. The only city traffic was the few brave souls trudging through the new powder on the sidewalk as he was. He'd missed his chance to fly with Dani to the ranch and was trying to decide if he should attempt the drive. Katrina Collins' confession and testimony would finish off Warden's murder spree. Katrina would have to serve some time; she needed to. But her confession had also brought his own failings into clear view. When he consented to participate in a relationship with Ellen for convenient sex, he had disregarded her needs and feelings. Lying to himself that theirs was a casual and uncommitted liaison when he knew better had set circumstances in motion he'd never considered possible. He would have to live with that.

When he arrived at the St. Clair building, he used his key to open the parking garage gate, passed through, closed and locked it. He was stuck in the city for the duration of the storm, probably all weekend, and he missed Dani already. He pushed the call button for the elevator. Anyway, he could catch up on his reading, and get ahead of next week's cases—a small consolation. He hated the idea of being without Dani. He entered the elevator, pushed the button for the twenty-sixth floor, and inserted his special key when prompted. Dani had sounded just as disappointed as he was when he'd called her from the police station.

She'd had big plans. She'd had Mark and the boys ready snowmobiles. The trails they'd ridden horseback all summer would now become a winter wonderland. The elevators doors opened into the penthouse lobby. The lights were on--he hadn't expected that. But the whole place was controlled by computer, he assumed when he pressed the button for the floor, it had readied everything for his arrival. He removed his gloves and stuffed them in his overcoat pocket, peeled off his coat and hung it on the rack. He loosened his tie and unbuttoned the top few buttons of his shirt. He was going to slip into a comfortable pair of sweats and pour himself a whiskey. Then he'd call the ranch to talk to Dani.

He grabbed the remote off the coffee table in the living room and started the gas fireplace with a click of a button. Outside the window the snow created a lace-like curtain and he watched transfixed for a few minutes before heading to the bedroom to change his clothes.

He flipped on the light by the bedroom door. Dani sat in a chair looking out of the floor-to-ceiling window; she didn't turn to face him, and he noticed one of his file folders on her lap.

"Baby, you didn't go to the ranch?" He walked over to her and squatted beside her chair. She turned to him; her cheeks were wet with tears. She let the folder fall to the ground, and the papers spilled onto the floor. Tim stood. Had he left that folder out on the home office desk? He didn't remember doing it. What a total screw-up he was! Dani had read all about her father's alleged indiscretion and the paternity lawsuit.

"You've pulled all my family's skeletons from their closets." She rose from the chair, turned, and searched his eyes. Was she worried that it would change things? She wasn't angry, but her spirit was crushed. The father she'd idolized had feet of clay.

"I did." He couldn't say he was sorry, he'd need to. "Every family has skeletons, Dani." He faced her. "That was their deal, not ours."

"Did your father cheat on your mother?"

Tim knew his father had never cheated. He was sure his parents had had their problems. But by the time Tim was born, they'd worked them out. All he remembered was their devotion and love for each other. "I don't think so. If he has, he hasn't been caught."

She sighed, and a little laugh left her throat. "Mine did. With his best friend's wife."

"We don't know that. Your father isn't here to defend himself." He tipped her chin with the back of his fingers so she'd would look at him. "But you knew about the diary long ago, didn't you?"

She closed her eyes as if remembering pain and nodded. "Katrina and I found her mother's diary when we were kids. I was broken hearted. My mother was desperately ill and I couldn't believe he would do it. So I asked him. He denied it and I was forbidden from seeing Katrina again. I wondered why Mrs. Collins would have accused him?"

"Money," Tim answered softly. "The world's number-one motive, for good or for ill. Baby, every family has skeletons."

"What skeletons does your family have?"

"You know about all of mine. Ellen." Tim thought for a moment, then remembered this morning. "Okay. How about this one: Both of my brothers *had* to get married, and in my Irish Catholic family, that's still a big deal. Their girlfriends--now wives--were both pregnant."

Dani sucked in a breath and started sniffing back her tears all at the same time. "Neither of my brothers-in-law work, they just live off my sisters."

Tim chuckled. He had to bring her out of this. "Okay. When I told my father we were engaged, the first words out of his mouth were: 'is she pregnant.' Not 'great news', not 'congratulations', not 'when do we get to meet her', or even 'super, we were wondering if you were gay.' No. It was: 'is she pregnant.'"

"My older sister was caught shoplifting a candy bar," she answered him.

He picked her up and twirled her around. He carried her to the bed, set her gently down and lay down beside her. "I've got better. My mother sabotaged all my relationships with girls, because she wanted me to be a priest—me a priest!? And I'm a complete disappointment to her. Skeletons, all." He turned on his side and gazed into her eyes. "I'm glad you stayed. I wasn't looking forward to being alone."

"I couldn't go without you." They kissed.

"I have an idea. Want to open a bottle of champagne, watch it snow, and make love by the fire on a bearskin rug?"

"We don't have a bearskin rug," Dani laughed.

"Darn, why not? Ahh, the sofa, then?"

"I love you, Tim."

"I love you, too, baby."

Suddenly the lights waned and flickered and they were plunged into darkness.

"Power outage!" Tim exclaimed.

"Just stay here, the generators will kick in. It takes about thirty seconds." She nestled against him. "I don't mind the dark, if you're here next to me," she whispered.

NINETY-SEVEN

This was the opportunity he'd been waiting for. The hospital lights flashed briefly before the room went dark and all the equipment noise died with it. Warden pulled the I.V. from his left arm and the heart rate and oxygen saturation monitor from his finger. He knew he probably had a minute before the back-up generators restored power. He wrestled the side rail down and clambered from the bed. He went to the one small closet where Margie, his little nurse, had left street clothes for him. He grabbed them and a number 10 scalpel from the equipment drawer and opened the sterile wrapper. He carefully checked out the hallway for his police guard. The floor was bedlam. Nurses and techs were scurrying about in the semidarkness. The guard was attempting to help restore order and wasn't paying attention to his post. Warden slipped up behind him, reached around his shoulder and quickly sliced through the flesh at his throat with the scalpel. He held tight as the man struggled. When his body went limp, he dragged the body into his hospital room and fought the impulse to stay until he bled out. He wanted to watch, but he had to go while he had the cover of darkness. Peeking out of the door he realized no one had even noticed the murder or the pool of blood on the hospital floor. Taking advantage, he skirted the confusion and slunk along the wall to the janitor's closet he'd scoped out earlier, where the bulk of his outer wear was stashed. Once he closed the door behind him, he knew he was halfway to freedom. He heard the whoosh of the heating system starting back up and the lights in the closet turned back on, but not quite at their normal brightness. He couldn't even imagine what kind of generators it would take to restore full power to a hospital.

Quickly, he stripped out of the hospital gown and dressed in his street clothes. Margie's brother was almost his size. A little bigger was better that than smaller. At least he'd talked her into buying the boots in his size. He opened the package of socks she'd stashed in the back of the closet next to the bleach and cleaning supplies. He rummaged under the sink for the navy-blue hooded ski jacket and gloves she'd told him would be there. He slipped them on. He felt through the pockets for the knife he'd asked her to buy, but only found a single key and a sheet of paper with an address written on it. Hers.

So she hadn't believed him entirely. He chuckled to himself. He remembered the skeptical expression on Margie's face when he told her

McAndrews had set him up. But as he wove his tale, he described all the evidence they had and how McAndrews had manufactured it, she started to believe him. He'd left out the statistics, the mathematical probabilities of the DNA. By then she'd wanted to believe him--and even with all the science nursing required, she was trafficking only in emotion. She needed a lover more than she needed reality. She'd been as gullible and willing as Ellen and Katrina had been. He was going to reward her. When he got to her house, he would make love to her. He would love her in a way she would never forget. He looked at the simple round clock hanging on the janitor's closet wall. It was eight. He could make it to Margie's apartment, show his appreciation, be at the fire station for the penthouse keys by eleven and to the St. Clair building by midnight. He couldn't stop it now. He was going to kill McAndrews, and the thought made him salivate.

NINETY-EIGHT

Warden used the key he'd stolen from Fire Station 123 to open the underground parking garage of the St. Clair building. He slipped through the iron gate, closed it, and relocked it. Once inside he brushed away the snow from his jeans and boots.

Getting this far had been a challenge. Already, he crossed paths with two police cruisers on his way from Margie's apartment. They were chained up—he heard them jingling and rattling against the snow long before he saw them, and hid long before they could see him. He assumed the police hadn't discovered he'd escaped from the hospital. That was a stroke of genius on his part. He'd easily convinced Jenny Mattison he was too helpless to be a threat and she'd gotten a court order to remove the usual handcuffs a prisoner would be expected to wear. Women like Jenny and Margie with their bleeding-heart compassion were incredibly stupid but equally useful.

Silently, he made his way to the large equipment room on the western edge of the parking garage. He removed his backpack and took out the tablet computer he'd stolen from Margie. Weeks ago, when he'd first discovered Daniela was here, he'd prepared. It had been no easy task. He'd followed Ramos--the security guard closest to his size--home one afternoon. The man dropped off his uniform for dry-cleaning and Warden had picked it up for him. His first plan was to break in, like he had Daniela's home on the edge of the city and McAndrews' apartment, but the penthouse proved to be a fortress. Before the incident at the ranch, he had planted a small camera in one of the emergency stairwells. They all looked exactly alike, so he only needed one camera. He'd recorded an hour of empty stairwell. He recovered the small thumb drive with the video on it from its hiding place--taped behind some shelves full of cleaning supplies. With the tablet computer, he hacked into the building's security system and installed the false video, overriding the live feed streaming into the security cameras. The security guard on the lobby floor would notice a brief flicker on his monitors but would assume the snow storm was still messing with the power. The new tape played a continuous loop—only the most highly trained security personnel would be able to tell the difference. As a precaution, though, he'd had Margie buy a simple can of black spray paint. On his way up to the penthouse suite, he'd spritz each camera. If security could restore the live feed, they'd see nothing but black. He was as prepared as anyone could be.

Margie had been a great partner. He'd given his little nurse a special send-off. Enduring the pain, he'd saved five OxyContin tablets from his hospital stay and had crushed them into powder, destroying their time-release properties. He'd dissolved them in her glass of that lovely petite syrah she'd bought for their celebration of his freedom. He didn't understand what all her whimpering was about when he'd duct-taped her to a chair and forced her to drink it. He'd made love to her before—like she'd wanted—hadn't he? It wasn't his fault she hadn't admitted the truth to herself. Surely, underneath it all, deep in her unconscious mind she'd known: he was Death.

He shouldered his backpack and started up the stairs. Twenty-six floors would be a hike, but he could plan and savor how he was going to kill McAndrews. Hate and rage drove him on, and he unclenched his fists. He tested his shoulder. There was still pain, but not enough to interfere. He imagined killing McAndrews as he had the gay boy. His mind raced back to the rush he'd felt as he watched the blood mixing with rain and spilling over the curb in a pink-tinged waterfall as it raced into the storm sewer. He'd almost stayed too long that night. Tonight, on the top of the world, in the St. Clair penthouse suite, he would wait until he could see McAndrews take his last breath. He hadn't decided what he was going to do with Daniela. He guessed that depended on her.

The emergency stairs were wider than he remembered. They spiraled up one half a floor at a time. He'd climbed lots of stairways like this during his time with the fire department--mostly in drills, loaded with equipment. His body was primed and ready. Once again, his thoughts drifted to McAndrews. The man had turned out to be a more formidable adversary than he'd first imagined. It had only made it more fun. Losing to McAndrews wasn't an option.

NINETY-NINE

Tim had always been a light sleeper. Tonight, the glow from the city reflecting off the snow kept him awake. He thought about closing the bedroom blinds, but he didn't want to disturb Dani, resting warm and content against his side. He closed his eyes and tried to drift off, but for some reason Katrina's confession kept playing over and over in his mind.

He heard it, as soft as a breeze—a hiss--as the air from the penthouse and the emergency stairway rushed to equalize. No one else had a key to the emergency stairs other than Scott, and he would never intrude without calling. Tim sat up and listened. It wasn't right—something wasn't right. Like a shot, he was out of bed. Noiselessly, he crossed the bedroom, and closed and locked the door. Dani was startled and sat up blinking at him.

"Get dressed," he whispered, but with an urgency that made her instantly obey. He pulled on his sweats and scrambled into the T-shirt he'd thrown on the floor last night. He grabbed the .380 Walther. He heard his cell phone vibrating against the wooden top of the nightstand and dashed for it—stopping the noise. He couldn't give their presence away. "Get behind me," he commanded, as he pressed ANSWER.

"McAndrews," he quietly said. Dani rushed behind him and held on. He could feel her trembling against his back.

"It's Scott. Warden has escaped. We don't know where he is. We think--"

Tim's mind raced through the possibilities and settled on reality. "He's here! Warden is here!" He didn't wait for an answer and calmly set the phone on the dresser. He didn't hang up. With resolve, he released the safety on his pistol and pulled back the slide. A .380 hollow-point self-defense round clicked up into the firing chamber.

ONE HUNDRED

The penthouse was quiet. The soft flickering light from the gas fireplace made shadows dance on the walls. Warden crept into the living room. But even as quiet as he tried to be, the rubber soles on his snow boots clomped against the hardwood floor. A confrontation with McAndrews could be dangerous. He'd learned that lesson the hard way. McAndrews wasn't the kind of man that would back away from a fight. Surprise was Warden's ally.

There was an open bottle of expensive champagne, two half-empty glasses, and a fleece-lined throw on the floor between the sofa and the coffee table. He picked up the throw and Daniela's perfume wafted on the air. Warden had always loved her scent. The lovers had retired for the evening. He glanced around the room. Behind him was a kitchen and to his left a hallway led to three rooms. All three doors were open. To his right another hallway and three doorways. But one of the three was closed. *I choose ... door number three!* He felt a smile curl his lips. He crept down the hall and when he reached the shut door he slowly turned the knob. It was locked. Carefully, he felt along the top edge of the molding. As always there was that tiny brass key—the emergency key--in case the kids locked themselves in the bedroom and couldn't get out. All firemen knew to look for that key. *Everyone else forgets about that little key.* He slipped it into the lock. When he heard the tumblers tick into place, he removed the key and replaced it. Now when he twisted the knob, there was no resistance, and the door soundlessly opened a crack. Warden removed the switchblade knife from his jacket pocket. He pushed the small button on the handle and the blade swept into place with a snap. He pressed his weight gently against the door opening it wider.

The faint light from the fireplace spilled into the room. Warden blinked as a memory overwhelmed him he wasn't prepared for. A sense of sadness and unbidden grief forced him to hesitate. Quickly, uncontrollable rage followed those emotions. Warden lunged for the bed and plunged his knife into the body sleeping there. Images from the dream flashed through his mind like a slide show; swirling now, he was home in the dingy, dirty apartment, tattered wallpaper, shadows wavering in the pale light. He was Death. He would kill his rival and take Daniela with him to safety. Over and over he drove the knife home.

ONE HUNDRED-ONE

Tim flipped the light switch. Warden stumbled backward and blinked with surprise as pillow stuffing drifted weightlessly in the air.

"Gary Warden. When did you get out?" Tim announced himself. Warden wheeled to face him. Obviously, he'd thought he'd killed him. The laser sight on Tim's Walther painted a neon green dot on Warden's jacket. Tim could see he was stunned. But that would only last a second. "Drop the knife! Now! Drop it. Don't you ever learn?"

They were locked in a stare. Tim wasn't sure what Warden would do. Wondered briefly if he had on body armor. Scott and the police were on the way, but would they make it in time? Tim knew when caught; many criminals chose "suicide by cop".

"What's it going to be, Gary?" Tim growled a warning. He felt his jaw tighten and heard Dani softly cry out as she tightened her grip around his waist. The same disturbing grin Tim remembered from the interrogation room slowly spread across Warden's face. *Was it surrender?* Tim didn't relax.

Tim heard the smooth roll of the elevator doors opening into the penthouse lobby.

"Cops are here. What's it going to be?" Tim asked again. Warden leveled his gaze at him. His eyes were wild and frenzied--darting back and forth. He was mumbling to himself, something about his mother. In that instant Tim knew. Warden lifted the knife and charged.

Tim squeezed the trigger. Two shots rang out. He pulled Dani to the right with him, as he watched Warden's body jerk as the rounds hit him. Warden kept coming. Tim adjusted his aim. He made certain these next shots were ones Warden could not survive. Tim fired again. Warden crumpled to the floor, stabbing at the air where Tim and Dani had been as he fell.

"Shots fired! Shots fired!" Tim heard Scott yell and the sound of footfalls running down the hallway. Scott stood in the doorway, gun drawn. He quickly assessed the situation and lowered his weapon.

For a moment, Tim felt staggered. He had known this was one of the possible outcomes when it first started. He'd hoped for another. He felt Dani's arm around his chest, gripping tight, her face buried against the back of his shoulder. He set his pistol down on the dresser and spun to take her in his arms.

"Everybody all right?" Scott came into the room.

"We're okay. Warden isn't," Tim answered. He exhaled and helped Dani to the safety of Anna, who steered her to the living room.

Scott bent over the body and felt for a pulse. He patted Warden down and removed the knife grasped in Warden's lifeless hand. He motioned for the medics to come into the room. When the medics confirmed the death, Scott walked over to Tim. "I guess no one told that asshole you never bring a knife to a gunfight," he said.

ONE HUNDRED-TWO

Tim folded the last of his sweaters he planned to take on their long-awaited ski trip and placed it in his suitcase. Dani pulled the blinds shut to the penthouse bedroom. She walked over to him and wrapped her arms around him, pulling him back against her. He closed his eyes, savoring her touch.

"We need this vacation," she whispered against his neck.

He nodded his agreement and turned to face her. This had been a grueling week. First he'd tackled the county review board and Miss Gracie Rose. She'd been certain Tim could've handled his confrontation with Warden without violence. Even when confronted with the fact that they were in bed in their own home. Tim reminded her of the Castle Doctrine and that he had the Constitutional right to defend his home against someone breaking in with the intent of doing him and his family harm. She ignored him. Saying so had only made her defensive. He remembered wondering how she'd react to having an armed killer bent on murdering her, knife drawn and charging full speed. Would she pull the trigger? He also knew she would vote to have him dismissed. Tim had said nothing more, but Goddard sure had. He'd won his reelection--and with four more years to look forward to, he'd earned the right. He'd tossed the crime scene and autopsy pictures of Candy Johnson and Alan Sharp's bodies at her and asked if she felt any differently after seeing those.

Elias Cain had asked Tim if he'd consider joining the FBI if the review committee results didn't go his way. Tim had given it some thought. It was a good offer, and he'd make more money. But D.C. was a long way away and Dani's businesses were here in Seattle. Dani had told him she could make accommodations for living there if that's what he wanted. She had a jet, after all. It only took him a few days, and he knew he didn't want to go anywhere else. He was home in Seattle. He'd refused the offer. Elias had grinned and told him the offer was open ended if he ever changed his mind.

Brad Hollingsrow had also stepped up and invited him to join his prestigious firm. There, he would be involved in every aspect of the law. But Brad especially wanted Tim on his criminal defense team. Tim considered that offer very seriously. But in the end, Tim knew he was a prosecutor. With what he knew about most criminal defendants, he wasn't sure representing them was a leap he could take.

Goddard asked him to stay with the district attorney's office. He'd been honest; he couldn't offer more money. He had done what he could and was positive the hearing would exonerate Tim. Still, Tim could tell Goddard expected him to move on to greener pastures. Tim told him he'd review all the offers while on vacation and would give him his answer once they returned.

Tim had finally taken Dani to meet his parents. At first, he wasn't sure his mother was going to accept her. But by the end of the weekend, they'd become tentative friends. It was true, his mother had never liked any of his girlfriends, because she'd wanted him to be a priest. It had been a family tradition since St. Patrick had rid Ireland of the snakes. A McAndrews son had always been dedicated to the Church. When his mother started to protest, told him he could annul the marriage and do his duty; Tim made it clear, she could have her opinion, but the only one that mattered was his. Dani was his wife and that was an end to it.

"I'm looking forward to this. Two whole weeks of best friends, skiing, and most of all--you." He took her in his arms. "No bad guys, no court, just peace and quiet," he breathed out a satisfied sigh.

"Umm. Sounds like heaven," Dani purred.

"Where is it we are going, anyway?"

"Idaho. Schweitzer."

"I've never skied there."

"You'll like it, deep powder," she smiled.

He remembered the soft feel of powder snow under his skis and how it would rooster tail out behind him. Skiing in powder was pure fun. He couldn't stop the grin. Finally, he asked, "One of your houses?"

"Yes," she answered almost defensively.

He nodded and chuckled.

"222 Snow Country Lane," she said.

Printed in the United States
By Bookmasters